W9-DDQ-737

THE
ABDUCTION

ALSO BY JONATHAN HOLT

The Abomination

THE
ABDUCTION

A NOVEL

JONATHAN HOLT

HARPER

www.harpercollins.com

HarperCollins books may be purchased for educational, business, or sales promotional use. For information, please e-mail the Special Markets Department at SPsales@harpercollins.com.

This book is a work of fiction. The characters, incidents, and dialogue are drawn from the author's imagination and are not to be construed as real. Any resemblance to actual events or persons, living or dead, is entirely coincidental.

First published in the United Kingdom in 2014 by Head of Zeus Ltd.

FIRST U.S. EDITION

Library of Congress Cataloging-in-Publication Data has been applied for.

ISBN 978-0-06-226704-7

14 15 16 17 18   OFF/RRD   10 9 8 7 6 5 4 3 2 1

In order for a war to be just, three things are necessary. First, the authority of the sovereign. Secondly, a just cause. Thirdly, a rightful intention.

– Thomas Aquinas, *Summa Theologiae*

PROLOGUE

IT WAS THEIR biggest night of the year, although you would have been hard pushed to find it advertised anywhere – anywhere, that is, apart from certain obscure internet bulletin boards and special-interest websites, where previous years' efforts were still talked about in the ecstatic tones usually devoted to cup finals or rock festivals. It certainly wasn't listed in the official programme of Venice's annual Carnevale, although it was inextricably linked to that event in spirit as well as timing. Many of the attendees had flown in specially; for them, this night was as close to the official celebrations as they would come.

At midnight, the club's two thousand square feet of inter-linked dance floors – and, even more importantly, the warren of dimly lit rooms that lay behind them – were almost deserted. But by half past, the queue of people waiting to use the lockers thoughtfully provided by the management stretched out almost to the parking lot, where security personnel in tuxedos and bow ties were checking names against the list of ticket-holders. By 1 a.m., the main dance floor was full.

To anyone unfamiliar with these occasions, it made an incongruous sight. Every participant wore a carnival mask, ranging from the classic blank white Volto, topped with a tricorne hat, to more elaborate affairs modelled on the rays of the sun, the birdlike beak of a medieval plague doctor, or the jewelled visage of an eighteenth-century courtesan. But in almost every case, these costumes ended at the shoulders. From the chest down the partygoers were dressed more conventionally; the men in smart trousers and expensive loose shirts, the women in short skirts and tops, in accordance with the club's strict dress code.

By two, the reason for this had become clear. The clothes were starting to be discarded. Women danced topless except for their masks. The men tended to keep more on – at least, until they joined the throng making their way to or from the smaller rooms. There were more bars back there, where you could strike up conversations with other couples before making your choice. But most headed directly to the playrooms, where the dim lighting was colour-coded to signify when a particular room was dedicated to a particular pleasure. In some, knots of bodies joined and re-joined, their masks still in place. In others, the masks themselves were an impediment to the enjoyments being sought, and were discarded.

In every playroom discreet stacks of towels, and bowls of flavoured condoms and mints, fulfilled the promise on the club's website to provide an impeccable standard of hygiene as well as the best music, lighting and atmosphere in Europe.

The slim female figure wearing a gold Columbina mask with grey feathers paused at the entrance of one of the playrooms. Inside, half a dozen couples were making love, the whole scene illuminated only by the jerky flashes of a strobe. Behind the feathered mask, her eyes were wide as she took it all in.

A voice in her ear said, amused, "Shall we join them?"

Without turning round she said, "You can if you want. I'm just going to watch."

The man reached for the hem of her T-shirt. "Let's take this off, at least."

"No," she said, putting her hand on his to stop him. "You have fun if you want. Just not with me. That was the deal, remember?"

Slipping away without a backward glance, she made her way to the next room. In the lemon-coloured light, two women knelt in the middle of a small circle of masked male figures. The girl watched for a while, then moved on.

Another room was completely dark: a notice by the door invited those who entered to take off their clothes and use their sense of touch. Almost regretfully, she turned away. In a small bar she stopped to look at a long-legged blonde who was lying on her back across a low table, a man at either end. Several couples stood around, drinks in hand, watching.

"Hey, beautiful." A man with a thick body-builder's torso, improbably tanned for the time of year, spoke to her in guttural English. "My wife thinks you're hot."

Shaking her head with a quick, regretful smile, she headed back to the dance floor. There was a platform at one end where two professional dancers, one male and one female, performed non-stop, their bodies gleaming with oil and sweat. The male dancer's chest was thin as a rock star's, but rippled with muscle. She watched him for a while, copying his movements, abandoning herself to the pulsing beat.

"Hiya." A masked girl a few years older than her smiled a greeting over the music. "Having a good time?"

"The best."

The girl leaned in closer. "You need anything sorted? Pills, coke, cheap cigarettes…"

"Uh… Maybe some cigarettes."

"Talk to him." The girl pointed to where a young man with

3

striking blond dreadlocks and a Trifaccia mask stood slightly apart. "Whatever you need. He's cool."

Nodding her thanks, the girl in the feathered Columbina made her way over to the young man. "Hey," she said casually.

Looking round quickly, he pushed open a fire door and motioned for her to step outside. She did so, shivering as the cold, foggy air hit her. "I hear," she began, but the words were hardly out of her mouth before she felt strong arms pinning her from behind. The Carnevale mask was plucked from her face, and some kind of bag made of heavy cloth dropped over her head in its place. More hands fastened round her calves, the two-man team lifting her as effortlessly as if she were a shop mannequin being moved to a different window. She felt herself propelled forwards, then lowered onto a hard surface that gave beneath her assailants' weight as they clambered in after her, rapidly securing her legs and arms with what felt like plastic strips. *I'm in a van*, she thought. *They've put me in a van. It must be the police.* Then, moments later, came the realisation that the Italian police would never hood her like this. "Dad?" she said hesitantly, just before a thick strip of tape was wound round her mouth, hood and all, muffling even the scream that belatedly escaped her. Terror and panic flooded her limbs, but though she bucked and jerked frantically, like a landed fish, she was too tightly secured to free herself.

She heard doors slam, felt the van move off. The whole thing had taken less than thirty seconds.

A hand held her down, and a male voice spoke close to her ear, crooning some words in Italian before switching to heavily accented English.

"Stay still, Mia. Stay still and I promise you'll be all right."

He knows my name, she thought, and the realisation was even more terrifying than anything else that had happened so far. She felt her bowels clench and unclench, and struggled without success to keep control of her bladder. Then a sweet-smelling liquid soaked the hood around her nose, and the darkness came racing towards her.

DAY ONE

ONE

COLONEL ALDO PIOLA of the Venice Carabinieri woke with a start, unable at first to remember where he was. Nearby in the darkness a white screen flashed, and a tinny speaker played a pop song. He recognised the tune as one his nine-year-old son had been listening to recently, by the American singer Pink, and felt a twinge of annoyance. Claudio must have changed his ringtone as a joke, or – more likely, he thought, his irritation replaced by a sudden surge of tenderness and guilt – in the hope of getting his father's attention at work.

There was no light by the sofa, so he answered by feel. "*Pronto?*"

"Colonel, it's Saito. Apologies for waking you at this unfortunate hour."

Piola had no idea what the hour was, but if something was serious enough to require a call from his *generale di brigata*, the time was hardly relevant. So he said only, "No problem."

"We've been asked to oversee an investigation at Vicenza. Some human remains have been found at that new American military base they're building."

Piola noted the curious use of "human remains" instead of "body". "Who found them?"

"A local boy, engaged in some kind of protest. Hence the ungodly hour. Unfortunately there's no one of your rank available over there – Serti's on a training course, and Lombardo's assigned elsewhere." General Saito hesitated. "There's a sense it should be someone senior, so that it's clear we're taking it seriously."

Ah: so it was a matter of politics. If it involved the US Military, perhaps that was no surprise. "Speaking of commitments, you're probably aware there are some administrative matters taking up my own time just now." Piola crossed to the door and flicked on the light switch as he spoke. The sofa, covered with one of his son's cast-off AC Milan duvets, sprang into view, along with the alarm clock balanced on one of the arms. It was 4.32 a.m. He reached for his trousers, the phone still clamped between his shoulder and ear.

"Indeed. To be frank, Aldo, that's why I thought of you. A quick and professional investigation, tactfully handled by an experienced officer, is all that's required here. It shouldn't be too time-consuming. And it won't hurt with Internal Affairs to have the Americans putting in a good word."

"I understand. Thank you." Through the open door Piola caught a movement across the corridor, a nightgown ducking back behind a doorframe. It was Gilda, his wife, trying to overhear. "Sir," he added, to make it clear that it was work. The nightgown disappeared.

"Thanks. A car's on its way. Keep me informed, won't you?"

By the time Piola had rung off, his wife had gone back to bed, her door shut against him. He knocked softly. "I have to go out," he said through the wood. "I'll see you tonight, shall I?"

There was no reply.

*

So that he wouldn't disturb his family any more than he had to, he went and waited in the street, hoping the driver would have the sense not to use his siren. The *caìgo*, the fog which blanketed Venice and the surrounding Veneto region most nights at this time of year, was especially thick tonight. It had drifted into Venice the day before from the direction of the sea, slipping up the canals and their smaller brethren, the *rii*; sliding over pavements and door sills into cloisters and courtyards, so that what had started around 4 p.m. as nothing more than a faint opacity in the air turned, as dusk fell, into a dense, other-worldly miasma that muffled church bells and gave every streetlamp a hazy aura, like a dandelion-clock. It brought with it a salty, numbing cold, the cold of the lagoon and the Adriatic, and Piola kept his jacket well zipped up. Normally he wore plain clothes for investigations, but since this one involved the US Armed Forces he'd opted for the working Carabinieri uniform of dark, pleated trousers, well-polished black shoes and dark blue windcheater. The lapels of the windcheater bore three silver stars above a three-turreted castle. Not that the Americans would be impressed by his rank, but it would do no harm to remind them that the Carabinieri, like themselves, were a military organisation. He placed his colonel's hat under his arm, making a mental note not to forget it when he put it down, as he usually did.

He was in luck: the car had its blue light on but no siren. The driver, Adelmio, had even thought to bring coffee. Tipping the contents of the tiny carton down his throat, Piola was also pleased to discover that it was laced with a generous *corretto* of grappa.

"Who's there so far?" he asked as they drove.

"Dottore Hapadi, sir. He was the one on call. And a few of our lot – I think they're the local boys."

"Know anything about it?"

Adelmio shrugged. "Not much. A skeleton, I heard. But it was on the construction site, and it was protestors who found it, so..."

Piola nodded his understanding. The new American base being built at the disused Dal Molin airfield, just a few miles from the existing garrison at Caserma Ederle, was one of the biggest building projects in northern Italy, matched only by the flood barriers in the Venetian lagoon. Both projects were controversial, but in the case of Dal Molin the controversy had quickly turned to something more.

Many local people had already been uneasy about the number of US Military installations ringing their city, from underground missile silos to vehicle compounds. Others had been riled by the way the Americans appeared to have been able to bypass the usual planning procedures, their very presence sanctioned by secret agreements dating back to the Second World War. In 2007, a hundred and fifty thousand people had joined hands around the centre of Vicenza – a UNESCO World Heritage site – symbolically forming a wall around their city to show that it would be defended. A proposed referendum on the new base had been mysteriously cancelled at the last minute by the courts; undeterred, the Vicentini vowed to go on protesting, even establishing a permanent "peace camp" adjacent to the construction site. It seemed to make no difference whatsoever to the work, which according to the local papers was due to be completed in record time. But Piola had no doubt that a Carabinieri investigation would be seen as a significant event by both sides.

If it *was* a skeleton – which would certainly explain Saito's reference to "human remains" – it might of course be an ancient one, in which case no criminal investigation would be required. Such skeletons turned up quite often during construction work in the Veneto, which was densely populated even before the time of the Roman Empire. But Piola also knew that a body buried in the region's damp soil could be reduced to bare bones in months, and building sites had long been favoured by the Mafia as a convenient place to get rid of their victims. It was best to make no assumptions.

The drive took about forty minutes. They left the deserted A4 *autostrada* by the Vicenza Ovest exit, then sped up Viale del Sole.

The fog had thinned a little as they came inland, so Piola was able to get some glimpses of the old airfield as they approached. The perimeter had mostly been boarded off, providing an irresistible temptation for fly-posters and graffitists. Slogans denouncing the Americans – "*Vicenza Libera!*" "*No Dal Molin!*" "*Fuori Dalle Balle!*" – were in turn partially covered by banners depicting smiling men in crisp black suits. There were elections coming up for the regional parliament, and these gameshow-host faces were the candidates. But access gates and stretches of chain link also allowed a glimpse of what lay within. Jagged spills of mud, like frozen waves, were proof of the pace of construction, as were the clusters of metal cranes that climbed into the fog like fairytale beanstalks. What caught the eye most, however, were the great corkscrews of coloured smoke – green, white and red – that fizzed up into the night sky, turning the fog itself into a giant, glowing Italian flag.

"I heard the protestors let off flares," Adelmio said. He pointed to a blue pulse over in the distance. "That'll be us."

Sure enough, by a gap in the boarding marked "Gate G" they found two parked Carabinieri vehicles, one with its light still flashing. A uniformed *appuntato* saluted Piola as he got out of the car, but it was a man in American grey-green combat fatigues who hurried forward, greeting him in passable Italian.

"Colonel Piola? Sergeant Pownall, Military Police. I'll be escorting you to the scene. If you wouldn't mind putting these on." He handed Piola a fluorescent jacket, a hard hat, and a laminated card on a ribbon. On it were the words "VISITOR – TEMPORARY PASS". Piola put it all on without comment, then followed the man to a waiting Jeep.

When they were under way, bumping and sliding over the rough ground, the sergeant spoke again. "Nothing's been moved or disturbed. Your medical people got here around an hour ago."

"When were the remains discovered?"

"Approximately two-thirty. We had a security ingress – protestors cut through the padlocks and forced open a gate. The gates are alarmed, and our cameras have night-vision capability, so we were well prepared for them. They let off these flares you can see, sprayed some graffiti, then split up. Two chained themselves to cranes – those are my biggest headache; we'll have to call in abseilers to cut them loose. My men followed another to a 319D – that is, one of the big excavator trucks. By the time they caught up with him, he was on his phone to the police, saying he'd seen a skeleton in the tipper. One of them went to check, and it turned out he was right. At least, there *was* a skeleton."

Piola noted the implication. "You don't believe the rest of his account?"

"Well, sir, I don't want to pre-empt your investigation. But on the cameras, we could make out that he was carrying a large holdall when he broke in. It seems possible he brought the skeleton with him, threw it in the truck himself, and then reported it, in the hope of holding up construction." Pownall glanced across at Piola. "No offence, Colonel, but Italian bureaucracy can be notoriously slow, and it wouldn't be the first time the antis have tried to get us tangled up in red tape. That's why we made sure we got the Carabinieri, rather than the State Police, to run this investigation. You people get that this is a military schedule we're dealing with."

Piola chose not to respond directly to that. "Have the protestors broken in before?"

"Negative – this would be the first time since Transformation began."

"*Trasformazione?*" Piola echoed.

Pownall shrugged. "That's what the consortium call it. I guess you'll see why. It's rather more than your typical building project."

In fact, Piola could still see very little. Tattered fronds of fog greyed the Jeep's headlights as they drove. He thought he glimpsed some earthmovers to their left, through a gap in the fog, but appearances were deceptive: it was at least another minute before the Jeep drew up beside them.

As he followed Sergeant Pownall towards the vehicles, stepping gingerly through the mud in an effort to preserve his shoes, he realised why he'd been confused about the distance. The machines were vast – at least twice normal size, the tyres alone the height of a man. On the door of the nearest one, some graffiti had been sprayed – a round circle with an A in it, like the anarchy symbol, except that there were also a smaller D and M nestled between the A's feet. The graffiti was very recent, the black paint still running in the moisture-laden air.

The truck was so big that to see into the tipper he had to

climb a ladder that was placed next to it. Peering over the edge, he saw two white-suited figures crouched amongst a heap of rubble, examining some bones by the glare of a portable arc light. Piola made out a skull, brown with age, and below it the hoops of a ribcage. Nearby, but separate, was a leg, still attached to a foot.

"Good morning, Dottori," he greeted them. One of the figures looked up.

"Ah, Colonel. I was beginning to think we wouldn't see you before breakfast." Hapadi's voice was muffled by his mask.

"I'm not sure why I'm here at all," Piola said. "As opposed to someone more local, I mean. What can you tell me?"

The forensic examiner pulled down his mask and stood, stretching to ease the stiffness in his back. "I'd say it's a man, from the size of the pelvis. DNA will confirm it – we'll have to use mitochondrial, there isn't enough adipose for a conventional assay."

Piola nodded, although he barely understood these technical details. "Any idea when it dates from?"

They both knew this was the crucial question, and Hapadi's voice when he answered was cautious. "Well, I doubt it's pre-medieval. But neither is it fresh – the discoloration's too evenly spread for that. There are some fragments of fibre that might help, probably from a khaki jacket, and he has an interesting distortion of the left wrist that could indicate pre-vaccination poliomyelitis – he'd have had a distinctive withered left hand, by the way. To be honest, dating skeletons is specialist work. I'll have to find someone who's more familiar with the tests than I am."

"Any thoughts on how it got here?"

"It looks as if it was tossed in by someone on the ground – the bones are clearly positioned on top of the spoil, not amongst it. The force of the impact is what caused the femur and pelvis to separate, I imagine."

"So it could have been thrown in only a couple of hours ago?"

"Possibly. I'm aware that's what's being hypothesised." Piola caught the wariness in the doctor's voice. "But you should be able to prove or disprove it easily enough."

"How, Dottore?"

Hapadi crouched down again. "See here, how earth has filled the pelvic cavity? If it was carried here, some would have fallen out along the way. Your skeleton will have left a trail of crumbs, Colonel. Like Hansel and Gretel."

"Thank you, Dottore. That's very useful."

As Piola started back down the ladder, Hapadi added, "You didn't ask about cause of death."

Piola stopped. "That's because I didn't think you'd be able to tell me."

"Normally, perhaps. But when it's like this it's not difficult." The doctor lifted the skull in white-gloved hands, rotating it so that Piola could see the neat circle just behind where the left ear would have been. "That's how I know it isn't medieval, Colonel. They didn't make holes like this before they had bullets."

TWO

MIA WOKE UP in a warm, comfortable haze that receded abruptly as the memory of what had happened came flooding back. It had been this way for a while now – sleeping from the drugs they'd given her; waking, her panic momentarily surfacing through the fog in her brain, then drifting back into oblivion again. How long exactly, she had no idea.

She vaguely remembered the motion of the van, and sensing when it pulled off a smooth, fast road on to bumpier, more rural ones. From the way her body had rolled from side to side, she'd guessed they must be climbing up into the hills. Eventually they'd turned onto what felt like a farm track, crawling over potholes.

She'd drifted off again, waking only when the van finally stopped. Doors banged, and cold air rushed in around her feet. A male voice spoke, the Italian dialect too thick and fast for her to make out the words.

A second man, close to her head, answered – he must have been in the back with her the whole time. Hands lifted her, the two men sliding her out and carrying her between them. There was some quiet conversation – "*Lentamente*", "*Attenzione alla porta*" – as if they were simply moving furniture or a piece of rolled carpet. Then she was somewhere that felt both small and echoey. The men's boots scuffed on a rough floor as she was lowered onto a mattress.

A sharp sting in her wrist had brought back the panic, only for sleep to claim her once more.

When she woke, it was to discover that the hood had been replaced with goggles – large ones, like skiing goggles, but with the lenses blacked out. She tested her hands. Handcuffed. Bile rose into her mouth.

"Looks like you're awake, princess," a voice said in heavily accented English.

A hand clamped around her wrist – not roughly, but resting there. She flinched at the touch, as light as a caress, but he was simply taking her pulse.

"OK," the same voice said at last. "*Cominciamo.*"

She didn't speak much Italian, but she understood that, and her body stiffened in terror.

Let's begin.

THREE

AS HE CLIMBED back down the ladder Piola caught the sound of raised voices. Looking over his shoulder, he saw four people standing under the arc lights. One was a young Carabinieri lieutenant who Piola didn't know. He was flanked by Sergeant Pownall and a big, thickset man wearing a bulging business suit, incongruously topped with a high-visibility jacket and a hard hat several sizes too small. The fourth was a woman.

"… which is why I need to examine the remains *in situ*," she was saying forcibly. "There are clear procedures for moving bones, and the most important one is this: don't move anything at all until it's been sifted and mapped."

"Well, it's in the hands of the Italian police now," the big man said.

"Or rather, the Carabinieri," Piola agreed, joining them. "Good morning. I'm Colonel Piola."

The big man stepped forward, effectively using his bulk to mask the woman, and thrust out a meaty hand. "Sergio Sagese, Transformation Director." Although his Italian was fluent, there was a twang that told Piola he was more used to speaking American. "Do you have what you need? We want to facilitate a speedy resolution for you people any way we can."

"Thank you." Piola looked around Sagese's shoulder to the woman, who now appeared even more furious. "And you are?"

"Dottora Ester Iadanza, forensic archaeologist." Piola noticed her unusual use of the female "-a" ending, as opposed to the more usual "Dottoressa". Some feminists, he had heard, had started avoiding the latter, which had traditionally been used to denote any woman with a university degree, or even a doctor's wife. "I'm attached to this construction project," she added. "Supposedly."

"Only for the preparatory stages," Sagese interjected. "And as it turned out, your involvement was never actually required."

Dr Iadanza spoke directly to Piola. "It was a condition of work going ahead that my team be given access. Not surprisingly, having been given not a shred of cooperation, we've found very little."

"Did you think you might?" Piola asked, curious. "I hadn't realised this area was of particular significance."

"Archaeology doesn't just mean ancient history, Colonel. This airfield was used by both the Italian and German air forces in the Second World War. Anything relating to that might be of great interest to a historian."

"And what is it – exactly – that you want, Dottora?"

"I want to examine the remains, and sift the soil they were found with, metre by cubic metre," she said promptly. "And if there's any evidence that they actually came from a different part of the site, I want to do the same in that location too."

"Surely there's no suggestion—" Sagese began, but Piola cut him off.

"Speak to Dr Hapadi, Dottora. He's already expressed a desire to work with a specialist on this. If he has no objection, neither do I."

"Thank you. I'll get suited up." She turned and headed off into the mist.

Sagese cleared his throat, although the sound that came

from his thick neck sounded more like a growl. "This won't affect construction, Colonel, will it?"

"In what respect?" Piola said.

Sagese jerked out his elbow to inspect the watch strapped to his massive wrist. "In exactly seventy-five minutes, our next shift comes on site. I just want to be certain there'll be no obstacles to them doing a proper day's work." He gave the word "obstacles" a disdainful sneer.

Clearly, Piola thought, any Carabinieri investigation of more than a few minutes would represent just such an impediment in Sagese's eyes. "It will be necessary to stand them down, for the time being," he said politely. "I'll let you know how soon you can expect to resume work when I have a better idea myself."

Sagese shook his head in exasperation. "Let me just explain what we're dealing with here, Colonel. This project involves the construction of over four hundred buildings across a site of one hundred and thirty acres. Structures on the east side are being completed even as groundworks are initiated here in the west. And each day my workers stand idle costs half a million dollars in overheads and penalty clauses – not least to the Italian government, who are co-financiers of the project and receive regular updates at the *very highest level*. Halting work is simply not an option."

Piola felt a flash of irritation at the man's tone, although he tried hard not to let it show. "We'll be as quick as we can."

"What the hell does that mean? An hour? A morning? A *day*?" Sagese demanded, pulling out his phone as threateningly as another man might pull out a knife.

"It's much too early to say. In the meantime, I'd like you, and all your people, to clear this area. Whoever threw that skeleton in the tipper may have left evidence on the ground, and we're trampling it."

As Sagese stamped off, already punching in numbers, Piola turned to the *carabiniere*, who had so far said nothing. "What's your name, Sottotenente?"

"Panicucci, sir."

"Do you know how to establish an investigative perimeter, Panicucci?"

"Yes, sir."

"Then please do so. One-hundred-metre tapes in every direction, with a single entry and exit point. Carabinieri guards front and rear. Every authorised visitor to be logged in and out, and make sure they wear microfibre overalls. Those remains may or may not be recent, but they didn't climb inside that tipper by themselves. And now," he said, turning back to Pownall, "I'd like to speak to the protestor who called this in."

The site guardhouse was like every guardhouse Piola had ever been in – too warm, and smelling of microwaved food. But the interview room where the protestor was being held was well equipped, with a table and chairs bolted to the floor, heavy-duty bars on the window, and a CCTV camera mounted behind a protective grille. Clearly, the US Military Police didn't do things by halves.

"Bring me his bag," Piola instructed. "And anything else he had with him."

The American guard hesitated, then, as Piola had intended, left Piola and the protestor alone.

"Luca Marchesin?" The young man with the straggly goatee sitting across the table nodded. "I'll need to see your ID."

He wrote down the details in his notebook. The date of birth was ridiculously recent – only nine years before his own son's. "Tell me what happened here, Luca."

Luca shrugged, affecting a bravado that Piola suspected he

no longer felt after several hours of being incarcerated by men in American uniform. "Five of us broke in just after two a.m. We all had different tasks – mine was to get right to the centre of the site, to leave a sign we'd been there. I had to move fast – the MPs were after us within seconds. I found a big excavator truck, so I climbed up the steps to spray the door. And that's when I saw it."

"Saw what?"

"A skeleton, lying right there in the tipper. So I called 112."

"You didn't touch the remains, or disturb them in any way?"

It was important to establish whether Luca was admitting any forensic contact with the bones. But the boy was shaking his head emphatically. "I never went near them. Check the film from my GoPro if you like."

The soldier had returned with a black holdall and a tray containing the boy's things: a watch, an iPhone and a small video camera on an elastic strap, like the ones worn by snowboarders. Piola picked the camera up. It was completely wrecked, the housing almost in two pieces and the innards spilling out.

"Your camera seems to be broken," Piola said neutrally.

Luca gave a hollow laugh. "So it is."

Piola unzipped the holdall. Inside were four aerosol cans, but otherwise it was empty. It was also perfectly clean, with no crumbs of earth like the ones Hapadi had said would fall out of the skeleton when it was moved.

"That graffiti you were spraying. 'ADM' – what's that all about?" he asked, turning the lining inside out to check.

"Azione Dal Molin." Luca looked defiant. "Our new group. The only thing the Americans understand is direct action. So that's what we're going to do."

"'Direct action'? Trespass and sabotage, you mean? What's wrong with legal forms of protest?"

Luca snorted. "Marches, petitions, protests – we've had all that. The decision to give this land to the US was made behind closed doors, by Berlusconi and his cronies. Why should we respect the law, when our own government ignores it?"

Piola looked at the young man thoughtfully. "You're making this very difficult for me, Luca. On the one hand, you say you've done nothing wrong. On the other hand, you're telling me you broke into the site with the express intention of breaking the law."

"I told you. Check out the footage."

"And as I told *you*," Piola indicated the broken camera, "that doesn't appear to be possible."

Luca's face cracked into a smile. "That's what the people who smashed it thought. But this isn't a conventional video camera, Colonel. This part *here* connects directly to the internet, via the personal hotspot on my iPhone. As soon as I broke into the site, I was streaming the film to our group's Facebook page."

The technical details meant nothing to Piola, but he understood the gist. "Can you show me? On your phone, for example?"

"Sure." Luca entered a passcode, then placed the phone in front of Piola, turning his head sideways so he could see too. "Ninety views already. Not bad."

The footage was often blurry as Luca, unseen behind the camera, scrabbled over obstacles, but the section by the excavator was clear enough, as was the sudden force with which the boy had been wrestled to the ground. The part where a burly figure – Piola couldn't be sure, but it looked like Sergeant

Pownall – yanked the camera off Luca's head, placed it on the ground, then lifted his booted foot and stamped on it, turning the image into flickering visual porridge, was almost comic. It was, Piola guessed, the kind of thing that would go round the internet like wildfire.

"OK," he said. "Stay here. And for your own sake, try not to antagonise anyone."

He went and found Sagese and Pownall.

"Well? Did the kid confess yet?" Sagese demanded.

"I need to confirm something," Piola said. "In the meantime, can you find me whoever was driving the excavator truck yesterday? And get me his documents, along with a plan of where he was working?"

There was the briefest of pauses before Pownall said, "Of course."

"Good. I'll see you in about twenty minutes."

The peace camp was about five minutes' walk, on a piece of waste ground to the north: half a dozen old Portakabins clustered around three marquees decked with rainbow flags and "No Dal Molin" banners. Going into the largest tent, Piola found the usual detritus of a long-running protest – a makeshift stage, posters, an industrial-sized cooking pot being stirred by a brawny woman with a stud through her nose. But it was also well swept and neat, with bins marked for every imaginable kind of recycling. Tables that looked as if they'd been liberated from a school or college held laptops, printers and tangles of wiring. Despite the earliness of the hour, half a dozen people were gathered around one of the computers.

"Good morning," he said to no one in particular. Faces turned towards him warily. "I'd like to speak to whoever's in charge."

"No one's in charge." The voice belonged to a ponytailed man of about thirty with a girl sitting on his lap.

"Then I'll talk to you," Piola said. "Your name?"

The man scratched his ear, revealing a faded Betty Boop tattoo on his forearm. "First things first. Before I say anything, I need to see *your* ID, Colonel. In case you've forgotten, you work for us, not the other way round." A couple of the onlookers grinned.

Piola doubted the ponytailed man had ever contributed much by way of taxes to the running costs of the Carabinieri, but he inclined his head courteously and took out his wallet. "Certainly."

The man pushed the girl off his lap and carefully copied the details of Piola's ID into a logbook before producing his own. It showed that his name was Ettore Mazzanti, and that he was a student, aged thirty-two.

"Quite old to still be studying," Piola commented.

"I'm writing a PhD. On the erosion of civil liberties by the police."

Piola chose to ignore that. "I take it you were part of last night's protest?"

"I was."

"Would you mind telling me what it was about?"

Mazzanti reached for a folder. "Read it for yourself, Colonel. Our mission statement, timetable, a list of objectives, and statements of intent from all participants. Oh, and photographs of each of us showing that we were sound and unbruised before we went in."

Piola took the folder and looked through it. It was all just as Mazzanti described. There was even a letter from a firm of lawyers arguing that the break-in fell within the category of democratic protest on public land. "May I keep this?" he said, impressed despite himself. To have documented their action so thoroughly wouldn't give the demonstrators immunity from prosecution, but it would certainly help if they ever found themselves in court. He couldn't remember when he'd come across a protest group as well organised as Azione Dal Molin appeared to be.

"Colonel Piola!"

Piola glanced over his shoulder. A man of about forty with a mop of curly grey hair was advancing towards him. Piola couldn't quite place him, although his manner and use of Piola's name certainly suggested they'd met.

"Raffaele Fallici, Lega della Libertà," the man added.

Piola knew where he'd seen him now. Not as an acquaintance, but on TV. Fallici was a blogger-turned-politician, a self-styled man of the people who'd come to prominence as part of Beppe Grillo's Five Star Movement. Subsequently setting up his own party, he had a reputation as a demagogue who spoke out against vested interests and corruption. On many occasions he'd also criticised the incompetence of the Carabinieri.

"I understand you're investigating the desecration that has occurred here," Fallici continued.

"I'm looking into this situation, yes," Piola said non-committally.

"Do you have enough resources? Are the authorities treating this with the seriousness it deserves? We must ensure that this unfortunate individual receives the same respect in death that any other Italian citizen would be entitled to." Fallici half-turned to the room. "To be frank, no one was surprised to discover that those responsible for Dal Molin have been treating human remains with disdain," he said in a louder voice. "They have been treating all of us, living or dead, with indifference, ever since the people of Vicenza made clear their democratic opposition to this development."

Faces nodded, and a few fists punched the air.

"What can I do for you, Mr Fallici?" Piola asked wearily. The sofa wasn't the most comfortable of beds, and even before Saito's pre-dawn call he hadn't been sleeping particularly well.

"I just want to be certain due process is being followed," Fallici said emphatically.

"Of course."

"By which I mean," he continued as if Piola hadn't spoken, "that a full survey must be done of the entire site: environmental, archaeological and anthropological, just as was demanded at the outset. Questions that were previously brushed aside by the developers in their indecent haste to get under way will now have to be answered fully."

Piola was beginning to see now why the local Carabinieri hadn't been keen on getting involved, and why Saito had wanted someone experienced on the case – not just to handle the pressure from the Americans, but to take the heat for having done so. The US might have plenty of clout in Rome and Milan, but there were few local votes in appeasing them. The protestors, on the other hand, were clearly a bloc worth courting.

"It's still too early to say what investigations will be appropriate, Mr Fallici," he said. "But rest assured, whatever needs to be done, will be." To his relief he saw Panicucci heading his way, holding a phone. "Yes, Sottotenente?"

"It's General Saito, sir."

Piola took the phone and walked outside.

"Any progress?" Saito's voice said.

"Some," Piola said, wondering what the man expected after

just a few hours. "That is to say, it looks as if the protestors had nothing to do with it."

"Good. Aldo, I've had five calls already about this case, and I haven't even had breakfast yet. One from the base commander in charge of the Vicenza garrison. One from our own *generale di divisione*. One from the mayor, and two from government officials in Rome who are so damn important I have absolutely no idea who they are."

Piola sighed inwardly. "The issue, as you're probably aware, is that the consortium are in a hurry to get their men back to work. But first I need to establish how the remains got into the tipper truck. And that would have happened a lot quicker, frankly, if they'd cooperated from the start, instead of trying to pin it on the boy who called it in." He hesitated. "There's something else you should know. That politician Raffaele Fallici's here, talking about environmental surveys, legal challenges…"

"Oh, that's to be expected. Where there are votes, there are vultures. We're caught in the middle, as usual. Keep me updated, won't you? It would be nice to have some progress to report back to Rome."

As Saito rang off, Piola realised it hadn't been news to him that Fallici would be there. He had the curious feeling that he himself was like an actor at the first rehearsal of a play, being fed his lines one by one, told where to stand and when to move, precisely so that at some later date everyone could point to him and say, "There. See what he did?" But that was often the way of these things – the top brass far more concerned with making sure no one could blame them for some procedural irregularity than actually solving crimes.

As he got into the car, spreading muddy stains over the carpet, he also realised that, sometime over the course of the morning, he'd managed to mislay that damn hat.

FOUR

THE WOMAN SLIPPED out of bed, careful not to wake the sleeping body at her side, and stepped into the bathroom. Scanning the hotel toiletries with a practised eye, she reached for a bottle of shower gel. Bulgari's Thé Vert, indeed. Her companion certainly hadn't spared any expense on the room.

She hadn't bothered with her clothes, just her phone. Checking the screen, she saw she had four missed calls and a voicemail, all from the same person. She ignored them and turned on the shower.

When she came out, wrapped in two big towels, the man in the bed was awake. He watched her as she dressed – quickly and efficiently, so unlike the night before, when the same clothes had come off slowly, piece by piece, their progress interrupted by kisses, sweet talk and mouthfuls of *prosecco*.

"Good morning, *cara*," he said at last, when she sat on the bed to put on her stockings.

She eased a kitten-heeled shoe over one foot. "Good morning," she answered just as evenly.

"I enjoyed last night."

"Me too." Although her words agreed with him, her tone was casual.

He reached out and ran a hand along her thigh. "Will we do it again?"

"I don't know. Perhaps. It's difficult for me." She stood up abruptly. As if unconsciously, she looked down at her left hand. Reaching into a pocket, she took out a wedding ring and slipped it back on.

"Yes, of course. Your husband. But if you ever find yourself in need of another little adventure…"

"I'll get in touch through the website."

The man, whose name was Riccardo, said, "I'll look forward to it. I mean it. That was something really special. And people like you and me… We have to take our fun where we can."

She nodded, her hand already on the door handle. "*Ciao* then, Riccardo."

"*Ciao*, Rita."

She passed through the hotel lobby, ignoring the night porter's polite "Good morning, *signora*." When she reached the street she looked at her watch. Still time to go home and change. As she walked through the fog-filled streets she pulled off the wedding ring and put it back in her pocket, then flicked her phone off silent. She was only a hundred metres from her apartment when it rang. Glancing at the screen, she saw it was the same person who'd been calling repeatedly all night.

Holly B.

Clearly Holly B wasn't going to give up. "*Pronto*," she said in her most businesslike voice.

"Kat?"

"*Si*, this is Katerina Tapo," she said, pretending she didn't already know who was calling.

"Kat, it's Holly."

"Yes?"

At the other end of the line, Second Lieutenant Holly Boland of the US Army's Civilian Liaison section pulled a face. She'd known this call would be awkward, but she hadn't expected it to be quite as difficult as this. "Kat, I'm calling on a semi-official matter. We have a military family over here at Vicenza whose daughter's gone missing. The local Carabinieri have been told, but... well, they don't seem to be taking it too seriously. The family have asked Liaison if there's anything we can do."

"How long's she been gone?"

"Two nights. She was meant to be on a snowboarding weekend with her class – at least, that's what the parents thought. When the coaches came back, it turned out she hadn't actually signed up for the trip."

"So she lied to her parents. And she's how old?"

"Sixteen. Almost seventeen."

"Have they checked with her boyfriend?"

"She doesn't have a boyfriend." Even over the phone, Holly caught Kat's snort of disbelief. "Apparently it's totally out of character," she added.

"Well, the local officers will know what to do. Check the hospitals, call her friends. Chances are she'll turn up."

"They did all that before they called it in," Holly said patiently. "And all the local officers have done is go through her bedroom, looking for drugs."

"Did they find any?"

"No. The thing is, Major Elston and his wife don't speak Italian, so—"

"Oh, he's a *major*, is he?"

"He happens to be an officer, yes. But they're understandably upset, and they could really use someone who can talk them through the Italian system."

Kat sighed. "Who can hold their hands until their precious daughter crawls out from whichever bed she's in, you mean."

"Is that so unreasonable? Put yourself in their shoes—"

"I'd have to ask my superiors," Kat interrupted. "And I should tell you it's highly unlikely they'll agree. I'm involved in a number of urgent cases at the moment."

"OK," Holly said, accepting defeat. She understood the source of Kat's hostility, and the almost permanent sense of anger the Carabinieri officer carried with her these days, but it was no easier to deal with for all that. "Let me know what they say, will you?"

"Of course. *Ciao.*"

Kat had let herself into her apartment and started changing into her uniform while she was still on the phone. Not long ago, when she was on a homicide team, she'd worked in plain clothes. Going back into uniform – even the beautiful Valentino-designed skirt and jacket of the Arma dei Carabinieri – had felt like a snub; and, she knew, had been intended to feel that way by those who had ordered it. Nor, despite what she'd said to Holly, were the cases she was currently engaged on much more than glorified filing. Stolen cameras, cloned credit cards, pickpockets dipping into open backpacks in Piazza San Marco – by the time she'd written up the crimes, the tourists who'd reported them were usually long gone, making any kind of investigation impossible.

She slipped the wedding ring onto the coat hook on the back of the bedroom door, ready for its next outing. It had cost a hundred euros and was one of the best investments she'd ever made – that, and the subscription to the Married and Discreet message board. Coupled with an anonymous account on Carnivia.com, it allowed her to conduct her sex life without any emotional entanglements whatsoever.

If only she'd found Married and Discreet before, she thought. If she had, her career might not be in such a total mess.

*

Leaving her apartment, she caught a train for the short hop across the Ponte della Libertà. As she strode out of the vast, imposing Stazione Santa Lucia – the only Fascist-era building in Venice, it was considered a monstrosity by most, although Kat secretly rather liked it – she was lucky enough to step straight onto a number two *vaporetto*. Even though this was the fast line, the boat made slow progress as it chugged its way up the Grand Canal. During Carnevale Venice attracted up to a million extra visitors, and crowds of people – some in masks and costumes, despite the early hour – surged on and off at every stop. A few surreptitiously raised their phones to take pictures of her. But she was used to that. A *capitano donna*, a female captain of the Carabinieri, was still a rare enough sight that even some Italians did a double take.

The Carabinieri headquarters were in Campo San Zaccaria, just behind the waterfront at Riva degli Schiavoni. Once, these cloisters had been part of Venice's largest convent. And the people who worked here now, Kat thought viciously as she passed through the entrance lobby, would probably prefer it if their female colleagues still behaved like nuns. But even though the comparison gave her some satisfaction, she knew it was actually a flawed one. The convent of San Zaccaria had been famous for the licentious behaviour of its inmates, many of whom had been dumped there by noble families unwilling to pay their daughters' dowries. Having escaped the crushing social confines of their family *palazzi*, the young women soon realised that the convent afforded them their first opportunity to take a lover. Like so many things in Venice, appearance and reality were two subtly different things.

There was nothing subtle, though, about the graffiti she found scrawled across her locker in the female changing room.

Va' a cagare, puttana.

Piss off, whore.

A few weeks back, when the insults had started appearing, she'd meticulously cleaned each one off with lighter fuel. Now she tended to leave it until three or four had accumulated before bothering.

She rarely used the locker these days. It had been a while since she'd opened it to find dog shit inside, though more than once someone had tried to urinate through the keyhole. When you made a complaint of sexual misconduct against one of the most popular male officers in the division, and a colonel to boot, this was the kind of thing that happened.

At her desk, she logged into her computer without acknowledging the officers on either side. They in turn ignored her, just as they did every day. She wondered which of them had written the graffiti.

She could tell from her inbox that it was going to be a morning of yet more tedium. On top of everything else, someone had forwarded a request from the Guardia di Finanza to investigate whether the handbags sold by the hawkers around Piazza San Marco were counterfeit. *Of course they are*, she found herself shouting inside her head. The bags cost a few euros from a homeless Nigerian on a street corner. Did anyone really imagine that was how Louis Vuitton and Dolce e Gabbana chose to sell their goods? Even if she arrested someone, the counterfeiters would simply find another vagrant, while the Carabinieri provided bed and breakfast to the first. It was utterly pointless.

Discreetly checking that no one was watching, she opened a web browser and typed a familiar URL.

A screen appeared. Below a white Bauta mask – which, despite having no mouth, somehow seemed to be grinning mischievously – was a login box.

Enter Carnivia.

She typed in her username and password.

Welcome, Columbina7759. Where in Carnivia would you like to go?

She typed "Rialto", and found herself standing on a perfect, 3D simulacrum of the bridge she'd passed under earlier. Every detail was accurate, right down to the current level of the tide, with one difference: here every passer-by was wearing a mask.

With a few clicks of her mouse, she propelled her avatar through the *pescheria*. The market stalls in Carnivia, she knew, actually sold much more than fish, but it was something else she was after now. Heading over the Ponte delle Tette – the "Bridge of Tits" – she entered what had once been Venice's red light district. In both the real Venice and Carnivia, it was still the centre of Venice's nightlife, with people crowding into the tiny bars. She went into one of the smaller establishments and approached a booth towards the back.

The canals and buildings of Carnivia appeared to exactly replicate those of the real Venice, to a level of detail bordering on the obsessive; it was said, for example, that if you counted the panes of glass in any real Venetian window, you'd find that its equivalent in Carnivia contained precisely the same number. But inside the buildings, space behaved rather differently, in a way that she'd read somewhere was based on string theory, but which always reminded her of a line of poetry she'd come across at school – something about seeing infinity in a grain of sand. Every table in a bar, for example, could host a dozen different chat rooms, each of which might link in turn to a thousand cyber lockers, peer-to-peer torrents and individual web pages, all created by Carnivia users eager to make the most of the extraordinary new world in which they found themselves.

The booth she sat in now contained a link to a site she'd visited many times: the Married and Discreet message board. She clicked on some graffiti scratched into the wooden panelling, and it materialised in front of her.

Riccardo hadn't wasted any time, already logging on under his own Carnivia identity of Zanni2243 and reviewing their encounter. He'd given her five stars, along with the comment: *Wow! Un'esperienza incredibile!*

Smiling to herself, she added her review of him. *Anche tu non eri per niente male.* Not bad yourself. Four stars.

She'd noticed she usually gave her partners lower scores and more ambivalent comments than they gave her. But there was no point in letting praise go to their heads. After all, it wasn't as if she was going to see any of them a second time.

Venice was a small city. Everyone knew everyone, and everyone gossiped. Ironically, it was the sudden success of Carnivia that had exacerbated the problem, by making it possible to post rumours about friends, colleagues or neighbours without being identified as the source. Kat's reputation had been so bad – Carnivia's infamous gossip ledgers now contained over a hundred and twenty anonymous comments about her, few of them favourable – that she'd decided Married and Discreet was the only way to ensure her partners had as much reason to keep quiet about their encounters as she did.

It was easier in other respects as well. The men she met didn't know her real name, her real email address, or what she did for a living. And generally, she'd discovered, married men didn't bombard her with texts, send her flowers, or demand attention and ego-stroking like single men did. It suited her to be able to concentrate on what was going on at work, whilst also being able to let off steam occasionally.

Or so she told herself. A nagging voice at the back of her head – which sounded suspiciously like her mother's – disagreed. But then, Kat and her mother had never seen eye to eye about such matters.

Her desk phone rang. Quickly, she closed the browser. "Tapo."

"Capitano, it's General Saito."

"General," Kat said, surprised to be called directly by such a senior officer. "What can I do for you, sir?"

"The American Civilian Liaison Office at Vicenza has called about a missing person, a teenager. I understand they've already approached you informally?"

"Yes. Of course I told them it would have to go through the proper channels—"

"That's fine," Saito interrupted. "You can go over there straight away. Give them any assistance they require."

"Really?" She knew the top brass were always sucking up to the Americans, but she hadn't imagined that would extend to relatively trivial family matters.

"There's another investigation going on – nothing to do with this, it needn't concern you directly. But the upshot is that I'd like to do them a favour. If this family want a female officer, I'm happy to help."

Ah, so that was how Holly, or one of her superiors, had spun it. Kat could just imagine the phone call. *"It's a job for someone sensitive. A female, perhaps. I believe we know just the officer…"*

Well, she'd show them how sensitive she could be.

"Of course, sir," she said sweetly. "It'll be a pleasure to get my teeth into something useful."

If Saito noticed the implicit complaint, he didn't mention it. "Good. Any problems, come to me direct." He rang off.

Kat picked up her mobile and texted Holly. *Spoke to my boss and managed to swing it. With you in an hour.*

She hesitated, wondering if she should add something to clear the air before they saw each other in person. The incident that had caused their falling-out – abruptly terminating not only their friendship, but also Holly's temporary residence at Kat's apartment – was not one either would forget in a hurry.

But then, she reasoned, the American had made it clear that this was a purely professional request. And there was no one better at keeping her own feelings in check than Holly Boland. Better, perhaps, to do the same, and keep their personal history out of it.

The matter decided, she pressed "Send".

FIVE

"GONE?" PIOLA REPEATED incredulously. "Gone where?"

"No one knows," Pownall said. "It seems he left without picking up his pay." He indicated a grizzled man in work clothes. "According to his foreman here, when the driver heard the Carabinieri wanted to speak to him, he asked for permission to go back to the accommodation cabins to fetch something. That was the last anyone saw of him."

Behind Pownall, Sagese's face was impassive.

Piola sighed. It confirmed what he'd suspected all along, even before it had become apparent that the Azione Dal Molin protestors had nothing to do with the skeleton's appearance. Any construction worker coming across a pile of old bones might be tempted to get rid of the evidence rather than face up to the bureaucratic tangles that would ensue if he reported it. He might even be tacitly encouraged to do so by his bosses, who would certainly be unenthusiastic about having their site shut down for days or even weeks while the archaeologists did their work. But it would have been nice to have heard it from the excavator driver himself, rather than learn that he had simply been allowed to walk out.

"Did you get his papers?" he asked. "And the plan of where he was working?"

Silently, Pownall handed over some documents. The top

one was a photocopied work permit for migrant EU workers, issued by the Sportello Unico per l'Immigrazione in the name of Tarin Krasnaki. It appeared to be in order. But peering closer, Piola saw that some of the individual letters were of microscopically different thicknesses. It was a forgery, albeit a very good one.

Again, that many of Italy's foreign workers were in the country illegally was hardly a revelation. He'd heard that these days you could even get false papers from the Mafia on easy credit, with payment deferred until your first pay packet – the catch being that only then did the illegal worker discover he was being charged an exorbitant rate of interest on top of the original amount, carefully worked out so that he'd never quite be able to pay off the debt.

Such an arrangement meant the criminals had a hold over the worker that could be exploited in other ways, too, Piola reflected; such as making him take the rap for some minor misdemeanour – throwing away a skeleton, say – that was holding up work for them all. "Do we know his real nationality?" he asked.

The foreman shrugged. "He said he was Albanian. I noticed he didn't talk much with the other Albanians, but he had the right papers, and he was vouched for by the agency, so..."

He spoke confidently enough, but Piola noted the flash of anxiety in the glance he gave Sagese afterwards, as if to check he was saying the right thing. Something was wrong here. But what it was, and whether it was relevant to his investigation, he doubted he'd ever find out.

Feeling his phone vibrate, he pulled it out. Hapadi's name was on the screen.

"Ah, Doctor. It will be nice to hear some real facts for a change," he said, stepping away from the construction workers.

"Don't say that too hastily," the forensic examiner said. "I don't have anything definitive for you. But I've taken a first look at our friend, here in the mortuary. As I suspected, the distortion to his left wrist is from polio, which means he was born prior to the vaccination programme in the 1950s. Taken together with the fragments of khaki, it seems likely the remains date back to the war."

"Thank you," Piola said. "That's very useful."

"There's something else that might interest you. We recovered a bullet from his right glenohumeral joint – that is, the right shoulder. The shot passed right through his head. There was an exit wound very close to the jawbone, which was why I didn't spot it at first."

Piola tried to picture how that could have happened. "So he must have been kneeling?"

"That's right. With his head forced to one side, and his jaw pressed against his shoulder by the pressure of the muzzle. The gunman would have been standing just behind him, to the left. I've sent the bullet for further analysis."

Thanking Hapadi again, Piola rang off. He knew exactly what he should do now – call Saito and tell him the case was effectively closed. Whether Krasnaki had really found the skeleton, or whether someone else had ordered it thrown into the excavator before it could hold up work, he didn't know. But it hardly mattered now. The point was, a scapegoat had been found, and had apparently confirmed his guilt by running away. The bones themselves dated back to a conflict almost seventy years ago. There was no reason not to allow the consortium to resume construction while Piola took himself back to Venice to write up his report in the warmth of his office.

"Well?" Sagese demanded. "Can we get back to work now, Colonel?"

JONATHAN HOLT

Piola turned back to Pownall and Sagese. "Not yet. First I need to speak to the archaeologist."

For the second time that morning he climbed the ladder up to the tipper. Inside, it had been taped into a grid, each square labelled with a reference number. Dr Iadanza was crouching amidst the rubble, carefully photographing each square.

"Any progress, Doctor?"

She looked up. "Well, I'm certain the remains weren't scooped up with this spoil."

He indicated the tapes. "Is all this strictly necessary, then?"

"It might be useful to prove it, at some point. I'm always asking myself what the archaeologist called by the other side might say in court."

"Of course," he said, a little surprised at her assumption that this might end up in a court. But perhaps that was just proper professional caution. He rather liked her, he realised; not just because of the way she'd resisted being browbeaten by Sagese, but because she hadn't made a big deal of it afterwards. "I was just going to inspect the area where the driver was last working, and it occurred to me that you might be able to tell rather more from it than I could. Would you like to come with me?"

"Certainly. Although to do a proper survey, I'll probably need ground sonar."

He climbed down the ladder again and waited for her to join him. Inevitably, he glanced up as she descended, and inevitably he couldn't tear his eyes away once he had. A little involuntary jolt of delight surged through him at the sight of her fine bottom, encased in the paper suit, negotiating the rungs towards him, followed almost immediately by a wave of irritation at his own predictability. Why did he always have to

42

look? And having looked, why did he have to like what he saw so very much? He had absolutely no doubt that Dottora Iadanza would be appalled if she knew the direction his thoughts had taken. As for his wife... well, he was in enough trouble in that direction already.

Annoyed with himself, he was initially silent as they walked over towards the far part of the construction site. The fog was lifting now; a faint glow from the east suggested that later, it might even be a beautiful day.

"There'll be an indoor swimming pool and gymnasium here, eventually," Dr Iadanza said, pointing. "Building number two hundred and forty-seven. And next to it, a cinema. Amazing what you need to fight a war these days. But I suppose you can hardly expect them to go to the *multi-sala* at Stradella dei Filippini with the rest of us to watch their war movies."

"You're no great fan of the Americans, I take it?" he said.

Her voice, when she replied, was careful. "I didn't say that. Of course we were frustrated not to be given proper access. But that was the Italian partners in the consortium, not the Americans themselves."

"Which partners are those?"

"Principally Conterno, plus a few others who deal with the specialist engineering."

Now Piola thought about it, he'd seen the Costruttori Conterno logo, a regal griffin's head on a heraldic shield, tacked to every entry gate, but it was so familiar it had barely registered. There was hardly a civil engineering project in northern Italy that didn't involve them in some way.

"One thing that being an archaeologist teaches you is that all empires fall eventually," she added. "I just wish the Americans appreciated that."

It took fifteen minutes of brisk walking to reach the far side of the site. Although mostly flat – this part had clearly been the runway, when it was an airfield – there was a small hummock to the side, perfectly round; almost, Piola thought, like an Iron Age burial mound. A huge bite had already been taken out of it by the excavators. "This is where the driver was working, according to the plan I was given," he said.

Dr Iadanza walked up close and peered at the face of the dug area, the way an art historian might scrutinise the details of a painting. "Quarried rubble," she said thoughtfully. "During the war, they probably kept a big heap here, ready to patch up the bomb craters." She pointed. "And that's where they came across the skeleton, I'd say."

Almost at ground level was a small cavity, hardly any bigger than the baskets the old ladies of Venice put their cats in. Something brown was hanging from its roof. She crouched down to examine it better.

"What is it?" Piola asked.

She took out a biro and used the point to tease away some of the earth.

"Well, well," she breathed. "You know what this is, don't you?"

He didn't, even when he squatted down beside her and she scraped away more soil to show him. It looked like a piece of folded cloth. Although faded now, it had clearly once been bright red.

"It's a *fazzoletto rosso*," Dr Iadanza said. "A red neckerchief. Our skeleton, Colonel, belongs to a partisan. Specifically, a partisan from one of the communist brigades."

"Somewhat ironic, then, that he ended up on an American air base."

"It may be rather more than that." She looked at him, her

eyes shining. "There's someone I'd like you to speak to about this, Colonel. I think we may just have helped to clear up a mystery."

SIX

SHE PACED HER cell anxiously. Six steps one way, three the other. It had clearly been built as an animal shed – the walls were of bare stone, the floor compacted earth. Part of a farm, then. A single window, high up in the roof, admitted the grey light of dawn, but it was barred with a metal grille that looked new.

She'd listened carefully, but she could hear no sounds of humanity – no hum of traffic, no chainsaws or church bells. Once, she thought she caught the distant clanking of cowbells, which made her think she must be high up in the mountains. Wherever they were, it was very remote.

The room contained a camping mattress, a blanket, a small chemical toilet like the ones used in caravans, an ancient gas heater, and a packet of Nuvenia sanitary towels. It was very cold, but the heater needed a special tool, so only the kidnappers could turn it on. In the corners of the room, too high for her to reach, were two small cameras. Between them they covered the entire room.

She wondered if they meant to rape her. To begin with she'd been certain of it – had assumed, with a sickening lurch of nausea, that that was why she'd been taken. But now she wasn't so sure. Almost the first thing they'd done was to make her undress, taking her into another, larger barn that led off this one,

46

where they'd photographed her from every angle. But there had been something oddly impersonal about it, as if it were all part of some ritual she didn't yet understand. Not that it was possible to read anything from their expressions – both kidnappers wore masks all the time, at least in her presence. One, the shorter, more thickset of the two, wore a Bauta, the classic plain white mask with an elongated chin and no mouth. The other wore a Harlequin, the red-and-blue diamond-patterned mask of a clown. The fact that they were Carnevale masks made her think of the club where she'd been snatched, but she couldn't work out if that was just a coincidence.

They'd paid particular attention to one of her legs, moving in and taking several close-ups. It was only when she glanced down that she'd seen why: it had got cut somehow during the kidnap, the blood crusting over the wound while she was drugged. They also took photographs of a bruise on her arm.

Noticing her trembling, one of them had fetched a blanket then, draping it round her shoulders like a shawl. It didn't stop her shivering – it wasn't just the cold, it was the nausea and the fear of what they might be about to do to her – but it was one of the things that had made her think that perhaps they weren't going to rape her after all. She remembered the many stories she'd read about Italian kidnaps. From what she recalled, they were usually carried out by the Mafia, who tried to look after their victims, at least initially, in order to protect their investment.

I didn't tell anyone where I was going, she thought suddenly. That was one of the precautions they taught you at the American High School, the school all the military teenagers attended, where it was drummed into you over and over that Americans made prime targets. *Always make sure someone knows where you are.* But the only person who'd known she was at the club was Johann, and he didn't even know her real name.

At home they'll know I'm missing by now. But not why. Not how, or where from. They'll have nothing to go on, until the kidnappers choose to make contact. The thought of home made her gulp back tears.

And there was another kind of fear gnawing at her now as well: fear of the unknown. After he'd brought her the blanket, the kidnapper in the Harlequin mask had placed something on the floor and gestured for her to step on it. Looking down, she'd seen that he was pointing to a pair of scales.

"The prisoner will be weighed," he said in his rough English.

The other man, the one in the Bauta mask, had lifted a hand-held video camera, the sort that plugged into a laptop's USB port, ready to film her again.

And immediately the terror had come flooding back, knotting her guts. Because in all the things she'd read about the Mafia, she'd never once heard of them weighing their hostages, let alone filming it.

SEVEN

THE YOUNG CLERIC looked up from his laptop and listened. From outside his office came the sound of applause, rippling around St Peter's Square. He knew what it meant: the crowds had glimpsed the Pope, on his way to his first engagement of the day. There was no double glazing in the tiny office – the cleric had already discovered that it was freezing in winter; doubtless it would be roasting in the summer months too – but he didn't resent the noise. In fact, he revelled in it.

What did air conditioning matter, when your ceiling was decorated with a biblical scene painted by Raphael? Who cared about heating, when your office was situated within the Apostolic Palace, only a short distance below the private apartments of the Holy Father himself? The room might be small, and the infrastructure on which he depended for his work, such as the broadband connection, almost laughably antiquated, but the fact that he was sitting in it was proof of his own meteoric rise within the Curia, and the power he now wielded.

A few months ago, at the age of just thirty-eight, the cleric – whose name was Martino Santini – had been plucked from his role running the press office of the archdiocese of Milan and appointed to the Papal Secretariat, a post that carried with it the automatic seniority of an archbishop. For years, he and other reformers had been arguing that the only way for the

Church to overcome its recent troubles was by becoming more open and transparent. The new Pope had evidently agreed – or at least, had seen the sense in drawing a line under the scandals of the past by appointing some of the more vocal reformers to key positions. In Santini's case, that meant being given responsibility for the Sala Stampa della Santa Sede, the Vatican Information Service. There could be no clearer signal that His Holiness wanted the Curia to abandon its centuries-old habits of secrecy.

Some of Santini's initiatives had been mocked at first – the Pope's Facebook page, for example, and his Twitter feed; not to mention Santini's own blog, updated daily. But they proved to be immediate hits with the faithful, just as Santini had predicted they would; particularly with the younger faithful, now seen as vital footsoldiers in the fight against secularism.

Santini checked his own Facebook page as he got to his feet. It took an age to reload; he really would have to do something soon about the Apostolic Palace's lack of bandwidth. But one battle at a time. Right now he had a meeting with Monsignor Verti, head archivist of the Archivio Segreto, the Pope's confidential library. He could guess what it was about. Ever since Santini had ordered that the library's entire contents be catalogued and listed online – again, giving a clear signal to the world that from now on, nothing was going to be concealed or kept hidden – the officials responsible for doing so had come up with reason after reason why it would be impractical. Needless to say, he was equally determined that they would do it.

He made his way along the corridor to where a small lift was tucked into a stairwell. The lift's interior was surprisingly modern, an airtight box of glass and steel that, once he'd put in his Vatican security card, sucked Santini down into the labyrinthine basements below the Apostolic Palace as smoothly and delicately as a component being pneumatically transported into a factory.

Four levels below St Peter's Square, the lift doors opened onto a long, low room that stretched away as far as the eye could see. Dim light, so cleansed of damaging ultraviolet it seemed almost colourless, seeped from concealed diodes in the walls. The hum of the air conditioning that kept the entire level almost as cold as a morgue, and the slight vibration underfoot from the dehumidification equipment, gave Santini the sense that he was in some sleek underwater vessel, moving purposefully but calmly through the depths of the ocean.

A series of glass-walled pens along both sides of the room contained books and documents too precious, or too fragile, to be kept in the stacks. In some, bookbinders and restorers worked with powerful magnifiers to repair microscopic tears. Scholars padded to and fro – access was granted each year to a privileged few with impeccable credentials and an orthodox religious outlook, although there was currently a ban on requesting any document less than seventy-five years old. It was one of the many arcane regulations Santini was determined to stamp out.

Everyone, whether staff or visitor, wore white cotton gloves. Santini pulled a pair from the dispenser in the airlock and tugged them on while he waited for the second door to open, the air in his lungs thinning with every breath he took. Even the atmosphere down here was different, constantly purged of any gases or humidity that might damage old documents. It was, Santini thought grimly, an appropriate metaphor for the place as a whole: they didn't even breathe the same air as the rest of humanity.

He strode into the glass meeting room, noting that despite the earliness of the hour the other attendees had clearly been there for some time; doubtless plotting how to outmanoeuvre him. As well as Verti there were two assistants, nervous-looking civil servants who avoided his gaze. And then there was the friar, Tonatelli. How old he was, it was hard to say – the baggy white robe and black mantle of the Dominican order concealed any stooping of his frame, while the blue eyes that looked at Santini from beneath frost-white eyebrows were fierce and steady. Quite how Tonatelli had come to be in charge of these archives, Santini had never been able to discover, but it was obvious from everything he'd heard that this lowly friar was the real power in this subterranean world.

"Gentlemen," Santini said, deliberately using a secular form of address to emphasise that this was to be a practical discussion. "You said there was a problem?"

"Indeed." Verti gestured to Tonatelli, as if they'd agreed that he would speak for them all. But the friar simply slid a flimsy sheet of paper across the table to Santini.

Santini turned sideways to read it, hitching his cassock and crossing one leg nonchalantly over the other to indicate that he had better things to be doing. It was a copy, made on an old manual typewriter with carbon paper: the letters had the telltale blue smudging he recalled from his childhood, and for a moment he was too distracted by that recollection to concentrate on the letter's contents. Then a name jumped out at him. He stopped, puzzled, and went back to the date at the top.

5th October, 1944

He started again, reading more carefully this time, feeling the blood draining from his face as he did so. He glanced around for water, but of course none was provided down here, lest it get spilled on their precious bits of paper.

"Who else knows about this?" he managed to say.

It was Tonatelli who replied. The friar's voice, unlike Santini's, betrayed no hint of dryness. "I should imagine," he said calmly, "that the other parties involved have not forgotten."

Santini's head was spinning with questions. But right now, he knew, he had to show firm leadership, focusing only on those facts which would help him lay down a clear plan of action.

"In theory, we don't need to make that letter public until 2019," Verti added. "Although if we were to release the archive early, in accordance with your instructions—"

"We won't be releasing it early," Santini said. "Clearly. We won't be releasing it at all. Is there anything else that points to the same, the same..." He struggled to find the right word. "Scandal", "betrayal", "catastrophe" – none of these was adequate. "The same conclusion," he said euphemistically.

Tonatelli shrugged. "There are eighty-five kilometres of shelving in the Archivio Segreto. We haven't even counted the number of documents that relate to the war years yet. Almost certainly, that letter's just the tip of the iceberg."

"Then you must find the rest. Immediately."

"Destroying documents now, if that is what you are intending, will only give the impression later that we had something to hide," the friar said mildly.

But we do, Santini thought. "Do you have a better suggestion, Reverendissimo?"

Tonatelli looked at him calmly. "I think your policy of openness is the right one – in fact, I think in the long term it is the *only* one. But we should adopt it in the knowledge that the conclusions people draw from our transparency will not necessarily be favourable."

Santini picked up the sheet of paper again, staring at each brief paragraph as if somewhere in the wording he might find room for ambiguity or reinterpretation. Transparency was surely unthinkable now. "People will say that if it happened then, it could have gone on happening." He glanced up, horrified. "It didn't, did it?"

No one replied.

He looked again at the bottom of the letter, where the author had both signed and typed his name. The handwriting was familiar to him from a thousand documents and decrees, although he usually encountered it using a different name.

Giovanni Battista Montini
Protonotary Apostolic for Extraordinary Affairs
5th October, 1944

He was looking at the signature of the man who had gone on to become Pope Paul VI, attached to a document that, were it to become public, would surely blacken the name of his papacy for ever.

EIGHT

KAT HAD BEEN to the American base at Vicenza before, but not to the military housing area that lay to the south of it. Following the directions Holly had texted, she turned off the ring road on to Viale della Pace – "the Road of Peace"; was it already called that when the Americans came, she wondered, or had some town planner with a sense of irony renamed it since? – and came to a security barrier manned by an American MP. The sight of her *gazzella*, as the Carabinieri's cars were universally known, wasn't by itself enough to get the barrier raised. She had to show her ID and have the vehicle checked underneath with mirrors before she was allowed through.

The place was vast. She drove past institutional-looking barracks, then street after street of apartment blocks, interspersed with a medical clinic, a veterinary centre and two schools. After that came individual houses, each one with a small square of lawn and a white-painted fence. These must be the officers' homes. Some had garages as well as gardens, an almost unheard-of luxury in Italy. The American flag seemed to be everywhere.

Struggling with Holly's directions – *It's 611: that means the eleventh house after the Sixth Street intersection* – she was relieved to come across another *gazzella*, parked outside a house that was otherwise indistinguishable from its neighbours. The bell was answered by a man of about forty-five. His buzz cut seemed a little too youthful for his face, but under his uniform she could tell that his lean body was granite-hard.

"I'm Elston," he said without preamble. "Come in."

He led the way into the kitchen – which was like no kitchen Kat had ever been in. A central island was surrounded by high stools, like a cocktail bar. Gleaming marble surfaces bore so many gadgets – a food processor, bread maker, juicer, some kind of coffee-making machine – that it resembled an industrial workshop. There was a fridge the size of a wardrobe, complete with an ice dispenser. There was, however, no sign of any food.

The petite woman sitting at the island had to be Mrs Elston. There was no mistaking the haggard, red-eyed expression of a mother ricocheting between terror and despair, nor the way hope flooded into her face at the sight of Kat's Carabinieri uniform, only to drain away again as she realised there was no news. Next to her sat a familiar figure – a wiry blonde woman in her early twenties, also wearing military fatigues. The front pocket had "Boland" written across it, while her shoulders carried the single pip of a second lieutenant. Her geeky face, devoid of any make-up, wore a sombre expression.

"I'm Captain Tapo," Kat said in English. "Second Lieutenant Boland's…" She hesitated, stumbling over the word "friend". "Her contact in the Carabinieri. I'm sorry to hear about your daughter's disappearance."

"This is my wife, Nicole," the major said. "Your colleagues are upstairs."

Kat drew up a stool. "I'll talk to them in a minute. Tell me what happened first."

The major spoke for both of them. "We thought she was on a school trip, but it seems she… we may have been wrong about that. No one's seen her since Saturday."

"Does she have a phone? Bank cards?"

"Yes and yes. We've tried the phone, of course, many times, but it's switched off."

"Has she taken any clothes?" Kat asked. "Luggage? A backpack?"

Major Elston glanced at his wife. The woman stirred. "I don't think so. It's hard to be sure, what with laundry... She's a teenager, she's pretty independent..." Her voice tailed off.

"And is there anyone you can think of who she might be with? I understand she doesn't have a boyfriend at the moment."

Major Elston was on surer ground here. "No. And not just 'at the moment'. She won't be seventeen for two weeks. She—" At the implicit reference to his daughter's future, he stopped short. A muscle twitched in his cheek.

Kat thought it curious that he would link not being seventeen to not having a boyfriend, but chose not to pursue that for the moment. "What about other male friends? Anyone who'd recently come on to the scene you weren't sure about?"

Again Elston shook his head. "She has a soldier friend, Specialist Toomer, who escorts her to social events. I trust him completely. I'd also trust him to tell me if she was mixing with the wrong crowd."

"Could she have simply got lost?"

"I doubt it. We've been here three years now. She knows her way around."

"Any problems at home? Arguments, rebellions?"

"We don't have arguments," he said flatly. "Mia accepts that in any family, civilian or military, there has to be discipline. We've brought her up to respect the boundaries of the house, and that includes not speaking back to us."

"May I talk to her teachers?"

"If you really think it will help," the major said. The muscle in his cheek twitched again. "What are you going to *do*?" he exploded, slamming his hand down on the marble counter. "People should be out looking for her, not asking questions."

Kat waited a moment. "Does she have any brothers or sisters?"

He sighed. "I'm sorry. You'll appreciate this is difficult for us. One brother, Michael. He's in ninth grade. He's at a friend's, getting ready for school. We thought it best he stick to as normal a schedule as possible until she's… until Mia's back."

"Is there a recent picture of her I can take?"

The major handed her a framed photograph. It showed a pretty, smiling girl in a mortarboard and gown, holding some kind of school diploma.

"I have these," Holly said quietly, before Kat could say anything about the usefulness or otherwise of the major's photograph on the streets of Vicenza. From a folder neatly labelled "Mia Elston" she produced a shot of the same girl surrounded by friends in a pizza restaurant. She was dressed up and wearing a little discreet eyeliner. Kat was struck by how much older she looked than in the other picture.

"Will you circulate that?" the major said. "I mean, immediately, to all the police forces? And trace her phone and so on?"

Kat said carefully, "I'll do what I can. The difficulty is that there's no evidence yet of any crime."

He looked puzzled. "We don't know where she is. Isn't that enough?"

"Until seventy-two hours have gone by, she isn't officially a missing person. And checking her phone records at this stage would breach data privacy laws."

"She's a child, for Christ's sake. How can her privacy be more important than her safety?" he demanded.

Kat asked a few more questions, jotting down the names of some friends she could speak to. It was certainly curious. With most reports of missing teenagers, there was a back-story that instantly explained things – a boy the parents didn't approve of, a group who were a bad influence. Neither seemed to be the case here.

Her eye was caught by a chart pinned up next to the cooker. It was headed "KP Duty" and listed various household chores – cleaning, laundry, garbage. Along the top were the children's names, Mia and Michael. Each box contained a silver or gold star to show what had been done. In the case of Mia, she noticed, the stars were all gold.

Major Elston followed her gaze. "She's a good kid," he said simply.

Holly got to her feet. "I'll show you her room."

The two women went upstairs in silence. Somehow the moment had passed to say hello to each other.

"Thanks for coming," Holly said at last. She spoke Italian, as she'd always done with Kat when they were alone. Having grown up on an army base near Pisa herself, she was as fluent as any native.

"It's no problem. My bosses were fine with it in the end. Anything for our friends the Americans, in fact."

"I'd hoped we'd see each other under different circum-stances—"

"But we didn't," Kat interrupted brusquely. "Is this her bedroom?"

Holly sighed. "Yes."

Kat had been expecting a typical princess's boudoir, filled with posters of teenage heart-throbs. But Mia's bedroom was nothing like that. A bookcase, meticulously organised, held a row of framed photographs, mostly of Mia doing various sports. There were a couple of posters, but they'd been properly framed and hung on the wall. The only clutter was on the bed, on to which two drawers of underwear had been emptied. A young *carabiniere* sat going through them. Another stood by the window, his back to the room, gesticulating angrily.

"You need to clean the carburettor before you look for the leak. No, listen to what I'm telling you. The filters were new three months ago—"

The *carabiniere* on the bed scrambled to his feet and saluted. Hearing him, the other one turned, slipping his phone away and saluting Kat in one practised gesture.

"Found anything?" Kat asked pleasantly.

The men looked at each other and shrugged.

"Well, what exactly are you looking for?" she prompted.

"Clues?" the first one said tentatively.

"Such as?"

Both men looked blank. Kat gave an inward sigh. "Clueless" would be a more fitting description. "OK, I'll take it from here."

When they'd gone she started putting underwear back into the drawers. "All right, I can see why you called me," she conceded.

Holly nodded. "Bad enough when it happens in your own country, but here…"

"Amongst the savages, you mean?" Kat said, more sardonically than she'd intended. Holly didn't reply, which was probably wise.

Kat picked up a pair of panties. Like most of Mia Elston's things, they were quite plain – there was none of the extravagant, lacy lingerie an Italian teenager would buy. The front bore some kind of slogan. Not a joke, but "Timothy 4:12", written in flowery script.

"Strange," she commented. Putting the panties down, she

picked up a silver bracelet and read out the inscription. "'True passion is purity. True commitment is abstinence. True love waits.' What does *that* mean?"

"It means she's joined an abstinence movement." Seeing Kat's incomprehension, Holly added, "No sex before marriage."

Kat frowned. "Why join a movement? Why not just decide when the time comes, like everyone else?"

Holly shrugged. "They're pretty popular in the US right now. Look."

She showed Kat the photo album she'd found in the bookshelf. Inside someone had pasted an invitation to "The Fourth Annual Ederle Purity Ball. Dress code: Prom!" Opposite was a picture of Mia, several years younger than in the photo Kat had. She was wearing an elaborate white dress, almost like a wedding gown. Alongside her stood her father, in full ceremonial uniform. On the next page were their pledges: in his case, "To support and protect you in your purity"; in hers, "To keep myself chaste, as a special gift for my Creator, in honour of my father, and as a solemn commitment to the man I will one day marry".

"Weird. But how come she needs this, if she's such an *asmodello di virtu*?" Kat held up a laminated card she'd just found, hidden inside a CD case.

"What is it?"

"A student ID. According to which, she's twenty-one." Kat looked at the card again. It was a terrible fake. "However little she paid for it, she got ripped off."

"Kids in the US get them off the internet. Usually so they can buy alcohol."

They searched the rest of the room methodically. There was a laptop, but it was protected by a password. In the closet hung a dozen outfits, including a cheerleader's frilly skirt and top. Two posters hung above the bed, neatly framed. One showed the American flag, with the slogan "These Colors Don't Run". The other was headed "Rules To Be a Lady". Kat stopped to read it.

A Lady Doesn't: Answer "Yep" or "Nope".
A Lady Does: Answer "Yes, please" or "No, thank you".
A Lady Doesn't: Let others down.
A Lady Does: Keep her promises.

Holly held up a slip of paper. "Take a look at this."

Kat took it. It was a receipt from a mask shop in Venice, showing that two weeks earlier Mia had spent twenty-eight euros on a feathered Columbina.

"I'm just thinking – we haven't seen a mask anywhere, have we?" Holly added. "Maybe she went to something to do with Carnevale."

"Good thought." Kat pulled some more books from the bookcase and compared the flyleaves. "She changed her name," she commented. "Up until last year, she signed herself Maureen Elston. Then she starts calling herself Mia. Her signature changes too. Like she's trying to be more grown-up."

"Lots of girls do that. After all, you stopped using Katerina."

"And in my case, it was round about the time I started doing things my parents disapproved of." Kat bent and retrieved a small foil packet that had fallen from between the pages of one of the books. "Ah!"

"What is it?"

"A condom." Kat examined the packet. "'Strawberry flavour.' That hardly fits with the abstinence bracelet, does it?"

"But the very fact it's still there, unused, shows we can't infer that she was sexually active," Holly pointed out.

"*Goldoni* come in packs of three. Where are the rest?"

"If it's flavoured, maybe she was just practising. You know – so she'd be good at it when it comes to the real thing."

"American girls do that, do they?" Kat said, shooting her an amused glance.

"It's hard to generalise about American girls," Holly said frostily. "Since there are around fifty million of them."

"Oh, of course. You're a *superpower*, right?"

"So what are we going to do?" Holly said with a sigh. "Can you help? Or do the parents just have to go on waiting?"

"Doesn't this look odd to you?" Kat demanded, glancing round the too-neat bedroom.

"In what way?"

"It's so... tidy. So perfect." She gestured. "She's even made the bed. What teenager does that?"

"Oh." Now it was Holly's turn to look amused. "Kat, it's a military family." She nodded at the rows of houses beyond the window. "They'll all be like that. My own bedroom—" She stopped, aware that she was straying back towards an area better not discussed right now. "It just becomes routine."

Kat grunted, also conscious that this was probably not the time to go too deeply into the subject of Holly's domestic habits. "Well, I guess it can't hurt to talk to her friends."

"What about her phone?"

"I can put in a request. But it will take eight weeks to get anything back."

"Eight weeks!" Holly looked aghast.

"This is Italy. We may not be a superpower, but we do have certain checks and balances. I'll have to apply for a warrant – that means getting a prosecutor appointed, then proving to their satisfaction that a crime has been committed, and that there's a reasonable chance of convicting someone."

"But how can you say who committed the crime if you haven't been allowed to investigate it?" Not for the first time, Holly found herself wondering if the Italian legal system hadn't been deliberately designed to obstruct criminal investigations, rather than facilitate them.

Kat, who had come to exactly that conclusion long ago, shrugged. "That's the law."

Holly hesitated. "What about Daniele Barbo? Could we ask him to help?"

"Are you joking?"

The founder of Carnivia might be an acquaintance of theirs, but he wasn't someone you could just ask a favour of. Not that the illegality of accessing someone's phone records would bother him – Daniele had his own, somewhat idiosyncratic, concept of morality – but the notion of doing another person a good turn would, Kat suspected, be completely alien to him.

"If it wasn't for us, he'd be in prison," Holly said. "I thought perhaps – in an unofficial capacity, of course..."

Kat considered. Saito had, after all, asked her to help in any way she could, and since there was no chance whatsoever that Daniele would say yes, it could do no harm to ask. But she thought it significant that Holly – normally a stickler for doing things through official channels – was worried enough to suggest something as desperate as this.

"Well, as a Carabinieri officer, I can't ask him. But there's nothing to stop you doing it – so long as I don't know, of course."

"I'll send him an email," Holly said. "Whatever he's doing, he's almost certainly doing it in front of a screen."

As they left the bedroom Kat picked up the fake ID again. "You say teenagers in the US use these to buy booze?"

"That's right. Why?"

"Major Elston said they've been in Italy for three years. Mia and her friends can buy alcohol here quite legally at sixteen. So what else was she doing, that she needed to lie about her age for?"

NINE

SHE HEARD THE rattle of a chain at the door. The man in the Harlequin mask came in, carrying a tray. Behind him was Bauta, once again filming everything.

On the tray was a bottle of nutrition drink. She recognised the brand – Ensure. Some of the jocks at school used it as a supplement.

"The prisoner will eat," Harlequin said flatly, setting the tray down. He stood back so that the other man could continue to film as she opened the plastic bottle. It was banana flavour, sweet and sickly. But she was hungry, so she drank it all.

It seemed strange to her that they were so interested in watching her do this. What was so special about the Ensure?

Unless it's drugged. A terrifying scenario flitted into her mind. She would now fall unconscious, then they'd undress her while she was out and do whatever they wanted to her. Perhaps they'd even film themselves. Maybe that was what this was really all about – making some kind of snuff movie. Or they could be traffickers, and this would be the first step in forcing her into prostitution.

She must have been staring at the bottle in horror, because Harlequin said quietly, "It's not drugged."

She looked at him, surprised that he'd been able to guess her thoughts. She realised that, whatever else he was, he was

66

intelligent – too intelligent, surely, to be just some Mafia hench-
man. And his English, although he spoke it with a strong
accent, was grammatically correct.

So: an educated man, then. She wasn't sure if that made her
situation more or less terrifying.

But at least he'd spoken to her, so she seized her chance.
"I'm an American citizen. I demand to know who you are and
why you're keeping me here." As soon as the words were out,
she wished she'd said, "I respectfully ask" instead of, "I
demand".

But Harlequin only watched her thoughtfully. "It is because
the prisoner is an American citizen that she is a prisoner."

"Who are you? What do you want me for?"

"Our name is Azione Dal Molin – in English, 'Action for
Dal Molin'." He glanced at his watch. "As for what we want
you for, you're about to find out."

TEN

DANIELE BARBO HELD up his hands, fingers spread, so that they were exactly opposite the hands of the young woman sitting across the table from him, his left palm facing her right and vice versa, with only a few millimetres separating his skin from hers.

"Begin," a quiet voice said behind him. He heard the click of a stopwatch.

He looked directly at the woman, flinching minutely as they established eye contact. But he'd made good progress since the first time he'd done this exercise. Now he was able to meet her gaze without panic or distress, although he felt his breathing quicken.

Long seconds passed. Where their hands almost touched, his palms and fingers seemed to throb, as if his pulse was reaching out to hers. It was, he knew, an illusion, but the sensation was not unpleasant.

"Good," the voice behind him said.

If he could manage it, the exercise required him to stare directly into her eyes for six whole minutes. Gradually he relaxed, and it became easier. She was, he supposed, attractive; her eyes especially so. Around the pupils, her irises were light grey, flecked here and there with variations of colour. Magnified by the curve of the cornea, he could make out intricate white lines within each one, like the pattern inside a Murano glass paperweight. Involuntarily, his skin prickled at her closeness, and blood thickened in his groin.

The eyes opposite him seemed to widen minutely, as if she knew. Or, he realised, as if something similar was happening to her. His hands twitched, ready to break away, but the fractional distance between their palms still held.

As their breathing deepened and synchronised, he became aware of the regular rise and fall of her chest. Now, somehow, he understood that it was her turn to feel self-conscious. He could feel her wanting to drop her gaze; the inner struggle as she told herself she couldn't. It felt as if the two of them were having the most intimate conversation, but without speaking a word. He wondered if it was the same for her. Every fibre of his body told him that it was, that this intense bond was being reciprocated. But a small, rational part of his brain knew that, unlike him, she had probably done this many times before, and with other patients besides him.

He also knew that the exercise they were carrying out, apparently so simple, was the result of extensive research. In a 1989 study at Clark University, psychologist James Laird had established that mutual eye gazing for just two minutes could produce rapid increases in sexual empathy, even between strangers. The physical proximity of their hands was based on a similar discovery by Leon Festinger and Robert Zajonc at Stanford.

"Sabrina, make a gesture," the voice behind him said.

Without taking her eyes off Daniele, the young woman moved one of her hands sideways, down towards the table. Immediately, Daniele copied her, so that their hands remained opposite each other. She did the same with her other hand, then turned her head from side to side. Each time he copied her, their eyes still locked together.

After two minutes of mirroring each other's movements –
again, based on research which demonstrated that it increased
feelings of closeness – the voice behind him spoke again.

"Now truth," Father Uriel said. "Daniele, you first."

He thought. What secret did he want this woman to share
with him? Under the rules of the exercise, she had to answer
any question honestly, no matter how intimate or revealing.

"Sabrina, why are you here?" he asked.

The young woman reflected, picking her words carefully.
"Father Uriel is my PhD supervisor. When he asked for volunteers to help with his clinical work, I thought it sounded
interesting."

"Are you being paid?"

"We get term credits for participation, in the same way any
research assistant would. So, yes, you could say I'm getting
paid."

"Do you work with his other patients too?"

She frowned, and he guessed that if she hadn't been obliged
to keep her eyes locked on his, she'd have looked to Father
Uriel for reassurance that this wasn't off limits. "I don't think
I can talk about that."

"I need the truth," he reminded her. Father Uriel remained
silent.

"I have done this with others, yes."

"Did it feel like this?"

She shook her head minutely, her eyes still fixed on his.
"Not exactly, no."

Father Uriel's voice said, "Sabrina, your turn."

She looked at Daniele in a different way now, assessing him.
"Today I felt you were attracted to me. Were you?"

"Yes," he said honestly. He waited for her next question.

"Why are *you* here?" she said, and he sensed that she

really wanted to know; sensed, too, that had the answer to the previous question been different, she wouldn't have asked this one.

"You mean: am I a woman-hater, or a paedophile, or one of the other categories of offender Father Uriel usually works with?" he said slowly. "And the answer to that is 'no'. But for various reasons, I've never found it possible to be close to other people."

"Are you autistic?"

"I have been called that, and by some very eminent doctors. But Father Uriel believes my condition is acquired, not inherited." He wondered if she realised how hard it was for him to talk about this; wondered, even, if the psychiatrist had put her up to it. "I was kidnapped as a child. They kept me locked up for several weeks."

"Is that how you lost your ears? And your nose?"

He tensed involuntarily. "Yes. The kidnappers... They did it to put pressure on my parents."

"Why didn't you have cosmetic surgery? Afterwards, I mean?"

He took a deep breath. "I was offered it, of course. But I refused. I told my parents I wasn't ready. But the truth was, my father loved beautiful things – artworks, his palace in Venice. I wanted him to look at me and see what he'd done. To remember that all his wealth had created something ugly."

She nodded calmly. He felt the rush of mental connection that came from sharing a secret he had never divulged to anyone else. It both excited and terrified him.

"What made you seek help now?" she asked.

"I realised I was never going to form a relationship – to love someone – unless I did."

"Are you in love with someone?"

It was getting to be too much now. Surely the six minutes were up? He shook his head. "No."

"But there's someone you're interested in?"

The silence drew itself out. Behind him, he heard the click of the stopwatch. He no longer had to answer.

"There *is* someone, yes," he said slowly. "Perhaps it's not possible. But I think I'd like to find out."

"Thank you, Daniele," Father Uriel said quietly. "You too, Sabrina. That's all for today."

Sabrina stood, pulled on a woollen cardigan, smiled briefly at Daniele, and left. He watched her go, feeling how the consulting room suddenly seemed a little emptier, a little drabber, for her absence. He thought: is this what people feel? Is this what normality means? To make a brief connection with a fellow human being, only to experience the wrench as it was broken?

And what if the connection wasn't a brief one, and breaking it hurt something fundamental in you? What then?

"You're making good progress," Father Uriel was saying. "I think you might soon be ready to move on to the next exercise. Perhaps even to some real-world socialising."

"A date, you mean?"

"If you like. It would be a big step, I know."

Daniele indicated the door. "Will I see her again?"

Father Uriel considered. "Usually I try to rotate the surrogates, to minimise the danger of my patients forming an emotional attachment to them. But in your case, that's hardly likely. Why? Would you *like* to see her again?"

"I don't know. I want to see her. But I want to meet the other surrogates, too."

Father Uriel laughed, confusing Daniele. Had he said something funny? "Well, I don't have that many research assistants.

Not ones as pretty as Sabrina, anyway. So I imagine you may well see her again." He consulted his computer screen. "The same time next Monday?"

As he left the consulting room Daniele flicked his phone back on, attracting a curious glance from a passing monk. He barely noticed these days that he was almost the only person at Father Uriel's Institute who wasn't wearing a religious habit.

Daniele didn't believe in God, except as a principle of higher mathematics. But he did appreciate the way that the sex scandals currently enveloping the Church meant greater resources for doctors like Father Uriel who were quietly exploring new ways of treating sexual deviance as a form of dissocial personality disorder. It was Father Uriel who had suggested that the reverse might also be true – that the same behavioural techniques he used to reprogramme a priest's sexual attraction to children, say, could also be used to develop empathy in people like himself. The treatment was highly experimental, but when Daniele had checked it out by hacking into the archives of a few peer-reviewed journals, he'd been reassured to discover that it was based on sound science.

He scanned his messages. Most were automated alerts from the Carnivia servers, notifying him of surges in traffic or attempted security breaches. The others he deleted rapidly one by one without reading them.

From: Holly Boland
Subject: Can you help?

He hesitated, then marked that one to read later.

It was another message, a little further down, that he stopped at. It had been sent to a hidden message board that, in theory, was only accessible to Carnivia's administrators. The sender was someone who until a few days ago he'd never heard of. The subject line read:

Dan, a generic description of the process

He opened it.

On arrival at the detention site, the prisoner finds herself under the complete control of her captors. She is subjected to precise, quiet and almost clinical procedures designed to underscore the enormity and suddenness of the change in environment, her uncertainty about what may happen next, and her potential dread of captivity. The captive's own clothes are removed and destroyed. Her physical condition is documented through photographs taken while she is nude.

The captive is shackled and placed in solitary confinement. No toilet items, reading matter or religious materials are provided. No communication is permitted with the outside world. Guards are usually masked and do not communicate more than the bare minimum, including giving commands in the third person ("The prisoner will exit the cell" etc.).

The captive is subjected to dietary manipulation. This involves substituting a bland, commercial liquid meal for a captive's normal diet. Calorific intake will always be set at or above 1,000 kcal/day. The captive's weight is monitored to ensure that she does not lose more than 10% of bodyweight.

The threshold question is whether this behaviour is so egregious, so outrageous, that it may fairly be said to shock the contemporary conscience.

It was the third email in a similar vein he'd received in forty-eight hours. Had it not reached him on that particular account, he'd have taken it for spam. But he was quite certain there was no way a Carnivia admin board could be spammed.

As he stood there with the phone in his hand, considering, it rang. Holly Boland's name was the caller ID. He hesitated, then pressed "Answer".

"Yes?"

Holly didn't waste time on small talk, knowing how much it both irritated and confused him. "Daniele, a teenager has gone missing. We believe her phone records may help to locate her."

"So?"

"It needs to be done quickly, which rules out conventional channels." There was a long silence. "Daniele?" she prompted. "Are you still there?"

"I'll help," he said slowly. "But I want something in return."

"Such as?"

This time the silence was even longer. "I want you to have dinner with me."

"Dinner?" she echoed. Now it was her turn to hesitate. "That would be great."

Next to her, Kat stifled a grin. It had been perfectly apparent to her when she'd last observed them together that Daniele fancied the blonde intelligence officer. It had also been apparent that Holly had been oblivious to it. Well, Kat had her own theory about why that might be.

"I'll text the girl's details," Holly said.

"A name will be enough. And her phone provider, if you have it."

"It's Elston. Mia Elston. She's—"

"I know that name already," Daniele interrupted. "She has an account on Carnivia. An account that's been hacked."

At the other end of the phone, Holly was confused. The one thing everybody knew about Carnivia was that it wasn't possible to hack it. That was the site's whole *raison d'être* – not for Daniele, perhaps, who preferred to see his creation as a kind of abstract mathematical model, but for the millions of ordinary users. On Carnivia, wrapped in the anonymity of its military-grade encryption, you could buy anything, from the secrets of your colleagues' sex lives to a new identity; sell anything, from a stranger's credit card details to your own body; gamble anything, from your wage packet to your life; and say anything, from a declaration of passion sent via an anonymous email that self-destructed after a few minutes, to a whistleblowing denunciation of a corrupt politician or government. Some people called it evil, others a force for good. Most, however, were coming to realise that it was neither, but rather that, like Twitter, Google or the internet itself, it was simply a new reality of the information age, one whose true impact would be gauged only in hindsight.

Assuming, of course, that it survived, instead of disappearing like so many other internet sensations before it. Carnivia's success was inextricably linked to its ability to remain secure. The implications of it not being so were enormous.

"Hacked?" she repeated. "How?"

"I don't know. Someone's sending fake messages from Mia Elston's account to an administrator's board. Whoever it is has a working knowledge of scripting tools – the source code has been rewritten in Python to ensure I can't trace it back to the IP. But that's relatively simple. Getting into Carnivia itself would mean learning the domain-specific programming language—"

"Daniele," she interrupted, "you lost me after Python."

"Sorry. The point is, just because someone appears to have hacked a website, it doesn't necessarily mean they've broken the coding. It's far more likely to be social engineering – in other words, stealing someone's password." He hesitated. "These messages I've been getting. They make no sense to me. But they sound like some kind of threat."

ELEVEN

"DO YOU KNOW where you are, Mia?"

She shook her head. *No.*

"Louder, please. Do you know what might happen to you here?"

No.

A hand smashed the table in front of her, making her jump. "Don't lie to me, Mia. Think about your answers. Can you imagine the kind of things that might happen to you here? I'm sure you don't like to think about them. But I'm sure you can. Correct?"

After an hour or so in her cell, she'd been taken back to the bigger room. A bed sheet had been draped across the end wall, like a banner. It had some kind of symbol painted on it, a big black circle with an A inside, similar to the anarchist symbol but with a smaller D and M just below the A. In front of it they'd placed a table with a chair on either side.

The man wearing the Bauta stood somewhere in the shadows, filming it all.

"Yes," she said in a small voice.

"List them."

"You might… hurt me."

"Go on."

"Kill me. Beat me." A pause. "Rape me."

"And if we did any of those things, what would you be able to do about it?"

Nothing.

Had she said that out loud, or just in her head? But the man opposite, the one in the Harlequin mask, repeated it, so she must have said it aloud.

"*Nothing.* That's right. You can do nothing. But I have some good news for you, Mia. Do you want to know what it is?"

Another nod. Then, remembering his instructions, "Yes."

"The good news is that none of those things will happen if our demands are met. Do you understand?"

"Yes."

"Now stand up and take off your clothes."

She hesitated, but only for a moment. As she removed the clothes she'd been wearing at the nightclub, he took a pair of scissors and cut each one into small pieces. When she was down to her underwear, he placed something else on the table. Looking down, she saw a pair of overalls and a roll of grey duct tape. Relieved, she reached for the overalls, but he put his hand on them to stop her.

"Uh-uh. In here, Mia, you have to earn the right to wear clothes." He picked up the duct tape. "And that means first, you have to help us make a little movie."

TWELVE

"I'M AFRAID I can't possibly discuss Mia Elston with you," the student counsellor said, accompanying his words with a self-important frown. "My conversations with the students are privileged. They have to know that they can speak to me about anything, without fear of it getting back to their parents."

"We quite understand," Holly said.

The counsellor, Mr McConnell, was the last on their list of people to talk to at the American High School. So far, they hadn't made much progress. Everyone had painted the same picture: Mia was hard-working, sporty and bright, although Kat thought it interesting that several of her friends had also implied she could be reckless. "You can dare her to do anything and she'll do it," one girl told them. "She's braver than any of the boys round here, no question."

"Actually," Kat said now, "it's *you* who doesn't understand, Mr McConnell. 'Privilege' is a legal term which, in this country, can properly apply only to a lawyer, doctor, or state-licensed psychologist. I'm assuming you don't fall into any of those categories."

"I am a fully certified—"

"You can have all the certificates in the world," she interrupted. "The law takes precedence. That means you're required to comply with any criminal investigation ordered by the Italian courts, or be in contempt of those proceedings and suffer the consequences – up to eight years in prison." She deliberately used somewhat formal language, in the hope he wouldn't challenge whether or not the courts had ordered any such thing. "So tell me, counsellor, what is it that Mia Elston confided in you?"

McConnell blinked. "It's, er, nothing specific, as it happens."

"Then be non-specific."

"Sometimes… how can I put this?" He looked up at the ceiling awkwardly. "It's not unknown, actually. But not exactly common. She… *taunts* me, is the only word I can use."

"In what way?"

"Students know I can't repeat what they say. Sometimes that gives them a sense of power – they get a thrill out of trying to shock me. In Mia's case, she tried to tell me about which male teachers she has a crush on." McConnell made a gesture. "Oh, it was all under the guise of saying that she's been having trouble concentrating, you understand. But she went into a little too much detail, if you take my meaning. And then, when I was trying to get her to open up a little, she tried to tell me she'd developed a crush on *me*. I don't believe for one moment it was true. She simply wanted to see what my reaction would be."

"What *was* your reaction?" Holly asked.

"I told her she'd have to see a different counsellor – which, since I'm the only one here, would mean my junior school colleague, Mrs Morales. Mia backtracked pretty quick after that, I can tell you. Came back next day and told me she'd decided it was just psychodynamic transference, if you please. She must have read it up on the internet – she knew all the jargon."

"So she prickteased you a little," Kat said. "It doesn't explain why she might go missing."

"Indeed. And your language, Captain… I don't mean to suggest that her behaviour was anything more than a young woman starting to realise how attractive she is, and testing the limits of that. But I was struck by the way that she seemed able to inhabit both versions of herself simultaneously, if you like: the demure honours student on the one hand, and the girl who's growing up fast on the other. Mia can flip between the two in a heartbeat."

"Have there been any boyfriends?"

He shook his head. "Not that I'm aware of, although I'm sure she could have her pick."

"Major Elston mentioned a soldier who takes her to parties."

"Oh, yes. Specialist Kevin Toomer. Her father's 'guard poodle', Mia called him. I got the impression she wasn't very keen on him."

The two women exchanged glances. Getting to her feet, Kat said, "We'll talk to him. Thank you for your time, counsellor."

"You were right. She *was* too good to be true," Holly said as they left the school for the base.

Kat made a face. "Winding up that lecherous creep hardly makes her a devil child. I'll bet it was *se non è zuppa è pan bagnato* – six of one and half a dozen of the other. Did you see the way he was looking at my legs? I think she riled him by calling his bluff."

"You're thinking maybe this soldier felt something similar?"

"Could be. It can't have been easy, being the father's hand-picked bodyguard-cum-boyfriend substitute. Maybe he'd had enough."

Specialist Toomer was waiting for them in an interview room. Kat was struck by how young he looked. It turned out he was nineteen, a couple of years older than Mia.

He wasn't an easy interviewee. Every answer was replete

with military jargon and delivered in a depersonalised mono-tone, as if Kat and Holly were sergeant majors on parade. Yes, ma'am, he sometimes accompanied Mia Elston to barbecues and movies. It was an honour to do so, ma'am. He had never personally served under Major Elston but it was his ambition to apply for Recon training just as soon as he had achieved sufficient seniority. Recon Red, the major's troop, was known to be one of the tightest units in the 173rd.

"What did you and Mia talk about?" Kat asked.

Toomer looked blank. "Army stuff, mostly."

"Were you romantically involved?"

The boy seemed shocked. "No, ma'am."

"What about sexually?"

Toomer looked as if he might explode. "Major Elston entrusted me with his daughter's honour. And Major Elston is, like, a legend."

"But you do find her attractive?"

The soldier hesitated.

"You're gay, aren't you, Kevin?" Kat said. Next to her, she sensed Holly stiffen. Toomer only stared at her, speechless.

"I know it's not something you usually talk about in the army," she continued. "But you see, I need to understand the relationship between you and Mia. From what I've heard, she was pretty good at picking up on things like that."

After a moment Toomer nodded. "Yes, ma'am, she was."

"So you two were just friends?"

"Kind of," he said warily.

"Meaning?"

"Once Mia had worked it out..." Toomer hesitated. "Mostly she was fine. But occasionally she'd go off on one. You know, 'Why couldn't my dad find a straight guy to take me out?' Kind of like a joke, but not a joke. And she'd say stupid stuff."

"Like?"

"Like, maybe she'd give me a blow job to find out if I really am gay," he mumbled.

"So she *is* sexually active?"

Toomer squirmed uncomfortably. "Maybe. I know she's told her dad she's going to stay a virgin. But she's into some sexual stuff, for sure. She'll talk about things she's seen on the net, y'know? Like, 'Oh, I saw this hot gay clip, you should check it out.'" He made a face. "It's to shock me, mainly. But I don't think she's making it up. She told me one time about a message board on Carnivia where you can post pictures of yourself and people rate them. Like, semi-nude, but you don't show your face so people don't know who you are. That gave her a thrill, I think."

"What about drugs?"

"I don't know anything about that," he muttered.

"Yes, you do. Or do you want me to tell your platoon buddies about you?" Kat felt, rather than heard, Holly's involuntary indrawn breath.

Toomer bit his lip. "I know she's tried a couple of things. I've never talked to her about it. I hate drugs. Her father does too. He told Mia he'd thrash her if she so much as touches them. I don't think that's stopped her, though."

"Why did you go on taking her out, if you're so different?" Kat asked curiously.

He shrugged. "Her dad, I guess."

"What about last weekend? Did she tell you what she had planned?"

"I knew she had something on – she said she needed to give her dad the slip. I told her I couldn't help. She kind of laughed and said, 'Don't worry, it's not something *you'd* want to go to.'"

"'To go to'? As if she was talking about a party?"

"Yeah... or maybe a rave. I think she'd been to a few things like that without her parents finding out."

When they'd sent Toomer back to his unit, Kat stood up abruptly. "Come on. It's lunchtime."

They walked in silence towards the main gate. "Kat—" Holly began.

"Yes, I know," Kat interrupted. "'Don't ask, don't tell.' And as for threatening to tell his platoon, that probably isn't in the rule book either. But you wanted my help. So that's what you've got."

Their route was taking them through Main Street, the base shopping mall. All around, people were carrying bags from the concessions on either side. Kat was reminded of a medieval citadel: soldiers and their families all billeted together in one defensive encampment, but instead of carrying regimental flags, these were marching behind the banners of modern retail: American Apparel, Gap, Old Navy.

As they passed a Baskin-Robbins she noticed how the flavours that were available in her favourite Venetian *gelateria* just then – blood orange, hazelnut *gianduiotto,* artichoke – were replaced here by over a dozen varieties based on cookies, many proudly proclaiming themselves to be low in fat. Next to it was a Burger King.

"I take it you don't want to recommend somewhere to eat on base?" she enquired innocently. Holly only laughed hollowly.

They found a little family-run *trattoria* a few minutes away, in Stanga. Inside, there was space for no more than half a dozen tables, and the menu chalked on the blackboard consisted of just three items. One was *bigoli al ragù d'asino.* "Let's have the pasta," Kat suggested.

"Great," Holly said, perfectly aware that Kat was testing her. "Which wine, do you think? Would Amarone or Valpolicella go better with donkey?"

"Valpolicella, for sure." Kat gave Holly a sideways look. "That's if you don't think it's a crime to drink wine at lunchtime?"

Holly chose to ignore that. "So... I take it we don't think either McConnell or Toomer has anything to do with Mia's disappearance?"

Kat shook her head. "But it still seems significant to me that she lives this double life – being one thing to her parents, and another to those who really know her."

"I think it's often the case in army families. My dad wasn't as strict as Major Elston. But you were always made aware that any trouble you got into would go on your parents' record. So you learn to keep your private life very private."

And sometimes it's a hard habit to grow out of, Kat reflected. But she kept the thought to herself.

Their wine came quickly, and the pasta soon followed – the sauce dark as duck, but with a gamey tang similar to venison. Rather to Kat's irritation, Holly ate it with every sign of enjoyment. Donkey and horse meat were considered delicacies in the Veneto, and although tourists tended to turn their noses up at such dishes, it was rare to find a *trattoria* that didn't offer *sfilacci*, smoked shredded horse rump on a bed of rocket, a *primo* of donkey meat pasta, or a main course of *spezzatino di cavallo*, a hearty stew made with tomatoes, horse steak and paprika. Perhaps, Kat thought, the second lieutenant was actually more Italian than her uniform would suggest. Not that it made any difference. Their friendship was still definitely over.

"Not bad," Holly said when she finished. She took a deep

breath. "Kat... I think we should talk about what happened. When I was staying with you, I mean."

Kat considered. "Why?"

"Because I miss your friendship," Holly said simply.

There was a long silence. "Then let's be friends," Kat said.

"Great. But we should discuss—"

"No, we shouldn't," Kat interrupted. "Don't be such a tight-assed American *sboro*. We had a stupid row over a frying pan, that's all. And now we've made up. So let's just forget it and find Mia."

Holly said nothing. The row had been over rather more than a frying pan, but if that was how Kat was choosing to remember it, so be it. "You don't still think she's gone off with a boy, do you?" she said quietly.

Kat shook her head. The fact was, ever since she'd seen Mia's too-neat bedroom the certainty had been growing in her that this was more than just another teenage runaway. Daniele's comments about Mia's Carnivia account being hacked had only reinforced that.

"No," she said. "There's something more to this. I'm sure of it."

But she wasn't yet ready to admit that her own reaction to that growing certainty wasn't simply alarm at the fact that a young woman was missing – at least, not entirely.

What she felt was, in part, a reaction to all the faceless men back at the Carabinieri headquarters, the ones who scrawled "Piss Off Whore" across her locker, or who thought that investigating fake handbags was a productive use of her time.

What Captain Kat Tapo of the Carabinieri was feeling at that moment was a mounting sense of excitement.

Mia Elston, you may just be the opportunity I've been waiting for.

THIRTEEN

"PROFESSOR TREVISANO?"

The man who had opened the door to Piola nodded. "Yes?"

"I'm sorry to disturb you," Piola said. "Dr Iadanza suggested I talk to you about a skeleton that was found this morning near Vicenza."

"Of course. Come in."

An affable man with a shock of curly black hair, Professor Trevisano ushered Piola inside his room at Ca' Foscari, Venice's university. Books lined the walls, and more books and files were piled high on the floor, but in the middle, like an island, was a group of three armchairs. Piola sat in one, amused to discover that he felt as if he should be producing an essay, and explained why he was there.

"A withered left hand, you say?" Trevisano interrupted. "And wearing a khaki jacket, as well as a red neckerchief?"

"Yes."

"Max Ghimenti. Commander of the Marostica Garibaldi Brigade," the professor said promptly.

"You're sure?"

Trevisano nodded. "As Dr Iadanza will have told you, the Second World War is my period. Uniform was scarce amongst the partisans, though they all wore the neckerchiefs, of course: red for communist, green for republican and so on. But to have had a jacket would have marked him out as an officer. And the twisted left hand is mentioned in several accounts. It's definitely him."

"Can you tell me anything that might explain how he came to be buried at the old airfield?"

"Well, that's the interesting thing," Trevisano said. "I can't. Ghimenti's death is one of the great mysteries of the months before Liberation. It was a chaotic time, of course: the Allies had invaded from the south and the Germans were retreating yard by yard, but here in the north, things very much hung in the balance. Together with a few of his officers, Ghimenti had left his base in the Marostica hills to attend a meeting with the American OSS unit that was coordinating resistance activity in this area. According to the OSS officer, they never made it."

Trained in the nuances of presenting evidence himself, Piola caught the implication. "'According to'?"

Trevisano shrugged. "The story was, they were surrounded while they were sleeping and, after a brief firefight, gave themselves up. There's even a plaque on the wall of the church where it's supposed to have happened. They were never heard of again – it was suggested they'd been sent to a death camp, back in Germany. But almost immediately, questions started being asked. If the Germans had really captured a partisan commander, they wouldn't just send him away. He'd have been tortured for information, and if – when – he died, his corpse would have been hung from a lamp post for everyone to see. To simply vanish like that... it was highly unusual, to say the least."

"This meeting they were on their way to – do we know what it was about?"

"According to Ghimenti's men, Allied weapon drops to them were more often than not landing in the wrong place. Yet at the same time they were being ordered to undertake missions so hazardous that large numbers of casualties were inevitable. Ghimenti had asked for a meeting with Major Garland, OSS's most senior agent in Italy, to discuss what they perceived as a deliberate attempt to sideline them in favour of other partisan groups."

"Were they right, do you think?"

Trevisano smiled ruefully. "Well, it's certainly possible.. We Italians are understandably attached to the idea that, after the shame of the Mussolini years, we all rose up as one against the Nazis. But partisan politics were in some respects even more messy, and more ruthless, than what had gone before. You had socialist brigades, Catholic brigades, republicans, monarchists – and the biggest grouping of all, the Garibaldini."

"Who were communists."

"Indeed. To say that the different groups didn't always get along is something of an understatement. But in the case of the communists, there was another problem too. Long before the end of the war, the Americans started turning their attention to the new threat posed by Russia. Officially, of course, the two countries were allies. But in practice, both were trying to grab as much territory and influence as they could before hostilities came to an end. Some historians even believe the reason the Americans invaded Italy in the first place wasn't just to drive the Germans out, but to deny it to the communists. After all, communist partisans under Tito already dominated Yugoslavia; if they'd got Italy too, the whole strategic balance in the Mediterranean could have shifted in Russia's favour. If the Americans saw an opportunity to weaken a communist brigade's influence, they might well have taken it."

"Interesting." Piola stood up. "Well, thank you for your time, Professor. I'll see if we can trace one of Ghimenti's descendants and get their DNA compared with the remains. Doubtless they'll be pleased to give him a proper burial after so long."

Trevisano put out a hand to stop him. "Wait, Colonel... I just want to be sure you've understood the implications of what you've told me. According to your forensic examiner, Ghimenti couldn't have died in a firefight. That means the original version of his death can't be correct."

"That may or may not be the case, Professor," Piola said, doing up his jacket. "But it's a matter for historians like yourself now, not for the Carabinieri."

"Ah," Trevisano said quietly. "That's where you may be wrong, Colonel. Tell me, how much do you know about the Hague Convention?"

Delayed by his conversation with Trevisano, Piola was late getting back to Campo San Zaccaria, where he was meant to be in a meeting with Internal Affairs.

"There you are, Colonel. Shall we make up for lost time by beginning immediately?" Colonel Lettiere said without looking up as Piola took a seat, muttering apologies. He gestured to his sidekick, Endrizzi, who took one of the half a dozen files in front of him and opened it at a page marked with a yellow Post-it note, placing it reverently in front of his master.

Piola knew his lateness would look like arrogance and, arrogantly, found he hardly cared. Colonel Lettiere's investigation into the allegations of sexual misconduct made by Piola's former subordinate, Kat Tapo, seemed to have been going on for ever now, an endless labyrinth of questions and insinuations. *"I suggest to you, Colonel..."* *"Do you see how it looks when..."* *"Are you really claiming that..."* Lettiere insisted on harvesting every detail, no matter how intimate – how often

Piola and Kat had slept together, the dates and times, whether Piola had stayed the night; even whether the complainant had exhibited, as Lettiere prissily put it, "signs of sexual fulfilment". When he'd asked that one, Piola had simply stared at him, in mute fury and outrage, until Lettiere, unabashed, had moved on to his next question.

"Today I intend to focus on a particular discrepancy between your statements and those of Captain Tapo," Lettiere continued. "The captain says here that on one occasion, the night of January 21st, she resolved to break off the relationship. Yet your own recollection of that evening..." Here he turned to another page, also marked with a Post-it. "Is that you went to her apartment and had intimate relations as usual." He peered at the page. "Along with *bigoli con ragù*, cooked by Captain Tapo herself. How charming."

"If you say so," Piola said, trying to suppress a sigh.

"What I'm wondering, Colonel, is how you persuaded her to change her mind. What inducements or pressure you might have exerted."

"None whatsoever. If Captain Tapo had wanted to end our..." Piola hesitated. "Our *affair*, she would of course have been free to do so at any time. She did not express any such intention to me on the evening you refer to, or indeed any other occasion. It was ultimately me, not her, who broke it off."

"Yes... So it follows that she didn't tell you *why* she intended to end it?"

Piola shrugged. He had long since given up trying to work out what tortuous chain of logic Lettiere's questions were following. "No."

Lettiere's eyes glinted as if he had scored an important victory. He gestured to Endrizzi, who placed a new file in front of him, open at yet another Post-it. With a sinking feeling,

Piola saw that there were at least half a dozen more yellow slips protruding from its pages. "Can you tell me how Captain Tapo came to assist you on the investigation in the first place?"

"I requested her."

Lettiere raised his eyebrows. "By name?"

How else? Piola thought irritably. "Indeed."

"Because she had previously caught your eye, as it were?"

"Because she's a Venetian. I've lived here a long time, but it isn't the same. I thought having a local person on the team would be an asset."

"A local person with no previous homicide experience, I understand?"

"We all have to start somewhere."

"Indeed. And you must have known she would be grateful for the opportunity."

"I had no intention of seducing her at the time, if that's what you're implying," Piola said coldly. Which was the truth, almost. Certainly, he'd had no expectation on that first day that the relationship between them would ever be anything other than professional. But he'd felt himself falling for her almost from the start, when she'd taken off her galoshes to wade barefoot across the flooded pavement in front of Santa Maria della Salute to examine the body of a murdered woman; a woman who was dressed in the robes of a priest. He'd caught a glimpse of the bright red polish on her toenails as she stepped without fear or hesitation into the freezing salt water, and his heart had skipped a beat.

And that had been the real problem, of course. Love, a word that hadn't been uttered once during this pointless post-mortem. If the two of them had simply slept together, regretted it, and resolved to pretend that it had never happened, everything would have been fine. It had been precisely because of the strength of their feelings that continuing to work together after the affair was over would have been impossible. When the criminals they were investigating had sent photographs of the two of them to his wife, in an effort to undermine the investigation, it had worked; given an ultimatum at home, he'd been forced both to end the affair and to ask her to step aside. It had deprived her of an important step up in her career, but he still believed he couldn't have come up with a better solution.

"Look," he said, suddenly weary. "None of this was her fault. So if you want me to say I put pressure on her, or abused my position, then just put the statement in front of me and I'll sign it."

Lettiere smirked faintly. "If only it were that simple, Colonel. The reason such relationships between ranks are forbidden is precisely because of the complex issues they throw up. It may be, for example, that you thought you were exploiting *her* for sexual favours, whilst she simultaneously believed that she was manipulating *you* for reasons of professional advancement. The breaches of discipline here are not in question. But it is the motivations behind those breaches that will determine my recommendations." Almost cheerfully, he reached for another Post-it. "Turning now to your relations with other subordinates—"

The door opened, interrupting him. "Ah, Piola. And Colonel Lettiere. How are you getting on?" General Saito said. Lettiere started to answer, but Saito simply continued over him. "I'm afraid you'll have to finish this another time. I need a word with your victim here, and although I'm sure the details of his love life could occupy us for days, the Carabinieri do have some other matters to attend to."

"Of course, sir." Lettiere stood up, motioning to Endrizzi to gather up the files. "As it happens, General, my report is almost complete. And although the outcome will of course be up to the disciplinary board, I will be making some very clear recommendations. What happened here is a familiar story. A woman scorned; rejection turning to thoughts of professional revenge... I think you can rest assured that Colonel Piola will be back to his regular duties very soon."

Surprised, Piola said nothing. He could only assume that Lettiere had been waiting to see which way the political wind was blowing before revealing his hand. Saito's tone had provided, at last, a clear indication of what his superiors actually wanted to hear, and Lettiere had seized on it.

"Indeed," Saito said carelessly. He turned to Piola. "It seems everyone is pleased with you, Aldo. The Americans have lodged a small complaint, more for form's sake than anything else. Fallici's Lega della Libertà has done the same. So you have succeeded in upsetting both sides equally, without making either feel that there is anything to be gained from kicking up a real fuss. A delicate balance, elegantly achieved, and hardly any loose ends. Given that the archaeologist is attached to the consortium, I suggest that we now leave it between her and her employers to negotiate how long she should continue her remaining investigations. Our job there is done."

"Not exactly," Piola heard himself saying.

Saito looked surprised. "Oh?"

"I was talking to a historian a little earlier. A man who's made a study of the war years. The thing is, the victim was wearing a khaki jacket when he died."

"So?"

"It seems that, as he was wearing uniform, he was entitled to the protection of the Hague Convention – which, unlike Italian civil law, has no statute of limitations. Cause of death was a bullet in the head at close range. An execution-style killing, in other words – a war crime. I've already opened a case file."

Saito stared at him. "Naming who as your suspect?"

"It's tentative. But initial indications are that the person responsible may have been a Major Bob Garland of OSS – the Office of Strategic Services."

"Is he even still alive?"

Piola shook his head. "He died five years ago, after a long career working here in Italy for the same organisation – or rather, the organisation that OSS became after the war."

"Which was?"

"The Central Intelligence Agency. Bob Garland was their Section Chief for Italy."

Saito laughed disbelievingly. "Colonel, you are priceless. You want to accuse a dead CIA officer of killing someone three-quarters of a century ago, in the middle of a war? What possible good can come of that?"

"I know," Piola said, matching the general's smile with an apologetic half-smile of his own. "But an allegation has been made, and we have the forensic evidence supporting it, so…"

Saito sighed. "Very well. Write up a report, if you must, and take it to a prosecutor. It won't get any further than that, and at least that way the paperwork will all be in order. But don't spend more than a couple of days on it."

"Of course not."

Saito clapped him on the back. "And try not to get too near to anyone in a skirt while you're at it, eh? We don't need any more junior officers' hearts being broken."

FOURTEEN

DANIELE BARBO SAT in front of his computer and prepared to hack into TIM, Telecom Italia Mobile. It was a relatively simple matter: a few minutes' research on a hacker site had turned up a description of a known buffer overflow vulnerability in TIM's system. In layman's terms, it meant that the pro forma boxes on TIM's website where users entered their names and email addresses in order to pay their bills would also accept raw HTML code. When Daniele pressed "Next", the code would enter TIM's system just as if it were being written directly into the mainframe. He was using it to grant himself root administrator privileges, but he could just as easily have used it to insert a logic bomb that would wipe hundreds of thousands of phones, steal customers' identity details, or flood their email addresses with spam. It always amazed him that companies could be so lax about a portal into their systems which they themselves had created, yet buffer overflows were amongst the most common vulnerabilities on the net.

As he waited for the code he'd written to turn up Mia's phone records, he considered the various messages he'd received purporting to be from her. Some barely made sense, which was why he'd disregarded them at first. That had been a mistake, he now realised. If someone had really compromised her Carnivia account, it made the hack he was performing now look like child's play. The messages would have a meaning; or if not, their very lack of meaning would form part of their intended purpose.

He grouped them together on his screen. The first one said, in English:

> Let no one have contempt for your youth, but set an example for those who believe.

Next came several emails describing procedures for dealing with captured prisoners, including the one headed: "Dan, a generic description of the process". The latest, which had arrived only twenty or so minutes ago, was headed "Update":

> The captors conduct an initial interview in a relatively benign environment and fashion. The captors take an open, non-threatening approach but can rely on non-specific fears, such as by asking, "You know what can happen to you here?" The captive may be offered clothing or other inducements in return for cooperation.
>
> Taken together, these techniques reduce the captive to a baseline. Establishing this baseline state is important to demonstrate to the captive that she has no control over basic human needs.
>
> *The threshold question is whether this behaviour is so egregious, so outrageous, that it may fairly be said to shock the contemporary conscience.*

As he read, another message arrived from the same account. Immediately, he clicked on it. It said simply:

Daniele, your website is pathetic. I've seen better security on a nightclub VIP rope.

The first message, he quickly discovered by typing it into Google, was a quote from the Bible. Specifically, it was Timothy 4:12, the version used in American schools. The repeated phrase about "shocking the contemporary conscience", however, was a legal one. According to Wikipedia:

> "Shocks the conscience" is a phrase used as a legal standard in the United States and Canada. An action is understood to "shock the conscience" if it is perceived as manifestly and grossly unjust, typically by a judge, and thus violates the due process requirement of the Fourteenth Amendment to the United States Constitution.

The remainder of the emails appeared to be extracts from a leaked U.S. government document on extraordinary rendition, the CIA procedure in which terrorist suspects were abducted in one country, then flown to another for interrogation – not least, to avoid the legal implications of the Fourteenth Amendment.

Why would someone go to the lengths of getting his attention by hacking into a secure email account, only to send him an American government memorandum on rendition? It was clearly some kind of puzzle, designed to tease and provoke him – which meant, in turn, that it might well be a riddle without a solution, left deliberately opaque by its creator.

On the other hand, Daniele reflected, even if someone thought they were writing gibberish, the gibberish they chose to write could still tell you a lot about them.

The computer chimed, alerting him to the fact that it had succeeded in accessing Mia's phone records. He switched his attention to the rows of entries on the screen. Perhaps there was something here that would make sense of it.

FIFTEEN

PIOLA DROVE THROUGH an iron gate topped with barbed wire and past a row of crumbling wooden huts. A sign announced that this was Internment Camp 73. Underneath, in smaller letters, it said: "Twelve thousand men, women and children passed through these gates en route for Nazi concentration camps, punishment battalions and forced-labour factories."

Trevisano had said there might be some photographs of Max Ghimenti in the archives of the Resistance Museum at the old Carpi Internment Camp, and although it would, strictly speaking, add little to the evidence, Piola knew all too well the value of such visual aids when it came to convincing a prosecutor that a crime was worth pursuing.

The museum – or, as it now called itself, the Visitor Education Centre – was a gleaming modernist extravaganza held up by steel girders as dramatically twisted as the strands of sugar in a Venetian dessert; a curious contrast with the decaying wooden huts around it. Another sign, rather larger than the first, thanked Costruttori Conterno for their generous support in providing it. It was odd, Piola thought, how that name was suddenly cropping up in so many places. But then he checked himself. Of course, it wasn't cropping up any more than usual: it was simply that today he was noticing the heraldic griffin and regal typeface more than he usually did. One had to be careful not to see patterns that weren't really there.

Inside, the Centre had the hushed feel of an art gallery or a private bank. Piola explained his mission to the elegantly dressed woman behind reception, who made a call and told him an archivist would look into it.

While he waited he wandered round the foyer display, entitled "Industry at War". It was, he soon realised, simply a payback to Conterno for their sponsorship. Expensively put together, with old black-and-white photographs blown up to billboard size, it told the story of the war years from the firm's perspective; specifically, that of Ambrogino Conterno, its founder. There was a grainy shot of the tractors Ambrogino had been manufacturing before war broke out, then a portrait of the man himself, standing proudly next to a prototype racing car. A caption read: "Like many Italian industrialists, the young Ambrogino was forced to help the German war effort. His factory was moved to the caves under the hills at Longare, out of range of Allied bombs, where it produced aircraft parts and armaments for the Nazis. Having seen at first hand the conditions endured by forced-labour gangs, Ambrogino secretly began to help the Resistance."

The next picture showed Ambrogino with a detachment of cheering partisans. At the right was a tall, stooping man in American military uniform. "Ambrogino Conterno with partisans of the Trentino Brigade on Liberation Day, together with Major Robert 'Bob' Garland of OSS."

Piola stopped. So that was his suspect. He peered at the American's face, but the photograph was too lacking in definition to give any sense of the man's personality. Further along, he found some more pictures of Garland. One showed him amongst a larger group, including Conterno, dressed in robes as if for some religious ceremony. The caption read: "Ambrogino Conterno and his partisan colleagues in Rome, April 1948, on the occasion of their induction into the Order of Melchizedek, an ancient chivalric and charitable order of the Catholic Church." In an adjacent cabinet were laid out the actual robes Ambrogino was wearing in the photograph, along with various medals and other honours. Many, Piola noticed, featured the same emblem: a cross, the down-bar of which ended in the point of a sword, and the motto *"Fidei in Fortitudo"*.

The Order of Melchizedek... He'd come across that name before, during the ill-fated investigation with Captain Tapo, the one that had started with a dead woman wearing the robes of a priest and had ended with the revelation that NATO and the Vatican, amongst others, had been secretly stoking the civil wars that followed the break-up of the former Yugoslavia. The Order hadn't been implicated in those crimes, though; or at least, not directly – he only remembered them now because of a turn of phrase Kat had used when looking at their website: something about how Italians were suckers for snobbery and ceremony when combined in the name of charity.

"Here you are." He turned. The receptionist was coming towards him, holding an envelope.

"Thank you. Would it be possible to get copies of these as well?" He indicated the display in front of him.

Reaching behind him, she handed him a glossy brochure from a stack. "It's all in there. And a CD as well." She turned her attention to where a group of schoolchildren were surging through the doors.

Opening the envelope as he walked back to his car, he found it contained three photographs. The first showed a handsome young partisan holding a rifle, a bag of ammunition dangling insouciantly from his other hand. Piola peered closer. The reason the bag appeared to dangle like that was because it was looped over his wrist. The left hand was curled inwards, a useless claw. Below the photograph the caption said: "Massimilio 'Max' Ghimenti, commander, Marostica Brigade. At its height the brigade numbered over two thousand partisans. Their many achievements included the destruction of bridges, roads and other infrastructure used by the Germans."

The next photograph showed Ghimenti with three other young men, their arms looped around each other's shoulders. All were grinning for the camera. Their chests were bare, but each still wore his red neckerchief. "'Max' Ghimenti with other officers of the Marostica Brigade, summer 1944, shortly before they were captured in an ambush and deported to the death camps."

Puzzled, Piola turned back to the brochure the receptionist had given him, and found the picture of the men in ceremonial robes. One was the same man as the partisan Max Ghimenti had his left arm around. He compared the two faces side by side, just to be sure. Definitely the same. Whoever the man was, he appeared to be proof that at least one partisan had survived the ambush.

Not for the first time that day, Piola wondered if he were mad to try to investigate Ghimenti's death. Quite apart from the practical difficulties of doing so, the war had claimed the lives of over a quarter of a million soldiers and two hundred thousand civilians in Italy alone. Only a few academics like Trevisano could possibly be interested in this one small incident amongst so much slaughter.

And yet Piola had an old-fashioned view that, just as every human being had the right to a proper burial, so every victim of violence had the right to justice. What had Fallici said? "*We must ensure that this unfortunate individual receives the same respect in death as any other citizen.*" Empty words, perhaps, in the mouth of a politician, but that didn't make them any less true. The fact that the crime had happened so long ago, at a time when all of Europe was engaged in killing, only made the choice more stark: when there was no reason to investigate other than principle, not to do so would be a clear betrayal of that principle.

But ultimately, he knew, it would be up to a prosecutor, not him, to determine what resources would be assigned to the investigation. And as Saito had said, few would think it a matter worth expending much energy on. Piola would have to assemble his case quickly, and well, before it was subjected to a colder scrutiny than his.

SIXTEEN

HOLLY WAS MAKING enquiries with Kat among the Elstons' neighbours when Daniele called back. "I've got the phone details," he said without preamble.

"And?"

"I take it you know how these things work? Basically, whenever your phone's turned on, a switching centre sends it small packets of data to find out which mast it's nearest to. The phone companies only keep that information for twenty-four hours – unless you make or receive a call. Then they attach it to your billing record. Mia's phone was turned off just before midnight on Saturday, but she'd received a text a few minutes before."

"Suggesting she was meeting someone?"

"I guess so. Anyway, it means we can identify the cell she was in at the time." Daniele hesitated. "Where are you, Holly?"

"Just outside Camp Ederle. Why?"

"Her phone was switched off just to the south of the sector you're in now."

Holly digested this. "We have an idea that wherever she went, it might have had something to do with Carnevale. If you're at a computer, can you see if there were any events listed just south of here?"

"Maybe that's what he meant," Daniele said slowly.

"Who?"

"'I've seen better security on a nightclub VIP rope' – that was one of the messages the hacker sent me." She could hear the click of his keyboard. "There's a nightclub less than a kilo-metre to the south of you. Club Libero." He clicked again. "According to its website, it's a *club privé*. And it just held a special party night for Carnevale."

The area south of Ederle was flat and featureless, a sprawling suburb of industrial buildings and retail units. Club Libero's entrance was down a side road, tucked between a motorbike shop and a warehouse selling swimming-pool parts. If they hadn't had the address, they'd have gone straight past.

"Not the most glamorous location," Holly commented.

"On the other hand, no problems with neighbours," Kat said. "I bet this area's deserted after dark."

Their banging eventually produced a cleaner. "We need to speak to someone in charge," Kat told her. The woman hurried off, returning a few minutes later with a man in his thirties.

"I'm the owner," he said. "Edoardo Pagnotto. How can I help?"

"We're looking for a missing teenager. Her phone was last used in this area on Saturday, just after midnight." Kat showed the photograph of Mia.

Edoardo frowned. "Saturday was a big night for us. But we operate an over-21 door policy."

"She may have had fake ID. Look, we're not accusing you of anything. But if you have any information that could help us, you should tell us immediately."

"As a private club, we have to make everyone sign in. We can check the list, if you like."

They followed him into the reception area. There was a long counter, and a side room containing rows of lockers.

Apart from the CCTV camera over the door, it looked, Holly thought, more like a private gym than a nightclub.

"What's she called?" Edoardo said, opening a ledger.

"Mia Elston."

After a moment he shook his head. "Not here."

"Again, she may have used a false name."

Edoardo looked up, suddenly thoughtful. "There is one thing." He gestured towards the side room. "We provide lockers for our guests. They keep the key with them, on a bracelet, then give it back when they leave. Occasionally people forget, so we have someone on the door, checking no one's still wearing a bracelet when they go. Usually that works fine. But there's still one locker from Saturday that hasn't been opened. I thought whoever it was would come back when they realised, so I haven't opened it."

"You've got a master key?"

He nodded.

"Let's open it, then."

Producing a key, Edoardo led the way to the lockers and fitted it into the only door that was closed. As it swung open, Kat and Holly craned to see inside.

A coat, a small bag, a wallet. And a mobile phone in a pink case.

Kat reached for the wallet. Inside was a University of Milwaukee student card with Mia's photo, giving her name as Mia Cooper and her date of birth as 1992.

"Looks like she managed to buy some better ID after all," Holly said quietly.

Kat looked at Edoardo. "We'll need to go through your door tapes."

"Of course. I'll call the man who looks after our security." He got out his phone.

While he was calling, Holly went back to the reception desk, her eye caught by a big bowl of what she'd assumed were sweets. "Kat," she said carefully. "Are these what I think they are?"

Kat looked over. "Yes. Condoms."

"What kind of club is this?"

"A *club privé*." Seeing Holly's look of incomprehension, she nodded at a discreet sign, "*Solo Coppie*", to one side of the door. "Couples only. It's a swingers' club. Which means Mia must have come here with someone. I'm hoping the tapes will show us who."

While they waited for the security director, Kat and Holly took a look around. In many ways it seemed hardly different from any other nightclub, Holly thought, struggling to equate what she was seeing with what she now knew actually happened here. The cleaner was vacuuming the dance floor. An electrician was working on a smoke machine that had blown a fuse. Only in the smaller rooms at the back – some of which contained oversized beds, wooden frames, and in one case a padded floor – was there any indication that the clientele didn't come just to dance.

A woman in her late thirties was putting out piles of freshly laundered white towels in one of the rooms. Coming over, she introduced herself as Jacquie, Edoardo's wife.

"Oh, you're American," she exclaimed to Holly in English. "Me too."

"How long have you had the club?" Kat asked.

"Four years. It's been our dream ever since we met, though." She made it sound as if they were running a sweet little café by the sea. "Somewhere clean and safe and glamorous, where everyone would feel welcome. I hope you find that poor girl soon," she added anxiously. "It's awful to think she might have been here."

When she'd left them, Holly turned to Kat. "Are there many places like this round here?"

Not so Italian after all, Kat thought wryly. "Every city has one or two. I've never had much to do with them, professionally speaking. The clientele are usually affluent and well behaved. And the clubs invest in good security because they don't want any hassle."

"'Professionally speaking'? You're not saying you've been somewhere like this in your personal life?" Holly couldn't help sounding shocked. She'd just peeked into another of the back rooms as they passed. It was bisected by a partition with a number of holes cut into it at around waist height. She tried not to think what they were for, although the paper-towel dispenser on the wall gave some indication.

Kat laughed. "Sure. It was a while ago now, when I was in Roma. I had a boyfriend who was into it, an older guy. He made it sound fun. So I went along a couple of times out of curiosity."

"And?"

She shrugged. "It was lots of people having sex. Once you get over the novelty, it's no big deal. But it's also pretty superficial. You meet, you say hello, you fuck, you say goodbye – it's like fast food. Me, I prefer a slow-cooked *ragù*." She glanced at Holly. "Not to mention a few arguments over the recipe."

"And Italians generally? They just accept these places?"

"Holly, until recently we had a prime minister who openly boasted of holding orgies. And every time he did, his approval ratings went up. If Italy ever starts to get prudish about sexual matters, it won't be because of clubs like this."

At the front desk they found a man working with Edoardo

on the CCTV machine. He didn't look up as they approached, which immediately made Kat suspicious.

"It seems there's a problem," Edoardo said. "The footage is meant to be stored on the computer. But there's some kind of glitch. We're working on it." He addressed the security man. "How long, Giù?"

"Maybe an hour or so," the man mumbled, his head still turned away from the two women. "I'll take it away, see if I can fix it—"

As soon as he opened his mouth, Kat realised she knew him. "You're a *carabiniere*!" she exclaimed. "One of the local boys."

"So?" Giù said belligerently. "A man's got to make a living, hasn't he?"

"Sure. But a man's also got to clear any part-time jobs with his *generale di divisione*. And I'm willing to bet yours has no idea you spend your nights doing security here. In fact, I'd bet that if I took a look at your duty roster, I'd find you magically manage to be in two places at once from time to time. So let's cut the crap, shall we, and tell me what you know."

Giù sighed. "All right. Get off my balls, will you? There *is* something, as it happens."

"Go on."

"I have four guys who work for me here. All good people. Anyway, on Saturday one came to me and said he thought there was someone dealing."

"That can't be unusual, surely?"

Giù bristled. "Dealers know to stay away from this place."

"That's why I employ him," Edoardo added. "Having a *carabiniere* on the premises, even off-duty, it lets people know you're serious. We operate a zero-tolerance policy – the guys search anyone they think might be bringing something in."

It seemed unlikely to Kat that the club would be allowed to survive very long if the Mafia really had no way of selling drugs to its customers, but she only nodded and said, "Go on."

Giù continued, "Anyway, I went looking for him – it was a young guy, they told me; white, but with dreadlocks. But he was already gone. I thought he must have realised he'd been spotted. Tino in the parking lot said he'd seen a van with blacked-out windows driving off fast. So that seemed to fit."

"But something didn't?"

Giù went over to the desk and opened a drawer. "We found this in the car park," he said, pulling out what looked like a tangle of knotted ropes. He shook it, and it became a wig of long white dreadlocks. "If he was a dealer, it seems weird that he was wearing a disguise."

Kat's phone rang. It was Daniele. "Yes?" she answered.

His voice sounded tense. "I've been sent another message." He paused. "A film clip. Kat, you need to see it. Mia's been kidnapped."

SEVENTEEN

"THERE'LL BE A press conference tomorrow at nine a.m.," Saito told the packed room. "In the meantime, no one else is to see this unless I've cleared it." He gestured to a technician to start the tape.

The Carabinieri team had been assembled in record time. Already, eighteen officers and sixty regular *carabinieri* had been allocated to the case. Kidnap specialists were driving down from Milan, and several Americans whose job titles were as vague as their names were uncatchable had set up a secure communications centre in a side room. Kat spotted Colonel Piola in the crush of officers and looked away, determined not to catch his eye.

The first thing on the film was a crude title, typed on basic video-editing software.

FOLLOWING CAPTURE, THE CAPTIVE IS SHACKLED AND DEPRIVED OF SIGHT AND SOUND THROUGH THE USE OF EARMUFFS, GOGGLES AND HOODS.

The film cut to a grainy image of a figure, hooded and bound, lying on the floor of a van. It had been filmed with a phone, or some other unsophisticated camera: the picture was shaky and slightly out of focus. Almost immediately, it cut to another title.

THE RECEPTION PROCESS GENERALLY CREATES SIGNIFICANT
APPREHENSION.

Now the camera was moving through the doorway of a small stone-built room, like an animal pen. A figure was sitting on the floor, handcuffed. The hood had been taken off, but only as she looked up did it become clear that it was a teenage girl. She looked terrified.

SLEEP DEPRIVATION AND DIETARY MANIPULATION ARE USED AS
STANDARD PREPARATORY STEPS.

Then there was a brief shot of the same girl drinking from a plastic bottle of Ensure. Again, it was only on screen for a few brief seconds.

THE INITIAL INTERVIEW IS RELATIVELY BENIGN.

Next came a shot of the girl's face in close-up. The camera pulled back jerkily to reveal that she was sitting in a chair. There was a murmur of disquiet around the briefing room as they saw that she was stripped to her underwear, and that her limbs had been secured to the chair's arms and legs with duct tape.

The framing was adjusted by an unseen hand, and the background came into view. On a kind of banner behind the girl was a crudely daubed circle containing a giant A, with a smaller D and M immediately beneath. To one side, a man wearing a Harlequin mask stood impassively.

THE CAPTIVE MAY BE OFFERED CLOTHING, FOOD OR OTHER
INDUCEMENTS IN EXCHANGE FOR COOPERATION.

The man spoke through the mask in strongly accented English. "Mia, do you have something to say?"

"Yes." The girl looked directly at the camera. In her terror she spoke too fast to begin with, so that it was hard to make out all the words. "Azione Dal Molin demands that a referendum be held immediately, so that the people of the Veneto can determine for themselves the following. First, whether all work be halted on the Dal Molin military base with immediate effect. Second, whether plans are drawn up to demolish the buildings already finished." She paused and took a breath, slowing herself down. "Third, whether the site is returned to public ownership by the end of the year. And fourth, whether all American troops engaged in the illegal occupation of northern Italy should be gone by August first." Her voice faltered. "I've been told I can add a short message to my parents. Mom, Dad—"

Abruptly, the picture cut. Another title appeared.

TO BE CONTINUED.

As the screen went blank, all the Carabinieri officers in the briefing room collectively exhaled.

"Her name's Mia Elston," Saito said. "Sixteen years old, the daughter of an American officer based at Caserma Ederle, reported missing last night. As for Azione Dal Molin, we hadn't heard of them until this morning, when some of them broke into the construction site and sprayed graffiti around in what now appears to be a coordinated attempt to publicise themselves ahead of this film." He nodded to where Piola stood. "By a stroke of good fortune, we were asked to investigate that incident, and Colonel Piola has already gathered the names and addresses of the ringleaders. We'll go in at four a.m. for maximum surprise and disorientation, and bring them in for questioning – all of them. One four-man team to each address, and an additional three-man unit to remain in each location to search for any evidence that might indicate where she's being held. Clear?"

Around the room, people were nodding.

"Coscia will lead a team that will analyse the film. Flamini will activate the official protocols and liaise with specialist advice units. Horst's unit will follow up on a van that was glimpsed driving away from the probable abduction site. Everyone else has been assigned to one of the arrest groups – there's a full list on the table, along with briefing packs detailing what little we know."

The officers filed out of the room, talking quietly amongst themselves. Having looked at the allocation list, Kat hung back.

"Yes, Capitano?" Saito said, noticing her.

"The list doesn't say which team I'm on, sir."

"That's because you're not on any of them. You can return to your other duties."

Kat couldn't believe what she was hearing. "With respect, sir, if it wasn't for me, we wouldn't have the leads to the club, or the van, or the girl's telephone." She thought it best not to mention her role in contacting Daniele Barbo, or in persuading him to pass on the film to the authorities. "I think I've proved I can be of use."

"Possibly. But you're forgetting one thing." Saito gestured towards the door. "Colonel Piola is playing a key role in this investigation. And I have instructions from Internal Affairs that the two of you aren't to work together until your complaint against him has been resolved."

"But that's crazy," she said furiously. "It was because he tried to move me off a case that I made the complaint in the first place. And now Internal Affairs are effectively doing the same thing."

"So make a complaint about them," Saito said, turning

away. "Make a complaint about me. Perhaps if you make enough complaints, Captain, your career will get back on track. But personally, I doubt it."

She went back to her desk still seething. Glancing at her emails, she saw that the list of petty crimes to be processed had almost doubled in her absence. She clicked on the top one.

CF56431A. Tourist camera missing from café.

Not for the first time, she found herself regretting ever having made the complaint about Aldo. She'd been right in principle, of course; but almost certainly wrong in practice. Looking back, she realised she'd probably been trying to emulate Piola's own somewhat idealistic attitude to his work. Well, that was a lesson well and truly learned. If you were a man, and a colonel, you could get away with romantic notions about fairness and justice. If you were female and a captain, you had to work the system.

"Fuck it," she said aloud. She reached for her phone. "It's Kat," she said when it was answered. "How's it going your end?"

"Crazy," Holly replied. "People flying in from all over. And the Elstons still in complete shock. You?"

"They're trying to take me off the case, just because Aldo's on it. Will you speak to Major Elston? If you can get him to insist, I reckon my bosses will have to let me stay."

"If you want." Holly's voice was guarded. "But Kat, what *about* Aldo? Wouldn't it make more sense to keep some distance?"

"He'll be fine. It's a big investigation, and what matters now is finding Mia. There's plenty of room for both of us."

EIGHTEEN

WITHIN AN HOUR Piola was told that the texts sent to Mia's phone on the night of her kidnap had been traced. They'd been sent from a phone registered to one Johann Vicaro, whose address was listed as an apartment in Vicenza.

"Who's bringing him in?"

"A local unit. He should be here in forty minutes."

Someone handed him a printout of the texts, along with Mia's replies. The first had been sent at 11.57 p.m.:

Meet you in the restaurant on Via Zamenhof. I'm wearing a jacket and blue silk shirt. Johann

Thx! I'm in a red T-shirt. M

Ten minutes later Vicaro had texted Mia again:

I'm at the bar. Want a drink?

Coke pls! Be there in five.

Apart from that, the two of them had exchanged just one phone call, a week previously, which had lasted twenty-two minutes. Before that point, they appeared never to have contacted each other; at least, not by phone.

His own phone rang, the caller ID one he didn't recognise. "Piola."

"Hello, Colonel, how are you? It's Dottora Iadanza." The archaeologist's voice was friendly.

"What can I do for you, Dottora?" Aware of how much

had to be done before the night was out, he spoke a little more briskly than he'd intended. In response, her own voice also became more businesslike.

"I thought you'd want to be told straight away – I managed to get some ground sonar out to the dig site, and there are what appear to be two further objects in the soil. It looks very much like two more skeletons. Of course, I'll make sure they're excavated properly this time."

"Ah." Piola thought hard. "How long will that take?"

"A week, perhaps more."

"You may have to let the construction work go on around you," he said, knowing that she'd assume he'd caved in to pressure from her bosses. But there was no way, now, that work could be halted – it would look as if the Carabinieri were giving in to the kidnappers' demands.

"But that could totally compromise the lift."

"I'm sorry, but we're not going to be able to hold off any longer. I'm afraid I can't explain the precise reasons just at the moment." There was silence from her end. He added, "Look, you know Professor Trevisano at Ca' Foscari, don't you?"

"Of course. It was me who gave you his name."

"Would you do something for me? The professor provisionally identified the first skeleton as a partisan commander by the name of Max Ghimenti. It's a fair bet the other two will be the partisans who vanished with him. But there was another man with them who survived – he was photographed after the war, standing next to an American intelligence officer. If I send you the photographs, could you pass them on to the professor? If he can put a name to the survivor, it would be a great help when I do come back to the case."

"Certainly," she said with a sigh. He could tell she thought he was fobbing her off. "We'll see what we can do."

He rang off, a little regretful. But wartime skeletons would keep, whereas a kidnap needed to be solved in the golden hours and days immediately after the victim was taken. It was when such cases dragged on, and frustration mounted on both sides, that tragedies occurred.

By the time Johann Vicaro was brought in, Lieutenant Panicucci had also arrived, and had surprised Piola by speedily assembling a sheet of background information on their subject. Vicaro was Swiss, twenty-eight years old, and ran his own business exporting wine. The company appeared to be doing satisfactorily: the rent on apartments in the building where he lived was around four thousand euros a month. A passport check showed that he travelled regularly around Europe, flying business class or taking the high-speed train. He had no criminal record and his residence permits were up to date. He was, in fact, the very model of a hard-working young entrepreneur.

Armed with the sheet, Piola stepped into the interview room. The young man sitting at the table was better-looking than his passport scan had suggested. He was expensively dressed in Ermenegildo Zegna knitwear, while his tanned face and general air of athleticism suggested that he spent much of the winter skiing. He hadn't asked for a lawyer, and didn't seem especially nervous, just bemused and frustrated at the sudden interruption to his evening.

"Do you know why you're here?" Piola asked as he sat down.

"No," Vicaro said. "Some bureaucratic nonsense."

"It's to do with a young woman. Can you guess who I mean?"

Vicaro looked thoughtful. "Not Mia Cooper?"

Piola put a photograph of Mia on the table. "Is this who you're talking about?"

Vicaro nodded. "Yes, that's her. Mia Cooper."

Piola chose not to correct him. "How do you know her?"

"Well, I don't, not really." For the first time, Vicaro seemed a little awkward. "That is, we met on a dating site. We had one date, but it didn't go so well. We haven't been in touch since."

"Where was this date?"

"At a nightclub in Vicenza."

Already Piola could see that Vicaro was the sort of intelligent, educated man who would finesse his answers so as to show himself in the best possible light, and might well leave out important details in the process. He decided to give him a rapid push towards disclosure. "You took her to a swingers' club. Do you know how old she is?"

Vicaro blinked. "Twenty-one. I saw her ID when we signed in."

"She's sixteen."

"Jesus!" Vicaro looked worried now. "But it's not illegal, is it? I haven't done anything wrong."

"That depends on exactly what you did."

"Because it was her who wanted to go there, you realise that? That was the whole deal." Vicaro was talking quickly now, desperate for Piola to understand. "It was a special party for Carnevale. But they only let in couples, and she needed someone to go with."

"Why you?"

Vicaro shrugged. "She liked my profile picture, I guess. And she trusted me."

"In what way?"

"Not to hit on her. That was the arrangement." He was still

gabbling, but his eyes were steady as they met Piola's. "I had to promise I wouldn't touch her."

"You mean…" Piola was trying to get his head around this. "She recruited you to go to a sex club, but she made you promise that you wouldn't have sex?"

Vicaro nodded. "It seemed strange to me too. In fact, I thought she was just playing it safe, in case she didn't like the look of me when we met, and that she'd change her mind once we got there. But it was no big deal to me if she didn't. Places like that, there's always more than any man can handle."

"And that's what happened?" Piola said slowly. "You had sex with… others?"

"Yes. Don't get me wrong, she's a nice-looking girl and I asked, but she knocked me back. So I thought: fine, you do your thing and I'll do mine. What with the masks and everything, we lost touch – it was pretty busy in there. I looked for her at the end of the night, but she wasn't around. I thought she must have decided the scene wasn't for her after all."

"Her name's Mia Elston, and she was abducted that night," Piola said. "Her coat and phone were left in a locker at the club. I think you were angry that she'd led you on. So you followed her outside. Perhaps you'd planned it that way from the start."

Vicaro looked genuinely puzzled. "Why would I leave a club full of women who wanted to have sex with me, to go after the one person who didn't?"

Why indeed, Piola thought. "Have you heard of an organisation called Azione Dal Molin?"

"Not that I recall."

"So you never signed their petition to close the American base, or visited their website? We'll check, you know."

"Political protests aren't really my thing," Vicaro said. Piola didn't doubt it.

"Where have you been since Saturday?"

"First thing Sunday morning I went down to visit a new supplier in Sicily, a wine grower. I got back today."

"Can you prove it?"

"Of course. I have receipts for petrol, *autostrada* tolls, my hotel room, the dinner with the grower…" Vicaro was opening his wallet, pulling them out as he spoke.

Piola took him over his story one more time. But he was already certain Vicaro was telling the truth.

"Just one more thing," he added when the man was done. "What made you assume it was Mia we wanted to talk to you about?"

"Oh." Vicaro thought. "I suppose because of the website. I don't usually meet girls on the internet – I find them in bars, or clubs, or just wandering about. But recently I've been working hard, travelling a lot, so I joined a couple of dating sites. But even those, you have to send girls messages, wait for them to get back to you, spend time chatting… The girls on those sites are looking for love, or at least for a boyfriend, so of course they choose carefully. Me, I was just after some fun. So I went on Carnivia – do you know it? It's the website where you don't have to say who you are unless you want to. There are different areas for everyone: singles, married people, gays, swingers; whatever you're into. I went to a swingers' chat room and saw there was a girl asking for someone to accompany her to the masked Carnevale ball at Club Libero. I sent her a photo, and we took it from there."

"And?" Piola asked.

"A couple of days after Mia and I talked, I went back to the same chat room. I thought maybe I'd contact a few more girls and arrange to meet them too – not all at the same time, obviously, but over the next couple of weeks. Like I say, I'm busy, and it seemed an easy way to line up more dates. But when I went back, the message thread had disappeared. So I did a search, and it didn't come up that way either. And then I tried typing in the actual page address. And that was even weirder, because I got this error message saying it hadn't even been registered yet."

NINETEEN

SHOWING MAJOR ELSTON and his wife the film of their daughter was one of the hardest things Kat had ever done. But even as she was doing it she felt the satisfaction that came from doing well something that most other people would find impossible.

Am I a monster? Should I be crying too? Or is it good that I'm clear-headed and focused at times like these?

She recalled the conversation she'd had earlier with Saito, when he'd phoned to tell her the Elstons wanted her kept on the investigation. "Which makes me wonder how they even knew you were coming off it. You're trouble, Tapo." But he'd said it without rancour, only a grudging admiration. "Since they like you so much, you get the shitty job of telling them what's happened."

"Of course, sir. I'll be glad to."

Well, "glad" might have been a slight exaggeration. As well as showing them the film, Kat had to explain that their daughter had been abducted from a swingers' club. Her father had managed to sit through the video without breaking down – unlike his wife, whose animal howling had echoed round the house – but he flatly refused to accept that Mia would have gone to such a place voluntarily.

"There must be some mistake. Either she was lured there,

or she didn't know what kind of club it was. She's underage, for Christ's sake," he added furiously. "A child."

"Actually, the age of sexual consent in Italy is thirteen," Kat said. "Fourteen, if one partner is several years older. Sixteen if a priest or teacher is involved, and eighteen for prostitutes. Club Libero operates an over-21 door policy, but that's discretionary. And all the evidence we're hearing suggests Mia went there of her own accord."

In response, the major only clenched his fists, visibly struggling not to hit something.

It was Holly who said carefully, "Sir, I'm an officer's daughter myself, and I grew up on a base very much like this one. Sometimes you can find yourself caught between two different cultures – between trying new things, and being the person your… the military wants you to be. So you do your experimenting in secret. My bet is that Mia didn't go to the club for the same reason as the other patrons. I'm guessing that when she found out there was a place like that almost on her doorstep, it seemed different and exciting, and her curiosity simply got the better of her. Think of it as proof that she's a brave, bright, curious young woman, not that she's disrespecting you."

The major shook his head in disbelief.

"There's something else I need to inform you of," Kat said. "It appears that Mia's kidnap is politically, rather than financially, motivated. But a kidnap protocol has been put in place, all the same."

"'Kidnap protocol'? What's that?"

"If the kidnappers ask for a ransom, it's illegal to pay it."

The major stared at her. "But that's madness. We'll pay anything, do anything…"

Kat shook her head. "That would leave you open to prosecution. And to prevent it, your bank accounts have been frozen."

"But... how do we buy groceries? Food?" the major said, stunned. "How do we live?"

"You'll be given a small allowance by the state. I must warn you not to try to circumvent this system. It's for everyone's good, and the penalties for ignoring it are severe." It was true that the number of kidnaps in Italy had fallen dramatically since kidnap protocols had been introduced, but she thought it better not to mention the tragedies that had also occurred, when criminal gangs had assumed that people who were desperate enough would somehow find a way round them.

"Civilian Liaison will make sure you have everything you need," Holly said quietly.

"And I'll need to take Mia's laptop," Kat added. "Our specialists will look for anything on it that might be relevant."

Major Elston shook his head. "There's nothing there. Only homework and emails from friends."

"How can you be sure?"

He hesitated. "I was... keeping an eye on it."

"In what way?" she said, puzzled.

He fixed her with a steady look. "I installed some software that monitored her internet use."

"You mean, like a filter?"

"This is more thorough than a filter. It actively scans for questionable activity and sends me daily reports, or alerts me in real time if anything untoward is happening. If necessary, I can see everything she's seeing, watch what sites she visits, read her messages..."

Kat was too surprised to respond. Holly said, "Was Mia aware you were doing this?"

"She knows that unregulated use of the internet worries me, and that I'm a responsible and pro-active parent. But I never specifically shared with her that I was monitoring what she did online." He caught Kat's expression. "There are dangerous people out there, Captain. So-called friends who aren't really who they seem. Sites dedicated to explicit materials, gambling, subversive philosophies. And then there are the security implications. Imagine if a teenager mentioned online that her father's unit was being deployed to a particular country. That information could be useful to America's enemies."

"You could have talked to her about the dangers," Kat said. "Explained how to stay safe."

"I did. The software was just a backup. And in the event, it was never necessary. Her online activity never gave me any cause for concern."

"Nevertheless, we'll need the laptop," Kat said firmly. "Yours too, if you have logs of the sites she'd been visiting."

Upstairs, as they bagged Mia's computer, Holly said, "You think he was being overprotective, don't you?"

Kat nodded. "Yes. But it's more than that – I think he's got it completely wrong, somehow. Remember what Toomer said? Mia was teasing him about explicit things she'd seen on the net. Then there was her Carnivia account. And it's a fair bet she found Club Libero online too, just like Daniele did. If her father was using spy software, how come he didn't pick up on any of that?" She gestured at the computer. "Somehow, whatever's on here must be part of it."

TWENTY

AFTER SHE'D MADE the film setting out the kidnappers' demands, they took her back to her cell. On the mattress was her reward: a plate with some bread and a piece of cheese.

Harlequin had watched her eat, then taken the plate away. "Rest," he'd ordered.

She'd tried, but there were too many thoughts going through her head. So now she knew why she'd been kidnapped: because of the new base, Dal Molin. She was aware that it was a contentious issue with some of the locals – the walls surrounding Camp Ederle were covered in graffiti about it, and the bigger demonstrations and rallies got a paragraph or two in *The Outlook*, the base newsletter – but she'd assumed it was only a small minority who cared one way or the other. Most of the Italians she met seemed really friendly.

All the same, the discovery gave her hope. She had an idea that if they'd been asking for a ransom, it might have been more difficult; she knew the Pentagon didn't pay out for kidnaps, in case it encouraged others. And her own parents were hardly wealthy. But her captors, it seemed, just wanted some kind of local referendum. That, surely, was no big deal – no one could object to a democratic vote, could they?

But even as she thought about it, she realised that was precisely why the authorities might not like it. She didn't know much about Italian politics, but presumably being forced into a democratic exercise by what was effectively a terrorist group would be a humiliation for the government. And if a majority voted for the Americans to leave, it would create a problem for both countries. America would have to ignore the wishes of the host nation's citizens, which in turn would fan the flames of the protest for years to come.

Far easier, perhaps, just to leave her here.

She wondered if the kidnappers were prepared for that. It seemed like they were prepared for most things.

The chain rattled at the door of her cell. It was Harlequin, beckoning her.

"Come."

As directed, she walked into the larger room, where she stopped short at the sight of a rope, hanging over a thick roof beam. On the floor was a coil of hosepipe that also hadn't been there earlier. Bauta stood to one side, watching.

"Move." Harlequin pushed her, making her walk to where the rope was. When she was in position he said, "Take off your clothes. All of them."

Startled, she didn't react immediately, and he shouted furiously, "The prisoner will remove her clothes."

She did as he ordered, trying not to look at either of them. When she was finished he produced the handcuffs he'd used on her before. "Wrists."

Obediently she held up her wrists for him to cuff, although her heart was racing.

He tied the rope to the short chain linking the handcuffs, then reached for the other end, pulling on it to raise her hands until they were above her head. Then he tied the free end to a bolt in the wall.

The flash of anger she'd witnessed when she'd been slow to obey him had vanished now. He seemed calm – almost, she thought, as if he were deliberately steeling himself for something.

He said stiffly, "I regret that this is necessary."

He turned and gestured to Bauta to start recording.

DAY TWO

TWENTY-ONE

AT PRECISELY 4 A.M. all known members of the Azione Dal Molin protest group were roused from their beds. Their computers and phones were seized, and their partners and families told to leave so that search teams could take apart their homes.

The suspects were brought back to the Carabinieri headquarters. Because there were so many of them, the interviews were still going on at 9 a.m. when Saito went into the press conference.

Flanked by the prosecutor on one side and Mia's parents on the other, he read out a short statement. A teenage girl, the daughter of an American officer based in Vicenza, had been abducted. A group calling itself Azione Dal Molin, which had recently come to the attention of the Carabinieri in the context of another investigation, had claimed responsibility. All known members of the group had now been taken in for questioning.

Saito looked around the room, confident that everyone there understood the implications of what he was saying: the Carabinieri had acted swiftly and decisively. "Needless to say, this is a very fluid situation, against an enemy who is not afraid to use terror tactics on an innocent victim. However, the

Carabinieri remain confident of an early arrest, and of course Mia's safe return."

Holly, sitting just behind Major Elston and his wife, translated the general's words for them. They seemed almost mesmerised by the barrage of flashes from the photographers' cameras.

Saito paused. "Although there are no indications that Mia has been harmed, I should warn you that this film is not pleasant viewing." He turned to the screen behind him and nodded to a technician to start the video.

The Elstons had their backs to the screen, as did Holly, so it was only when she saw the shock on Saito's face that she realised something was amiss. She looked round.

The film they'd seen yesterday had started with Mia in the van, hooded and bound. But it was a different image that was on the screen now. Mia was standing. Her shackled arms had been pulled over her head by a rope attached to the ceiling, forcing her up onto her toes. She was naked.

A crude caption appeared:

NUDITY IS USED TO CAUSE PSYCHOLOGICAL DISCOMFORT, PARTICULARLY IF AN INDIVIDUAL, FOR CULTURAL OR OTHER REASONS, IS ESPECIALLY MODEST.

The picture held on Mia shifting her weight uncomfortably from one leg to the other. Another caption appeared:

THE WRISTS ARE SHACKLED TO A BAR OR HOOK IN THE CEILING ABOVE THE HEAD FOR PERIODS RANGING FROM TWO OR THREE DAYS CONTINUOUSLY, AND FOR UP TO TWO OR THREE MONTHS INTERMITTENTLY.

The film cut back to Mia. A figure wearing a Harlequin mask entered the frame from the left. He was holding a hose. As water gushed from the end, he sprayed Mia with it, causing her to shriek in terror and shock.

THE MINIMUM PERMISSIBLE TEMPERATURE OF THE WATER USED IN WATER DOUSING IS 41°F, THOUGH YOU HAVE INFORMED US THAT IN PRACTICE THE TEMPERATURE IS GENERALLY NOT BELOW 50°F SINCE TAP RATHER THAN REFRIGERATED WATER IS GENERALLY USED.

Holly turned to the Elstons, who still hadn't looked round. "Sir, Mrs Elston, you need to come with me," she said urgently. "Now."

The major took one look at her face, then put his arm around his wife and bodily pulled her to her feet. "Follow Boland."

She got them out by the nearest door as quickly as she could, trying to ignore both what was happening on the screen and the cameras that turned to follow their progress.

When they were outside, Major Elston took a deep breath. "Thank you, Second Lieutenant. I take it that wasn't something my wife would want to see?"

"I don't think it was, sir, no."

"What was it?"

"Really, sir, I don't exactly know." She hesitated. "The kidnappers appeared to be spraying her with water."

But she didn't tell him about the last thing she'd seen, just as the door closed on the conference; another title flashing onto the screen, above the heads of the assembled journalists.

HAVE YOU WORKED IT OUT YET?

TWENTY-TWO

"IT SEEMS THE original film wasn't a clip at all, but a kind of embedded link," Holly said. "In other words, when the kidnappers updated the footage on the server, the original was replaced by the new film."

"Where's this footage being hosted?"

"Carnivia – a social media site based here in Venice. The site's owner, Daniele Barbo, is being questioned."

"They think he had something to do with it?"

"Not necessarily, but the Carabinieri want to examine his servers to see if the source code gives any clue to the kidnappers' location. So far, I understand, Barbo is sticking to his blanket policy of not cooperating with the authorities."

She'd been summoned to update Colonel Carver, Major Elston's commanding officer. He sat in the middle of a long table, flanked by serious-faced staff officers and a sprinkling of men in dark suits she assumed were kidnap specialists. She wasn't introduced, but she knew a council of war when she saw one.

Carver shook his head angrily. "I spent a lot of time and money trying to contain the anti-Dal Molin activity. Instead, it looks like they've managed to get the whole world looking our way, and put a young American's life in jeopardy at the same time. I suppose the Italian media are all over the story?"

"Affirmative, sir." She took some printouts from a folder and placed them in front of him. Carver picked up the top one. It was from the blog written by the political campaigner Raffaele Fallici. Entitled "Persona Non Grata", it usually consisted of an angry polemic against the various failings of the establishment. But today, perhaps because he was mindful of his own putative role in the affair, it was entirely devoted to a denunciation of Azione Dal Molin's tactics – "From which, for the avoidance of all doubt, I hereby distance myself unreservedly. Indeed, there is nothing more likely to turn the sound judgement of the Italian people against the anti-Dal Molin movement than the damaging and irresponsible hijacking of a worthy cause by those whose overriding mentality is simply that of terrorists. In one reprehensible action, they have handed the moral high ground in this affair straight to Washington."

"Well, that's something, I suppose," Carver said, passing it on.

Many of the papers already had the story up on the breaking news sections of their websites, illustrated by photographs of Mia taken from the internet. As most of the pictures were several years old, they had the effect of making her look even younger than she actually was. The headline in *Il Gazzettino* was fairly typical: "*INNOCENZA RUBATA*", it screamed, above a particularly fresh-faced shot of the stolen innocent in question. The writer had somehow discovered that Mia had signed up to an abstinence movement; she was, he went on to say, the embodiment of the religious values that, more than anything, continued to unite their two nations.

"Several papers have asked us for a quote," Holly said. "Do you want me to draft something?"

Carver fixed her with his gaze. "Tell them that America will hunt down and destroy our enemies wherever we find them."

"Roger that, sir." She hesitated. "Although technically, it will be the Carabinieri who'll do the hunting down here, since this is Italian territory."

Carver waved the objection away. "Then you'd better write some of that soft-soap stuff you people in Liaison always write. Just try not to be too obsequious to America's adversaries, will you, Second Lieutenant? Every sign of weakness here is another haji emboldened to blow up our troops over there."

"And Richard and Nicole? How are they holding up?" one of the staff officers asked quietly.

"Mrs Elston is in a bad way," Holly said frankly. "The doctors are keeping her heavily sedated – they think it's the best thing for her at this stage. The major's coping pretty well, all things considered."

"Major Elston is one of the toughest fighting men who ever served in this brigade," Carver said. "A decorated hero and an inspiration to his men. He won't buckle, no matter what pressure he's put under."

Holly said nothing. Mia was clearly the apple of her father's eye, and it seemed to her that no man could fail to be destroyed by the knowledge that his daughter was being treated in such a way.

"But you're to come to me personally the moment he shows any signs to the contrary," Carver added. "I want daily updates. And I particularly want to know any details of the Italian investigation that aren't being placed in the public domain."

One of the men in suits said, "The Carabinieri's record for pulling off successful rescues in situations like these stands at about sixty per cent."

There was silence while the rest of the room digested this. "And the other forty per cent?" someone asked. "Are they killed by the kidnappers?"

The specialist shook his head. "Most die during rescue attempts."

This time the silence went on even longer.

"So we offer what we'll call 'training and support'," Carver said at last. "Effective immediately. That is to say, when they do locate her, we'll jump in and take over as necessary. Meanwhile, we'll have a team of our own people double-tracking the Carabinieri investigation, in the hope we find her before they do."

"Affirmative, sir. I take it you don't want the Carabinieri to know that's what we're doing?"

"Too right, Second Lieutenant. When the life of an American innocent is at risk, diplomatic niceties come second. Mia's safety is our only priority now."

She saluted. "Roger that, sir." He nodded to show she was dismissed.

Leaving the war room, she headed over to the far side of Camp Ederle, to the Education Block. In theory, three different American universities offered courses here, helping soldiers gain the qualifications that would get them jobs when their military careers were over. In practice, those who used these facilities were mostly wives and retirees; as, indeed, were many of the teachers.

She found a small classroom marked "CH12 – Roman Civilization" and knocked.

"Come on in," a familiar voice said.

She smiled a greeting to the white-haired man by the window. She often consulted Ian Gilroy about matters relating to her work, given his long experience of running the CIA's Venice section before his retirement, but it was something more specific that had prompted her to arrange this meeting today. One of his cases, back in the period of turmoil in Italy known as the Years of Lead, had concerned the kidnap of the young Daniele Barbo, whose mother was American. Daniele had been mutilated by his kidnappers, but she knew that many in the intelligence community believed that, had it not been for Gilroy's behind-the-scenes counsel, the outcome could have been far worse. Daniele's father had evidently agreed, subsequently appointing Gilroy to the board of his art foundation, a role he had continued to hold ever since. Daniele himself, though, took a rather different view. Since the Foundation controlled all the family's wealth, Gilroy was now effectively Daniele's guardian in financial matters, something the younger man deeply resented.

She updated him on the Carabinieri investigation, just as she had Carver, with the difference that this time she added a summary of Colonel Carver's remarks as well.

"An interesting situation," Gilroy said thoughtfully when she'd finished.

"In what way, sir?"

"It just seems curious that the kidnappers should have chosen Daniele as their conduit, given his own history. It gives a strange kind of... *symmetry* to the story, doesn't it?" He mused for a while. "Do any of the news reports mention Carnivia?"

"Most of them. But it's Fallici who's going the furthest, on his blog."

Gilroy got out his reading glasses as she handed him the printout. "'It is literally incredible,'" he read out loud, "'that an organisation can be permitted to exist whose sole purpose is to facilitate the propagation of pornography, to make possible anonymous slanders, to facilitate tax evasion and petty crime, to break all the laws of our country, and to spread malicious innuendo and rumour. That it has the effrontery to reside right here, in our own country, rather than in some desperate and despotic tax haven, says more about the inherent corruption and political apathy of our nation than even the ongoing scandal of our crime statistics. For the crimes on Carnivia.com are potentially numberless. Even now, it could be that the abduction and subsequent brutalisation of a thousand more Mias is being planned within its darkest corners. I have long supported the freedom of the internet. But with great freedom comes great responsibility. Is it too much to ask that the authorities finally exert themselves to bring this festering cyberslum under something resembling control?'" He raised his eyebrows. "Fiery stuff."

"It sure is."

"What is it, Holly?" he said, noticing her hesitation.

"Daniele spotted that some of the messages he was sent were lifted word for word from CIA directives. It seems a fair bet that the captions on the films were, too." She gestured at the printout in his hand. "Assuming the kidnappers have more material to quote from, and that it's all going to be blown up by the media, what are the political implications of this?"

"Ah, Holly. As ever, you've thought about the bigger picture that your more gung-ho colleagues have missed. It was a great loss to Langley when you decided to enter the military, I hope you know that." He considered. "In answer to your question, it probably depends on what else the kidnappers have, and how they choose to use it."

"Think I should do some more digging? See what else might be coming out?"

"Indeed I do, Holly. It's what you're best at Let's try to figure how this might play out for Mia, before any of these hotheads unleash their dogs of war."

TWENTY-THREE

AFTER THE DOUSING she'd been left to stand there, naked and wet. Soon she'd started to shake uncontrollably, both from the cold and the pain in her stretched arms.

It was as if they'd been waiting for her to do exactly that. At a word from Harlequin, Bauta lifted the camera and filmed her for a minute or so, before Harlequin gave another command.

"*Quanto basta.*"

Was it her imagination, or did Bauta seem almost reluctant to obey? Whatever the reason, Harlequin had to repeat the instruction a second time before Bauta stopped.

A sound came from the laptop – a familiar four-note bubbling refrain: the Skype call tone. It was so reminiscent of all the times her father called home from foreign deployments that for a moment she thought, *It's dad*. Hope leapt in her chest. Even if it wasn't her father, it could be someone trying to negotiate. Her nightmare, surely, couldn't last much longer.

"*E' lui,*" Harlequin said. Picking up the laptop, he left the room.

E' lui. That meant "It's him". So it was a call the kidnappers had been expecting, not an offer of negotiation.

As they waited for Harlequin to return, she could hear Bauta's breath rasping in his nose. For some reason, it made her uneasy. She suddenly felt acutely aware of her own nakedness.

Bauta moved, coming closer to her, and she tensed. He walked all around her, but without the camera this time, close enough to touch. Her skin crawled as he went behind her, out of her line of sight.

When he appeared in front of her again, his face was so close that she could see his eyes through the mask. Deliberately, his gaze dropped to her breasts. Then he reached for his crotch, closed his hand around it through his trousers, and shook it at her.

She'd seen that gesture before – here in Italy leering old men, particularly in the countryside, used it almost like a wolf whistle. But she'd never experienced it when she'd been help-less like this. She gasped, pulling as far away as the rope would allow.

Chuckling at her reaction, he put a hand on her shoulder and squeezed. It was calloused and leathery, the hand of a working man. "*Carinissima*," he breathed. Cute.

She kicked him away. But without shoes on it was hard to inflict much damage, and he only laughed again. The second time she tried to kick him, he simply caught her by the ankle and pulled, forcing her to hop towards him on one leg.

"*Bella sgualdrina*," he breathed, sliding his hand up her calf.

The door opened. Taking in the situation at a glance, Harlequin spoke sharply, in a stream of Italian too fast for her to follow.

Bauta shrugged sulkily and mumbled a reply. But he let go and took a step back, away from her.

Harlequin came and untied her wrists. "We do not do that," he said, anger thickening his accent. "Only what is necessary."

Going to a bag in the corner of the room, he took out some overalls and placed them on the table. "From now on you wear these." He hesitated. "Unless I order it. But not him. You understand? And if he does that again, you tell me."

She picked the overalls up. As the full length of them unrolled she realised something she hadn't before. They were bright orange, made of heavy cotton, like those worn by the prisoners in Guantanamo Bay.

TWENTY-FOUR

IN THE AFTERMATH of the second film, the atmosphere in the operations room was feverish. Almost immediately, Saito was summoned to a high-level meeting – to be given a bollocking, Kat suspected. In his absence, the colonels allocated tasks as best they could.

"Captain Tapo. Have you been assigned yet?"

She turned. It was Colonel Lettiere from Internal Affairs. She'd known they were putting every available man on this investigation, so she wasn't surprised to see him. But it was an effort not to let her dislike of him show.

"Not yet, sir. Why?"

"I need someone to compile a list of all the people who were in Club Libero that night. They will have to be contacted individually, in case they saw anything. Of course, being swingers, some of them may be wary of talking to the Carabinieri, so we should send someone they can relate to… I should imagine that's a task you could accomplish, isn't it?"

Behind him, someone sniggered.

"Of course, sir," she said blandly. "But Club Libero was at full capacity that night. Tracking down all of them could take one person weeks."

Lettiere's expression didn't waver. "Then it should keep you out of mischief for some considerable time, shouldn't it, Captain?"

She drove back to Club Libero in a foul mood – not at Lettiere's needling, which was no worse than anything else she'd been on the receiving end of recently, but at his instruction. She already knew that Club Libero made its guests sign in, so unless they'd used false names she should be able to trace them easily enough. But to tackle such a huge task on her own meant she'd effectively been once again sidelined from the main investigation. And it wasn't even likely to generate any leads: Lettiere knew full well that on the night of the kidnap all the patrons had been masked, so the chances of getting anything useful from the clubbers was negligible.

She saw blue lights in her rear-view mirror and pulled over to let a fire engine past. It was rapidly followed by two more. Only as she neared her destination did she see that they'd been heading for the same place she was. Black smoke was billowing from a jagged hole in Club Libero's glass door. Another fire engine was pouring foam from its hoses through the exit doors that gave onto the car park.

Edoardo and Jacquie stood to one side, watching, their faces ashen. Kat went over to them. "What happened?"

Edoardo gestured. "A firebomb, they think. We got the call an hour ago."

"Has anything like this ever happened before?"

He shook his head. "Never."

"Have you ever had any trouble with organised crime? Anyone asking for protection money that you haven't paid out on?"

If that was what had happened here, she knew they'd be unlikely to tell the Carabinieri. But Edoardo shook his head emphatically. "We've never had any trouble. Giù makes sure of that."

She found Giù at the local Carabinieri station. "I suppose you've heard?"

He shrugged belligerently. "It's not my fault. Someone decides the *scambisti* were spoiling the neighbourhood, there's not a lot I can do about it."

"Maybe. But that fire was started right by the front desk. I'm thinking that perhaps they wanted to be sure of getting the signing-in book. And the computer with the CCTV images on."

"It's possible," he said grudgingly.

"The computer you said you were going to take away to fix," she reminded him. "Where is it now?"

"In my locker," he mumbled.

"Let's take a look, shall we?"

As he set the computer up, she said, "Let me give you a hypothesis, Giù. This laptop's working fine, and always was. You just didn't want me to see the tapes."

"I mended it," he protested.

"Pull the other one. You've got a nice little sideline here, and you didn't fancy having the club's guests bothered by a Carabinieri investigation."

"So?" he said aggressively. "Important people come to the club. Why drag them into it unless we have to?"

"Like who?"

He shrugged. "Vivaldo Moretti was in that night."

She laughed out loud. "The politician? He must be nearly seventy."

"He's an old rogue, for sure. But a good tipper. Turns up with two or three girls on his arm and asks for a table on the far side of the dance floor, one where you can see everything without being seen too much."

"When you say 'girls', I take it you mean hookers?"

Giù shrugged. "Hookers, weather girls, *veline*... it's a fine line these days, isn't it? Anyway, when I thought we were just talking about a missing schoolgirl, there didn't seem any point in bringing his name into it. Last night, when I heard about the kidnap, I realised I was going to have to tell you."

Or realised there was no point in tapping Moretti for a bung to keep his name quiet, she reflected cynically.

The club's CCTV camera was positioned just over the reception desk, so the images on Giù's screen showed the patrons coming off the street. But, just as she'd expected, most had put their masks on before entering the club, making identification impossible.

"There," Giù said, freezing the tape. "That's the one I was talking about. Dreadlock Guy."

Kat peered at the screen. The image was relatively high quality, but the wig, along with the mask, obscured the man's features completely.

"Who's he with?" she wondered aloud. The woman behind him was also wearing a mask – a Volto, a full-face mask of white plaster decorated with elaborate Venetian gilding, together with an oversized tricorne hat that hid her own hair from the camera. Whoever these people were, Kat thought, either they were consistently lucky, or their planning was remarkable.

Giù let the tape roll. Sure enough, the camera had taken one more image of the couple as they left the reception desk. Dreadlock Guy was almost out of shot, but the woman had been caught in profile.

"What's that?" She pointed.

There was a tattoo on the woman's arm, partly revealed by her sleeve as it rode up. Kat made out the bottom part of a skull with two wings emerging from either side, and under that, some writing – it looked like three words, a motto of some sort. "Can we print this?"

"Sure." Giù pressed a button.

Mia and her date were on the tape a little later. It was hardly surprising that the club had accepted her ID at face value, Kat thought. While most of the clubbers were in their thirties – she recalled from her own brief experience on the scene that it mainly consisted of married couples battling domestic boredom – there were plenty of younger patrons too. With her feathered mask on, Mia didn't stand out in the least.

Again Kat thought how well planned it all was. Dreadlock Guy and Tattoo Woman were already inside when Mia arrived. Which meant there would probably have been another team on the outside, tracking them in.

"Who's that?" she asked, noticing a young man on the tape who wasn't wearing a mask.

"Him? That's Roberto, the podium dancer."

"Do you have an address for him?"

"Sure – he lives just behind the hospital. I could drive you there in ten minutes."

"Thanks, I'll talk to him. Maybe he saw something no one else did."

Roberto was extremely pretty. He was also somewhat stupid, his inanely cheerful smile oddly robbing his face of the attractiveness a sulkier expression would have lent it.

He was only doing the dancing, he explained, to support himself through his personal-trainer exams. But it was a good job – after all, if he wasn't being paid he'd still be out dancing anyway. "This way I get into clubs for free!" he exclaimed. "And most of them charge forty euros for admission!"

"Is Club Libero the sort of place you normally go?" Kat asked.

Roberto shook his head. "I've got a steady girlfriend. But if you don't go into the back rooms, it's not much different from anywhere else. In fact, in some ways it's better. At Libero, no one has to try too hard to get laid, so people aren't bothered if you tell them you're not interested."

"Did you see this girl on Saturday night?" Kat asked, showing a picture of Mia. "She may have been wearing this." She added a picture of a feathered Columbina mask she'd printed out from the internet.

He studied them, frowning. "Maybe... Yes, while I was doing my first shift. I remember because she was kind of flirting with me, you know? Copying my moves."

It was interesting, Kat thought, that Mia had flirted with the only unavailable young man in the whole club. It seemed to confirm Holly's theory that she'd only gone there as a kind of dare. "Then what?"

"I saw her with a guy with blond dreadlocks. They went outside, through the fire door."

"Could it have been a drug deal?"

Roberto shook his head. "The usual dealers weren't around on Saturday."

Kat's ears pricked up. "What do you mean?"

"There are a couple of dealers who are always there – they don't give any trouble, but they make sure everyone's got what they need, you know? On Saturday, I couldn't—" He stopped short.

"Don't worry," she assured him. "I don't care if you're in the habit of getting yourself a little pick-me-up from time to time. But I need to know if you're sure – the usual guys had vanished?"

He nodded.

"Thanks, Roberto," she said. "You've been very useful."

Back in the car, she turned to Giù. "You didn't tell me you have an arrangement with the local Mafia as well."

"I don't know what you mean," he blustered, starting the engine.

"Yes, you do. I thought it was crap, when you said dealers know better than to come to the club when you're there. Which suggests to me that it's you who lets them in. That's why you search people so thoroughly, isn't it? Not to keep drugs out, like Edoardo thinks. It's to make sure no one else brings anything in, so your friends can maintain their monopoly."

"A man's got to live," Giù said truculently. "I've got less than two years to go, and my Carabinieri pension won't feed my family."

"Correction," Kat said. "You've got less than two days to go. Just as long as it takes you to write out a letter of resignation, in fact. A moonlighting *carabiniere*'s one thing. Moonlighting for the Mafia's something else."

"Everyone does it," Giù said with a snarl. "You will too, one day."

"No, I won't."

"Want some advice?" he said, pulling abruptly into the traffic.

"Not really."

"Don't chase this one too hard. You don't know where it'll lead you."

"What do you mean?"

"If the local *spacciatori* don't turn up to Libero's biggest night of the year, it's for a good reason. Someone put the word out – someone who gets listened to." He gave Kat a sideways glance. "That means someone who knows how to shut up nosy bitches like you, as well."

TWENTY-FIVE

PIOLA RAN THROUGH the stack of statements one more time. Together they occupied eight box files – nearly four hundred pages of evidence, gathered in record time.

Not a single page of it contained any useful leads.

All the members of Azione Dal Molin claimed to know nothing of any kidnap plan. Such tactics, several said vehemently, were completely abhorrent to them. Yes, some of them had been prepared to break the law to protest against the Americans' presence; but that was a far cry from being prepared to adopt the same methods as those they protested against.

Not that Piola had expected the interviews to provide a breakthrough; at any rate, not immediately. Azione Dal Molin was too well organised for that – as evidenced both by the remarkable efficiency of the break-in at the construction site, and the almost military precision of the kidnap itself. If the organisation followed the same model as, say, the militant animal rights groups he'd come across, they should be looking for one or two people who'd been involved in the wider anti-Dal Molin movement some time previously, but who'd appeared to move away from it just as frustration among the rank and file had led to the formation of a smaller, more radical group. On the face of it, there'd be no connection between them. In reality, one or two members of the group would act as cut-outs, carrying messages to the hard-core activists in the kidnap cell.

It meant that, unless they generated some more leads quickly, they could end up with a pool of over a hundred and fifty thousand suspects – every single person who had ever signed a petition against Dal Molin.

He picked up Luca Marchesin's statement. It was very similar to all the others. No, he would never dream of doing anything like that. He was a pacifist. He would have turned anyone who even thought about doing a real kidnap over to the police...

"Sottotenente Panicucci?" he called.

"Sir?"

"Come with me. We're going to go and speak to Luca Marchesin. I want to check something."

Luca lived with his parents in Padua, not far from the university. When his mother opened the door and saw the two Carabinieri officers, her face darkened.

"I know he already spoke to my colleagues," Piola said. "But I just want a quick word with Luca. Can we come in?"

"It's OK," Luca told her, appearing at the door. "He's the one I told you about, the one who got me out of the guard-house."

Somewhat reluctantly, she let them in.

"Luca," Piola said. "There's a girl about your own age who's terrified right now that she's going to be killed by her abductors. And there are people holding her – quite possibly well-intentioned, if misguided people – who could get killed themselves during the rescue operation. This whole thing is a tragedy waiting to happen."

"I know that. But I already told them – we never planned anything like this."

"I believe you. But what I want to know is, did anyone ever mention the idea of a kidnap? Even just as a suggestion, perhaps one that was immediately discounted?"

Luca hesitated.

"It was you, wasn't it?" Piola said. "In your statement, you talked about never having thought about doing a real kidnap. That suggests to me kidnapping did get mentioned, somehow."

"That's what's so crazy," Luca said slowly. "Because it was nothing – not even an idea, just a throwaway remark."

"Such as?"

"We were having a… I guess you'd call it a brainstorming. Trying to come up with some neat protests, stuff that would go viral. I was doing most of the talking – I'm good at all that; social media and so on. There were a few ideas I was really keen on. Like having a flash mob at Vicenza station, with guys in American military uniforms wearing Playboy bunny ears."

Piola frowned. "That would work?"

Luca nodded confidently. "For sure. Anyway, I had this other idea too. That we should all dress up in orange jumpsuits and Guido masks and pretend to be American prisoners. Someone said it had been done already. So *I* said, so let's just take one prisoner, then, and do a rendition on them. I wrote it on the board, but it was never mentioned again. It was just one idea in amongst lots of crazy stuff."

"But someone made it a reality?"

He shrugged miserably. "I guess. Or maybe it's just coincidence. I'd hate to think they got it from me."

"Who else was at this meeting?"

"The whole group. It was when we first started."

"OK, Luca. Thank you for being honest with me about that."

"Will I get I into trouble?"

Piola shook his head. "Having an idea doesn't make you a criminal. It's doing it that counts."

He was in a thoughtful mood as they went back to Venice. Despite what he'd said to Luca, recent legislation had blurred the lines between thought and action: conceiving and planning a terrorist action was now a crime in itself, and who was to say what counted as conceiving?

But perhaps that kind of step was necessary, now that crimes didn't have to take place in the real world either. It was something new and quite alien to him, this world in which a protest could take the form of a flash mob or a firebomb, or both.

"I suppose you do all this stuff?" he said to Panicucci. "Facebook virals and so on?"

Panicucci seemed surprised by the question. "Some of it, sir. I'm not a heavy user. Just Facebook and Twitter. And Instagram and Flickr. Oh, and Storify, Tumblr... maybe a few others."

"Carnivia?"

Panicucci hesitated. "And Carnivia, yes. But that's different. People don't really talk about their Carnivia accounts. But everyone has one. It's like a guilty pleasure."

A guilty pleasure that could be exploited by criminals, Piola thought. How did one police a city in which no one had a name or a face? How did one solve crimes that transcended the boundaries of the physical and the digital?

Back at his desk, he reached for the stack of files and prepared to go through it one more time. As he did so, he was struck by another thought.

Military precision – it was ironic, really, how that phrase had come into his mind earlier, given that the abductors ostensibly stood against everything that the US Army stood for.

Ostensibly.

Could it be anything more than that?

Piola was professionally trained to scepticism. And so he found himself examining this most sceptical of thoughts from every angle, turning it over and over in his mind, before deciding that there was, at this stage, no reason to entertain it any further.

Though not, perhaps, to dismiss it altogether.

TWENTY-SIX

HOLLY SAT AT her computer and swiped her CAC card through the reader. The Common Access Code software immediately compared her movements around the base that day with those she was authorised to make. Satisfied that she was who she claimed to be – a junior intelligence officer stationed at Camp Ederle in Italy – it granted her access to SIPRNet, the US Defense Department's own version of the internet.

She brought up a secure search engine, Intelliseek, and began entering each of the phrases that had accompanied the video of Mia. She'd expected this to be a lengthy process. But almost immediately, a plethora of hits came up on regular news sites, relating to the 2009 release of a number of CIA memos after a Freedom of Information action brought by the American Civil Liberties Union. One was a fax sent by someone at the CIA – in the published version, the sender's name had been obliterated – to the Acting Head of the Justice Department's Office of Legal Counsel, Dan Levin. The cover note said simply, "Dan, a generic description of the process".

Holly exhaled. Daniele Barbo had assumed "Dan" meant him, but actually the sender had been talking about a different Dan altogether.

She vaguely recalled some newspaper articles at the time about the "torture memos", as they'd been dubbed, but she'd never actually read the originals. Now, on the Huffington Post website, she found an article with links to the documents. Written in the bland, reassuring language of bureaucrats, they detailed a series of over thirty techniques that made up the process known as "enhanced interrogation".

The Red Cross, the website pointed out, had carried out its own investigation into these techniques, and had described them as torture. During his election campaign Barack Obama had appeared to adopt a similar position, saying:

"To build a better, freer world, we must first behave in ways that reflect the decency and aspirations of the American people. This means ending the practice of shipping away prisoners in the dead of night to be tortured in far-off countries, of detaining thousands without charge or trial, of maintaining a network of secret prisons to jail people beyond the reach of the law."

Most people had interpreted this to mean that under his administration such practices would end. But other, more cynical, commentators had pointed out that by rolling several clauses together, he was effectively leaving himself some wiggle room. Thus, "ending the practice of shipping away prisoners in the dead of night to be tortured in far-off countries" might be said to have been achieved if those prisoners were taken in the daytime, say, or if it wasn't far-off countries they were shipped off to.

In fact, the Huffington Post article said, the Obama administration had later quietly decided that while the old system of "extraordinary renditions" – that is, kidnapping a foreign national and flying them to another country such as Syria or Libya for interrogation – might be indefensible, "ordinary" renditions should continue. In other words, foreign nationals could still be seized and interrogated without trial or the protection of the law, so long as it was Americans who did the interrogating, rather than some foreign regime. And whilst Obama had said that the Army Field Manual should be used as the basis of future interrogations, he'd stopped short of actually declaring any of the old CIA techniques illegal. The article gave several examples from the Obama years of people who alleged that they'd been subjected to procedures identical to those summarised with clinical precision by the CIA's lawyers in the torture memos.

The slap is delivered with fingers slightly spread, which you have explained to us is designed to be less painful than a closed-hand slap. The slap is also delivered to the fleshy part of the face, further reducing any risk of physical damage...

She saw what the kidnappers were doing now, and just how clever it was. They were simply going to do to their own captive everything the Americans did to theirs, from illegal detention onwards. People would be horrified – but they would also say the US had no right to cry foul. Together with the demand for a referendum, it gave the kidnappers a spurious figleaf of morality, whilst at the same time reminding their audience of all the reasons why they might not want the US Armed Forces in their country in the first place. It was a kidnap perfectly designed for the internet age; a kidnap in which page views and public opinion, not cash, was the currency being sought.

Holly had never devoted much time to considering whether America's rendition programme was ethical. As a soldier, you signed up to an honour code that, perhaps ironically, left such judgements to others. Even before that, as a military brat, she'd been steeped in a culture fixated on conduct, not conscience; valour, not compassion. Yet many generals, she knew, were quietly disparaging about intelligence gleaned from harsh interrogations. Some even went so far as to question whether, by using such techniques, America wasn't betraying the very principles it claimed to be fighting for.

In Hawaii once, during her training, she and three other female officer cadets had been asked to help with "an intel matter". They'd been taken by truck to a military camp fifty miles away. Surveying her fellow volunteers, she couldn't help noticing that they were among the prettiest in that year's intake. There was much joking about whether the matter would actually turn out to be dinner and beers with some sex-starved intelligence officers.

In the event, they'd been asked to go to different huts "and observe". Inside her hut, Holly had found a man with his hands shackled to the ceiling in a manner not so very different to Mia's. He was naked. Incongruously, there was an expensive-looking stereo system and an iPod on the floor nearby.

The man looked exhausted. Holly learned later that his interrogators played the *Sesame Street* song at full volume whenever it looked as if he might fall asleep. His head and face had been shaved, very roughly, leaving patches of black hair and scabs of dried blood.

On seeing her, a man in American uniform standing next to the captive had turned and flicked his victim's penis.

"What d'you think, Cadet Boland?" he demanded. "Would you fuck a dick as pathetic as this?"

"No, sir," she'd answered dutifully.

"That's right. You'd fuck a proper Yankee dick, not a

shrivelled Muslim pecker. No wonder you people screw little boys," he said to the prisoner. "No wonder your Muslim women won't fuck you. No wonder your wife begged my buddies to have a go on her."

The detainee had raised his head and met Holly's eyes. His expression, which had been blank and distant, changed somehow. Later, she came to the conclusion that it hadn't been the sexual and religious humiliation, or even the reference to his wife, but simply that he'd caught sight of Holly's own look of horror – and, just for a moment, had seen himself through her eyes. A tear ran through the coarse, badly shaved stubble of his cheek.

"Good job!" the interrogator had exulted. Turning to Holly, he high-fived her. "First blood, Cadet Boland!"

But a tear isn't blood, she'd found herself thinking. The treatment being meted out to this man seemed more like hazing or playground bullying than the defence of the homeland.

Afterwards, all four women had made light of what they'd seen. If any of them were troubled, none wanted to admit it: being sensitive or squeamish about such matters was tantamount to confessing to unmilitary, female weakness. It was only much later, after the inevitable dinner and beers with the interrogators was over, that Holly had found herself wondering for whose benefit she'd really been in that hut: the defeated, exhausted enemy, or the high-fiving, overexcited officer? It was one of the reasons why she'd steered herself into intelligence, believing herself better suited to analysis than the brutal realities of the battlefield.

But, of course, the whooping interrogator had been an intelligence officer too. Before she left that evening, he told her that their captive had been caught red-handed with a car-load of explosives.

The pros and cons of using force without due process was a debate that would never be settled. The important thing was to take what she had found back to Ian Gilroy. If she was right, and Mia was going to be subjected to an exact replica of a CIA rendition, those page views were soon going to be rising exponentially.

TWENTY-SEVEN

KAT WENT BACK to Venice. But instead of going straight to the Carabinieri headquarters, she made her way to Palazzo Balbi in Dorsoduro.

This sprawling old building overlooking the Grand Canal was the home of the Veneto parliament, the Giùnta Regionale. She found Vivaldo Moretti's office and sent in her request via the startlingly curvaceous secretary.

At last a TV crew came out, talking animatedly amongst themselves. Shortly after, the man himself appeared with some papers, then vanished again. He must have communicated with the secretary by email, however, as a few moments later she said, "You can go in now."

Moretti's office was small and comfortable, with fresh flowers on the low coffee table that stood between two elegant B&B Italia sofas. As he rose and escorted her to one of them, she recalled a newspaper interview in which he'd said he liked to do his work on the sofas and have sex on his desk, instead of the other way round like most of his colleagues. The quip had reinforced his public image as an incorrigible old goat. But it also bolstered his reputation as someone who brokered alliances and got things done, rather than simply pushed paper.

He was shorter than he appeared on television. The facelift, too, was obvious, but somehow the tightened skin behind his eyes enhanced rather than obscured the expression of twinkling amusement, while the grid of hair plugs across his scalp reminded her of a neatly planted vineyard. Add to that a bulbous nose and a protruding chin, and the man could hardly be called handsome. Even so, she felt the extraordinary force of his charm.

"So," he said. "I think I already know what prompted this visit, Capitano."

"Giù called you."

Moretti gave a shrug, as if to say the loyalty of men like Giù was inevitable. "What I'm less clear about is how you think I can help."

"He said that you like a particular table at Club Libero, next to the dance floor, where you can see what's going on. It occurred to me that someone sitting in such a spot might have seen something useful."

"Ah. It's true, yes, that I was at the club last Saturday. Though sadly," he sighed theatrically, "one gets so little time just to sit back and observe. Even though at my age the attractions of an *ombra* of *prosecco* and some entertaining gossip are perfectly sufficient, my companions last Saturday were more energetic, and I was soon dragged into the fray. I'm afraid I saw nothing but some young people having a good time."

"Did you come across either of these two?" She showed him the pictures of Dreadlock Guy and Tattoo Woman.

He pulled out a pair of glasses and scrutinised them before shaking his head. "Regretfully, no."

"How often do you go to that club?"

He considered. "A few times a year, no more."

"Aren't you worried it might get in the papers?"

"It's a risk, certainly," he said with a shrug and an easy smile. "But after all, what is life without risk? I can think of nothing worse than avoiding all pleasure in the hope of appeasing public opinion. Have you come to blackmail me? If so, I should warn you that you're going to be disappointed."

The question took Kat aback. "Of course not. Are you going to ask me to keep your presence at the club a secret?"

He looked equally surprised. "Of course not. Although I would hope that you won't publicise it unless it becomes necessary to your investigation."

"I can't see any reason why it would."

"Excellent. Since we find each other so *simpatico*, Capitano, I find myself wondering how we should continue this conversation. Will you have dinner with me?"

She laughed, and Moretti affected to look hurt. "Have I said something amusing? I was thinking perhaps at the Hotel Metropole, which has recently gained a second Michelin star. But not in the restaurant – people are so very friendly, they would want to pass by our table and talk about politics, whereas I would much rather get to know *you*. There's a charming suite on the second floor with a lovely view across to San Giorgio. And it's just round the corner from the Carabinieri headquarters."

She shook her head. "I don't intend to go to bed with you, Mr Moretti."

"Vivaldo, please. And although I very much regret your answer, I quite understand. Perhaps we might have a drink together in any case. I collect interesting people, Captain, and I think that you would interest me greatly."

It was on the tip of her tongue to tell him to fuck off. "Maybe one day," she found herself saying. Since he'd taken so little offence at her refusal, it was hard to get worked up about his pass. Perhaps, she thought, that was the secret of his success with women: good manners, persistency, and the element of surprise. "Getting back to these tapes… What's puzzling me about Club Libero is why anyone felt the need to firebomb it. At first I thought it might be because someone like yourself had heard about the investigation and wanted to make sure they weren't exposed as a patron. But having spoken to you, I feel reasonably confident you wouldn't do such a thing."

He inclined his head. "Thank you."

"Then who?"

He thought. "You know, crime isn't so different from politics, in the end. In both, you sometimes make decisions not because of the effect they have, but because of the message they send."

"What do you mean?"

"Perhaps someone wants to draw attention to the club's role in this kidnap. Perhaps it is all part of their plan to make this one of the great mysteries of Italy."

She was silent, digesting this.

"That interview I just gave…" he said, gesturing at the door. "The journalist wanted to know if I agreed that this website, Carnivia, should be shut down. Already, apparently, people are saying that if we can just deny the kidnappers a platform, Mia will be released."

"You don't agree?"

"I think it's a simplistic answer. But this case will be all about public opinion, it seems to me. And at times like this people want action, not caution."

"The website hasn't done anything illegal."

He shrugged. "Some means will be found. It always is. And with the elections coming up, I think you can depend on there being more than the usual amount of nonsense talked. " He stood up. "Goodbye, Captain Tapo. I hope our friendship will continue to blossom."

"I hope so too," she said, and was surprised to discover that she meant it.

"Until we meet again, then." He held out his hand for hers, and when she took it, raised it to his lips and kissed her fingers.

As she left his office, she could have sworn the curvaceous secretary winked at her.

TWENTY-EIGHT

SITTING ON THE thin mattress in her orange overalls, Mia wrapped her arms around her knees and sobbed. As hour followed hour with nothing but her own thoughts to distract her, terror had been replaced by an aching, dull despair.

I'm such a fuck-up.

She saw now how the kidnappers were going to prevent this from dragging on: they were simply going to escalate her torment, little by little, and film themselves doing so. The onus would be on the US to find a solution before things got really nasty.

She didn't kid herself that her parents would have any say in what happened then. Her father was a soldier. He obeyed orders, just as he expected those under his command to obey the orders he gave.

At the thought of her parents, her despair worsened. They'd know by now where she'd been snatched from. What must they think of her?

She got onto her knees and tried to pray. At home her family did this together every week; it was one of the things her father insisted on. She wasn't sure if she really believed – not that she'd ever dare tell *him* that – but right now it felt reassuring, as if it weren't God she was getting in touch with, but her family.

The sound of the chain rattling at the door alerted her to the fact that the kidnappers were coming for her again. She pressed her hands even tighter together, squeezing her eyes shut too, whispering soundlessly into her fingertips.

She heard the door open, but no command came.

She went on praying. Still there was no sound. A minute passed. When she did eventually look up, she saw Harlequin standing there, framed by the doorway, waiting for her to finish.

"Get up," he said. "We have work to do."

She was strung up by the wrists again, her arms supporting almost all of her body weight, the metal of the cuffs digging into her flesh.

Suddenly, without any warning, Harlequin grabbed her by the lapels of her overalls and pulled her violently towards him, then threw her backwards in the same manner. As she rocked back against the rope he slapped her, hard, across the cheek, with an open palm.

She screamed. It wasn't just the pain; it was the sudden, shocking violence of it. After he'd given her the overalls to wear, she'd convinced herself that he didn't intend to hurt her. Whimpering, she pulled away as far as the rope would allow.

Bauta filmed it all impassively.

Harlequin was breathing heavily now. He swung her round on the rope, then yanked her forward and grabbed her head in both hands, bringing it very close to his own so that she could see right into his eyes. As he released her, he slapped her face again.

"*Aspetta. Voglio fare un primo piano.*" It was Bauta. He seemed to be telling Harlequin to do it again, so that he could get a closer shot.

Harlequin turned and, in one fluid move, smacked the camera clean out of Bauta's hand. It seemed to shock all of them – not least Harlequin, who muttered curses as Bauta scrabbled after the camera.

She wondered whether, if it was broken, they'd let her go.

It was fine. Bauta was telling Harlequin it was fine.

For the first time she realised how deep, and how unpredictable, the rage in Harlequin was.

It was her praying, she realised with a flash of insight, that had made him so angry. Could he be religious? She tucked the question away for future reference. There was no time to think about it now. They were untying her. Her aching body sagged with relief, but it wasn't back to her cell that they were dragging her, one on either side. It was towards the chair.

Evidently, work wasn't over for the day.

TWENTY-NINE

DANIELE LEFT THE Carabinieri headquarters in a fury, the Carnevale crowds only worsening his mood. Venice's six million tourists were invariably so starstruck by the city's beauty that they wandered around at a snail's pace, looking everywhere but the narrow pavements. Venetians in a hurry had long ago learned to barge past with a cursorily muttered "*Attenzione!*", their natural courtesy hardened by necessity.

Today Daniele Barbo dispensed even with the mutter.

He'd been interviewed by the man in charge of the investigation, General Saito, who'd blithely told him that it would be in his best interests to provide any information he could.

Daniele had tried to explain. "It's in Carnivia's best interests that it remain independent. I have a responsibility to my users to deny requests for information that they can reasonably expect to remain confidential. And in the case of Carnivia, that means everything."

"What about Mia Elston?" Saito had said.

"My responsibility to Mia is exactly the same as to anyone else. That is, to keep her account out of the hands of the government."

In response Saito had rubbed his hand over his face. He'd been up all night, and he wasn't in the mood to let some skinny computer nerd get in the way of his investigation. "Then take it down," he demanded.

"What?"

"Close Carnivia yourself. Why not? You'll have denied the kidnappers the publicity they crave, but you won't have compromised your precious data by sharing it with us."

Daniele closed his eyes. "I can't do that."

"Of course not. That would be far too selfless." Saito stared at Daniele. "Why you?"

"What do you mean?"

"Why did the kidnappers choose to alert *you*, in particular, to Mia's abduction?"

It was a question that had been troubling Daniele too, but he didn't intend to let Saito know that. "I've no idea. Since you're the Carabinieri, why don't you investigate and tell me?"

"I'll tell you what I think." Saito leaned across the table. "I think it's because this stuff isn't coming via Mia's account at all. I think you're putting it out there yourself."

"That's ridiculous."

"Is it? You're a convicted computer hacker, I understand."

"I was found guilty of a minor offence a long time ago when I was a student, yes."

Saito picked up a briefing sheet. "'The 1994 Comcast hack,'" he read aloud. "'One of the first attacks by what came to be known as "hactivists". The damage to Comcast's reputation was estimated at millions of dollars.'"

"Your researchers shouldn't believe everything they read on Wikipedia, General."

Saito ignored him. "I should imagine that kind of attention-seeking is quite addictive. Do you miss those glory days? Mounting hacks against *American* companies? How much more satisfying to get the US Military dancing to your tune. And by hacking into your own website, you can make it look like it's nothing to do with you."

"This is total fantasy," Daniele said, shaking his head.

"You were kidnapped yourself as a child, I understand." Saito nodded at the note. "According to my researchers – who are very thorough, by the way – that's when you started to develop your obsessive tendencies." His gaze travelled over Daniele's facial deformities. "Is this all just some kind of twisted revenge?"

"I won't bother to answer that."

"Your refusal to deny the allegation is duly noted."

"Can I go now?" Daniele said coldly.

"Yes, for the time being. But I'm going to arrange for your medical history to be evaluated by a police psychiatrist. If the profiler agrees you're capable of orchestrating Mia's kidnap, we'll apply for a warrant on that basis. One way or another, Mr Barbo, you *will* help us."

Back at Ca' Barbo, Daniele went up to the old music room and, with a sigh of relief, logged on to Carnivia. It was something he did every time he got home almost without thinking, as automatic and as welcome as closing his front door on one world and slipping into another.

Ordinary users, he'd heard, found entering Carnivia the first few times a bewildering, almost overwhelming experience, their exhilaration at being able to interact with others in complete anonymity tempered by fear at the realisation that others could act equally freely. But for him, a world in which the only laws were those of mathematics made perfect sense. He only wished the real world could be as straightforward.

He checked his messages. Most were from his fellow administrators, concerning relatively mundane matters of housekeeping. There'd been a higher than usual number of attempted hacks on Carnivia in the last twenty-four hours, but that was no particular cause for alarm: there had been a higher than usual volume of traffic, too, as word about the Mia films had spread. Some of the attempts were so amateurish they made Daniele smile, the way an adult smiles at the bravado of a toddler.

Just as he was about to navigate away, another message arrived.

From: Mia Elston
Subject: Help

He opened it.

Daniele, won't you come find me? Unlike Casanova, I can't escape.

Daniele stared at the message. With a sinking feeling, he realised that, in one sense at least, he knew exactly where Mia was.

Setting off from Ca' Barbo, he crossed the Grand Canal by the Accademia bridge, its wooden boards shaking slightly under his feet. Looking down, he saw it was currently low tide: you could just make out a faint line of green weed along the sides of the palaces bordering the canal. As he continued on to Piazza San Marco, a light shower made the *masegni*, the stone tiles that paved the narrow thoroughfares, a little slippery.

The route was almost as busy as it had been earlier, when he'd walked in the opposite direction, but it was an easy matter to slip through the crowds – not least because he was now invisible, and those around him were all avatars.

Carnivia's version of Piazza San Marco was filled with masked and hooded figures. Many were deep in conversation; others were just passing through. Beyond them rose the

Byzantine grandeur of the Palazzo Ducale. Daniele knew it well: he'd built it himself, taking the measurements of the real palace room by room and obsessively coding the wireframe of its Carnivian equivalent, line by line.

He was heading for the "leads" – the space under the lead roof that had once housed the Republic's prison. The real palace had been built by Venice's shipmakers, who constructed the roof as if it were an upside-down hull, leaving plenty of room in which to accommodate prisoners, though not in comfort. It was also where the Doge's inquisitors once tortured on behalf of the state. The windows of the tiny, cramped cells looked inwards to the torture chamber, rather than outwards to the lagoon, in order to weaken the prisoners' resistance even before it was their turn. It was from one such cell that Casanova had famously escaped.

In the middle of the torture chamber stood a female avatar wearing a Columbina mask. She was bound, her shackled wrists pulled above her head by a rope that hung from the ceiling. As he took a step towards her, some words wrote themselves in fiery letters across the wall:

According to America, this isn't torture.

A film started, embedded in the wall of the Doge's Palace as if on a giant cinema screen.

It began with Mia being violently grabbed by the lapels with both hands. A title appeared.

ATTENTION GRASP: THE INTERROGATOR CLASPS THE INDIVIDUAL WITH BOTH HANDS, ONE HAND ON EACH SIDE OF THE COLLAR OPENING, IN A QUICK AND CONTROLLED MOTION. IN THE SAME MOTION, THE INDIVIDUAL IS DRAWN TOWARDS THE INTERROGATOR.

Next the film showed the kidnapper grabbing her head, his palms over her ears and using it to pull her around and shake her.

FACIAL HOLD: ONE OPEN PALM IS PLACED ON EITHER SIDE OF THE INDIVIDUAL'S FACE TO KEEP THE HEAD IMMOBILE. THIS IS DONE TO INTIMIDATE THE INDIVIDUAL.

Then came the sudden, sickening violence of a slap, delivered as if he were driving a squash ball down a court. Its force spun Mia right around.

FACIAL OR "INSULT" SLAP: WITH THIS TECHNIQUE, THE INTER-ROGATOR SLAPS THE INDIVIDUAL'S FACE WITH FINGERS SLIGHTLY SPREAD. THE INSULT SLAP IS USED PRINCIPALLY TO DISPEL ANY NOTIONS IN THE CAPTIVE'S MIND THAT SHE WILL NOT BE STRUCK.

But it still wasn't over. As they dragged her to a chair, fastening her arms and legs to it with duct tape, Mia looked up in horror at something they were bringing towards her. A moment later, Harlequin pulled some electric clippers into shot.

Sickened, Daniele couldn't watch any more. Abruptly, he reached out and turned off his computer.

Then he sat for a long time in front of the blank screen, his head bowed in what would have looked, in any other man, like prayer.

THIRTY

HOLLY DROVE OUT to the magnificent Palladian villa in the Veneto countryside where Ian Gilroy lived, his rent and all expenses covered by the Matteo Barbo Foundation. As she mounted the great cascade of oversized steps that led to the entrance she felt, as the architect had no doubt intended, almost insignificant – as if the ten-foot-high double doors might be thrown open at any moment to reveal some imposing high priest in his robes, instead of the amiable and slightly frail ex-spy who actually lived there.

In the dining room, four men in dark suits got to their feet as she entered, not out of courtesy but to remove themselves and their satellite equipment from her view. She waited until they'd gone before turning to Gilroy. "Friends of ours, I assume?"

He nodded. "Indeed. There are still a few of the old hands who remember me. I'm trying to be the voice of restraint."

"That may get harder." She pointed at the TV behind him. It was tuned to a news channel with the sound down, but the titles scrolling across the screen told their own story. "It was just on the radio. They've released another film. From the sound of it, her treatment is getting worse."

Cursing softly, Gilroy picked up a remote and raised the volume. The film showed a series of quick shots of Mia being manhandled and struck, intercut with more titles.

He watched what was being done to Mia without apparent emotion. Holly guessed that over the course of his long career he must have seen far worse than this – indeed, had probably been present at many such scenes himself.

"What are they doing *now*?" he murmured, almost to himself, as Mia was led towards a chair. A moment later, a hand appeared, holding a pair of electric hair clippers.

THE CAPTIVE'S HEAD AND FACE ARE SHAVED.

"Oh, dear Lord," Gilroy said. Brown hair fell in clumps into the lap of the orange jumpsuit as the kidnapper went to work. In less than a minute of screen time, Mia's head had been completely shorn.

THAT CONCLUDES THE PREPARATORY STAGES.

The film ended on the by now familiar Azione Dal Molin logo. When the TV channel cut back to a studio interview with a "kidnap expert", Gilroy turned it off. "What have you learned, Holly?"

She handed him a dossier she'd prepared about the torture memos. "As yet, the pressure seems to be on Carnivia rather than the US," she concluded. "Several bloggers besides Fallici are calling for it to be taken down, and the Italian news channels seem to be lining up the same way. It may be that the kidnappers won't be able to release more films in any case."

"Hmm." Gilroy sank into a chair and flipped through the dossier.

While he read, she examined the room, pacing softly so as not to disturb him. The walls were divided by marble pillars into panels painted with *trompe l'oeil* fauns and nymphs cavorting in a mythological garden that, she realised, cleverly continued the actual views of the park outside.

Then she noticed something else. The marble columns were not marble at all but painted wood and plaster. It was an illusion within an illusion.

"Palladio's genius was to realise that in Venice, everything is façade – even an interior," Gilroy's voice said behind her. "Do you know the story of the Villa of Dwarves?"

She shook her head.

"Well, it's a very Venetian anecdote. Not far from here, a nobleman had a daughter who was a dwarf. To save her from the pain of realising how different she was from others, he built her a house in proportion to her small size, even hiring dwarf servants to wait on her. It worked so well that she grew to adulthood completely unaware of the deception that had been played on her. Until one day, she spied a handsome young nobleman in the woods, picnicking. Approaching him, she discovered the truth. And she felt, for the first time, her father's disgust and horror at what she was."

"What happened?"

"She climbed to the top of the villa and threw herself off."

Ian Gilroy's career, she knew, had been in counter-intelligence: the endless game of mirrors played between great powers – moles and counter-moles, double- and triple-agents. But the story he had just told was a parable of the futility of deception. She wondered if that was why he'd told it.

"Carnivia is interesting," he said, and she knew from his tone that he was no longer making idle conversation. "What do you know about the underweb?"

"'The underweb'?" she repeated. "It's not a term I've come across."

"Many people haven't. But what we think of as the 'world

wide web' is, despite its name, only a very small part of the internet. Like an ocean on which our ships cross only the surface, the internet has huge depths, inaccessible to most, where strange, misshapen creatures dwell, far from scrutiny. Some call it the dark web, some the invisible internet. Others know it as the underweb."

He got to his feet and began to pace, his liver-spotted hands clasped donnishly behind his back. "Paywalls, servers without IP addresses located in countries run by corrupt regimes, virtual computers hidden within virtual proxies – there are many ways of hiding online, if that is your goal. And yet, increasingly, the inhabitants of the underweb want access to the vast resources and population of the regular web as well. And so, cautiously, they seek out the places where the two overlap."

Not for the first time, Holly wondered just how retired Ian Gilroy actually was. For a man of his age, he seemed remarkably well informed about these arcane developments.

"Which brings us to Carnivia," he continued. "Daniele Barbo has built a city out of code – code, that is, in both the new and the old meanings of the word; an encryption algorithm so sophisticated, no one has been able to penetrate it. Carnivia is like Lisbon in the Second World War, or Berlin during the Cold War: a city between frontiers. Such places are highly attractive to a certain kind of person. Amongst other things, it's a city where those with secrets and those who wish to acquire them can meet on equal terms." He looked at her to see if she understood what he was saying.

"The US has spies in Carnivia!" she said, realisation dawning. "Of course!"

He nodded. "There are currently more analysts and what one might loosely call field operatives assigned to Carnivia than there are to any physical country, with the sole exception of China."

"If Carnivia's closed down, they'll be shut out."

"And we'll lose an important portal to the underweb. It's in America's interests that the Italian authorities find some other way of rescuing Mia."

"That's why you watch over Daniele," she said softly. "It's because he *is* Carnivia."

Gilroy nodded. "Of course, I could never have known, when I promised his father I'd keep an eye on him, that he would one day create Carnivia. Matteo believed Daniele wasn't capable of functioning in the real world." He shrugged. "In many ways, he still isn't. He's paranoid, obstinate, reclusive, obsessive... Yet somehow those same qualities which make him a flawed human being, when translated into code, become the wonder that is Carnivia."

"I find him fascinating," she said.

"That's good," he said, glancing at her. And although she knew that he would never dream of making a direct suggestion on such a matter, she could tell that with those words he was giving her his blessing to take that thought and pursue it to its logical conclusion. "The very best outcome, I think, would be if Daniele were to voluntarily, and privately, relinquish the kidnappers' data, whilst publicly maintaining that he refuses to work with the Carabinieri. That way, the criminals and spies will continue to believe in Carnivia's independence, and we would have consolidated a useful toehold in his world."

"I think..." She hesitated. "I think, from our past interactions, that I have some kind of rapport with him. In as much as any person can, of course."

"Really?"

She blushed. "He's asked me on a date. With everything

that's going on, I was going to cancel. But maybe it would be a chance to see if he'll help us."

"Good," he said again, drawing out the word until it almost became two syllables. "But, as ever, don't mention my name. For some reason, he's never trusted me. If he knows we've been talking, he may become suspicious."

THIRTY-ONE

SHE PACED HER cell. Two strides one way, three the other. But this wasn't like the agonised, hand-wringing pacing of the morning.

Mia was thinking.

As she walked, she lifted her hand and ran it over her scalp. The soft, shorn bristles felt cold and unfamiliar. It reminded her of kissing her father's cheek, the rough rasp of his stubble.

When Harlequin had brought her back to her cell, she'd caught sight of the laptop screen. On it was her own dazed face, frozen in close-up. Without the familiar mane of long brown hair her head looked tiny, her eyes strangely huge. But that, too, had reminded her of something.

When young recruits arrived at Camp Ederle, their high and tight buzz cuts were hardly any more generous than this.

Some words were running through her mind. A conduct code – not that crap about being a lady her father had framed and given her two Christmases ago; she'd only hung *that* on her bedroom wall to please him. No, what was going through her head now were some phrases from the Soldier's Creed.

I am an American soldier.
I am a warrior and a member of a team.
I am trained and proficient, physically and mentally tough.
I will never accept defeat.

Normally her father was reticent about his work, but when her brother was little he'd tried to answer his questions, however dumb or bloodthirsty, because like most officers he hoped his son would follow him into the forces. And Michael had asked once what the duty of a serving soldier was if he were captured: try to escape, in order to tie up enemy resources, or accept his fate, and that way save the US from risking more lives coming to get him?

Her father had said without hesitation, "The duty of a captured soldier in any of my units is to survive, period. He knows we'll get to him in the end, no matter how long it takes or how high the cost. So his sole job is still to be there when we do."

Remembering that moment, courage came to her, flowing into her veins from some hidden reservoir. It had always been there, she knew, waiting for an occasion such as this. From an early age she'd been aware that she was far braver than Michael. When it came to jumping off a high board or standing up to a bully, she was the one who never hesitated. Yet in families like hers, it was the boys who were encouraged to call their fathers "sir", to have their hair cut at the soldier's barbershop on base, to take part in the zip-wire exercises and parachute jumps the military laid on every summer.

They'll get to me in the end.

My sole job is still to be here when they do.

She heard the rattle of the chain as the door was unlocked. But this time, instead of cowering, she stood up and turned towards the sound, ready to face her captors.

I am a warrior and a member of a team. I will never accept defeat.

THIRTY-TWO

KAT WENT UP to the second-floor attic room where Malli, the Carabinieri's lead IT technician, had his office. As usual, every surface was a jumble of disassembled computers and tangled leads, although a space had been cleared amidst the mess for Mia's laptop.

"Let me show you something," Malli said, propelling his chair from one desk to another with a practised flick of his foot. "This isn't Mia's actual hard drive – I made an exact copy, just in case it had any self-destruct codes built in. And look."

He clicked something on his own computer and Mia's desktop appeared, complete with files marked "Homework", "Music", and "Cool Stuff".

"So this all seems pretty normal," Kat said, unsure what it was that Malli was showing her.

"Exactly. On the face of it, just your regular Windows laptop. But now take a look at the operating system." His fingers flew across the keys and the screen filled with flickering characters. "As you probably know, the different versions of Windows are really just a skin – a nice-looking interface between you and MS-DOS, the operating system that does the real work." The flickering froze. "Notice anything odd?"

Kat looked closely. "Is that *Russian?*"

Malli nodded. "It's an OS called DEMOS. The Russians didn't have access to MS-DOS, so they developed their own alternative."

"But why would Mia Elston have a Russian computer?"

"She doesn't. At some point, her machine has been wiped clean of MS-DOS and replaced with DEMOS, whilst all the time appearing as if nothing has changed."

"What would be the point of that?"

"It's just a guess, but these days Russia breeds some pretty nasty hackers. And just as American nerds grow up fluent in MS-DOS, so a Russian hacker might have cut his teeth on DEMOS."

Something clicked in Kat's brain. "What about the father's computer?"

"The same. Why?"

"Elston said he installed parental spy software on Mia's laptop. It sent him regular reports on what she was seeing on the internet. But the strange thing is, the reports don't appear to have reflected the reality."

Malli looked thoughtful. "If it was some kind of spear-phishing exercise—" He caught Kat's expression. "That is, if the hacker sent Major Elston an email warning him about the dangers of letting his children access the internet unsupervised – making it look like it was an offer from a bona fide computer magazine, say, along with some spurious five-star reviews and a link to their recommended product – then when he down-loaded it on his own computer and installed it on Mia's, it could have infected both of them."

"It's that easy?"

"Oh, yes. The neat thing, though, is using the father as an intermediary. Most teenagers these days are pretty clued-up about not downloading unverified software, but their parents are a much easier touch. Is he a protective dad?"

"Very, where Mia's concerned."

"Which suggests the whole exercise was specifically tailored to them. That's a sophisticated operation. As are the films, incidentally. That trick with the embedded link isn't something your average computer geek could set up."

A sophisticated operation. She'd made a similar observation herself, she recalled, about the way the kidnappers had snatched Mia from the club. And now here was further evidence of their cunning. But what did it mean? It was exactly the kind of vague but promising lead that, once upon a time, she would have loved to have discussed with Aldo Piola.

Back at her own computer, she did a search for the skull-and-wings symbol she'd seen tattooed on the woman's arm in the Club Libero tapes. It was, she learned, a symbol that had been used many times throughout history, from the Harley-Davidson logo right back to seventeenth-century gravestones, where it symbolised the transition between the physical and the spiritual worlds. For a similar reason, it had frequently been used by Freemasons and other secret societies.

It was always tempting to look for some kind of weird, esoteric meaning in a symbol, but somehow she doubted that was the right thing to do here. The artwork on the woman's arm was crude – hardly the kind of thing you'd use to mark your induction into some cabbalistic cult.

Then she came across another reference.

The first combat mission of the 490th Bombardment Squadron was flown in 1943 in B-25 Mitchell bombers bearing the "Skull and Wings" emblem, an adaptation of

*the personal insignia of the commanding officer. For this
reason it is sometimes referred to as "Death from Above".*

Death from Above... The phrase seemed familiar somehow.
Something she'd glimpsed on the base, perhaps? She tried to
wind her mind back to the shopping mall on Camp Ederle's
Main Street. But it was no use, the memory had gone.

It was after nine, and she was exhausted. The operations
room had long since emptied. It was time to go home and get
some sleep.

She was reaching for her computer to turn it off when she
saw that her browser was showing an updated newsfeed.

MIA: FOURTH FILM RELEASED

Shit. She brought up a news site.

Mia, wearing the orange jumpsuit, was once again standing, her shackled arms stretched above her newly shaved head.
Her eyes gazed at the viewer. They were dull with pain and
fatigue, but there was also something in them Kat hadn't seen
there before: a mixture of defiance and pride.

Kat recognised that look. It was the expression she herself
wore when she was taking too much shit and didn't intend to
take much more. It was a look that said, *You can do what you
like to me. But you won't take away my self-respect.*

The image cut to a title.

THE DETAINEE IS PLACED IN THE VERTICAL SHACKLING POSITION
TO BEGIN SLEEP DEPRIVATION.

The rope attached to Mia's wrists was tightened, pulling her
arms up so that she was lifted almost onto her toes.

THE MAXIMUM DURATION OF SLEEP DEPRIVATION AUTHORIZED
BY THE CIA IS 180 HOURS, AFTER WHICH THE DETAINEE MUST
BE PERMITTED TO SLEEP FOR AT LEAST 8 HOURS.

A third title faded up:

GOOD NIGHT!

Her own exhaustion vanished instantly. If Mia wasn't going
to get any sleep, then neither would she. She'd get some food,
then come back and continue trawling through what slender
leads they had until something shook itself loose.

THIRTY-THREE

AS SHE LEFT the Carabinieri building, Kat hesitated. In her life, she had tackled armed men and been blown up. She cleaned sexist insults off her locker on a regular basis, and worse things too from time to time. She had no difficulty approaching a man she liked the look of and telling him she wanted to go to bed with him, or telling one who wouldn't take no for an answer to crawl back up his mother's vagina and fuck her instead. But she found herself reluctant to do something most Italian men did almost without thinking: to eat alone in a restaurant. It was something Italian women just didn't do.

Screw it. I'm hungry.

There were a dozen *trattorie* within a hundred yards of Campo San Zaccaria. Most *carabinieri* went to the nearest, Da Nino on Campo San Provolo. For that very reason, she headed a little further away, to Alla Conchiglia on Fondamenta San Lorenzo. She took along a file of paperwork, so she could occupy herself while she ate.

As she stepped inside she saw Aldo Piola at the nearest table, a fork in his hand and a similar file open in front of him. He looked up, and saw her too.

Quickly, she turned to leave. But then she turned back.

"I don't see why I should go somewhere else just because

you're here," she told him. "And it's going to be really strange if we sit at different tables. Besides, I want to talk to you. So I might as well sit down, and if you don't like it you'll just have to get up and walk out. Which would be crazy when you've already got your food. Are those *moleche*? I didn't know the season had started."

He didn't tell her she was talking too much, or that they weren't allowed to do this. He just gave a wry shrug and gestured to the chair opposite, which she still hadn't quite had the courage to pull out.

"Not that I mean anything else by this, of course," she added as she sat down. "We've both moved on, as they say."

Given the havoc their affair had wreaked on both their lives, it perhaps wasn't the most tactful way of putting it. But he didn't point that out either, just pushed the bowl of *moleche* towards her.

"Have some."

She speared one and took an experimental bite. The shell of crisp batter – sprinkled with salt and a squeeze of sharp lemon – exploded in her mouth, the rich, sweet crab juices bursting down her throat. For a long moment she said nothing, concentrating on the flavour that, more than any other for her, marked the end of winter.

Twice a year without fail, Kat's grandmother Nonna Renata would head off to the market to buy a basket of live spider crabs during the all-too-brief season known as *la muta* – "the change" – during which the tiny crustaceans shed their shells in order to grow a larger one. Like most Venetians, she usually served this delicacy stuffed, with the unusual proviso that it was the crab, not the cook, which did the stuffing, the crabs having been placed in a bowl of batter mixture to gorge themselves for a few hours before being tipped into a pan of hot oil.

It might be cold and dark outside, but the first *moleche* of the year were as sure a harbinger of spring as the coming of Lent or the changing of the clocks. It meant that soon the market would be full of crunchy *castrauri*, tiny artichokes nipped off the stalks to make room for their larger brethren. There would be *bruscandoli* shoots too, the first sproutings of the hop plant, and then *sparasini*, tender white asparagus, and finally the fresh peas, grown in the salty soil of Sant'Erasmo, so crucial to a Venetian summer *risotto*.

Piola speared another crab himself. The restaurant owner, unbidden, came and poured Kat some wine. It was Vespaiolo, sharp and acidic; the perfect counterpoint to the rich, salty crab.

It seemed wrong to be eating and drinking like this while Mia was suffering. But it also made the food more important, somehow: a reminder of what really mattered.

"The thing is," she said, "I don't know what I'm doing. I'm desperate to impress General Saito, but I don't have anyone to tell me what's important, what I should be prioritising. I can feel myself getting frustrated, and that makes me even more aimless." She looked him in the eye. "I want you to be my boss, Aldo. Like you were before we screwed things up."

She thought he was going to tell her to leave. But he only said, "If I'm to be your boss, you'd better start calling me 'sir'."

"It's a deal. Sir."

He poured himself more wine. "I don't think I've ever been on a case that's more horrific, or one so cleverly constructed to have us chasing our own tails. Why don't you tell me what you've learned, and I'll do the same?"

She told him everything. Just the simple act of putting it all into words – of gauging from his expression when he was intrigued, or thoughtful, or puzzled; of seeing from his quick nods when he approved of various decisions she'd made, or from his frown when he disagreed – helped her to sort and order events in her own mind. His phone buzzed several times as she spoke, but he ignored it.

"But I keep wondering," she concluded, "if this whole thing isn't just too *slick*. Hackers, films, fires, masks… It just seems incredible that a bunch of amateurs could execute something as complex as this without making a single mistake. Am I being crazy, or is something more going on here?"

He looked at her. "I've been asking myself the exact same thing," he said quietly. "The link between Azione Dal Molin and the kidnappers, for example: if I hadn't been called to that investigation over the skeleton, I'd probably never have questioned it. But the more I think about it, the more suspicious I become. Was the break-in a simple publicity stunt, ahead of Mia's kidnap? Or a sleight of hand to make us think we know exactly who's behind this, when the reality is rather more complex?"

"But if it isn't the protestors, then who?"

He shrugged. "Terrorists? I doubt it – they wouldn't hide behind some local protest group; they'd want to claim it for themselves. The Mafia? Hardly – they'd be after a ransom, not a referendum. But who else is there?"

She said slowly, "The Americans themselves?"

He shot her a glance. "Are you serious?"

"I don't know," she confessed. "But there was a woman at the club who *might* have been one of the kidnappers, who had what *might* be an American military tattoo on her arm. And it seems to me there must have been more than one team tailing Mia, too."

"Military precision," he said, almost to himself. "And who's better at that than the military?"

"But if it *is* them, I don't see why they'd kidnap one of their own children, let alone subject her to what most people would call torture." She looked at him. "Should we take this line of enquiry to Saito? Ask him if we can investigate further?"

"No," he decided. "Saito's a political animal: I saw how nervous he got about upsetting the Americans over that skeleton investigation. If we go to him now, he'll simply order us not to pursue it."

She nodded, remembering how quickly Saito had offered her own services to the Civilian Liaison Office as a favour, and how he'd caved in to a request by Major Elston to have her reinstated.

"Better to follow up these leads ourselves, then go to him as soon as we find anything concrete," he added. "*If* we find anything concrete, that is. They've given us precious little to work with so far."

She hesitated. "What about Holly Boland?"

"Your American friend? How could she could help?"

"I don't know," Kat said truthfully. "She's certainly no maverick. But she wants to get to the bottom of this just as much as we do."

They discussed the case late into the night. The carafe of wine was emptied and replaced by one of grappa; and that was almost finished, too, before they were done.

THIRTY-FOUR

SHE WOULD NEVER have believed that standing still could be so painful.

It had been bearable for the first forty minutes or so. Then her muscles had started to cramp. To relieve the pressure in her legs, she sagged as far as the rope would allow. But that only put more pressure on her arms. After just a few seconds, the pain in her shoulders felt like white-hot blades. So she raised herself up onto tiptoe to ease that pain, which made her legs cramp all over again.

She tried to devise a programme of stretches, kicking out with first one leg, then the other, and jumping, so far as she was able, up and down on the spot. It worked for about twenty minutes. Then the pain returned, worse than ever.

The room was in darkness now, apart from the pool of light from one portable arc lamp. Sometimes she thought she glimpsed Bauta in the shadows, filming her, the red light of the camera a tiny dot in the blackness.

After two hours she was exhausted. She wanted more than anything to sleep. But if she relaxed her position even slightly, her weight pulled on her arms and the pain flashed through her shoulders and neck again, waking her up.

Hearing a sound, she opened her eyes. Harlequin was standing there, watching her, his masked face in shadow.

"Let me go," she begged him.

For a moment he didn't reply. Then he said, so quietly she could barely hear, "Your country believes that it is acceptable to do this to someone for seven days without letting them sleep."

"But I don't do those things," she wailed. "I'm not America. Why take it out on me?"

"You are not America," he agreed. "But you *are* American. You are what your country calls 'collateral damage' and everybody else 'an innocent civilian'. According to the United Nations, over twenty thousand people like you – twenty thousand! – have been murdered by your countrymen in Afghanistan alone." He took a step forward, and she could see the light of zealotry in his eyes. "Some were killed by drones sent from bases here in Italy. If your suffering saves a dozen such lives, will it have been worth it? What about a thousand? Ten thousand?"

"I'm sixteen. Doesn't that make a difference?"

"Oh, yes. Sixteen. In America, that almost makes you a child, doesn't it? Too young to drink, to vote. But not too young to imprison. Over two thousand children younger than you have been detained without trial during this so-called war on terror. There have been children in Guantanamo, did you know that? There were even two little boys captured by the CIA specifically to be used as levers against their father. Their names were Yousef and Abed and they were aged nine and seven. Or do you think you're unique because you're a woman? Then you can't have read the report by Antonio Taguba, the former US general, saying that in Abu Ghraib prison US guards filmed themselves raping female detainees. That was after they'd photographed their breasts and used their buttocks as paintball targets." He paused. "Think yourself lucky that we only do the official treatments. The ones that were authorised by your President."

"I can tell you're sincere," she said, trying to keep her voice steady. "But you've already made your point, with the films. Wouldn't it be even better if you let me go? You'll have proved you're different to America; more merciful, more humane."

He laughed – an incredulous bark. "And? You think your President will say, 'Oh, they let her go. I'd better close an air base or two.' Being merciful won't change anything."

The intensity in his voice frightened her, but she kept going. "Neither will keeping me here. America doesn't negotiate with terrorists. Everyone knows that."

"Yes? Then why are you pulling out of Afghanistan?" He shook his head. "They'll listen – they'll have to. But more importantly, so will others. You Americans are only in our country because every government we've ever had has been too scared and too corrupt to tell them to leave. But the Italian people aren't so cowardly."

"Or maybe the Italian people will be so ashamed of what you're doing that they'll go the other way," she said.

The sudden, searing anger in him erupted then. "Shame? Don't speak to me of shame! It's America that should be ashamed! And they will be!"

"What do you mean?" she said fearfully. "Ashamed of what? What are you going to do to me?"

He reached down to a package at his feet and pulled something from it. When he held it up she saw that it was a diaper, one large enough for an adult.

"From now on, you will wear this. It makes it more convenient for the guards, you see? Not to have to unshackle the prisoners during the night. And if it humiliates the prisoners too – well, that was never the intention. Oh, no. Just a coincidence." He gestured at her. "Sometimes they leave it on for days. Until the prisoner gets sores and broken skin from standing in their own shit."

She took a deep breath. "Wait. All you care about is what it looks like on film, right? So let me go back to my cell for now, then tie me back up in the morning. It'll look like I've been here all night."

"Why should I?" he demanded.

"Because you're not a bad man," she whispered.

He took another pace forward. She wasn't sure if he was going to hit her or release her.

For a long moment he did neither. She could see, behind the mask, the black depths of his own eyes; his long lashes.

Reaching up, he untied the rope.

"Thank you," she gabbled, rubbing her wrists. "I promise you won't regret it."

"Don't speak," he commanded gruffly. "Go to your cell. If you say another word, I'll tie you back up."

THIRTY-FIVE

HOLLY BOLAND TOOK from her closet a little-used Stefanel dress of clinging grey cashmere. Coupled with a bra from La Perla in Vicenza, the stretchy wool somehow gave even her sinewy body a suggestion of curves.

It had been weeks since she'd worn anything but fatigues; months since she'd used make-up or left her blonde hair unpinned. After her big Belleville boots, the kitten heels she also pulled from the closet felt like gossamer. Gossamer that, bizarrely, hurt like hell, whereas her Bellevilles were as comfortable and familiar as slippers.

She swapped the heels for some Timberland deck shoes, and told herself it was unconventional.

She got to Ca' Barbo around eight. It took four pulls at the bell, and several minutes, before Daniele appeared, dressed in his usual attire of sweatshirt and sneakers. She'd never seen an Italian man dress as casually as he did; but then, Daniele wasn't like most men, let alone most Italians.

He gave so little sign of recognising her that she actually felt the need to remind him who she was. "Daniele? It's me – Holly?"

"Of course. Come in." He didn't kiss her on both cheeks, as most Venetians would. She wondered if that was because of his deformities; if he liked to keep people at a distance from the missing ears and truncated nose that were the legacy of his own kidnap.

He led the way up to the first floor. Ca' Barbo wasn't big – indeed, it was probably no wider than a New York brownstone – but it was beautiful. Huge oak rafters supported a painted ceiling, and the floor was a geometric pattern of tiles that put her in mind of Escher. There were also some remarkable artworks dotted around, mostly from the twentieth century. Daniele's father had sold off the family's Old Masters to invest in modern artists, before bequeathing his entire collection, and the palace itself, to the art foundation that now bore his name. For his part, Daniele had sold the furniture – the only part of Ca' Barbo he actually owned – to fund the creation of Carnivia, filling the palace with cheap, functional pieces from IKEA instead. It made for a strange combination.

He took her into the old music room. It was warmer than the rest of the *palazzo*, heated not by a stove or radiators but by the four NovaScale servers ranged along one wall, their lights flickering in complex combinations. Cheap roller blinds hung between the marble barley-twist columns of the windows. A bottle of *prosecco* and two glasses appeared to be the only concession to the fact that this was meant to be a date.

"I brought you a gift." She handed him an A4-sized frame. Inside it was an equation.

$$K := \{ \ (i, x)$$

"The Turing Paradox," he said, nodding. "That's a great one. Thank you."

"I looked it up on the net. Turing invented the computer, didn't he? And this was one of the equations that made it all possible."

Holly was one of the few people who knew, from her previous work with him, that Daniele Barbo's equivalent of his father's priceless art collection was to decorate the walls of Ca' Barbo with his favourite equations – which to him were just as beautiful, and just as profound, as any painting.

"I just got another message," he said, changing the subject with his customary abruptness. "That makes two in the last hour."

"Can I see them?"

He pointed to one of the screens. She went and read the email that was open there.

From: Mia Elston
Subject: Torture?

"Any fixed position which is maintained over a long period of time ultimately produces excruciating pain. After 18 to 24 hours of continuous standing, there is an accumulation of fluid in the tissues of the legs. This dependent edema is produced by the extravasation of fluid from the blood vessels. The prisoner's ankles and feet swell up to twice their normal circumference. The edema may rise up the legs as high as the middle of the thighs. The skin becomes tense and extremely painful. Large blisters develop, which break and exude water serum…

"The accumulation of body fluid in the legs produces impairment of the circulation. The heart rate increases, and fainting may occur. Eventually there is renal shutdown, and urine production ceases. The subjects develop a delirious state, characterized by disorientation, fear, delusions, and visual hallucinations. As urea and other metabolites accumulate in the blood, the prisoner experiences agonizing thirst."

"Jesus," she said when she'd finished.

"I did a search – it's from a Defense Department research paper, written back in the Cold War," he said. "Ironically, it seems it was the communists who developed most of these techniques. At the same time as Stalin was ordering that men confess to plotting against him, he was also insisting that communism meant respect for the working man, and thus no torture. His secret police had to find ways of torturing people that didn't look like torture... The CIA studied what they did, and turned the results into a training programme on how to *resist* those techniques."

"SERE," she said. "Search-Evade-Resist-Escape. I did the basic level myself – all officer cadets do."

He nodded. "When President Bush demanded harsh interrogations after 9/11, it was the SERE psychologists he turned to. So the techniques that were developed during the paranoia about communism are now being used in the paranoia about terrorism. The wheel goes full circle."

"And the other message?"

He clicked on the screen.

From: Mia Elston
Subject: Torture?

So, Daniele, I take it you've found my little Easter egg. Now you have a decision to make, don't you? Close Carnivia down, and stop the show. Or sit back and watch, like the voyeur you are. What's it to be? I think I know which you'll choose. The trouble is, people aren't going to like it, are they? Maybe they'll decide it shouldn't be up to you any more. Maybe this is goodbye Carnivia.

"What does he mean by 'Easter egg'?" she asked.

"It's a gaming term – a hidden surprise that can only be unlocked by highly skilled players." He gestured at the screen. "He's referring to that last film of Mia. Inadvertently, I was the one who unlocked it."

He looked so pained that she asked, "Are you all right?"

"I feel like I'm torturing her myself," he said quietly. "Like I'm helping them, somehow." He looked directly at her. "What should I do?"

"You mean, should you close Carnivia? You'd really do that?"

"I believe in the freedom of the internet," he said. "But that shouldn't mean the freedom to do this. Perhaps it's time to admit that people will always use liberty for evil, not good."

"Wait – let's just think this through. It's like there are two different voices in these messages, isn't it? There's the kidnappers themselves – they want Carnivia to stay open; it's the only way they can achieve their objectives. But then there's this other voice that seems to be taunting you, almost as if he *wants* you to shut it down. For him, it's like the main objective isn't Mia at all. It's to draw Carnivia, and you personally, into what's going on."

"Yes. The *tone* is different." He said it hesitantly, as if tone were a concept he had only recently discovered. Then he nodded. "Of course. They must have recruited a freelance."

"A freelance? Is that possible?"

"Oh, yes. In Carnivia today, you can hire a hacker as easily as my ancestors could find a killer on the Rio Terrà Assassini. But you have to be careful. The hacker may well think himself cleverer than you – in fact, he undoubtedly *is* cleverer than you. He'll certainly have no hesitation in using whatever you've employed him for to pursue his own agenda."

"Which is…?"

"In this case, perhaps, to prove that he's cleverer than Daniele Barbo." He glanced at the servers. "It isn't just governments who object to Carnivia's independence. There are hackers who would love to take it down."

"Why?"

"Kudos. In that world, the prestige that would come from being the first to hack a website like Carnivia would be enormous. And this hacker is good – very good. Already he's sniffed out weaknesses that even I didn't know existed."

"So who is he? Is there a way to flush him out?"

He went to the long table and, pulling up a chair, began to type.

"What are you doing?" she asked.

"I'm crowdsourcing your question."

She leaned over his shoulder. On the screen was the familiar Carnivia home page – a smiling mask and the words "Enter Carnivia". But now there was also some text.

Fellow Carnivians,

A Carnivia user in Italy has been taken – kidnapped from her family in protest at the construction of a US Army base.

The kidnappers appear to have recruited an accomplice on Carnivia. Some of you may know who that person is. If so, I need you to tell me.

Daniele Barbo

"You should add a link to the messages he sent you. Perhaps here?" She pointed. "And maybe mention the films, and the webcast."

He typed some more. "There. That's done."

Reading the revised text over his shoulder, she felt him tense. Looking down, she saw that a strand of her hair was brushing his neck, just below the severed stump of his ear.

He glanced up at her. His gaze immediately slid away – he rarely held eye contact for long in any situation – but she sensed, in the suddenly charged atmosphere, that this was different.

She straightened, and the moment passed.

Daniele turned back to the screen. "I've never intervened before," he said quietly. "It feels like crossing a line."

"Maybe there's a middle way."

"What do you mean?"

"If there was some way of giving the authorities what they need," she said slowly. "That is, some information about the kidnappers – but without letting it be generally known. And it wouldn't just be to save Mia. They might be able to get this hacker off your back, too."

He shook his head. "A principle isn't a principle if you're prepared to drop it the moment circumstances change. Those who care about the freedom of the internet will see that message and try to help."

A pulse of blue light strafed the room.

"What's that?" she said, suddenly fearful. Crossing to the window, she saw three blue-and-white "Polizia" motorboats chugging rapidly towards Ca' Barbo's landing stage. "Daniele, there are police launches coming this way. What will you do?"

"I don't know. Stall them, if I can." He turned back to his computer and typed some more.

The sound of splintering wood from downstairs suggested that stalling was unlikely to be an option for long. Within moments, it seemed, the room had filled with men wearing full riot gear. But it was a woman in plain clothes who stepped forward, brandishing a piece of paper.

"Inspector Pettinelli, CNAIPIC," she said. Daniele raised his eyebrows. Amongst hackers, Holly knew, the National Computer Crime Centre for Critical Infrastructure Protection was generally considered something of a joke. "I'm authorised to take Carnivia offline." She glanced at the NovaScales. "Those are the servers, I take it?"

"If you don't know what those machines are, Inspector," Daniele said calmly, "I'm certainly not going to help you."

"I may not have your coding expertise. But I know how to pull out a plug," she assured him. She went around the back of the servers, searching for the power supply.

Holly's heart was in her mouth. *She's only shutting down a computer*, she told herself; but a part of her felt that it was much more than that. All those millions of users whose avatars would be extinguished – it felt, strangely, like a kind of murder.

Inspector Pettinelli flicked a switch. On the screen in front of Daniele, the image of the grinning mask went blank.

Then, seconds later, faded back up.

Like everyone else in the room, Holly turned towards the NovaScales. They were still without power.

Only Daniele and Inspector Pettinelli appeared to understand what was happening. "So you have a mirror site," she said.

"Sites," he corrected her. "More than one."

"But not many. I've seen your bank transactions. You can't afford multiple hostings." She was watching him closely. "And I can't see you entrusting a Carnivia mirror to some random regime on the other side of the world. You'll want them close at hand. Somewhere you think is safe."

Daniele didn't answer.

"Well, wherever they are, I will trace them. And I will take them offline."

"I'll see you in court, Ispettore," he said.

Pettinelli shook her head. "You're going to see a great deal of me, but it won't be in court. Under anti-terrorism legislation I am authorised to take you into preventative detention. You are not under arrest and you will not be charged, but you will remain in custody until we are satisfied that your liberty no longer poses a threat to this country's security. Daniele Barbo, you're coming with me."

THIRTY-SIX

ALDO PIOLA WENT to retrieve his car from the multi-storey at Tronchetto for the drive back to the mainland. It had been a long day, and he knew there would be many even longer days to come, but his mind was not now on the kidnap so much as the conversation he had to have with his wife when he got home.

He had promised Gilda that he would never again be alone with Kat Tapo. That meant not working with her, let alone having dinner with her. And it was no use, he thought ruefully, trying to pretend that conversations about work were different. It was precisely *because* work was different, because he and Kat had shared the all-consuming intensity of a big investigation, that their affair had started in the first place. If only work were more like the mundane, banal reality of marriage and parenthood – the daily grind of laundry and shopping and homework, and telling the kids not to look at their phones at the table – it would probably never have happened.

But Kat was also the best junior officer he'd ever worked with, and he, like her, needed someone to bounce ideas off. The problem with a case as big as this one was that you could end up as no more than a tiny cog in a massive machine, feeding it with scraps of evidence but never seeing the big picture.

For Mia's sake he needed to work with Kat. For the sake of his marriage, he needed to be honest with his wife.

Gilda would have to understand that this was a purely professional decision. And then, after the case was over, he'd put in for a transfer. It would probably mean moving to Milan or Rome, which would be a wrench for the children. But they'd make new friends soon enough, and it would be a new beginning for Gilda and him. Perhaps he could even wangle Genoa, where her parents lived. That would be the deal he would offer her, although he wouldn't put it in exactly those terms: he would work with Kat again now, but it would be for the last time.

Without being aware of it, he sighed. Although not a native of Venice, he had come to love this strange, stinking city. Of course, it was full of tourists in the summer, and flooded in winter, but there was something about these mist-filled canals, the improbable Byzantine palaces that floated up out of the black depths of the lagoon as if built by mermaids, that spoke to something poetic in his own soul. In Venice, it was possible to think a man could be a hero. In Milan or Genoa, he suspected, life would be more prosaic.

His phone buzzed. Pulling it out, he saw it was simply reminding him that he had a message. Whoever had called earlier, when he was in the restaurant, had left a voicemail.

Retrieving it, he heard a woman's voice. "Colonel, it's Dottora Iadanza. I wanted to tell you that I've been in contact with Professor Trevisano, as you suggested, and we think we've found something rather interesting. Could you call me back?"

This time it was him who got voicemail. He left her a message in turn saying he'd try again tomorrow. Then he started his engine and headed across the Ponte della Libertà, over the misty waters of the lagoon, towards Gilda.

THIRTY-SEVEN

AT HOME IN her apartment, Kat logged on to Carnivia and read Daniele's appeal. The final paragraph now read:

> As I write this, the police are downstairs. I have no doubt they will try to take Carnivia offline. I have taken steps to prevent this from happening, but no website is proof against a determined government. If they succeed in closing us down today because of this one case, tomorrow there will be another, and then another. The future of Carnivia is in the balance.

Looking up the anti-terrorism act, she discovered that the authorities could keep Daniele detained without charge for as long as they wished. The measure had been described as a last resort when it was introduced, but without legal precedent to define it, it seemed no one could say what that actually meant.

Kat doubted if anyone in authority really cared whether shutting down Carnivia would help or hinder the search for Mia. The media had demanded action, and since leaving the website up would look like inaction, closing it down had seemed the better alternative.

But then, she found herself on a different side of this debate from Daniele. Whether or not to close down Carnivia was, for her, a pragmatic question. Of course freedom of speech was generally a good thing, and censorship bad – but if what you were censoring included child pornography, drug deals and stolen credit card details, what was the big deal? In her professional capacity she'd had to watch films depicting sexual violence against women so sickening, it was impossible to think that any person who was aroused by watching them should be allowed to go on doing so. Daniele, she knew, would say that no individual should have the power to make such a complex moral judgement. But she wasn't sure that Daniele's moral universe was a place she particularly wanted to live in.

Out of habit, she checked her messages. Because she was now logged on to Carnivia, they included anything she'd been sent as Columbina7759. Some were alerts that new gossip had been uploaded about people she knew – since Carnivia could glean from your computer who you worked with and who your Facebook friends were, it could also alert you to any rumours that were circulating about them. Some were messages from strangers who'd come across her profile on Married and Discreet. Three, though, were from Riccardo, the last man she'd hooked up with. She scanned the headers:

Meet again?

Really want to see you

A lovely picture of you and me

Puzzled, she opened the last one.

As I haven't heard back from you I thought I'd send you a little reminder of the other night...

Attached was a photo – or rather, she realised, a still from a piece of film; the frame had that telltale letterbox format. A softly lit hotel room. A bed. Kat, naked, on top of an equally naked Riccardo.

Fuck, she thought as realisation dawned. *The fucking prick filmed it.*

Thinking back, she recalled seeing his phone on a table, casually propped against a bottle of wine. Why hadn't she thought to check it? But doing that would have meant not trusting him, and at the time she'd wanted to believe in the fiction she'd created around that evening – that instead of being a sad, furtive, meaningless encounter with a married man, it had been some kind of exciting, romantic adventure.

You stupid idiot.

Her immediate instinct, after the initial anger and disgust had worn off, was to email him back, arrange to meet, and then arrest him. Or at the very least, show him her Carabinieri ID and put the fear of God into him.

But there was no time for that now. Besides, it had taught her a valuable lesson.

On Carnivia, no one is who they seem.

The fact was, she realised, she'd only met up with men like Riccardo because she'd been bored out of her mind. The website had been an outlet, a hint of risk and danger – just as for Mia, the thrill of going to a swingers' club to see what went on there had seemed like a cool rebellion against her military family. Mia had been unlucky enough to get abducted; Kat had got away comparatively lightly.

But for her the real thrill came from doing the job she loved. That was far more satisfying, and far more addictive, than any night with a stranger.

Doing the job you love – with the man you love, a voice

inside her head echoed. But the voice was wrong, she knew that. There was nothing between her and Aldo Piola now, nor would there ever be.

She put her hands on the keyboard and, in a few quick strokes, closed down her account at Married and Discreet.

THIRTY-EIGHT

MIA CAME AWAKE at the touch of a hand on her shoulder. Harlequin was squatting next to her mattress.

"Wake up, Mia. We have work to do."

Her heart sank. "Work" was his euphemism for the things they did to her.

As if reading her mind he said, "I want you to know that this is not my choice. But your government and mine are leaving us no option."

She was given a piece of paper with what she had to say hastily scrawled on it. The red light on the camera went on. Facing it, she delivered the words in front of her.

"This is a message from Azione Dal Molin in response to the attempt by the Italian authorities to close down the Carnivia website. They want you to see what will happen if the channel of communication between my captors and the Italian people does not remain open."

The light went off. She waited.

A little later, she heard thumping from the room next door. It sounded like blows, a body crashing against a wall. *They're fighting*, she thought anxiously. But what about? Whether to release her? Rape her? Kill her? There was no way of knowing.

Something had clearly happened – something they hadn't been ready for. Whatever she was hearing, it was part of their response.

The chain rattled and the door opened. She tensed, then saw to her relief that it was Harlequin.

He came in and gestured silently for her to stand.

"What do you want?" she asked.

He put a finger to his lips, telling her to be silent. The he pointed to the zipper of the orange overalls and mimed for her to undo it.

Nervously, she complied. When she was down to her underwear he walked around her slowly, scrutinising her. She tried to force herself not to show fear. She was, she realised, unconsciously mirroring the postures of the fighting men she'd grown up around: standing straight, her shoulders back.

Harlequin chuckled. Placing his hands on her shoulders, he adjusted her position slightly, like a sergeant major on a parade ground.

Suddenly she realised, *It's not the same man.* The mask might be the same, but the person wearing it was an inch or so shorter than the kidnapper she thought of as Harlequin, and more stocky. All the relief she'd felt evaporated.

As he resumed his scrutiny, he whistled under his breath. At one point he picked up her wrist, examining it carefully.

He's seeing if the cuffs have done any damage. "Are you a doctor?" she said nervously. "*Dottore?*"

Almost casually his arm flicked out, his elbow close to his body and the forearm sweeping towards her, so that the back of his hand hit her across the stomach. She doubled up in agony, too winded even to make a sound. As she gasped for breath he put his finger to his lips again. *Don't talk.*

Then he reached for her head, wrapping his strong hands around it as if to snap her neck. She tried to scream, but he wasn't hurting her, just rotating her head this way and that.

She'd had a physical exam from a doctor once, after a

snowboard fall. He'd done something similar, to check her vertebrae.

Evidently satisfied, he stood back, gesturing silently for her to pull up the jumpsuit. He left, returning a few minutes later with Bauta. They were carrying between them a large piece of plywood and some lengths of timber.

She understood then that what she'd heard earlier hadn't been fighting. It had been *practising*. Whatever the wood was for, the whistling man had been instructing the others in the use of it.

DAY THREE

THIRTY-NINE

AS SHE NEARED Campo San Zaccaria next morning, Kat saw Piola. He was carrying an overnight bag and his face was unshaven. His wife had thrown him out, then. She hoped it wasn't because of their dinner, which, after all, had been strictly professional. But she feared it might be.

There was a time when she'd have asked him. But things were more complex now. So she only said, "Good morning, sir."

"*Buongiorno*, Captain," he replied, equally neutrally.

In the operations room she went straight to her computer. To her surprise, she appeared to have been logged out. As she retyped her password, she saw that others around her were doing the same.

"Some kind of IT problem," one of her neighbours told her with a shrug. It was the first time he'd spoken to her in months.

She hadn't even finished logging in when her screen abruptly went dark. The grinning Carnivia mask appeared, before cutting immediately to a piece of film. Mia, holding a piece of paper.

"This is a message from Azione Dal Molin…"

Around Kat, the same words were playing from every computer. She watched, appalled, as the film cut abruptly to Mia, standing in her underwear in the same room, blindfolded and cuffed, in front of a wall made of wood. A title appeared:

THE DETAINEE IS PLACED IN FRONT OF THE WALLING WALL. THE
DETAINEE REMAINS HOODED. THE DETAINEE REMAINS NUDE.

The man in the Harlequin mask entered the frame and
placed a towel around Mia's neck, locker-room style, looping
it over itself so it wouldn't come loose. The action, some of
them commented later, was strangely tender in its protective-
ness, given what was about to happen – like a parent fastening
a scarf around a child's neck on a chilly morning.

WALLING IS ONE OF THE MOST EFFECTIVE TECHNIQUES BECAUSE
IT WEARS DOWN THE DETAINEE PHYSICALLY AND CREATES A
SENSE OF DREAD WHEN THE DETAINEE KNOWS SHE IS ABOUT
TO BE WALLED AGAIN.

With sudden, shocking violence, the man grabbed Mia by
the head, one hand on either side, and flung her against the
wall, so that she took the full impact against her shoulders.
The force of the blow was such that around the room, hardened Carabinieri officers gasped.

As she fell forwards he caught her, pulled her to her feet and
threw her back against the wall again. This time, as she
rebounded, he slapped her across the face.

IF APPROPRIATE, AN INSULT SLAP WILL FOLLOW.

Almost without a pause, it seemed, Mia was thrown yet
again against the wall, as helpless as a rag doll, before the
image cut to another title:

A DETAINEE MAY BE WALLED TWENTY TO THIRTY TIMES
CONSECUTIVELY WITHIN A SESSION.

As the film resumed, Mia could be seen slumped on the floor.

THE TIME PERIOD BETWEEN SESSION ONE AND SESSION TWO COULD BE AS BRIEF AS ONE HOUR.

THE PROCESS OUTLINED ABOVE, INCLUDING TRANSITION, MAY LAST FOR THIRTY DAYS.

Their screens went blank. A moment later, the regular desktop screensavers were back.

"What the fuck just happened?" the man to Kat's right demanded. "How is that even possible?"

General Saito gathered them together, his face grim.

"It appears that when Malli connected a copy of Mia's hard drive to his computer, a virus entered our system, giving the kidnappers limited access to our network. The virus has now been found and removed. Needless to say, no word of this must leave this building." He paused. "The same film has been sent to *Corriere della Sera*, *La Repubblica* and various others. Therefore we needn't be specific about how it came to our attention."

"What will our response be?" someone asked. "Do we let Barbo go?"

"The decision has been taken at the highest possible level. Neither the American nor the Italian government negotiates with terrorists. Therefore, no action will be taken in response to these threats. Daniele Barbo will remain in custody. CNAIPIC will continue to locate and neutralise any servers hosting the Carnivia website."

"What about Mia?" Kat said, appalled. "What will this decision mean for her?"

"Freeing Mia and arresting her abductors was already our priority. Therefore nothing has changed," Saito said baldly. He paused. "Look, I'm as disgusted by what I've seen as any of you. But these were difficult conversations, particularly in light of the fact that we don't have any decent leads. We'll have to spread our net wider. That means locating and interviewing every single person who has supported the No Dal Molin movement since it began."

He passed a hand across his face, and for the first time it occurred to Kat what a strain this must be placing on him. "You should know that, as of last night, this is now officially a joint operation between the Carabinieri, the Polizia and Military Intelligence. Unofficially, questions are being asked of us – why we haven't found her yet. Within a day or two we'll probably be taken off the investigation altogether. I would appreciate your best efforts to find her, and quickly."

FORTY

PIOLA CAUGHT A *vaporetto* for the five-minute hop across to the island of La Giudecca, where he booked himself into the Molino Stucky Hilton. There were cheaper hotels in Venice, but he wanted to stay somewhere large and anonymous. And besides, he liked the view back over Venice from the upper floors.

He'd last been there a couple of years back, and remembered thinking at the time what a good job they'd done of converting the huge Stucky flour mill into a hotel. Once, La Giudecca had been home to Venice's heavy industries, the decline of which had left the area derelict, its former rope factories and boat-yards a haven for drug addicts and petty criminals. The Hilton's dollars, and their confidence, had helped the whole area turn the corner, bringing economic regeneration at a time when no Italian company would touch it.

At the desk they told him bookings had fallen by thirty per cent since news of the kidnap was announced. American families already here on vacation had simply packed up and gone. There was no particular reason to think the protestors would snatch another teenager, but no one wanted to take any chances.

Predictably, the papers this morning were full of nothing else. Most were still going with the line that Mia was as innocent as apple pie. One had even printed a recipe for that dish, which it claimed was Mrs Elston's own, while the Berlusconi-owned *Il*

Giornale – part of the same group that once caused an international furore by publishing topless photographs of Kate Middleton, the future British queen – had dubbed Mia "*la Vergine Rapita*", "the Stolen Virgin", its cover splashed with a picture lifted from the first kidnap video on which her bare breasts were clearly visible; the whole image, perhaps unconsciously, redolent of Michelangelo's *Madonna and Child*.

One paper, though, had scooped them all. "KIDNAPPED MIA A SWINGER?" screamed *Il Gazzettino*'s front page, the question mark an indication that the paper itself couldn't quite believe its own luck, let alone its own story. Underneath was a second, scarcely smaller headline: "SEX CLUB BURNS AS TEENAGER HELD".

Piola scanned the article. As he'd expected, an "anonymous source close to the investigation" had exclusively revealed where it was that Mia had been abducted from. The Carabinieri, the article said, were now investigating "whether Mia's secret life had any bearing on her kidnap". Lurid pictures from Club Libero's website accompanied the piece.

Piola remembered how quickly the Italian press had turned twenty-year-old Amanda Knox into "Foxy Knoxy" after the Meredith Kercher murder. He had little doubt the same thing would happen here. Journalists loved nothing better than a sexual enigma, and the question of whether Mia was a saint or sinner would surely occupy them for days, if not weeks.

He brought up Raffaele Fallici's blog. Evidently, the politician had also been sent the walling video: there was already a link to it on his website.

The decision to incarcerate Daniele Barbo was a typically ill-thought-out move on the part of the Carabinieri, an attempt to play to the gallery of public opinion with a quick, meaningless gesture more rooted in the world of politics than the harsh grind of real policing. When will they learn that there are no easy shortcuts? Mia will only be found through real intelligence – which means, in this modern age, employing the full panoply of electronic surveillance measures. One only hopes that the Americans themselves have not been so tardy.

Puzzled, Piola clicked on the archive – hadn't he recalled Fallici saying almost the exact opposite the day before? But that day's entry had been deleted. He clicked on the one for the day before that.

The situation at Dal Molin is a complicated one, requiring finesse, and is in danger of being bungled by the authorities. That is why I have been offering myself as a neutral conduit through which negotiations between the protestors and the authorities might be conducted – an honest broker who can be trusted by both sides, while holding no political view myself as to whether the Americans' presence here is a good thing or not. I only wish that, in this situation which could all too easily become a dangerous one, democracy should prevail, and prevail peacefully.

Piola snorted. Given the partisan speech he'd heard Fallici make at the peace camp, he doubted very much whether he was looking at a contemporaneous account.

To one side were links to other websites and bits of film – all the Mia videos were there, as well as the film Luca Marchesin had made when he'd broken into the camp. Piola clicked on it, watching again how the grainy night-vision footage jolted and jiggled over the rough terrain as Luca ran for the truck. The section in which he was abruptly brought down by Sergeant Pownall was just as filmic as Piola remembered. As Luca had said, he was good at this kind of thing.

A phrase came back to him, something the boy had said the first time Piola interviewed him. *"I had to move fast – the MPs were after us within seconds."*

Well, of course. But why did that particular phrase strike him as significant now? He thought again. Pownall had said something similar, he recalled, when Piola first arrived at the site. What was it, exactly? He tried to picture the scene – he'd been in Pownall's Jeep, bumping through the mud, the pre-dawn mist shredding in the vehicle's headlights, that colonel's hat on his knee...

Yes, that was it: *"The gates are alarmed, and our cameras have night-vision capability, so we were well prepared for them..."*

He called Kat.

"You were right," he said when she answered. "There's more to this. The Americans had someone inside Azione Dal Molin. Someone who was telling them what was going on."

"Who?"

"I'm not certain, but I have a pretty good idea."

He gave her a series of instructions, and told her he'd meet her in twenty minutes at Campo San Zaccaria.

They had their subject placed in an interview room, then went in together .

"Ettore Mazzanti," Piola greeted the ponytailed young man. He consulted his notes. "Thirty-two-year-old student. Writing a PhD on political studies. When did you last see your doctoral supervisor, incidentally?"

Mazzanti looked wary. "I check in with him occasionally. Why?"

"You didn't mention last time we spoke that it's the American College in Rome you're enrolled at."

He shrugged. "You didn't ask. Is it important?"

"How come the American MPs were ready for the break-in at Dal Molin, Ettore?"

Mazzanti stifled a yawn. "I don't know what you mean."

With his long hair and baggy college sweatshirt, he was the very picture of a perpetual student. But Piola noticed how his thin frame was padded with muscle, as if he worked out. And there was that Betty Boop tattoo, poking out from under his shirtsleeve. A strange tattoo for an anti-American protestor to have.

"Do you speak English?" he asked in that language.

"Some," Mazzanti replied, also in English. "Why?"

"You speak it with an American accent."

"Well, I lived in the US for a while."

"And joined the US Army when, exactly?" Piola enquired politely.

There was a silence. "Air Force, as a matter of fact," Mazzanti said. "Came out five years ago. Why are you so interested?"

"So you're still, technically, a reservist?"

Mazzanti leaned back in the chair and folded his arms. "Good luck to them if they ever want to call *me* up. I'm done with that shit. People change, Colonel."

"And sometimes people move on to more interesting things. Like undercover work."

Mazzanti didn't reply.

"So what are you then, Ettore? Defense Intelligence? CIA? INSCOM? Because the one thing I'm absolutely certain of is that you're not just another student agitator."

"This is paranoid bullshit," Mazzanti said. "Wow." He shook his head disbelievingly. "I don't know what you've been smoking, Colonel, but I want some."

Piola looked straight into the other man's eyes. "Come on, Ettore," he said in a low, urgent voice. "An American teenager has been abducted – the daughter of one of your own. Operational secrecy is all very well, but what matters now is helping us to find her."

"If I could help, I would. But I can't. Sorry."

Kat said, "There's a girl, isn't there, Ettore?"

"What do you mean?"

"You have a girlfriend in the Azione Dal Molin group." She indicated Piola. "My boss here remembers her sitting on your lap when he came to the peace camp. That's taking the under-cover thing to a whole new dimension, isn't it? But I can see how it must be hard not to. After all, there comes a point where it would look suspicious if you *didn't* have a partner."

"You've lost me," Mazzanti said with a grin. "What does Lucia have to do with all this?"

"Because if you *don't* give us what we want, the next person we'll go to will be her. I wonder if she's ever noticed anything suspicious about you? Any absences she can't explain, perhaps, when you're off talking to your handlers? Any little deceptions you may have been forced to carry out?" She leaned forward. "Of course, we'll explain to her that undercover agents are often married. Taking a girlfriend from amongst the protestors is just for a little extra cover. And then, if she can't stop crying enough to help us, we'll go to the others and ask them if *they've* ever noticed anything odd about you. Given how high-profile this case is, I'd be surprised if your picture isn't on the front page of *Il Giornale* tomorrow. That should be handy, in your line of work."

There was a long silence.

"Jesus," Mazzanti said disbelievingly. "What a bitch."

"What do we call you?" Piola said quietly.

"You can call me Mazzanti." He hesitated. "Sir."

"Thank you," Piola said. That one word, with its tacit admission that they were both military people, had changed everything. "So let's say you were tasked to infiltrate the protestors at Dal Molin. But you were much more than an observer – I saw that for myself. You were a leader; an *agent provocateur*, even. That's why the break-in was so well organised. And now I'm looking at a kidnap that was equally well organised. And I'm asking myself, what's the connection?"

Mazzanti hesitated again. Then he said, "I was giving them an outlet."

"Giving who?" Piola pressed.

"The protestors. When I first joined them there was all this talk about escalating it to another level. Flash mobs, sit-ins... crazy, random stuff, but some of it might have been quite effective. I thought if I organised a small break-in, it would make them feel like they were doing something."

"But you warned your handlers they were coming."

"Of course." Mazzanti smiled thinly. "Couldn't have them doing any serious damage. Those builders are on a schedule."

"And an American child was kidnapped anyway."

"Yes, but..." He looked puzzled. "I swear none of my protestors had the brains, let alone the balls, to do such a thing. Sure, there was some sounding off about stuff like that, but it was just wishful thinking."

"By Luca Marchesin, for example?"

Mazzanti nodded. "I knew he'd never have gone through with it. He wasn't even particularly serious at the time. It was more like, 'It would serve them right if we renditioned one of *their* kids.'"

"But you put it in your report?"

"Of course. But not as something that might actually happen, you understand. Just as an idea that had been discussed. So that they'd know how strongly people were starting to feel about Dal Molin."

"Who's 'they', Ettore? Who did you send the report to? Your handlers in Rome?"

Mazzanti shook his head. "Rome doesn't run this one. I'm on a short-term secondment here, building up my cover. My reports go direct to Colonel Carver and the Director of Transformation, Sergio Sagese."

FORTY-ONE

THEY MET HOLLY at the Stucky, in a quiet corner of the rooftop bar, under the guise of getting an update on her conversations with Daniele the night before. When she told them that he believed the kidnappers had recruited a freelance hacker, Piola and Kat exchanged glances. It seemed to support what they were already thinking: that the kidnappers were too well organised to be what they claimed.

"There was another reason we asked you here, actually," Piola said quietly. "It's possible the kidnappers themselves may have links to the US Army."

Holly stared at him. "*What?*"

"One of the Azione Dal Molin protestors is an undercover agent," Kat said. "He was sending reports back to Colonel Carver and the man who runs the construction consortium, Sergio Sagese. One of his reports mentioned an off-the-cuff remark by a young activist about kidnapping an American child."

Holly shook her head. "That's crazy. It's unthinkable – *unthinkable* – that we would ever be part of such a thing. Not to one of our own."

"Even so, it's a lead that has to be investigated," Piola said. He paused. "Somehow. We can speak to Sagese, but Carver…"

She stared at him. "Oh no. You're not thinking—"

"We can't even get on to the base without authorisation," Kat said. "We need your help."

"*My* help! I don't—" Holly stopped short. "'Without authorisation'? So this isn't even an official line of enquiry?"

"Not yet," Piola said. "But that's better, isn't it? Keeping it between ourselves for now… That way, if it *does* turn out to be nothing, it'll never reach the papers. Whereas something as big as this, if it were to be investigated officially, would be all over the media within minutes." He gestured at the copy of *Il Gazzettino* on the table. "Sadly, these journalists seem to have very good links to some of my colleagues."

Holly was silent. She could see that keeping this out of the papers would indeed be beneficial. "What exactly do you think the colonel and this other man might have done?" she said at last.

"We don't know. It may even be nothing." Kat explained how the MPs had known the demonstrators were coming, as a result of Mazzanti's report. "The point is, it makes Carver and Sagese part of a very small pool of people who even knew of Azione Dal Molin's existence."

"The colonel said something when I was there. About having spent a lot of time and money trying to contain the anti-Dal Molin protests. At the time I thought nothing of it, but I guess it fits with him planting Mazzanti. But why would he get involved in anything like this? Sagese too, for that matter? Surely the very last thing either of them wants is to hand the protestors a publicity coup."

"Unless it's to discredit the protest movement as a whole," Piola said quietly. "A couple of months ago, there was going to be a regional referendum about Dal Molin. It was cancelled by the courts days before it was due to take place."

"I recall that. But so what?"

"In the local elections, some of the candidates are – or at least *were* – standing on anti-Dal Molin platforms. If they'd done well in the polls, the protestors would have had a voice in the regional parliament. If *enough* of them did well, and there was even a majority prepared to vote against the American presence here... effectively, the anti-Dal Molin movement would have a democratic mandate. That could have made things pretty difficult, couldn't it? Three thousand troops and their families arriving here from Germany, just as the host nation turns against them at the ballot box?"

Kat added, "And I checked – the reason they're leaving Germany is because of a similar grass-roots protest movement there. The US is suddenly Europe's persona non grata, going from country to country looking for somewhere to put its bases. But it wants those bases more than ever: all America's strategic objectives, from Africa through the Middle East, depend on what they call power projection capability. That is, troops and planes stationed around the Mediterranean, on near-constant standby."

Holly couldn't fault Kat's analysis. But there was still too much that didn't make sense. "But it's precisely the... the so-called torture of terror suspects that's made us unpopular," she objected. "Why would we risk making ourselves more unpopular still?"

"We don't know," Kat said. "Maybe they've already planned how it could play out in a way that will end up with public opinion on the US's side. Or maybe they've simply misjudged the public mood."

"That implies the US would interfere in the domestic politics of one of our own allies. We don't do that kind of thing. Not any more."

Piola spread his hands. "Look, you may well be right. But

it's a lead. And there are precious few of those right now. All we're asking is that you help us investigate it."

She was silent, thinking. "You two aren't even meant to be working together, are you?"

Kat and Piola looked at each other. "That's correct," Piola said at last.

"Are you sleeping together again?" she asked bluntly.

"No," Piola said. "And nor will we be. You have my word on that."

Holly nodded. "All right. I'll ask some questions for you. But only because I think there's nothing in it, and I want to help you eliminate this line of enquiry and move on to something more realistic. Something that might actually help us find Mia."

FORTY-TWO

"SO NOW THEY think Carver could have something to do with it?"

Holly shook her head. "That's putting it too strongly. They're professionals – they accept it might be nothing more than a coincidence. But they've asked me to find out who else he shared his reports with besides Sagese."

"Hmm." Gilroy pushed himself up from the table he was propping himself against and took a turn around the classroom, his hands in his pockets. "So the implication is, far from it being an anti-American terror group behind the kidnap, it could be some murky scheme we're pursuing amongst ourselves."

She'd updated Gilroy on her abortive date with Daniele, but it was this new initiative from Piola and Kat he seemed most interested in.

"Could it?" she asked quietly.

"I don't see how." He looked at her. "But that doesn't mean we shouldn't investigate. Hopefully, as you say, it will be nothing more than due diligence."

She sighed. "But what I don't see is how I actually do this. It's not like I can just walk up to Colonel Carver and demand to interrogate him."

"No. But there are two parts to this hypothesis of theirs. One is that Carver himself could be the link. The other is that

Mia wasn't just picked at random. That might be your way in – tell Carver you're trying to establish why the kidnappers went to such extraordinary lengths to target *her*."

"I'll see what I can do."

"And the next question," he continued, "will be what to do if you find anything."

"Sir?"

"Even if you find something that vindicates their approach, it may not be in America's interest to pass it back to the Carabinieri. If it were something that discredits us, for example, and could thus put troops' lives at risk…" He paused. "It might be best for the Carabinieri to feel that this isn't a particularly relevant or fruitful avenue of investigation, at least for now."

She saw what he was telling her, and was silent.

He nodded. "In other words, Holly, you should give your friends the impression that the lead Mazzanti has furnished them with – that the USAF itself could somehow be involved with the kidnap – is a dead end. Whilst, of course, continuing to pursue it to the very best of your ability. Can you do that?"

"I think so," she said hesitantly. "If I can bring anything I find back to you."

"Of course. Share everything with me, and meanwhile let's be cautious who else we speak to."

As she turned to go, he said, "One other thing… How was it that a full colonel of the Carabinieri came to be investigating the break-in at Dal Molin in the first place?"

"Oh…" She told him about the skeleton. "It seems like that was the only unpredictable thing in the whole operation," she added. "When Mazzanti sent the protestors into the construction site, he could never have known they'd come across something like that."

"Indeed." He rubbed his hand thoughtfully over his chin. "If I was Colonel Piola, I'd be looking very closely at that."

"Why?"

"Why?" He seemed surprised at her question. "Because whoever's behind this operation, they clearly like and expect things to go exactly to plan."

FORTY-THREE

AFTER THE WALLING, they let her sleep for a few hours. She woke with her shoulders still sore and her arms covered in bruises where Harlequin had grabbed her.

She unzipped the jumpsuit and, experimentally, felt her back with the tips of her fingers. Nothing seemed to be broken. Like all the techniques she'd been subjected to so far, it seemed to have been carefully calibrated so as not to cause any lasting damage.

It was that – the considered nature of what they were doing – that almost made it worse.

The door chain rattled. It was Harlequin, bringing her food. It was real food today, or what passed for it here: a pastry and a can of Sprite. Her reward, she supposed, for enduring the walling he had given her last night.

"You're *evil*," she hissed as he put the tray down, no longer caring if she angered him.

"What was done to you less than half a dozen times would be done to a real detainee a hundred times or more in one session," he said calmly. "And with a great deal more violence."

"A real detainee could confess. Then it would stop."

"Only if they were guilty."

"America doesn't do this to people who aren't guilty."

"Please, Mia," he scoffed. "You're a clever girl. Today you

236

are understandably upset, but if you just think for a moment you will realise what a stupid statement that is. There are currently one hundred and sixty-four detainees in Guantanamo alone who have been interrogated – *tortured* – for over a decade. Yet in all that time they haven't provided the authorities with any evidence which would allow them to be tried in a court of law. Are they innocent? Or are the interrogation methods they have been subjected to ineffective? It must be one or the other."

"The President's already said he's going to close Guantanamo."

"Oh, yes." Behind the mask, she could tell he was smiling bitterly. "The 2009 Executive Order. We had such high hopes of Obama, you know, when he first took office. He said that Guantanamo would be closed by January 22nd, 2010. Such a precise date! You'd think if they were just a few hours late, there'd be trouble. But it's still open. And do you know why?"

She shook her head.

"Because he wasn't actually going to give the Guantanamo prisoners a trial, let alone release them. He was just going to transfer them to other American jails, but without legal rights. Even your Congress baulked at that. And so they stay in Guantanamo. In limbo." He leaned closer to her. "A decade, Mia. Think of that. There are people in that prison who were younger than you when they were taken, and who have now spent nearly a third of their lives in that place. Can you imagine their despair?"

"Yes," she said with quiet emphasis. "I can."

He stopped at that.

"Besides, America has the right to defend itself," she added.

He recovered. "And so do we."

"But if you accept that principle—" she began.

He stood up. "This is all very amusing, Mia, but it isn't you we need to convince, and I have things to do. You have one hour before we need to begin."

He took the tray and left. She noticed that there had been, once again, a tiny flash of anger – not when she swore at him, but when she'd challenged him.

He likes the sound of his own voice, she thought. *To preach. Not to debate.*

Interesting.

FORTY-FOUR

HOLLY WENT TO see Colonel Carver, saying that she needed to update him on Major Elston's condition.

It was only partly a pretext. Being told that his daughter was being walled had devastated the major, and hearing that her presence at Club Libero was now all over the papers as well had finished him off. Holly hadn't seen him break down before – indeed, the granite-hard military demeanour was so much a part of his character that when he collapsed, sobbing, she'd become genuinely alarmed.

"At one point he grabbed me by the arms," she reported to Carver. "He was saying over and over, 'I'll give them anything. Do anything, whatever they want.'"

"Hmm." Carver was thoughtful. "And the Italians? Are they any closer to finding her?"

Holly shook her head. "Negative, sir. The investigation is getting bigger every day. But the kidnappers don't appear to have made a single slip since they started." She hesitated. "One thing the Carabinieri *have* established is that one of the protestors, Mazzanti, is actually working for us."

Carver seemed unperturbed. "I thought that might come out eventually. And if the Carabinieri know about it today, doubtless it will be in the Italian media tomorrow."

Holly said nothing.

"Well, I don't imagine anyone will be very shocked to discover that we took steps to protect our installation. The fact that the group our asset infiltrated is also behind this kidnap simply proves how dangerous they are. If anything, we'll probably take flak for not having *more* people on the inside."

"If that group *are* behind the kidnap, sir."

He looked at her sharply.

"There's a body of opinion within the Carabinieri that's starting to wonder if Azione Dal Molin could be some kind of false trail," she explained.

"By who? And why, for Chrissake?"

"I don't believe they've worked that out yet, sir. But they're wondering who Mazzanti's reports went to. Besides yourself, of course."

Holding her gaze, he said, "I kept the distribution extremely restricted, Second Lieutenant. Sagese at Transformation. Mike Pownall in Site Security. One or two staff officers here who report directly to me. That's it."

She mentally filed that answer away for future examination. "Then it may be something quite different. Has Major Elston's unit ever been involved in any controversial actions – anything that might make him or Mia a particular target?

"Not that I'm aware of. Recon Red is the 173rd's RSTA."

Translated out of military-speak, Carver was saying that Elston commanded a company of around eighty paratroopers with special responsibility for reconnaissance, scouting and target acquisition behind enemy lines. "He's a proper fighting man," Carver added unnecessarily. "And a damn good one."

Holly understood him to mean that, as a mere liaison officer, and a woman at that, she was neither. "That's what I told them."

"Told who?"

"You know what these Italians are like, sir – they just love their bureaucracy. The Carabinieri want to interview all of Major Elston's troop, to see if they can find some special reason why his daughter might have been the one to get kidnapped. My worry is, if we let them start down that path it'll divert resources from the real investigation. But equally, we don't want to look like we're telling them how to do their job."

"I'm not having the men interrogated as if they were the criminals," Carver said. "Besides, Recon Red's on a training run, up at Asiago. If I start pulling troops off their deployments just to satisfy some *carabiniere* with a fancy hat and a red stripe down his pants, pretty soon my whole battalion will have ground to a halt."

"Maybe I could do it, sir – just get a few quick details, put it all into some official-looking files. That should be enough to keep them off our backs."

"Very well. But don't interrupt the men's schedule."

"Roger that, sir. I can drive up to Asiago, no problem."

"And keep me informed about Major and Mrs Elston." Carver nodded to show she was dismissed.

When she'd gone, he sat for a moment, thinking. Then he lifted the handset on his desk.

"We may have a problem," he said, when the other person answered.

FORTY-FIVE

KAT WAS GOING through the most recent film, the one of Mia being walled. It had occurred to her that, if it was an impromptu response to the threat of Carnivia being closed down, the kidnappers might have made some small slip-up or mistake that they hadn't in the others.

Piola came to stand by her shoulder. "Anything?"

She shook her head, frustrated. "Although there is a curious discrepancy between the titles and the film." She wound back to the very first title. "Do you see here, how it says, 'The detainee remains nude'? And then we see Mia, and she isn't. She's wearing those overalls."

"Which is correct?"

"The caption is an accurate quote from the CIA memos. So why give her clothing? The whole point of the kidnap seems to be to sensationalise the CIA approach. It seems strange that they wouldn't take the opportunity to get a few extra ratings."

"Maybe she'd done something to earn a privilege. Or maybe they just got tired of humiliating her."

"Which is interesting in itself," she said thoughtfully. "It suggests they're not quite as ruthless as the people they're copying." She looked up at him. "Did you speak to Sagese?"

"Yes." He sounded just as frustrated as she was. "Stonewalled."

The Transformation director had been no more cooperative than he had the last time they'd met, on the morning of the protestors' break-in. Flanked by Costruttori Conterno lawyers, he claimed to have done no more than skimmed Mazzanti's reports. Operational decisions about site security matters, he said, were entirely up to the military.

The lawyers had been more interested in making sure that the Carabinieri weren't entertaining any notion of giving in to the kidnappers' demands. Any attempt to do so, they emphasised, would result in an immediate claim for millions of euros' worth of damages from the construction firm. They had already sought, and received, assurances from the very highest levels of government that the existing policy of not making concessions to hostage-takers would be rigidly adhered to.

Piola had looked Sagese in the eye. "Just to be clear, if it came down to a straight choice between holding a referendum and leaving Mia to rot, you'd prefer her to rot?"

"But it isn't a straight choice, is it, Colonel?" Sagese had replied blandly. "There's a third option, which is that the Carabinieri do their job and find her. And in answer to your question, it doesn't matter how innocuous a kidnapper's demands appear: if you give in to them, next day you'll have a dozen more kidnaps on your hands."

Piola had cut his losses then and stood up. But as he was leaving, Sagese stopped him.

"By the way, Colonel, I thought I should give you this."

He was holding out a small red document. The cover bore a crest and the words "Република Србија: Пасош".

"The excavator driver left it behind when he absconded," he added. "I wasn't sure what to do with it after my men found it, so it's been sitting here in my safe."

Piola took it. It was a Serbian passport, in the name of Tarin

Krasnaki. That fitted with Krasnaki having forged work papers; whereas Albania was sufficiently advanced in the EU membership process for its citizens to work in Italy legally, Serbia wasn't. But it seemed strange that the driver would have left such an important document behind.

Remembering the passport now, Piola took it out of his pocket and handed it to Kat. "Open a Missing Person file for this man, will you? I doubt we'll find him, but you never know."

A voice cut across the hubbub of the operations room. "There's another film."

All the Carabinieri present gathered round one of the biggest screens. Someone clicked "Play", and the room went quiet.

The film began with one of the now familiar captions:

ACCORDING TO THE USA, STRESSFUL STANDING IS NOT TORTURE.

Then it cut to a shot of Mia, sitting on a chair. Her wrists were shackled, and she was wearing the orange jumpsuit, but otherwise there was no indication that she was being mistreated. More captions appeared, fading on and off over the image:

JUDGE FOR YOURSELF.

IN RESPONSE TO THE COWARDLY ATTEMPT BY THE ITALIAN GOVERNMENT TO CENSOR OUR EXPOSÉ, WE APPEAL DIRECTLY TO THE PEOPLE OF ITALY TO SUPPORT OUR DEMAND FOR A FREE AND FAIR REFERENDUM.

FOR THIS REASON WE WILL NO LONGER USE THE STATE-OWNED AND US-INFLUENCED MEDIA AS INTERMEDIARIES. FROM NOW ON, WE SPEAK DIRECTLY TO THE PEOPLE.

AT 9 P.M. TONIGHT MIA ELSTON WILL NOT BE TORTURED.

WATCH IT LIVE ON CARNIVIA.

The Carnivia URL appeared. Then the screen went blank. That was all.

"What does it mean?" someone asked.

"It means they've changed their tactics," another officer replied. "It's like a film trailer. They're drumming up ratings in advance."

"It seems the kidnappers are setting the agenda, yet again," Kat said quietly to Piola.

He nodded. "Have you heard from Holly?"

"She left me a message."

"And?"

"She's spoken to Carver. There are no further leads but she'll keep us informed. She sounded like she didn't hold out much hope." As she spoke, she became aware that they were being glanced at. Doubtless, the news that the two of them were talking again had gone round the building within minutes. "Would you rather have this conversation somewhere else?"

He brushed the suggestion aside. "I've nothing to hide. What's next?"

"Well, there's one place we haven't really investigated yet."

"Where's that?"

"Inside Carnivia."

He raised his eyebrows. "Isn't that CNAIPIC's territory?"

"Technically, perhaps, but it seems to me that anything to do with Carnivia is going to require Daniele Barbo's cooperation. And I don't suppose, having been detained without charge, that he's going to be in the mood to assist CNAIPIC very much."

"You think he'll talk to you?"

"I think it's worth a try."

As Piola went back to his desk, his phone rang. "Pronto?"

"Ispettore Marino, from the Padua Polizia," a voice said. "Is this Colonel Piola?"

Piola agreed that it was.

"This may seem a strange question, Colonel, but do you have any connection with a Dottoressa Ester Iadanza?"

"Dottora," Piola corrected automatically. "She calls herself 'Dottora'. And yes, she's involved in an investigation of mine. Why?"

Inspector Marino's voice was guarded. "And Professore Cristian Trevisano?"

"Him too." Piola was beginning to get a bad feeling about this. "Why do you ask, Ispettore?"

"They're both dead," Marino said bluntly. "It appears he shot her, then turned the gun on himself. I'm calling because you left a message on her phone. I thought perhaps she was a 'person of interest', as we say."

"She was a forensic archaeologist," Piola said heavily. He had a sudden memory of her shapely rear descending that ladder, how he had looked up admiringly and then wished he hadn't. She had been clever, passionate and alive, and now she was dead. He sat down, suddenly sick to his stomach. "She was removing a skeleton from the Dal Molin air base for us. And Trevisano – he was someone I spoke to about the identification."

"Did you know they were lovers?"

Piola thought back. Of course, it had been Dr Iadanza who'd recommended the professor to him. But there had been no hint that they were romantically involved. "Are you sure?"

"Absolutely. They were found in his apartment, in bed. Of course, given the presence of the gun, we can't rule out rape, but it seems highly unlikely – there was a bottle of wine by the bed, as well as a bowl of olives that had been eaten, and the stones put to one side. My hypothesis is, after they'd made love she told him she was leaving him, and he couldn't take it." Marino's voice was fading in and out, and he was a little breathless: Piola guessed he was walking briskly as he told him all this, probably towards a bar for his lunch. "Anyway, I thought I should give you a call, as a professional courtesy."

"Thank you. I have to tell you, Ispettore, I doubt it happened as you describe. They were neither of them temperamental types."

"Well, who can say." Marino's voice was neutral. "When it comes to affairs of the heart, we all do strange things."

"But you're collecting more evidence? You'll look for any signs they were both murdered?"

There was a small pause. "Why do you say that? Was your investigation one that could have placed them in danger?"

"Not on the face of it, no," Piola admitted. He'd asked them to try to identify the missing partisan, he recalled, the one who'd survived the shooting of Max Ghimenti and the others. And in the message she left, Dr Iadanza had said they'd found something interesting. But her tone had been relaxed, with no hint that she might have considered herself to be in jeopardy. "I think you should investigate further, all the same."

Marino's voice became a notch frostier. "I don't know how you do things in the Carabinieri, Colonel, but in the Polizia we try to look at all the available evidence and make a professional judgement before spending taxpayers' money on unnecessary investigations. The team looking at the scene, I might add, were all extremely competent."

"Of course," Piola said. "I didn't mean to imply otherwise."

"We've had our leave cancelled in any case, so that we can concentrate on this American teenager's abduction." Marino paused significantly. "A Carabinieri investigation initially, I understand."

"Indeed. We're all very grateful for the Polizia's assistance," Piola lied. "Can I take a look at it?"

"At what?"

"The professor's apartment."

"It's a crime scene, Colonel. We can't have you contaminating it, can we? I'll send you the photographs."

He rang off before Piola had time to point out that, firstly, he could hardly contaminate it, since there were to be no more investigations, and secondly, it was curious that Marino was still calling it a crime scene, when he had just been at pains to point out that they were no longer bothering to treat it as any such thing.

FORTY-SIX

DANIELE WAS BEING held at the men's prison on Giudecca. Like so many of Venice's public buildings, it was a former convent, its beautiful but worn façade quite at odds with its present-day function. There was, Kat had heard, even an old walled garden nearby where the nuns once grew vegetables and fruit for their own consumption, and where today female prisoners grew produce for a weekly market on Fondamenta delle Convertite.

When she was shown into the interview room, she found herself shocked by Daniele's appearance. Even in this short space of time, his eyes had acquired a deep-set, haunted look, and he was rocking backwards and forwards in his chair. As she took a seat she saw that under his shirt his arms were covered with scribbles.

"Are you all right?" she asked.

"You need to get me out of here."

She spread her arms helplessly. "It isn't up to me. It isn't even up to the Carabinieri."

"There are things I need to do. Things that could help Mia."

"You'll have to let me do them for you."

"You!"

"Why not? I have a Carnivia account. I'm reasonably familiar with how it works."

He seemed to come to a decision. "Give me your phone."

She hesitated – what he was asking was almost certainly against prison rules – but only for a moment. He went to the web browser and from there straight to Carnivia, skimming rapidly through commands and shortcuts unfamiliar to her.

"How do you—" she began, but he cut her off.

"We'll talk in a minute. Right now I need to concentrate."

For several minutes she watched him skip rapidly through messages, replying to some and deleting others. Then he handed the phone back. "I've left it logged in with an administrator password. You'll be able to communicate directly with the wizards."

For a moment she wondered if he had suffered some kind of breakdown in here. "Wizards?"

"I don't run Carnivia on my own," he said impatiently. "The wizards are the administrators. Eric, Anneka, Zara and Max. You can trust them."

"Trust them with what?"

He took a breath, slowing himself down. "That crowdsourcing appeal – a Carnivia user has reported being offered films of Mia for sale. What's significant about these is that they date from *before* the kidnap. At least one shows Mia in her bedroom."

She frowned. "How's that possible?"

"A RAT."

"Daniele, you're going to have to explain."

"A Remote Administration Tool. It's a relatively simple program that allows you to take over another person's computer. You can open their email, go through their files, collect their passwords as they type them... Or you could turn on their webcam and film them through it without them realising. It explains how the kidnappers knew Mia was going to the club, too. They were following her electronically, as well as in the physical world."

"So that's how they got into her Carnivia account? By getting her password?"

"Perhaps. It doesn't explain everything they've done."

"Is there any way of establishing who this hacker is?"

"Not easily. But that's not to say you can't trap him."

"How?"

"He has at least one weakness – his ego. He showed it in his messages to me, and he showed it by trying to sell films of Mia. He wasn't doing that for the money – he was showing off to his fellow hackers. If we offer him a big enough prize, maybe he'll take a big risk for it."

"What prize?"

Daniele pointed at her. "You."

"Me!"

"Yes. Seek him out, flatter him, tell him you need his services and are prepared to pay for them. He'll almost certainly put a RAT on your computer to check you out. What he won't be anticipating is that the wizards will be able to use that as a tunnel back to his own machine. But you'll need to be careful. I'd advise making a complete backup of your computer, wiping it, then creating a totally new version of yourself. Clean out any data that could allow him to identify who you really are, or where you live, but leave enough to give a sense that you're a real person."

"How will I know when I've found him?"

"Don't worry, he'll want to boast." He took her phone and, opening a message thread, showed her. "This was one of the responses to my appeal."

So you want your friends to find me? That should be fun!

FORTY-SEVEN

HOLLY DROVE NORTH in her little Fiat 500, towards the mountain range that rose up out of the Veneto's northern plains like a huge, forbidding wall, its battlements topped with white. The drive took almost two hours, but she hardly noticed the time. She was thinking about her mission – which was, essentially, to spy on her own commanding officer.

The same unwritten code of loyalty that said you didn't question orders also said you didn't doubt the people who gave them. Your chain of command was always right: if subsequent events proved the opposite, you acknowledged that the burden of leadership was such that even a bad decision was better than none. And there had to be a fundamental breakdown of trust before you made any kind of complaint, official or otherwise.

To question the actions of a colonel was a breach of the code so severe, she'd probably be court-martialled if it ever became known what she was up to.

But then there was Mia. Holly hadn't told anyone that every time she looked at Mia in those terrible films, she saw herself. She knew what it was like to have grown up on an army base, part of the military world but not quite a soldier. She'd ended up going into the army, but there had been a time when she could just as easily have rebelled.

She knew, too, what it was like to feel smothered by others' expectations of what it meant to be a woman.

She even knew what it was like to have been tortured. As she'd told Daniele, her training had included a basic level of SERE – Search-Evade-Resist-Escape. The "Resist" module was meant to give you an idea of what to expect if you were captured by the enemy. After the first Iraq war, a module on sexual humiliation had been added for aspiring female officers, with the part of the torturers played by final-year cadets. Once the course was over, everyone involved pretended that they'd simply been playing their roles to the hilt. But she'd known that wasn't really the case. No method actor, let alone a young army officer, could have faked the excitement in her captors' eyes. For her, that had been the worst part – discovering what people she'd looked up to and considered her friends really thought of her. She'd known that female cadets were dismissively labelled "trous" – short for "trousers" – by some cadets, because they were considered only good for putting on and wearing like an item of clothing. She hadn't expected to have it chanted at her with quite so much venom, or at so much volume, or to hear cadets she'd trained alongside offering to warm up her frigid lesbian cunt while she hung, semi-naked and in chains, under the jets of cold water from their hoses.

If there was even the slimmest chance that what she was contemplating now could help Mia, she'd do it.

At Asiago she left the *autostrada*. Soon she was tacking up vast mountainsides on little roads, her right wheels never more than a foot or so from precipitous drops. The slopes above her were thick with snow, the branches of the pine trees sagging under its weight. She loved the mountains – her father had brought the whole family up here every winter, to ski – but more than once she had cause to be grateful for the Italians' preference for small, nimble cars as she encountered a coach or lorry, swinging out dangerously on a hairpin bend.

Red Troop were training in a wooded valley high above the snow line. She located the unit base in a secluded clearing and was unsurprised to find no one around, apart from a couple of cooks peeling potatoes. One told her that the unit – about sixty men – wouldn't be back until lunch time.

"That's if they don't mess up," he added. "Stick around, and you should see the balloons."

"Balloons?"

He nodded. "Skyhook. They're training for evade-evac. First pass was twenty minutes ago."

She looked at the snowy woods, interested to see this. Skyhook – or the Fulton Surface-to-Air Recovery System, to use its proper name – was rarely deployed these days except by reconnaissance units, who might be required to exfiltrate from enemy territory in regions inaccessible to helicopters. Instead, a plane dropped a pack for each soldier containing a weather balloon, harness and gas cylinder. One by one, each soldier inflated his balloon, which lifted him rapidly into the air. A yoke-shaped device on the plane then hooked the line and the soldier was pulled to safety. It was simple, crude, and required split-second timing – inflate too early, and you'd find yourself floating upwards with no plane in sight and nothing to stop you freezing to death; too late, and you'd either be captured by enemy forces who'd seen the package being dropped and could thus zero in on your location, or miss your ride completely.

"How's the exercise set up?" she asked. "One team does the exfil, the rest play the bad guys?"

He nodded. "And just to make sure they're motivated, the guys doing the chasing only get chow if they succeed. My money's on them. Not that I won't feel sorry for the runners. If they get caught, the bad guys do a little role-play on them."

Holly suppressed a shudder. Units most likely to be captured, such as reconnaissance troops, underwent SERE Level C. The "role-play" the man was talking about would undoubtedly be far worse than anything she'd experienced.

"Sounds like show-time now," he added, looking up.

She caught the sound of an aeroplane. The snow-covered woods bounced the noise back and forth, making it impossible to tell which direction it was coming from. Bang on cue, a red balloon – she judged it to be around a yard in diameter – rose from the distant trees, gathering speed as it ascended. After about ten yards it shuddered, then continued to rise more slowly. That would be the jerk as it took a man's weight, she realised. Sure enough, a figure in combat whites appeared above the woods, hauled up into the sky by the balloon's ascent. She could only imagine the force of that jerk as it took you off the ground, or the sensation of being pulled into the air like that.

"They say it's a hell of a buzz," the cook said, watching. "Mind you, they say that when they're safely back on the ground."

Another balloon appeared, thirty seconds behind the first. The plane was visible overhead now, swooping over the trees low and fast, the Y-shaped yoke on its fuselage aiming for the rope below the first balloon. Scooping the soldier up, it performed a tight turn and headed for the second. The gap between each soldier's ascent, she realised, was precisely timed to match the time it took the plane to turn. Another balloon was already appearing over the trees.

Four balloons went up: all four were rescued by the plane. The cook grinned. "Looks like my money's safe. It was a six-man team."

Thirty minutes later the first truckload of soldiers returned. While they ate, Holly explained to the lieutenant in charge that she wanted to talk to the men about Major Elston. She kept Carver's name out of it for now.

"Of course," he said immediately. "If it might help the major's kid, talk to them all you want."

She took the opportunity to ask him about Red Troop's recent combat.

"Five tours of Afghan in six years. In Wardak province mostly. Tough place." He gestured at their surroundings. "Everyone thinks Afghan's hot, but the mountains look like this four months of the year."

"Was Red Troop ever involved in anything…" She hesitated. "Anything controversial?"

"Like what, Second Lieutenant?"

"I'm not sure exactly. But anything which could have made Major Elston a particular target for reprisal. Anything that involved interrogations, or the death of civilians, for example."

He scratched his head. "Not that I know of. The last mission, we did pick up a few targets for the intel guys to question. They'd give us a name, photograph and location, then we'd go into Taliban territory and snatch them. But all we did was pick 'em up and hand 'em over. Glorified taxi service, with added bullets."

When she talked to the men, they all confirmed what the lieutenant had said. Major Elston, it was clear, enjoyed genuine respect. One man told her how the major had risked his life to save a farm boy caught in the middle of a firefight between the Taliban and his own troops. "Gave him a piggyback through no man's land, walking backwards so he shielded the kid with his body," the man said. "I saw it with my own eyes."

Carver's name drew shrugs and blank looks. They saw little

of him, was the general theme. While they were out in the forward bases, in Taliban territory, he was with the command units back at Bagram Air Base, or shuttling back and forth to the Pentagon.

Another soldier told her how Elston had looked after a wounded soldier. "Joe took a bullet in the leg and his army career was over. The major stayed in touch, helped him sort out his Tricare claims. Joe got into a bad way with drugs for a while, but the major helped him get clean. He still visits him every few months – Joe hasn't got any family of his own, so he stayed here in Italy. I think maybe he didn't want to move too far from the troop."

Holly could understand that. Her own father had intended to retire to a village in the Tuscan hills, visiting Camp Darby every week for the veterans' perk of tax-free shopping and petrol, until his first stroke had brought a premature end to his military service. "Do you have his address? I'd like to speak to him."

"Sure, it's on my phone." He showed her. "Up near Lake Como. Joe likes mountains. Personally, I've seen enough freaking mountains to last me a lifetime. Give me the sandbox any day," he added, using the soldiers' slang for the desert.

FORTY-EIGHT

KAT TOOK HER laptop back to the Stucky for her expedition into Carnivia. Daniele had given her a link to an administrator login, but the only difference she could see between it and the usual one was a box that appeared, asking:

Do you wish to be:

a) visible?

b) invisible?

She clicked "visible" and found herself in Palazzo Barbo, at the base of the staircase. Walking up amongst a throng of other masked avatars, she knocked on the door of the music room. Normally, this area was off limits, the door permanently closed. But today it opened for her.

Inside, two figures were waiting. One wore the mask of a Scaramouche, with spectacles and an exaggeratedly long nose. That, she knew, was Max. The other wore a black Volto with elaborate gilding. Daniele had told her this would be Zara.

Thank you for doing this, she typed.

No problem, Max answered. *We've already done some asking around. There's someone in the market we can talk to.*

We'll be right beside you, Zara added reassuringly. *No one else can see us, but we'll be there.*

It was a strange sensation to be walking the narrow canal-side pavements of Carnivia with the two administrators – she still couldn't bring herself to think of them as "wizards" – flanking her like two guardian angels. Although Daniele had told her that Zara had visited the real city only a couple of times in her life, and Max never, they knew Venice as well as she did, automatically picking the best route through the tangle of tiny streets towards the Rialto.

In the market, Zara and Max steered her towards a stall that appeared to sell nothing more interesting than lemons. But as she peered closer, the trays shifted and telescoped to become a series of tickets, each with a description written on it: "John the Ripper", "p0f SYN+ACK", "Kraken", "BlueCoat Proxy SG9000". She was, she realised, looking at the tools hackers used to carry out their work.

How can I help?

It was the stall owner, leaning in close so that their conversation was encrypted.

I'm looking for something specific, she typed.

Such as? Not everything I have is on display.

A RAT. One powerful enough to cover its own traces. Perhaps one that can be adapted to order.

There was a long pause, as if he was communicating privately with someone else. Then: *Look for Pulcinella379 in the bar.*

Looking round, Kat saw the entrance of the Bacaro al Mercato behind her. She went inside. An avatar with a Pulcinella mask sat at a counter, typing on a laptop. Feeling a little self-conscious, Kat approached him.

Excuse me, she typed.

Without looking up, the avatar responded. *What do you require?*

She repeated her request.

I have a NetBIOS RAT customised from the Gh0stnet source code, he replied.

Behind her, Zara typed privately: *[Kat, Gh0stnet was a Remote Administration Tool created by Chinese hackers – probably the most sophisticated RAT ever built. It's linked to cyber-espionage by the Chinese government. If he really has the source code, that would explain a lot.]*

To the Pulcinella, Kat wrote, *What's the price?*

20 BTC.

[Kat, BTC are bitcoins, a digital currency. They're currently trading at US $820. He's asking for over sixteen thousand dollars for a copy of the program.]

She thought, then said to the Pulcinella, *Can I have a sample? Some proof it really is what you say?*

No problem.

A text box appeared in the air between them.

Pulcinella379 has sent you an attachment. Accept?

[Kat, be aware that once you click on that attachment, you may not be able to limit how much control he has over your machine.]

[I understand.]

She clicked "Accept".

For a moment, nothing happened. Then the window in which she was viewing Carnivia abruptly minimised. A new page opened, a notepad program on her computer she'd never used before. Some words appeared, as rapid as typing:

The sample is you.

The screen filled with her own startled face, filmed by her webcam. Over the image, a myriad of windows opened and closed. He was inspecting every program installed on her machine – her web favourites, browsing history, recent documents, emails, even her photographs. As Daniele had instructed, she'd deleted everything that might identify her too precisely, but even so it felt uncomfortable.

As her screen filled with windows, he typed:

Tell me. Why do you want this RAT?

She was ready for this.

A scumbag who filmed me and him together. I want to get him back.

Hmm.

More windows opened and closed. He typed at the same time:

I'm just showing off, you understand. Normally, this part is completely hidden. There's no reason for the slave to realise they've been ratted.

Then:

I'm looking for the film. Why isn't it here?

She typed: *It was a still. And I deleted it.*

Shame. I was looking forward to watching it. You're cute, for a MILF.

Fuck off, Pulcinella.

*Call me Ethereal. And I *do* need to see that pic.*

Why?

Because I want some proof you're who you say you are. Everyone's a little jumpy just now. A still from the film will do just fine.

She could probably get a copy from her Carnivia message box. But every nerve in her body was telling her not to share that picture with the man who called himself Ethereal.

She typed: *I won't do it. Do you want the money or not?*

He didn't reply. Boxes opened and closed. One was black, and contained the command prompt *C:*. She watched as he typed a number of commands, culminating in *>unkill [Recycled]*.

A Windows message appeared. *Are you sure you want to restore the deleted file [Recycled]? Y/N*

Y flashed. Moments later, the names of all the files she'd deleted to clean her machine were flickering down her screen.

Shit. Daniele had told her to wipe her laptop, so she'd deleted everything and emptied her recycle bin – which, according to the warning message flashed up by her computer, would permanently delete all its contents. She hadn't realised such a command could be undone. She reached for the keyboard, intending to close down the internet connection to shut him out. But Ethereal was ahead of her. No sooner had she opened the wi-fi panel than it closed again. She tried going to the "Start" button, to click on "Shut Down", but that, too, closed before she could do anything.

She had no idea where in the hotel the internet router was. Short of running out into the street and losing the signal, she had no way of breaking the connection to Ethereal. And she knew he'd be done long before she managed that. He was scrolling down the list of deleted files, rapidly opening the ones he was most interested in. She watched in horror as her emails, photographs and even her search history filled the screen.

He stopped on the header "A lovely picture of you and me". A moment later, the picture of her and Riccardo in bed together filled the screen.

OK, Ethereal typed at last. *You've got my attention, Kat. Or do I call you Rita?*

FORTY-NINE

HOLLY MADE THE briefest of stopovers at Camp Ederle before heading north again. Joe Nicholls, the soldier invalided out of Red Troop, lived right up by the Swiss border. There were no east–west roads up there, so she drove inland first, before beginning the long journey into the mountains.

She drove alongside Lake Lecco, the road winding in and out of tunnels hewn through the rock as it climbed. Once again, she was soon above the snow line, the road signs – which were in three languages now – pointing her onwards to St Moritz and San Bernardino. At Chiavenna, she turned onto an even smaller road towards Passo dello Spluga, the Splügen Pass.

Nicholls lived at the base of Bocchetta del Pinerocolo, a massive col of snow-encrusted black rock that towered over the tiny village below like an ocean liner over a skiff. Technically, this was still within Italy, but she noticed how even the blackboard outside the village bar proclaimed tonight's specials in Swiss francs as well as euros.

She'd called ahead, so as to give him some warning but not too much. When she rang the doorbell at his isolated chalet he opened it readily enough, greeting her with a nod and a quick "Boland, right?" before leading the way past racks of skis and snow shoes into a pretty kitchen with a view of the mountain. Despite the snow outside he was wearing just a T-shirt and sweat pants, as if he'd been working out. He still had the muscular physique of a professional soldier, although he walked with a pronounced limp.

He made her coffee in a stovetop Bialetti while she explained why she was there.

"I've been following the news about Mia," he said when she was done. "Sent the major a message of support when I heard. This must be killing him."

She nodded. "It is."

"And you think his family may have been singled out for some reason?"

"That's overstating it," she confessed. "All I know is it's a possibility we should be considering."

"Major Elston saved my life twice," Nicholls said flatly. "Once in combat, when he got hold of my femoral artery and wrapped it around his finger to stop me bleeding out. And again a year later, when he helped me get clean from drugs. There's nothing I wouldn't do for him. But I can't think of anything that could be relevant. I'm sorry, you've had a wasted journey."

She asked him about Carver, and he shrugged. "RSTA, you're out in the field mostly. Carver's crew were based at Bagram. But people who worked with him said he was an OK officer. Not one to let red tape get in the way of the mission, unlike some of those other guys with silver eagles on their pockets."

"Since I'm here, mind telling me about the drugs?"

"It's the usual story. I started using to mask the pain, plus I was bored out my mind without the troop. Once the heroin had hold of me, it wouldn't let me go. The major heard about it. He came and found me, tore me a new one. Said I was a disgrace to Red Troop – which I was – that he'd get me into a programme if I supplied the will-power. Put like that, I realised I had to get my shit together."

"So you didn't start using while you were in the army?"

He shook his head. "My problem started after I got back – Italy's awash with the stuff." He stopped. "Look, I don't know if this is relevant, but…"

"Yes?" Holly prompted.

"Last time me and the major spoke was about two months ago, right after his last tour. He came up here to visit when he got back, check on how I was doing. And the answer's 'pretty good', as you can see. I asked if there was any special reason he was here, and he said he'd just wanted to remind himself what it was all about. I got the impression he was pissed at something."

"Something in the army?"

"He didn't say. But yeah, maybe."

"I'll speak to him," Holly said. "Ask him what he meant."

Nicholls nodded. "Do that." He gestured at the mountain. "Hey, if you don't mind, I'm late for my cross-country training."

"You do it every day? That's impressive."

He shrugged. "It's one reason I live up here. Nobody limps on skis, right?"

"Sure. Have a good one," Holly said, accepting defeat. She glanced at her watch. She'd been in Joe Nicholls' home less than thirty minutes. "Thanks anyway."

"No problem. Sorry I couldn't be more help."

FIFTY

BACK IN THE men's prison on La Giudecca, Daniele listened without comment to Kat's explanation of how Ethereal had gained access to her deleted information. "Have you brought the laptop?" he asked when she was done.

She indicated. "It's in my bag."

"Off, or standby?"

"Fully off." Zara had told her that if she simply put it in sleep mode, Ethereal could wake it at any time.

"Good. Let's assume he doesn't actually know you're Carabinieri yet. If we're going to turn the tables on him, we have to do it before he finds out."

"How do we do that?"

"I'll bury a file in your hard drive and make it look as if you've tried to hide it. When he opens it, it will upload a trojan directly to his machine." He paused. "I'll need to do this quickly – he may have an alert set up to notify him as soon as you turn the laptop on. Ready?"

"Absolutely," Kat said, uncertain exactly what she was meant to be ready for.

Daniele covered the webcam lens with a piece of card, turned on the laptop, and immediately accessed the internet. He appeared to be downloading and modifying some files, but it was all done so fast Kat couldn't follow it.

"That's the file set up," he said. "I'm nearly done."

A box appeared on the screen.

Why are you hiding from me, Kat?

"Finished," Daniele said, stepping away from the laptop and uncovering the webcam.

Good afternoon, Kat.

As her face appeared on the screen, she reached out and turned the laptop off.

"Why did you do that?" Daniele asked.

"I'll turn it back on later. Trust me, he won't go away."

As the time for the live webcast drew near, it was clear that once again the kidnappers had shown an innate understanding of how to make their material viral-friendly. By eight, the trailer announcing Mia's upcoming live appearance had travelled all round the world.

Shortly before nine, Malli set up a computer and a screen in the operations room so that the *carabinieri* could watch it. Within Carnivia itself, what looked like a giant cinema screen had been erected at one end of St Mark's Square. At 9 p.m. exactly, it flickered into life.

The screen showed Mia standing on a small box. She had some kind of blanket draped over her, with a hole cut for her head, and she was hooded. In each outstretched arm she held what looked like electrical wire.

Kat recognised it instantly – there could be no mistaking a re-creation of one of the most iconic images to have emerged from the Abu Ghraib prison scandal.

STRESSFUL STANDING IS DESIGNED TO INDUCE THE MILD DISCOMFORT ASSOCIATED WITH TEMPORARY MUSCLE FATIGUE. IT THEREFORE FALLS OUTSIDE THE PROHIBITION ON TORTURE.

The camera held on Mia, shifting awkwardly from foot to foot on the flimsy box. Someone behind Kat said, "Are those electrical wires?"

"It's something that was done in Iraq," another voice said quietly. "The prisoner was told that if he fell off the box, he'd be given a shock."

Compared with previous days' films, this was slow; uneventful, even. Its impact came from knowing that what you were seeing was unedited, live footage – that Mia was experiencing that abuse now, in real time. It gave the webcast a horrible, almost voyeuristic immediacy.

The screen went black.

#TORTURE?

#NOTTORTURE?

YOU DECIDE.

As the operations room erupted into discussion, Malli picked up a remote and switched over to Rai News24, the state news channel. The film was already being reported. A scrolling title along the bottom added that the number of people visiting Carnivia.com during the webcast had reached six million. Reactions to the film were easily the number one subject on Twitter.

Within moments, the channel had also put the original photograph and the re-creation featuring Mia side by side. They were almost identical. It was, thought Kat, a neat visual trick; one the kidnappers had almost certainly anticipated.

The female newsreader was explaining that Abu Ghraib had been a prison in Iraq famed for abuses by American guards, when she hesitated and put a finger to her earpiece. A new picture flashed onto the screen behind her: the masthead of the newspaper *La Stampa*. Underneath was a picture of Mia and the headline "REWARD: 1M EUROS".

"Turn it up," someone said to Malli.

"… has been revealed exclusively in tomorrow's edition of *La Stampa*. The reward, which is being offered by Marco Conterno on behalf of Costruttori Conterno SpA, is for any information leading to Mia's safe return…"

On every side of the operations room, a groan went up from the assembled Carabinieri.

"*Brutto bastardo figlio di puttana*," Piola said heavily. "Now we're really screwed."

DAY FOUR

FIFTY-ONE

THE SWITCH TO live webcasts, and the million-euro reward from Conterno, turbocharged still further a story that had been dominating the headlines even without those refinements. The Italian prime minister cut short a foreign visit to convene a meeting of the National Disasters Committee. The American Secretary of State gave an interview on the steps of an aeroplane, pointedly stating that finding Mia was a matter for the Italian authorities but that the United States was "ready to offer any assistance that might be required".

Whilst no one finds their methods more abhorrent than I,

Raffaele Fallici wrote on his blog,

there is a serious question raised by this protest which has so far been ignored. Last night on Twitter, a million people agreed that what they were witnessing was #torture. Let us not be too squeamish to say it out loud: if these "enhanced techniques" might be used at American bases in Italy, should we not have some say over whether those bases are situated here? The Americans choose to do their torturing abroad, in places such as Abu Ghraib and Guantanamo Bay, precisely because they believe it gives their interrogators some protection from their own Constitution. Why should it be one law for US soil, but another for Italian?

Il Gazzettino, not to be outdone, published a double-page photograph of Mia with the headline "MISSING", and asked its readers to put it up all over the country. Since there could scarcely be a person in Italy unaware of the story, Piola suspected it had more, to do with distributing the logo of the newspaper itself, prominently displayed in the bottom right-hand corner.

The kidnappers simply released another film. It was short – just seven seconds, making it easy to share on social media sites like Vine and Instagram. Mia, sitting on the mattress in her cell, waiting. And a title that said:

WALL STANDING IS NOT TORTURE.

AT 9 P.M. THIS EVENING, SHE WILL NOT BE TORTURED.

WATCH IT LIVE ON CARNIVIA.

*

It was clear that a senior member of the Carabinieri team was going to have to go and ask Marco Conterno to reconsider. No one expected that the request would be successful, so Piola wasn't in the least surprised when his offer to do it was accepted by General Saito.

Costruttori Conterno was headquartered in Treviso. Smaller and quieter than Venice, and situated a little way inland, the town attracted far fewer tourists than its larger sibling. Piola had no trouble finding Conterno's office: the sleek, Renzo Piano-designed cube loomed over the surrounding suburb like a spaceship in a public park. Whisked to the topmost floor in a steel-and-glass lift, he stepped out onto a carpet as soft and muffling as a duvet. In front of him, a wall of glass framed a view over the Sile river towards the distant Venetian lagoon. An assistant told him that Signor Conterno would be with him in a few minutes.

While he waited, he examined yet another display of photographs of the firm's founder, Ambrogino Conterno. They showed him as an older man than the ones at the internment museum, still remarkably handsome in a louche, leonine way, even after his hair had gone white, and still exuding charm and success. It was curious, Piola thought, how these big companies made such personality cults of their founders; almost as if the more faceless and corporate they became, the more they clung to the charisma of their past. He recalled the slogan that supporters of Juventus, the football club owned by Gianni Agnelli, used to chant at matches: "Agnelli is Fiat. Fiat is Turin. Turin is Italy". There was no doubt that, at its heart, Conterno was still Ambrogino.

In one of the cabinets was a sash embroidered with a motif he recognised, a cross with a stubby downbeam that turned into the blade of a sword, and the motto "Fidei in Fortitudo", just like the ones at the museum. His Latin was rusty: should that be translated as "My faith is strong" or "Faith in strength"?

"Good morning, Colonel," said a thin voice behind him.

He turned. Even though he knew that Marco, Ambrogino's grandson, was only thirty-nine, Piola's first impression was how ordinary he seemed. His suit was expensive – Brioni or Zegna, Piola guessed enviously – and almost certainly made to measure, and his glasses looked as if they not only cost more than Piola's car, but contained more precision engineering as well. But the eyes behind the glasses were blinking nervously, and the man inside all these beautiful accessories seemed somehow more like a bland, middle-ranking manager than the head of one of Italy's largest corporations.

They sat in two armchairs, either side of that endless view. Piola declined coffee but accepted water. A secretary, or perhaps a PR minder, poured iced San Pellegrino for them, then sat discreetly just out of their line of sight, tapping at her BlackBerry.

"You've come to talk about the reward, I take it," Marco Conterno began when they'd exchanged pleasantries.

"That's right," Piola said. "Specifically, to ask you to withdraw it."

Conterno blinked. "I thought the Carabinieri would be pleased. This could be a paradigm changer for the investigation."

If he'd really thought that, Piola reflected, it was curious that he, or his advisors, hadn't checked with the Carabinieri before splashing it all over the newspapers. "It will make the task of finding Mia far harder," he said flatly. "If not impossible."

"I don't see how."

"It's effectively offering a ransom to the kidnappers by the back door," Piola explained patiently. "By linking payment to Mia's release, rather than to a conviction, you're circumventing the laws designed to prevent people from profiting from these sorts of crimes. The kidnappers may even try to negotiate the amount upwards, by treating her even more appallingly. But of more immediate concern to us is that we'll have every conman and lunatic in Italy calling the investigation team in the hope of laying claim to a share. It'll be all but impossible to sift the useful leads from the chancers."

"In a purely cost–benefit sense, it must surely be better to have too many leads than too few," Conterno objected.

Piola noted how the other man slid into business-school jargon whenever he was challenged. "It will cripple our investigation." He watched Conterno closely. "But perhaps that's what you intended?"

"That's an insulting suggestion," Conterno said, bridling.

"Then withdraw the offer, at least until Mia's been found. You can say it's on the advice of the Carabinieri."

For a moment Conterno hesitated. Then he shook his head. "The deadlock needs to be broken. The Carabinieri have had their chance. If this reward salvages Italy's reputation – a reputation which your organisation's failure to find Mia has done so much to undermine – it will be money well spent."

He spoke firmly enough, but Piola thought his words seemed somehow second-hand, as if they were a speech he'd heard someone else make and was now repeating.

"Well, I can see that you're sincere, even if we disagree," he said politely, getting to his feet. "Since you won't change your mind, I suppose we must hope you're right, and that Mia is returned safely. 'Fidei in fortitudo', as it says on your grandfather's sash over there."

The effect of his words was extraordinary. For the first time since they'd been talking, Marco's face lit up – with an expression, Piola thought, of almost innocent joy. "Are you Brethren? You should have said—"

"Brethren?"

Conterno subsided. "I thought that perhaps you were a fellow member. Many senior *carabinieri* are, I understand."

"Of the Order of Melchizedek?" Piola shook his head, trying to hide his amusement. "Alas, I haven't had that honour."

"Well, you mustn't give up. To be proposed into the first

degree, after all, isn't so very arduous. You only need four supporters – and to show that you are a man of worthy and charitable endeavour, of course."

"Do I take it that you have the distinction of being eminent in that brotherhood?" Piola said, trying to employ the same tortured syntax as Conterno.

"I have the honour of serving humbly as Master of the House of the Venetians. As my father and grandfather did before me." The other man smiled wanly. "Both rose even higher in their time, of course. I can only hope I shall do the same."

"Indeed," Piola said. "Actually, I recently came across the names of some members your grandfather might have known. Bob Garland, for example?"

"It's possible – Grandfather knew everyone. If you're really interested, the archive would be the place to look."

"The archive?"

"In Palazzo Lighnier, the Order's headquarters. You must stop by sometime. Apart from anything else, it's a wonderful place to stay when you're in Rome. And very convenient for the Vatican."

"I'll certainly do so. May I say that you sent me?"

Conterno hesitated. "Yes. I think that would be permitted."

"Permitted" – he sounded like a schoolboy, Piola thought, worried about breaking the rules. "Did you discuss this reward with your fellow members of the Order, by any chance?"

Conterno blinked. "There are many eminent men amongst the Brethren. I'm not at liberty to name names, of course. But our symposia are an unparalleled opportunity to take soundings... I'd be foolish not to take advantage of that. And I have to tell you, Colonel, that out there, amongst men of action, the plan meets with almost universal support."

Translation, Piola thought: someone put the idea of that reward into your head, and bullied you into going along with it. Rather to his surprise, he found himself feeling almost sorry for Marco Conterno.

FIFTY-TWO

"THE SAME NAMES, coming up again and again," Piola mused. "Dal Molin. The US Armed Forces. And now Conterno."

"But Conterno's company has done well out of American contracts. It's not unreasonable that he'd want to help them now," Kat objected.

Piola's room at the Stucky had become their temporary operations centre. Now that the Carabinieri were – just as he had predicted – swamped by calls from the public claiming that Mia had been sighted in the caller's village just an hour ago; that Mia had appeared to them in a dream; or that a girl looking just like Mia was sitting in a café right now reading a guidebook, Campo San Zaccaria was best avoided.

"All the same, it was strange how little sense of *power* there was about him," he said. "Almost as if he were just a figure-head."

"I guess by the time these companies get to the third generation they're actually run by a board, and the heir is only there for his name." Pulling her laptop towards her, she typed some words into a search engine. "That's interesting."

"What is?"

"Holly's retired CIA friend Ian Gilroy sits on Conterno's board." She typed some more. "As his predecessor Bob Garland did before him."

"So it's not only the Conterno name that continues through the generations. The connection with the American intelligence services does too."

"Perhaps Marco's just being prudent. Conterno's an international company now. Geopolitical advice from an ex-intelligence chief would be hard to beat."

"True, but I wonder if it goes deeper than that. Garland and Ambrogino Conterno were both members of the Order of Melchizedek. When I mentioned it, it was the only time Marco Conterno became animated – he was clearly intensely proud of being the Venetian Master or whatever he called it."

"We never found any reason to think the Order was anything other than legitimate," she reminded him.

"But I seem to recall that you had your suspicions?"

She nodded. "It was through them that Father Uriel's psychiatric institute was funded. It always seemed to me that might be a way of buying his silence over the whole William Baker conspiracy. In which case, who ordered it? And where did the original funds come from?"

She picked up a photograph from the desk. "And this? What's this about?" The photograph appeared to show a couple in bed, but the blood spatter on the wall behind told a different story.

"That's the archaeologist, Dr Iadanza, and Professor Trevisano," Piola said. "I have no evidence whatsoever, but I'm certain they were killed to silence them."

"Because...?"

"I don't know." He got to his feet and started pacing. "If nothing else, it just seems too extraordinary to be a coincidence. Mia's kidnap links to the base; so does the skeleton. Mia's kidnap links to Conterno; so does the skeleton. And now two harmless academics who were investigating how the skeleton died are themselves killed." He clenched his fist and shook it, as if about to roll an imaginary dice. It was a gesture he only made when he was thinking hard. "All of which makes me wonder whether unravelling the mystery of how the skeleton came to be on that base might give us a fresh lead on the Mia case. When I saw him, Professor Trevisano told me about a researcher in Rome I could talk to who's made a special study of the partisans." He looked at her. "It might mean staying overnight. Do you want to come?"

She was torn. This mental intimacy, and the back and forth of ideas, was for her the greatest thrill of an investigation. But there was also Daniele's hacker to find, and for various reasons, she didn't want to tell Piola about that – not least because she still pictured herself going to General Saito with a breakthrough that was hers and hers alone, clear proof that he and his fellow officers had been wrong about her.

Piola took her silence for something else.

"My wife has asked me to stay away for a while," he said quietly. "She thinks I have to decide… to work out what my priorities are. My family or… or the job. And the truth is, I'm not sure any more. I thought I was, but I'm not."

She wondered if his wife knew about that small gesture he made with his hand; if seeing it gave her the same pleasure it gave Kat. And she remembered all the times they'd flowed so naturally from work to sex, and back to work again, their bodies fitting together just as their brains had done. It would be so easy to do the same again now. It might even lance the boil – one ecstatic coupling for old times' sake, and then perhaps they would both see things clearly enough to make a decision. About his marriage, about the mess they were in, about their future.

But she shook her head. "I've got enough to keep me busy here in Venice."

They both knew that wasn't what he'd really been asking, and both pretended it had been. But only one of them knew that her answer to that other, unspoken question had been at least half a lie as well.

FIFTY-THREE

HARLEQUIN BROUGHT HER hot food – pasta with a simple sauce of anchovies and onions. For fifteen minutes the smell had been wafting into her cell, making her mouth water.

But her anticipation was mixed with dread. Hot food meant he was feeling bad about something he'd be doing to her later.

After she'd eaten, the camera was set up in a new position. She was made to stand sideways-on to the big sheet with "ADM" sprayed on it. The kidnappers spent five minutes working out camera angles, so Harlequin could stand next to her without impeding Bauta's view.

Eventually, the camera was set up on a tripod and Bauta left them.

Harlequin indicated the orange jumpsuit. "Take this off."

She undid the zipper and stepped out of it. When she was standing in her underwear, he said, "Lean forward as far as you can against the wall."

She was about four feet from the wall he was indicating. If she reached forward as far as she possibly could, she could just support her weight with her hands.

"Don't move."

She heard him leave the room. By the time he returned, after about three minutes, her arms were shaking with the effort of holding the position.

He came and stood next to her. She could tell he was taking deep breaths, as if steeling himself for something.

What that was, she didn't want to think about.

Her arms were unable to take her weight any more. Inevitably, her knees buckled and she fell to the floor.

He hesitated – then, with a strange, inarticulate cry, turned on his heel.

She looked round, confused. The room was empty.

Five minutes went by. She heard raised voices in the next room. "*È troppo tardi per questo! Fai quello che sei venuto a fare!*"

She understood that much – someone was telling Harlequin he had to go through with it. And she heard Harlequin's response, his voice hoarse: "*Io non posso farlo. Non voglio.*"

I can't do it. I won't.

Footsteps approached the door. Instantly she resumed her position against the wall. She knew at once it wasn't Harlequin who entered – this man was whistling under his breath, the same tuneless whistle she'd heard before.

He stood beside her, and she saw his knees flex. Then, without warning, he slapped her in the belly, hard, with the back of his hand.

As she fell to the ground, howling, she saw him look down at her and nod, as if to say, *That's how it should be done.*

FIFTY-FOUR

IN ROME, PIOLA'S first stop was the Via Condotti, where he did some shopping. He told himself it was because he'd only had time to pack a few things when Gilda threw him out, but the truth was that buying beautiful clothes was his habitual reaction to stress of the marital kind. In the Armani store he toyed with a tie made of grey woven silk, before looking at the price tag and reluctantly putting it down again. He did, however, buy some shirts, along with some silk socks from Antonella e Fabrizio.

He'd got the address of Anna Manfrin, the researcher Professor Trevisano had told him about, from the electoral records, but there was no answer to the doorbell and he could see from the post amassing in the letterbox downstairs that she hadn't been home the night before. Then a curtain moved, and he saw a cat peering anxiously from a window. Someone, he thought, must be feeding it.

He showed his ID to a neighbour, who said she'd seen Anna dropping by a couple of times, but that it looked as if she hadn't been staying.

"Do you know where she works?"

"Oh, yes – she's often mentioned it. She has a researcher's pass to the Vatican library."

Piola took a taxi to the library, and asked the security guard if he'd seen Anna Manfrin that day.

"More than that," the guard said. "If she's here, I can tell you which desk she's working at. The new system logs everyone in and out electronically. Yes, she's there now. Desk 12C." He swivelled his computer screen so Piola could see.

"Do you have any idea how long she'll be here?"

"Until four, when we throw them out."

Piola looked at his watch. He had two hours to kill. Recalling that Marco Conterno had said Palazzo Lighnier, the headquarters of the Order of Melchizedek, was close to the Vatican, he asked for directions.

It was indeed very close: less than five minutes away, on Via Falco. Like many Roman *palazzi*, the exterior was nondescript, even anonymous; only the big wooden doors, opening onto a pretty little courtyard where a fountain splashed over an ivy-covered statue, gave any clue to the opulence of the interior. Piola wandered in, noting the discreet brass plate bearing the Order's name. There was no obvious reception desk, but the only door that was open led into a small room where an elegant, well-dressed woman sat at a desk, typing.

Producing his ID, he asked if he might speak to someone connected with the Order's archives.

"May I ask what it's in connection with?" the woman asked.

"I'm trying to identify some members from the 1940s and 50s."

"I'm afraid that won't be possible," she said with a smile. "Membership of the Order is never disclosed without the express permission of the member concerned."

Piola said politely, "In this instance, *signora*, the members are all deceased. So it really wouldn't be possible to ask their permission."

There was a pause while she considered this. "No," she

agreed. "It wouldn't." She turned back to her screen and went on typing.

When it became clear she wasn't going to do anything else for him, he said, "Of course, we could do this the hard way. I could go and get a warrant."

"No, you couldn't," she said. "Palazzo Lighnier was granted extraterritoriality in 1964."

Piola raised his eyebrows. "Extraterritoriality" meant that, like the Vatican itself or the Order of Malta's headquarters at Palazzo Malta, the building was exempt from Italian law. "May I at least speak to an archivist?"

"You can ask for an appointment, yes. But only in writing."

He sighed. "In that case, may I have a piece of paper and a pen, *signora*?"

Her smile still in place, she fetched both. He uncapped the pen. "To whom should I address my request?"

"I'm sorry. The archivist's name—"

"… is confidential," he finished for her. He wrote the note anyway, emphasising that he had dropped by at the invitation of Marco Conterno. "And do you have any information on the Order that I could take away?"

"It's all on our website," she said, putting his note in a drawer.

"Actually, your website claims to be under construction at present," he said mildly. He pointed. "I think I saw a brochure in that drawer."

Without a word she opened the drawer, removed a slim booklet, and handed it to him. He inclined his head graciously. "I'm very grateful to you, *signora*."

He went and sat in a bar to read the booklet. It was only twelve pages long, and consisted mostly of photographs of

Palazzo Lighnier, accompanied by a few scant paragraphs of text.

Dating back to 1393, the Order of Melchizedek is a chivalric and charitable order of the Catholic Church. Along with the Teutonic Knights, the Order of the Holy Sepulchre, the Knights Hospitallers and the Militia of the Virgin Mary, it is one of the "Great Five" ancient orders. Its members, known as "Brethren Knights" or "Worthy Companions", work principally to reinforce Christian standards amongst the priesthood.

Aspirant members must be practising Catholics of good character, recommended by their local bishop and supported by several existing members of the Order, and are required to make a generous donation as "passage money" (echoing the ancient practice of Crusaders paying their passage to the Holy Land). There are twelve degrees, each of which must be fulfilled before the candidate progresses to the next. Those of noble birth are automatically elevated to the third degree, Knight Emeritus.

There was a picture of the previous Pope being welcomed to Palazzo Lighnier by a group of men in ceremonial robes, and another of a robed man proudly holding an elaborate golden urn. Just visible inside it, through a kind of porthole, was a lump of black matter.

One of the Order's most prized relics is the incorrupt tongue of St John the Baptist, presented to the Brethren by Pope Sixtus IV in 1477. The tongue, which spoke the original prophecy of Christ's arrival, is reputed to warn whenever the Catholic Church is in danger of heresy or misjudgement.

If that was the case, Piola thought cynically, it must have been babbling non-stop of late. He turned the page.

The Palace offers Brethren accommodation and service of the highest standards whenever they are in Rome. The Order's fortnightly dinners, known as "symposia", are always well attended.

It sounded more like a gentleman's club than a charity, he thought sourly, still irritated by his encounter with the receptionist. But there was absolutely nothing here to implicate the Order in any wrongdoing. On the contrary, it all seemed rather benign.

He went back to the library and asked the security man to tell him when Anna Manfrin came out. Soon after four the guard nodded towards a woman in her late thirties, hurrying past with her head down. "That's her."

She was walking surprisingly fast. As he tried to catch up with her, she glanced over her shoulder, and increased her speed.

"Anna Manfrin?" he called, but she seemed not to hear him, turning a corner into a little square. By the time he got there, she'd vanished.

He dropped back into a doorway and waited. On the other side of the square was a bus stop. After about five minutes a bus arrived, the doors hissing open. And sure enough, there was Anna Manfrin, dashing towards it. She must have been hiding until it arrived.

He got on by the back doors and made his way to where she was sitting. As she looked up, startled, he produced his ID. "It's all right, Anna. I'm Carabinieri. My name's Colonel Piola."

*

They got off close to Piazza Navona and went to a café. He noticed how she checked out the interior before choosing a table right in the back, with a good view of the door.

"Is something worrying you?" he asked while they waited for their coffees – he'd initially asked for a *spritz*, the classic Venetian aperitif of *prosecco*, sparkling San Pellegrino and Aperol, but the waitress had simply looked blank.

Anna Manfrin's dark eyes were troubled. "If you're really Colonel Piola, you already know the answer to that."

He thought he probably did, but he waited for her to go on.

"Cristian Trevisano and Ester Iadanza," she explained. "Or do you also think he killed her, then shot himself?"

"I take it you don't?"

Her dismissive "Pff!" told him what she thought of the Polizia's theory.

"Did either of them speak to you about my investigation before they died?" he asked.

She nodded. "Ester emailed me the photograph of the man you wanted help with identifying. They thought I might have come across him in another context."

"And had you?"

She didn't answer him directly. Instead she picked up the brochure from Palazzo Lighnier. "Are you thinking of becoming a member, Colonel?"

"Of the Order of Melchizedek? Good Lord, no. Not that they'd have me. I get the impression it's all rather exclusive."

"Some *carabinieri* are members." She looked at him warily. "If they're senior enough, and of the right political persuasion."

Conterno had said something similar, he recalled. "The Order's name came up in the context of the investigation, that's all. Both Ambrogino Conterno and that unidentified partisan became members shortly after the war. How do you know about them? I got the impression they keep a pretty low profile."

"They're the black nobility. Or at least, they were."

He shook his head, frowning. "'The black nobility'?"

"The *nobiltà nera* – the old aristocracy of Rome. The princes and counts, most of them attached to the Papal Court, who in the early twentieth century quietly plotted to reverse the unification of Italy and restore the Papal States. Some became the Pope's Noble Guard, but those positions were formally abolished in 1964. The Order of Melchizedek, and a dozen or so other strange little fraternities, are all that's left."

Piola recalled that 1964 was when Palazzo Lighnier had been given extraterritoriality. "I got the impression it was mainly a talking shop for wealthy businessmen."

"Businessmen, yes... but also cardinals, newspaper editors, generals, right-wing politicians, all drawn in by the lure of mixing with the aristocracy. They even take the occasional gentleman from the olive-oil business."

"Mafia, you mean?"

She nodded. "Now, Colonel, you say 'a talking shop'. But when you think about that list, what does it remind you of?"

He thought for a moment. "P2?"

"Exactly."

It had originally been uncovered long before his time, but the P2 scandal had continued to dominate the newspapers throughout the 1980s. "Propaganda Due", to give it its full name, was a Masonic lodge run by a charismatic chancer called Licio Gelli. Those listed as members included the heads of all three intelligence services; the leaders of a Mafia-backed attempted coup; and the future Prime Minister, Silvio Berlusconi. It turned out to have been implicated in dozens of scandals, from the death of the Vatican banker Roberto Calvi in London to the massive system of organised bribery known as *tangentopoli*, the exposure of which had brought down the Christian Democrat party.

"But the Order of Melchizedek must predate P2 by centuries," he objected.

"You'd think so," she agreed. "At least, from reading that leaflet. But if it did exist before the Second World War, it was moribund. Membership had become little more than a courtesy title, conferred by the Pope. Then, after 1945, it suddenly turned into a vibrant, active organisation again – one might almost say, a *network*."

"And how does that relate to my investigation, would you say?"

Abruptly, she stood up. "I'd like to continue this conversation, Colonel, but I have to make some calls. Shall we have dinner together this evening, and talk about it then?"

"I'd like that. I take it you aren't staying at your apartment?"

She nodded. "It seemed a sensible precaution, after what happened to Ester and Cristian. Just for a week or so. Where are you staying?"

"I haven't organised anywhere yet. Is there somewhere you can recommend?

She thought for a moment. "Book into the same place I'm in, in Trastevere. There's a restaurant nearby we can go to. The food is good, and it's reasonably quiet. No one should see us there."

FIFTY-FIVE

ONCE AGAIN, KAT took the infected laptop to Piola's room at the Hilton and booted it up. Within moments, or so it seemed, Ethereal had swooped through the wi-fi and taken control, like some malevolent imp – turning on her webcam, opening her email program, flicking through her saved documents and scrolling through her browsing history.

You have a nice apartment, he wrote, adjusting the focus on the webcam.

Thanks.

And yet, according to your IP address, you're actually in a hotel. The Stucky, in Venice. Is that a Hilton bathrobe I can see?

She thought quickly. *I'm travelling on business. Didn't seem worth explaining.*

What's your job?

I'm a travel agent.

Hmm. In one corner of the screen, all her stored photographs were flickering open.

OK, Rita-Kat. Shall we RAT your ex?

Sounds like a plan, she typed.

Want to put that bathrobe on? This may take some time. You might as well get comfortable.

You wish! she wrote.

Indeed I do. And my wish is your command, remember? Besides, it's a little late to be getting shy.

Suddenly, the Carnivia home page was on the screen. *I need you to log in for me.*

So he couldn't hack into Carnivia, she thought, filing the information away for future reference. She hated typing her username and password for him, but there was nothing for it. She would just have to set up a completely new account when this was over.

You're following the Mia case, he observed, looking through her newsfeeds.

Yes. Isn't everyone? If his ego was as big as Daniele said, this is where he might start to boast. *The way the kidnappers have got the world's media jumping to their tune is incredible.*

They're idiots. They couldn't have done it without help.

Whose help? Yours?

He didn't answer directly. *What's this?*

On her screen, the mouse arrow had opened a file marked "Private" she hadn't seen before. Inside was a movie clip titled *Rita.mpg.*

It had to be the file Daniele had created. Quickly she typed, *I didn't mean for you to find that. Leave it alone, will you?*

Perhaps. Perhaps not.

She watched as the mouse arrow double-clicked on the clip. A screen appeared.

Loading movie

Of course, if you were to put on that bathrobe, maybe I wouldn't need to watch this film.

Why do I not believe you?

The progress bar inched towards 100%. She wondered when Ethereal would realise that it was taking a lot longer to load than a real movie clip.

A newsfeed updated.

LIVE MIA FILM ONLINE NOW

Immediately, Ethereal clicked on it.

Following the pattern established by the earlier films, this one began with a title:

WALL STANDING: THE INDIVIDUAL, WHO REMAINS NUDE, STANDS ABOUT FOUR TO FIVE FEET FROM A WALL, WITH HIS FEET SPREAD APPROXIMATELY TO SHOULDER WIDTH. HIS ARMS ARE STRETCHED OUT IN FRONT OF HIM, WITH HIS FINGERS SUPPORTING HIS BODY WEIGHT. THE INDIVIDUAL IS NOT PERMITTED TO MOVE OR REPOSITION HIS HANDS OR FEET.

Now Mia was revealed, in exactly that position. The shot dragged on for six or seven seconds.

WALL STANDING IS USUALLY SELF-LIMITING IN THAT TEMPORARY MUSCLE FATIGUE LEADS TO THE DETAINEE BEING UNABLE TO MAINTAIN THE POSITION AFTER A PERIOD OF TIME.

Without cuts or edits, it was agonising to watch. Mia was clearly close to the limit of her endurance. A figure stood next to her – it looked like the man in the Harlequin mask, although the camera didn't show his face or feet.

As she fell, he struck her in the belly with the back of his hand.

WITH HIS FINGERS HELD TIGHTLY TOGETHER AND FULLY EXTENDED, AND WITH HIS PALM TOWARD THE INTERROGATOR'S OWN BODY, USING HIS ELBOW AS A FIXED PIVOT POINT, THE INTERROGATOR SLAPS THE DETAINEE IN THE DETAINEE'S ABDOMEN.

THE INTENTION IS NOT TO CAUSE SIGNIFICANT PAIN, BUT TO STARTLE AND ALARM THE DETAINEE.

The assertion that the slap would not be painful was immediately contradicted by Mia's face, contorted in agony, as he pulled her to her feet. Then the whole exercise was repeated again, before the image finally cut.

UNTIL TOMORROW.

Neat, Ethereal wrote. He flicked over to a website reporting internet data. In a sidebar headed "Top ten sites by current traffic", Carnivia.com was number three. Only Google and Facebook ranked higher.

She looked at the download bar. Daniele's file was now fully transferred to Ethereal's computer. She reached for her laptop, relieved to be able to turn it off. But as she did so, she froze.

Ethereal had paused the slide show of speeded-up photographs on a picture her parents had taken, the day she became a captain. It showed her in her Carabinieri uniform.

That doesn't look like fancy dress to me, you bitch.

FIFTY-SIX

HE'D ARRANGED TO meet Anna in the hotel lobby. They took an aperitif at a bar that was a little too trendy for Piola's tastes, then walked to the restaurant, which was on a tiny island in the middle of the Tiber. It was reached by steps climbing down from the bridge, with a view of an older, crumbling bridge to the north – an oasis of calm in the middle of the city.

Much of the menu was unfamiliar to him – Rome being, if anything, even more fiercely regional in its cuisine than Venice – and he asked her advice. She guided them to *antipasti* of fried artichokes, a speciality of Rome's Jewish ghetto, and fresh fava beans mixed with crumbs of sheep's cheese. Then for the *primo*, it had to be meat, and specifically offal. Roman cooking had always been based on using odd cuts in interesting ways, Anna told him, a legacy of the days when there had been so many cardinals, nobles and courtiers in the city that all that was left to ordinary people was the *quinto quarto*, the fifth quarter – that is, the insides. He was intrigued to see on the menu dishes such as *milza* (stewed spleen), *cervello* (brain), *coratella* (fried heart, lung and oesophagus), and even *zinna* (cow's udder); all hard to find elsewhere these days, but clearly still devoured by Romans with gusto.

At Anna's suggestion – actually, it was more of a command – he ordered the *pajata*, rigatoni with boiled intestines, and then, because it was spring, *abbacchio alla romana*, suckling lamb cooked with anchovies. He tried to exert more influence over the wine, since it was apparent to him that wine from Lazio was vastly inferior to that of the Veneto, but she simply told the waiter to bring them some Cesanese, and that was that.

Actually the wine was rather good, he thought as he ate the artichoke, which had been flattened until it resembled a rosette before being fried. The grape was rustic, and had a faint whiff of the farmyard, but it went well with these strong, earthy flavours, which it had been accompanying for thousands of years.

They chatted amiably about this and that, not returning to the subject of the investigation until they'd reached the *secondo*.

"We talked earlier about P2," he began. "Do I take it, *signora*, that you believe P2 was run by organised crime?"

She considered. "Well, it was organised, and it was criminal. But even though P2 involved the Mafia, I don't believe the Mafia had the intelligence, let alone the resources, to instigate something so complex. So let me put my question another way. Who's behind the Mafia?"

The question made no sense to Piola. "No one. They're criminals."

"As a historian, Colonel, I look for patterns. For example, from around 1900 to 1945 the Mafia was all but extinguished in Italy. Do you know who brought it back?"

He shook his head.

"The Americans, during the war. When they were planning the invasion of southern Italy they went to an imprisoned Mob boss, a man called Vito Genovese, and asked for his assistance. The deal was that the Mafia would help the Americans to oust the fascists, and in return they would get to run the liberated towns and villages. It wasn't so very different from the CIA policy of arming the Taliban to fight against the Russians in Afghanistan, fifty years later."

He frowned. "Even if that's true, I don't see how it relates to the Order of Melchizedek."

"Well, let's just say it's an interesting connection. The Americans…" She picked up a glass. "Talking to the Mafia." She put the glass down so that it was next to the wine bottle. "Now, here's another question. *Why* did the Americans choose to invade Italy first – as opposed to France, say, or Greece?"

He recalled the answer to this from his conversation with Professor Trevisano. "In part, to deny it to Russia – to make sure the Iron Curtain came no nearer than Yugoslavia. And because otherwise the Pope might have found himself in a communist country."

She inclined her head. "So now we have another possible connection, this time between the Americans and the Church." She picked up the pepper pot and placed it next to the glass and the bottle. "What's next? Oh, the army." She picked up a knife. "The Allied Supreme Command was giving our armed forces orders long before the end of the war. Afterwards, the Allies became NATO, and the connection continued." She placed the knife next to the others and picked up a fork. "Politicians. Well, that wasn't quite so straightforward, was it? All those communist partisans, and the tens of thousands of little towns and villages that regarded them as heroes, particularly in the north… In the aftermath of the war, certainly by the 1948 election, it looked as if Italy might simply *vote* itself communist."

"And?"

"And the Americans simply couldn't have that. Their entire plan for post-war Europe would have been undone – and, to add insult to injury, at the ballot box of all places." She looked at him levelly. "Here's an interesting fact, Colonel. The first four directives from America's newly formed National Security Council to the CIA were all concerned, in one way or another, with Italy. Directive Number 4, for example, stated that the CIA was to disrupt the electoral success of the Italian communists by any means possible. In other words, to undermine the democratic process of an apparently sovereign nation in any way it could, legal or not."

He looked at her. She was telling him all these extraordinary things quite coolly, as if they were accepted facts. "How did the CIA go about it?"

"A variety of methods. But one of the most effective was to create a new centre-left grouping as an alternative to the communists, allying the socialists and the Church." She rearranged the pepper pot so that it was next to the fork. "The Christian Democrats."

"The Christian Democrats were a creation of the CIA?" he said, astonished.

She nodded calmly. "It cost them millions of dollars in project funds. Which, I imagine, is where their other friends came in." She indicated the wine bottle and the knife.

"And there's proof of all this?" he asked, suddenly a little sceptical.

"The CIA always intended it to be a clandestine operation. There *is* evidence, but it doesn't show the full extent to which our country was corrupted during those years. I've been trying to amass more."

He appreciated now why Anna Manfrin was being careful about her own security, if this was the kind of thing she researched. "And Professor Trevisano? He was going to put all this in his book?"

She nodded. "There's an informal group of academics and

researchers who collaborate on this. We call ourselves the Resistance. It's only half a joke."

"You were going to tell me how the Order of Melchizedek fits in."

She leaned forward. "If you look at the ownership of the Order's assets – that nice *palazzo* of theirs, for example – you find that before 1947 some of them belonged to a completely different organisation. Its name was the American–Italian Cultural Exchange."

"Another front?"

"I'd bet my life on it."

"In other words," he said, trying to get his head around this, "you believe that P2 wasn't the only CIA-backed network in Italy. You think there were others, and that the Order of Melchizedek was one of them."

"That's my working hypothesis, yes. Although when we say 'CIA', we should be a little careful. I'd imagine the bosses back in Langley never knew the exact details. Having passed the directive down the line, they'd have let those on the ground take care of the rest."

"And that ancient reliquary of theirs? The tongue of John the Baptist? Are you saying that's all a fake?"

She shrugged. "Define 'fake', Colonel. After all, there are at least four heads of John the Baptist scattered around Italy. I should imagine the Order got that tongue from some mouldering Vatican store, to lend itself a little authenticity. Oh, and to justify having a very secure strong room. All those project funds had to be stashed somewhere."

"I spoke to Marco Conterno. His passion for the Order seemed genuine."

"I'm sure it is. People love these exclusive societies, don't they? The secrecy, the ranks and levels, all that dressing up and mixing with Princes of the Church. It's a curious thing I've noticed about some men: the more power they have, the more they're attracted to the idea that there's some kind of exclusive club of the even more powerful."

"Very well," he said. "Let's assume you're right. How does it relate to my missing partisan?"

She took a mouthful of wine before replying. They'd almost finished the bottle, he saw.

"As I said, the focus of my research at the moment is how the CIA subverted the post-war elections. Getting proof of that has always been hard, not least because the Vatican officially doesn't release documents from the archives until after seventy-five years. But recently, it's been making more and more exceptions. When the new man, Santini, took over at the Vatican Information Service, he let it be known that he was going to start releasing documents early. It really looked as if, for the first time, we were going to get our hands on some cast-iron primary sources."

"I sense a 'but' coming."

"In the last few weeks, there's been a U-turn – almost, you might say, a panic. The seventy-five-year rule is being rigorously enforced; researchers with access to the Archivio Segreto have had their passes revoked; new security procedures are being put in place. But it's more than that. There's been frenzied activity – monks have been drafted in to go through the uncatalogued material, and they're taking boxes of documents to a meeting room for Santini to inspect personally." She hesitated. "Yesterday I saw a guard carrying out the packaging for a document shredder."

He raised his eyebrows. "Do you have any sense of what caused this?"

"No. But whatever it was, it was part of the ongoing

cataloguing process, and that's being done in chronological order. So it must concern my period."

He nodded thoughtfully. "Though it may be something entirely unconnected to what we've just been discussing."

"Of course. But anyway, it's unfortunate. I'd hoped to be able to track the missing partisan back through the archive."

"To do that, *signora*, I imagine you'd need a name."

"I know his name," she said quietly. "I recognised him as soon as Cristian emailed me the photographs. It's Sandro La Sala."

The name was familiar, although Piola couldn't immediately place it.

"One of the earliest members of the Christian Democrats," she added. "The deputy for the Veneto. He held a number of government positions over the years."

Piola remembered him now. A grey, slightly insignificant-looking politician who had always played a secondary role to more flamboyant figures like prime ministers Giulio Andreotti – eventually convicted for having longstanding links with the Mafia – and Giovanni Goria, whose resignation over corruption charges brought to an end the unbroken line of Christian Democrat leaders which had governed Italy for almost forty years. It was hard to connect the portly, balding figure Piola recalled from his own childhood with the grinning, whippet-thin fighter in the photograph.

He sat back, thinking. "So La Sala was a communist partisan, but moved towards the political centre after the war? And took advantage of those CIA project funds, presumably?"

"Possibly. But perhaps in his case it was the other way round. Perhaps high office, and membership of the Order of Melchizedek, were the rewards for his silence over the death of his comrade, Max Ghimenti."

He considered. "It's plausible, I suppose. But how would you ever prove it?"

"The same way any historian does. By looking for evidence in whatever sources are left to us." She looked suddenly sad. "That's why the idea that the Vatican could be shredding documents is so upsetting. To a historian, those few primary sources that remain are like a dwindling rainforest or an endangered species. To destroy even a single one is a crime against history."

"They may not have gone that far yet."

"Perhaps. But whatever this is about, it was serious enough for Ester and Cristian to be killed over."

"Tell me," he said curiously. "Like you, I have a suspicion your friends were murdered to order. But do you have any specific reason to doubt the official account – that he killed her in a moment of passion, then turned the gun on himself?"

She shrugged. "That simply wasn't the kind of relationship they had. They were old friends – we were all part of the same group at university – who ended up sleeping together occasionally. But out of affection and friendship, not passion. A civilised arrangement. The idea that he would murder her because she broke it off is just ludicrous."

He nodded. The waiter, unbidden, brought them two small glasses of grappa.

"Thank you for this evening, *signora*," he said. "It's been enjoyable as well as informative."

"Please, I'd much rather you called me Anna." She hesitated. "And actually, it's *signorina*." She waved away his apologies. "It's all right. Once you reach thirty, people just assume. It's fine."

"Anna, then. And please, call me Aldo."

She picked up her glass and swirled the colourless liquid

around thoughtfully. Her next remark was addressed to the drink. "Are we going to sleep together, Aldo?"

He hadn't seen it coming. That is, he knew he found her attractive, but their conversation had been much too serious for flirting, and he didn't think he had allowed his feelings to become obvious. Certainly it hadn't occurred to him that they might be reciprocated.

"I'd welcome the company, to be honest," she added.

"A civilised arrangement?"

"Exactly."

He hesitated, and she saw it.

"Please, forget I asked," she said quickly. She tried to make a joke of it. "Mrs Piola's a lucky woman."

"She doesn't think so," he said.

Some hint of his own pain must have crossed his eyes, because she said, "I'm sorry. I didn't mean to intrude."

She stood up, and he stood with her, regret at not taking her up on her offer already flooding through every fibre of his being. But it was nothing, he knew, compared to the regret he would have felt if he'd accepted.

FIFTY-SEVEN

KAT TURNED OFF her laptop the instant Ethereal worked out who she was. For good measure she also shut the lid, flipped the machine upside down, and took out the battery. Then she paced warily around the computer where it lay on the bed, as if it were a magic box inside which some evil genie was trapped.

Her phone buzzed with a text from Holly. *Kat, what's going on?*

She texted back. *What do you mean?*

Think you'd better check Facebook.

With a feeling of dread, she got her Facebook page up on her phone. According to her wall, she'd just organised an event.

Kat Tapo has invited 198 people to a swingers' party TODAY at Hilton Stucky, Room 696.

There was a grainy thumbnail – the picture of her and Riccardo. *Shit.* She pressed "Recall", then "Delete".

Kat Tapo just cancelled an event.

Her phone rang, the number one she didn't recognise. A slow, courteous voice said, "Good evening. This is Impresa Funebre Pavanello, in Cannaregio. May I offer my deepest condolences—"

"About what?" she interrupted.

"I understand your twin, Rita Tapo, has sadly passed away? We've been asked to make the necessary arrangements."

"It's a stupid hoax," she said, pressing "End Call". Reloading Facebook, she found herself being redirected.

RIP Kat Tapo...

Somehow he'd turned her page into a memorial.

Words cannot express the sadness we feel at losing one of Married and Discreet's most active members. A serving captain in the Carabinieri, Kat loved to party, in or out of uniform. Share your memories of Kat Tapo here.

The first comment was by Ethereal.

Let's kick this off. Captain Kat wasn't the sharpest tool in the box. In fact, even amongst the Carabinieri, her stupidity was legendary. Her colleagues still remember the time she was found staring at a carton of orange juice. When asked why, she replied, "The instruction says 'concentrate'."

Told by a junior there was no more space in the archive, she gave permission for him to get rid of all the old documents, so long as he made photocopies first.

"Oh, great," she muttered. But even while she'd been reading the feeble jokes, Ethereal had been busy again. Her phone buzzed with an automated text message from her bank.

Because of suspected fraudulent activity, your account has been suspended.

Her heart sinking, she checked her emails. As she'd expected, he'd hacked those too. And he'd not only resurrected her account at Married and Discreet, he'd set all the profile settings to "Public". Half a dozen men, and two women, had emailed her already, asking for a date.

The last email in her inbox was a message from *noreply@ ethereal.com.*

Are we having fun yet?

She thought. There was clearly no point in worrying about the laptop any more – he already had everything he wanted from it. Putting the battery back in, she booted it up and went straight to Carnivia. It took her only a few minutes to find the bar near the market, although she noticed that Carnivia's usually smooth interface seemed jerky and sluggish.

Going inside, she marched up to the avatar with the Pulcinella mask.

What the fuck?

Sorry, Pulcinella379 is sleeping. Back soon.

I don't believe you.

Ha! The Pulcinella woke up and looked around. *Oh, there you are. Something wrong?*

Leave me alone, she typed furiously. What was the convention? Oh yes – it was shouting if you used capitals. *LEAVE ME ALONE, CREEP.*

Or what? the avatar asked. *Going to put me in handcuffs?*

What you're doing is a crime. Identity theft, misuse of data, harassment— The screen froze in mid-sentence, leaving her typing impotently into nothingness.

Believe me, Captain, I'm wanted for more exciting things than that, he answered when it unfroze again. *But sure, I'll stop.*

You will?

Yes. If you and me have a cyberdate. There's a nice little video-chat function in the back room here. Clothing optional.

You must be joking.

Always. But one thing I'm very serious about. You tried to fool me. That really wasn't clever.

Suddenly, another voice appeared next to Ethereal's. [*Kat, it's interesting that he says fool, not hack. That suggests he hasn't realised Daniele's put malware on his machine.*]

[*Who is this?*]

[*Zara. You didn't log on as an admin, so you can't see me. Neither can he, of course. The point is, I think maybe he's been so busy punking you, he's missed Daniele's trojan. Inadvertently, you've created the perfect backdoor.*]

Well? Ethereal demanded. *Do we have a deal? Ready for a little cyberparty, Kat Tapo?*

There was a whirring noise from her laptop. She looked down. The eject mechanism on the CD drive was making the disc tray go in and out suggestively.

[*Keep him talking. I'm going to access the trojan from this end, see if we've got a link to his hardware yet. It may take a few minutes – I've never known Carnivia this laggy.*]

Maybe, Kat typed, switching her attention back to Ethereal's thread. *If you start behaving like a gentleman.*

Hmm. Not sure I really know what that means.

It's rude not to let me see your face, for one thing. Since you can see mine.

Two windows opened on the screen of her laptop. One showed Kat's own face, as filmed by the webcam. The other showed a skinny youth of about seventeen with pale skin and short red hair. He wore heavy glasses and a T-shirt covered in a slogan in Cyrillic script.

Better? he asked.

Much, she lied.

[Kat, this will take a few more minutes], Zara typed. *[I've made the uplink, now I need to FTP his data files.]*

So how does this work, Ethereal? I'm a stranger to cyber-dating, quite frankly.

Well, first you get a little more comfortable.

You mean, like find a cushion?

Hahaha. No, I mean lose the clothes.

She kept her smile plastered to her face. *You first.*

On the screen, Ethereal pulled off his T-shirt, revealing a thin, hairless chest. *Your turn.*

As slowly as she could, she unbuttoned her blouse. Underneath she was wearing a black bra from Superboom.

[Thirty seconds], Zara interjected.

And the rest, he typed impatiently.

Uh-uh. It's your turn now, remember?

On the screen, Ethereal stood up and shucked off his jeans.

Hey, you sure know how to woo a lady, Ethereal.

Your turn. Or do I have to come and get you?

My screen keeps freezing. I think there's something wrong with the connection.

It's this shitheap website. The word is, it lost another mirror site a couple of hours ago. Don't worry, it won't spoil our fun.

Close your eyes, then. And don't open them until you've counted to ten.

[Done], Zara typed.

[Thank God for that. Do you have some wizardy way you can get us both out of here?]

[Sure.]

Bye, creep.

A moment later, Kat was back in the virtual Palazzo Barbo, and Zara had materialised beside her.

Within an hour, with Zara's help, Kat had closed down her Facebook and Gmail accounts and sent a message to all her contacts explaining she'd been hacked. At Zara's suggestion, she'd said that the hacker had circulated some Photoshopped images purporting to be of her and could the recipients please delete them immediately.

It would, she knew, only increase the curiosity of those who hadn't yet viewed them, but at least it gave her a tiny figleaf of deniability.

Meanwhile, Zara had been working on the download she'd made from the hacker's laptop.

As we thought, she typed, *he's Russian. His skills aren't bad, actually – he's more of a script kiddie than a leet, but what he doesn't know, he takes the trouble to parse rather than buying OTS.*

I have absolutely no idea what you're talking about, Kat confessed.

Basically, he's not the master hacker he claims to be, just some bright kid who gets a kick out of using other people's programs. I wonder...

There was a long pause. When Zara eventually returned, she typed, *Interesting. It looks like Ethereal wasn't contacted directly by the kidnappers. There was an intermediary, another hacker. The name won't mean anything to you, but it's familiar to us: Mulciber.*

Who is he?

A former associate of Daniele's – that is, I don't know if they ever actually met, but in the pre-Carnivia days they collaborated on several hacks. When Daniele lost interest in that scene and started working on Carnivia, Mulciber was one of the very few allowed to contribute to the coding. But they fell out – Mulciber and the other hackers wanted Carnivia to be a sort of secret hang-out for leets, Daniele just wanted to build it and see what happened. I guess Mulciber saw working for the kidnappers as a chance to mess up Carnivia, and he knew enough about Carnivia's programming to make it look like he'd been able to hack the whole website.

If it was to mess up Carnivia, it's been pretty successful, Kat wrote. During her conversation with Zara, the screen had been freezing more and more frequently.

Ethereal was right when he said we're down to our last remaining server. If CNAIPIC find that one too, we're offline. But it might not even take that – if the number of viewers increases any more, we could go under from the sheer volume of traffic.

So now it's a race between us and Inspector Pettinelli, Kat wrote, only half joking.

I guess. Good luck.

An impossible race – and with the added handicap, Kat reflected, that Inspector Pettinelli knew exactly what she was trying to achieve, misguided though that might be; while Kat and the rest of the Carabinieri were still clutching at straws.

FIFTY-EIGHT

THE NIGHTS WERE very long and very cold. Although the kidnappers had given her a blanket, it wasn't nearly enough to stop her from shivering.

She'd tried asking Harlequin for more blankets. "You can have Gul Rahman's, if you like," he'd replied.

"Great, thank you. Who's Gul Rahman?"

"He was a detainee in Afghanistan, in a CIA prison known as the 'Salt Pit'. He froze to death after a CIA case officer ordered the guards to strip him naked, chain him to the concrete floor, and leave him there overnight."

"I take it that's a 'No', then," she'd muttered.

She couldn't make Harlequin out. Even when she was certain it really was him, and not the whistling man, he behaved towards her in ways that seemed inconsistent.

She'd been trying to decide if he was gay. To begin with, it had seemed like an obvious explanation for why, unlike Bauta, he hadn't tried to grope her. She reckoned she was pretty good at picking up on people's sexual orientation – she'd guessed that Kevin Toomer was homosexual, for example, even though he'd successfully hidden it from his platoon. But there was something about Harlequin that was more complex, something she couldn't quite fathom. When he made her undress, even just down to her underwear, it was almost as if he were forcing himself not to look at her. As if he were afraid of what looking might do to him.

If he were younger, she might have wondered if he was a virgin. But it seemed unlikely that could be the case at his age.

She sighed. She recalled reading about Stockholm Syndrome, the process by which a hostage could come to identify with their captors. She must be careful, she thought, not to project her own feelings onto Harlequin's impersonal mask. He really wasn't worth expending so much energy on.

It was only much later, as she finally drifted towards sleep, that a thought materialised in her brain and made her suddenly sit bolt upright.

When she'd read about Stockholm Syndrome, she'd also read about its opposite: Lima Syndrome, in which a kidnapper developed a powerful bond with their victim. It was named after a siege in which the hostage-takers had come to empathise so strongly with their hostages that they'd released them, unharmed.

Released them...

She cast her mind back for more details. Lima Syndrome, she remembered, started with a lonely captor discovering that his captive shared the same world-view as him.

She also recalled reading somewhere that the mask a person chose to wear for Carnevale, while it might conceal their identity, could also reveal something far more important: their personality. What did it say about Harlequin that he had chosen the persona of a crying clown? At times she sensed a kind of melancholy in him, but at others, he seemed implacable, quite resolute in his determination. If there was an inner division in him, what had caused it?

Lima Syndrome. She rolled the words round and round in her mind, her excitement mounting.

Could there be a way out of this after all?

FIFTY-NINE

HOLLY SAT AT the bar in the Ederle Inn nursing a *spritz*. She rarely drank alone, but that evening, on her return from the mountains, she'd been to see the Elstons. The stress was visibly taking its toll on both parents now. The major's fatigues hung off his frame, his face was gaunt, and his hands were shaking as he poured water into a glass.

"What can I do?" he'd said when she'd finished updating him. "How can I convince them not to do those things to her?"

"Sir, there's nothing," Holly had said gently. "But we still have every confidence the Carabinieri will find her."

"You try to do the right thing," he said. "Nobody's listening." He lifted up his eyes to the ceiling. "Not you. Not anyone." It had taken Holly a moment to realise that he was speaking not to her but to God.

"Sir," she said, "I went to see Joe Nicholls today."

His eyes swivelled to her. "Nicholls. A good soldier. A good man."

"He said the last time you visited him, you seemed angry about something."

"Did I?" He shook his head, as if trying to shake the memory loose.

"Can you tell me what it was?"

He stared at her, and for a long time it seemed to her that

313

he was in another place entirely. Then his eyes refocused, and he came back to her. "Oh. Budget cuts. Bureaucracy. The sort of stuff I used to care about. It all seems so trivial now."

"Is there anything..." Holly began, treading carefully. "That is, is there any reason you can think of why Mia might have been singled out? Why they might have taken her, instead of some other officer's daughter?"

He stared at her again, lost in his own private hell.

"Sir?" she'd prompted gently.

He'd only shrugged helplessly. "Ask him. The big man. God. He knows. Nobody else."

She finished her Aperol. It really wasn't very strong. Perhaps she'd have one more.

"Hey."

She looked round. It was the lieutenant she'd met up at Asiago, the one commanding the Skyhook unit. "Oh, hi there."

He was beaming, clearly pleased to have come across her again. "Bill Coyne. I was just about to get a beer. You want one?"

"Sure," she said with a sigh. "Why not?" And then, by way of explaining why she was sitting there alone, "I just went to see Major Elston."

"You find out anything? From the troop, I mean? Anything that helped?"

She shook her head. "Zip."

He sat down next to her. "Hey, you know you were asking if we were ever mixed up in anything controversial?"

"Yes?" she said, her interest quickening.

"Well, it wasn't controversial, which is why I didn't think of it when you asked. But it was classified, if that helps."

"It might do," she said cautiously. "What kind of classified?"

"You remember I told you we were basically the Taliban Taxi, snatching the bad guys and shipping them back to base? There was word that some of those guys were earmarked for some kind of transportation programme. Project Exodus."

"What's that?"

"SAP."

A Special Access Project – in other words, information about it was disseminated on a need-to-know basis.

"Whatever it was, it was pretty sizeable," he added. "Because it wasn't just those prisoners. I went through Bagram on my way home that tour, and there was a Globemaster on the tarmac being loaded for take-off. I went to take a look because I assumed that was what me and the guys were hitching a ride home in."

She nodded. The Boeing C-17 Globemaster was one of the biggest troop transporters in the US air fleet.

"But this flight was for people in orange overalls and restricted arm movement, if you take my meaning. About a hundred, hundred and fifty of them, all lined up on the tarmac on their knees, being guarded by a couple of our guys."

"Orange overalls," she repeated, turning it over in her mind. "Like Mia."

"Yeah... There couldn't be any connection, could there?"

She thought. Assuming that what he'd seen was some kind of prisoner-movement programme, she still couldn't see how it could have anything to do with Mia's kidnap. "Where was the Globemaster headed?"

"Aviano Air Base, just up the road. That's why I'd assumed it was our ride."

"Then where?"

He shrugged. "I saw it on the tarmac when we landed, with the doors open. Guess they must have already been transferred.

Probably to some black site in Libya or somewhere. That's what happens, right?"

She had another beer and listened to some of Bill Coyne's stories about Afghanistan. But with half her mind, she was processing what he'd said.

If Major Elston had been involved, however tangentially, with some kind of rendition programme, could that be a reason to target his daughter for a simulated rendition too?

There was a kind of logic to it. But the more she thought about it, the more she realised how little sense it made. First, the kidnappers had never made any allegation of a specific link between Mia and renditions. Second, it would be hard to find a Special Forces or intelligence unit that *hadn't* been connected, in some way, to the taking or transporting of prisoners. That was how the Afghan insurgency had been fought – by capturing thousands of suspects, tens of thousands even, interrogating them for any evidence that they were linked to the Taliban, and building up a picture of the enemy, piece by careful piece. What Bill Coyne had described sounded more like the routine movement of detainees around the prison bureaucracy than any kind of abduction.

It made far more sense to accept the kidnappers' motives at face value – that Mia had been snatched simply because she was perfect casting for what they had in mind. She was photogenic, female, young but in military terms an adult: the perfect proxy for America itself. In thinking anything else, Holly was chasing after a will-o'-the-wisp.

Even so, it gave her a pretext to go back to Carver. She could ask him directly about Exodus, and give him another chance to explain how it was that Mazzanti's report had coincided with the kidnap.

Thanking Coyne for the beers, she made her way over to Staff Command. As she'd expected, it was still busy. She was about to go inside when she saw Carver himself, strolling with another man outside the Command block. He was smoking a cigar. The other man, she realised, was Major Elston. Even better: she'd speak to the two of them together.

"You should have one of these," Carver was saying, pulling another cigar from his pocket. "To celebrate your daughter's safe return."

She'd been found! "Sir – is she back?" Holly said eagerly, stepping forward.

Carver turned, frowning when he saw her. "Is who back, Second Lieutenant?"

"Mia. I thought you said—" Holly stopped, confused.

"What you were eavesdropping on was a private conversation," Carver said icily. "But just so that you are completely clear, I was offering Major Elston a cigar to celebrate with *when* his daughter is returned to him, safe and well. Which I have every confidence she will be." He turned back to Major Elston. Holly heard him mutter "Dumb blonde" under his breath.

"Sorry, sir," she said, mortified at her mistake. "I misheard. I didn't mean—" But he had already walked on, resuming his pep talk, his arm considerately draped around the major's shoulders.

DAY FIVE

SIXTY

MIA WAS AWAKE well before dawn, thinking about how to initiate her new strategy with Harlequin.

He liked to preach, she knew. He disliked being challenged. So she'd take that on board, and stop challenging him.

He'd said something to her before, to the effect that it wasn't her he needed to convince. But what if he started to think he *was* convincing her? Would that, perhaps, create the bond between them she needed?

She'd pretend that she bought his whole upside-down version of reality, and see where that took her.

Eventually she heard the rattle as he unchained the door. Every morning he brought her Ensure and made her stand on the scales to be weighed. But today he'd brought a treat. A can of Coke, and a packet of Reese's Peanut Butter Cups.

As she popped the Coke she said casually, "I really want to understand why you're doing this. You personally, I mean."

"It's not your concern."

"Well, it kind of is." She gestured at the cell. "Since it's led to me being here."

He hesitated. "Very well. I suppose you have a right to know. Two years ago I was working in the Middle East. It was after... There were some changes I had made in my personal life, and I wanted to work with the poor. But it was in a country where Al Qaeda was active, and the CIA were launching drone strikes against those they thought were terrorists."

She nodded. "Go on."

"I had a friend, Hussein Saleh. He worked for the same international charity I did. His wife was expecting their fifth child. Anyway, he was distributing food in a very poor region when he witnessed a drone strike on a house. He went to help the survivors." He paused. "What he didn't know was that the CIA had recently adopted a 'second strike' policy. A short time after the first missile, they fire another at exactly the same spot."

"Why would they do that?" she said, confused.

"To make sure everyone's dead. And to discourage others from helping the wounded. Hussein was killed instantly. The charity made an official complaint. Do you know how the Americans responded?"

She shook her head.

"They said, 'We treat all military-age males in a strike zone as combatants, unless there is explicit intelligence posthumously proving them innocent.'"

"But that means—"

"Exactly. By the time they've decided you're innocent, it's too late. And this was at a time, incidentally, when President Obama was denying a drone programme even existed."

"That's terrible," she said, and meant it.

He nodded. "When I came back and found the US was building a new base outside Vicenza, I joined the protestors. But I soon realised they were deluded. They thought that if enough of them voted against it, the Americans would just pack up and go away. I knew different."

"So you decided to kidnap me instead."

"It wasn't quite that simple. But I gradually came to the conclusion that when good men are paralysed by their principles, then those principles are a kind of moral trap, laid by the Devil to weaken his enemies."

She opened the Reese's. "Want one of these?"

He hesitated. "We give you so little food."

"No, go ahead."

"I've never tried a peanut butter cup before." He unwrapped the candy and raised it to his mouth, but it wouldn't fit through the mask's mouthpiece.

"I'll look away." She turned her head.

When she turned back, he was chewing. "It's quite good," he said, surprised. Then, "I wish I didn't have to wear the mask when I talk to you, Mia."

"It has its advantages."

"I can't think of any."

"Well, if you developed feelings for someone in a mask…" she said. "If you felt you had a real connection with them… It wouldn't be because of what they looked like. It would be because of who they really were."

For a moment she thought she'd gone too far.

But the masked head only nodded. "It says a lot about you, Mia, that you look for the positive, even in this situation."

"I'm always positive," she said.

Lima Syndrome.

Later, thinking back over the conversation, there was much to occupy her. He'd lapped up all the hints she'd laid about how she was starting to come round to his point of view. But in part, that was because she *was* starting to appreciate it. He was wrong, of course, and utterly misguided, but that story he'd told about his friend at least explained why he was so angry with her country.

She wondered what the "change in his personal life" that he'd referred to had been. Divorce? Somehow he'd made it sound more significant than that. And there had been that slightly odd reference to working with the poor.

Then all the stuff about the Devil. Where had *that* come from?

Suddenly she realised.

He's a priest.

Or maybe an ex-priest – that might have been the change. Yes, it all made sense now: the theological references; the sexual awkwardness; the moral resolve; the occasional gentleness that seemed so incongruous for someone doing what he was.

A priest. She wondered how best to use that information. Because it was, surely, significant.

It was only much later, pacing up and down, that she realised she'd been so busy thinking about her new strategy she'd never thought to ask Harlequin what was so special about today, that it warranted the exceptional treat of Reese's for breakfast.

SIXTY-ONE

KAT FORCED HERSELF to walk into the operations room as if
nothing had happened. She was aware of the glances coming
at her from left and right, and found she didn't care.

When you'd been ostracised as she had, you developed a
pretty thick skin. The fact that all her colleagues had now seen a
picture of her straddling a stranger wasn't the end of the world.

Or so she told herself.

She busied herself with looking through the overnight evidence logs. There had been over a thousand phone calls now,
all of which, in theory, had to be followed up.

"Another film," a voice called. The speaker sounded unsurprised. It was getting to be a routine now: the kidnappers
releasing a trailer first thing in the morning, to build up anticipation ahead of their main feature later on.

Then, "Oh, *God*."

Kat looked up, as did everyone else.

The film this morning was not of Mia, but of an empty
room – the larger cell, the one with the sheet-banner hanging
at one end.

The man in the Harlequin mask and his Bauta-wearing
accomplice were carrying in some kind of bench or gurney. As
they set it down, it became apparent that it had been modified
so that one end was higher than the other. Straps, nailed to the
wood, were clearly intended as restraints.

The men placed two towels, neatly folded, on the bench, followed by a red plastic watering can.

A title appeared.

WATERBOARDING IS NOT TORTURE.

AT 9 P.M. TONIGHT SHE WILL NOT BE TORTURED.

There was a moment's stunned silence, followed by a sound that came from the throats of every single person in the room – a kind of murmured gasp, a collective groan of despair that was also an acknowledgement that this had always been going to happen, if they failed to find her.

And now they had failed, for it was upon them.

As if to emphasise that this threat was of a different magnitude to anything that had gone before, the film ended not with a blank screen but a grinning Carnivia mask and a counter, ticking down the hours and minutes until the broadcast. Almost immediately, it became clear that the same counter had been plastered right across the internet – not least on the home pages of CNAIPIC, the Veneto parliament, and USAF Ederle, all of whose websites had been hacked.

"Has anyone checked our own website?" Saito asked, bringing the pandemonium of the operations room to an abrupt halt.

Someone brought the Carabinieri site up on the screen. There, too, was the grinning mask and counter.

According to the counter there were, by now, less than twelve hours to go.

What we see here is not just the incompetence of the Carabinieri,

thundered Raffaele Fallici in his blog.

What we see here is a return to the dark days of the Years of Lead: an inability to understand and address the shame of our failure as a state. Italy has been tested, and Italy has been found wanting.

And what is to be done? It is simple. Of course, our government cannot negotiate with terrorists; therefore, there can be no question of giving in to their demands. However, wiser, more flexible governments than ours have been known to initiate dialogue, in order to come to a peace process, which is a very different thing. After all, the Americans themselves have held talks with the Taliban: could not something similar be done here?

"The number of people on Carnivia is at an all-time high," Kat told Piola, now back from Rome. "This morning, just after the announcement, it actually crashed." Instead of "Enter Carnivia", users had been greeted by the words, "Due to exceptional volumes of traffic, the page you are trying to reach is unavailable."

"Are there any new leads?"

"Not really. Saito's got us collating no-fly lists with people who have extreme left-wing views, that kind of thing... Trawling expeditions, in other words."

"Do you have any better ideas, Capitano?"

"Only one, and it's pretty desperate. I'm going to try Daniele Barbo one last time."

She found Daniele in an even worse way than before. His eyes were so deeply ringed with exhaustion that at first Kat thought they must have been bruised in a fight, and he seemed to have acquired a number of other nervous tics and twitches in addition to his habitual blinking.

"Daniele," she said urgently, "you were right about the hacker. But unfortunately, that still hasn't helped us find Mia. You *have* to give me something more to work with. Even if it means giving up confidential information."

He gazed down at a piece of paper in his hand. It was heavily creased from having been folded and refolded many times. Now, he unfolded it and spread it on the table.

"What's that? she asked.

"An equation."

Written on the paper was the formula:

$$K := \{ \, (i, x)$$

"Holly gave it to me," he added. "When we had a... When we met up. It's the Turing Paradox. I've been thinking about it a lot in here."

"And?" she said, impatient to bring him back to the subject.

"It's to do with sets." He saw her incomprehension. "There's a famous example about a barber who shaves every man in the village who doesn't shave himself. The question then arises: does the barber shave himself? Logically, he can't, because that would mean that instead of being in the group of those he shaves, he's in the other group, men who shave themselves. But if he doesn't shave himself, then he has to, because now he's in the group of people he ought to be shaving. And, unlike most problems of logic, turning it into mathematics doesn't help. The equation just chases itself round and round: the set of all sets that don't include themselves."

He held out his hand for a pen, and wrote:

$$\text{let } R = \{x \mid x \notin x\}, \text{ then } R \in R \iff R \notin R$$

"It was Alan Turing who realised that this was going to be a big problem for his Turing machines – in other words, computers. If you tell a computer to perform any open-ended task, you're effectively asking it to calculate infinity; it ends up devoting all its processing power to the impossible, and grinds to a halt. So all computer programs have to have a work-around built into them to avoid what's called the Halting Problem.

"Effectively, it's logical proof that logic is only a tool – a useful, but fallible, way of looking at the world, not some defining principle of the world itself. To go on using logic, in fact, even mathematicians have to find workarounds: logical disjunctions, fuzzy logic, or in binary code, bent functions."

He indicated the equation. "What Turing saw is that real life isn't classical. It's non-predicate, non-Boolean and non-Euclidean." He paused. "In layman's terms, it's a beautiful fucked-up mess."

Kat didn't understand the mathematics, but she did understand that he was wavering.

"Daniele," she said urgently. "Just think of a girl. Locked up – as *you* were once locked up. Think of her terror – the terror *you* must have felt, when the kidnappers held a knife to your ear. Think of what it turned you into. And don't let that happen to her."

He dragged his gaze to hers. She could tell what an effort it took; could tell, too, that when he achieved it – when their eye lines met and locked – he was considering what she had said.

For her part, she felt almost buffeted by the vulnerability and pain she saw there. *So this is why he doesn't let people look.*

He blinked. "It isn't as easy as people seem to think. I can't just hack into my own code: that would take weeks, possibly months, and Carnivia would simply fall apart when I was done. But there may be another way."

"Yes?"

He reached for the pen. "It's clear from the webcasts that the kidnappers are looking at the live feed on their laptop," he said, sketching a diagram as he spoke. "In other words, they see what everyone else is seeing – the image as broadcast on Carnivia – then fine-tune the picture accordingly."

"Go on," Kat said.

"Obviously, if we interfered with that image in any major way, they'd spot it immediately. But if we were to take the feed and zoom in on it, very, very slowly – so slowly that they're never aware we're doing it..." He paused. "It wouldn't be much. But after a while, if you compared it to the raw, unzoomed footage, there'd be a border all around the screen which the kidnappers would believe is out of shot, but which you could monitor."

She stood up. "How do I make it happen?"

"I can write a simple piece of code on your phone to add to the feed. It'll make the zoom happen automatically, in increments too small for the naked eye to spot."

In three minutes he'd composed a page of what looked to her like gibberish but which was actually, she guessed, the language he himself had invented; a language in which only a handful of people in the world were conversant – the unique, impenetrable code from which Carnivia was built.

"There," he said, handing the phone back to her.

"That'll do it?"

He nodded, exhausted.

"Daniele, thank you. You won't regret this."

*

She went straight to Saito and told him what Daniele was proposing. She left nothing out, although she glossed over several sections – the fact that her laptop had been infected by Ethereal's RAT, for example; and the strange gift from Holly that had somehow convinced Daniele to cooperate.

When she'd finished, Saito said, "I have absolutely no idea if what you've just done is criminally reckless or a breakthrough. Or possibly both." He lifted his phone and dialled a number. "Can you see how quickly Inspector Pettinelli can get here?"

It took her half an hour, during which time Kat was made to sit outside the general's office like a naughty schoolgirl. Then Inspector Pettinelli swept in, and Kat explained everything for a second time.

"Well?" Saito demanded. "Will it work?"

Inspector Pettinelli considered. "I doubt it."

"Why not?"

"This small ribbon of border we'll be able to see – *if* Daniele Barbo is telling the truth about that – won't actually show us anything new. The kidnappers wear masks at all times. And the camera's in a closed cell." She shook her head. "In my opinion, this is Barbo throwing us an insignificant bone in a last-ditch attempt to save his website."

"Which suggests that CNAIPIC's hunt for the servers is forcing him to play ball," Saito suggested. "If he's been prepared to offer the captain here this small concession, he may yet offer more."

"Perhaps. But I don't believe we need his cooperation now in any case. Yesterday we found a Carnivia server hidden on an industrial estate near Milan. Our feeling is he's probably got only one more, and that it's somewhere in this country. If we can find it, we can take him offline altogether."

"And what will the kidnappers do then?" Kat interrupted.

"Kill Mia? Cut off her ears and nose like Daniele's, to show us how angry they are? It's the most horrific gamble."

Pettinelli looked at her calmly. "We can't know what they'll do. But whatever it is, it will be their responsibility, not ours. Whereas leaving Carnivia up when we have the means to block it would be abetting them in their criminal activity. CNAIPIC's position is clear: broadcasting these films is itself a crime and should be prevented by any means possible."

Inspector Pettinelli's world was almost as black-and-white as Daniele's, Kat reflected.

Saito looked from the inspector to Kat, his eyes hooded. "Very well," he said at last. "We'll pursue both avenues. The zoom can do no harm, assuming that it's technically possible, so we'll set up a small team to monitor it. Meanwhile, Barbo stays in preventative detention, and CNAIPIC will continue their efforts to find his servers. Thank you, Inspector." As the two women turned to go, he added, "Captain, a word."

When the inspector had left them, Saito shut the door. "I thought you were assigned to family liaison with the Elstons. Not to negotiations with a man detained under anti-terrorism legislation."

"I saw the opportunity, sir. It seemed sensible to explore it."

"Did it indeed?" He fixed her with a withering look. "Let me explain what CNAIPIC are doing, Captain. They're making sure that everything they do is by the book, so that if this case has a tragic ending – which, let's face it, is looking more and more likely – no one is going to be able to say they were the ones who messed it up. In that situation, the very worst thing would be for the Carabinieri to seem as if we were charging around the place without any clear strategy or lines of authorisation. From now on, stick to your remit, Captain. Is that understood?"

SIXTY-TWO

SHE SAW THE gurney and the watering can through the door of her cell when they brought her lunch, and knew immediately what it meant.

"It wasn't my decision," Harlequin said, following her gaze.

She wanted to shout, *Oh, take some responsibility*. But she was determined to follow through on her new strategy. "And you think this will help you make your case?"

"I'm sure of it. Otherwise I'd never go along with it." He sighed. "We were certain that when ordinary Italians saw what your countrymen do to their prisoners, they would be so disgusted they would immediately demand a referendum. But it hasn't happened that way yet. We've been hoping this wouldn't be necessary. But we can't hold back any longer."

"Then do it," she said. "If it needs to be done, just do it."

"You mean that?"

Like I have a fucking choice. "Yes. Just… look after me, will you? I know how dangerous it is."

"I promise I won't let you come to any harm."

Really? How's that going for you, then? Because it seems to me you've already agreed to half-drown me. "Thank you. I trust you completely – I hope you know that."

As he turned to leave she said, "Wait… Are you – were you – a priest?"

He stiffened, but didn't reply.

"The reason I ask…" She took a breath. "I want you to hear my confession. Before you waterboard me. Just in case."

He turned, the dark eyes behind the mask searching her face. "You know I can't discuss who I am. Or say anything that might identify me afterwards."

"Then don't. But hear my confession. If you're not really a priest, I don't care. If you are, then that's good."

"And if I refuse?"

"But you can't, can you? It's canon law: 'In urgent necessity, or in danger of death.' And even if you've left the Church, that doesn't let you off the hook. Not in a theological sense. I learned that at school – the sacraments you took are embedded in your soul. Even if you've lost your own faith, you're still the conduit by which grace flows from God to me."

"Clever as well as brave," he murmured. "Your teachers must hate you."

"Some do."

"I won't tell you if I was once a priest or not," he said, shaking his head. "That's private. But I will hear your confession."

He sat on her mattress while she knelt beside it.

"Bless me, Father, for I have sinned."

"Have you examined your conscience?"

"I have examined my conscience."

"May God, who has enlightened every heart, help you to know your sins and trust in his mercy."

"Amen."

He reminded her of the passage from Luke in which Jesus defies the Pharisees and tells a sick man his sins are forgiven. "The scribes and the Pharisees began to reason, saying, 'Who is this man who speaks blasphemies? Who can forgive sins, but God alone?'"

She knew why he'd chosen that particular passage: both because it described a scene in which Jesus had broken the law, and because it was as the son of man, not God, that he forgave.

"I confess to Almighty God that I have sinned, through my own fault, in my words and deeds," she began quietly.

"Is something in particular troubling you?"

"Yes." She told him about Club Libero, how she'd thought it would be exciting to go and see what people did there. "And now my dad must know about it. He'll think I'm some kind of pervert."

"But you're not."

She shook her head. "All I did was take a look. I mean, don't get me wrong. I was only a kid when he made me take that stupid vow. I don't consider myself bound by it."

"Your father's views on sex and marriage are also the views of the Church," he reminded her.

"I know." She shrugged. "I don't care about that so much."

"Is it God's forgiveness you really want?" he asked gently. "Or your father's?"

She thought. "My dad's."

"Then I can't help you," he said, a little sadly.

He led her through the Act of Contrition, then the Absolution. "The Lord has freed you from your sins," he concluded. "Go in peace."

But as they sat there, neither of them appeared to have achieved very much of that.

SIXTY-THREE

From Rai News24:

ANCHOR: Tell me, Doctor, what is it about waterboarding that makes it so contentious?

DOCTOR: First of all, it can cause a range of very serious injuries. These include lung damage, broken bones due to the violence with which victims struggle against their restraints, brain damage from oxygen depletion, pneumonia, hyponatraemia – that's a rare but deadly condition caused by lack of sodium in the blood – right through to asphyxiation, choking on vomit, or dry drowning. But what makes it especially controversial is that, unlike other harsh interrogation techniques, it is specifically designed to take the subjects as close to death as possible.

ANCHOR: We have here a copy of the American so-called "torture memos" setting out in almost clinical detail how this practice works.

DOCTOR: Indeed, and it makes for unpleasant reading. [READS FROM MEMO] "After immobilising the detainee by strapping him down, interrogators tilt the gurney to a ten- to fifteen-degree downward angle, with the detainee's head at the lower end. They put a cloth over his face and pour water, or saline solution, from a height of about six to eighteen inches. The slant of the gurney helps drive the water more directly into the prisoner's nose and mouth."

ANCHOR: How long would this go on for?

DOCTOR: The flow of water onto a detainee's face is not supposed to exceed forty seconds during each pour. Interrogators could perform six separate pours during each session.

ANCHOR: And each time the interrogators just pour the water over the cloth?

DOCTOR: Exactly. According to the memos, it "closely replicates" the sensation of drowning.

ANCHOR: So the subject isn't actually in any danger?

DOCTOR: The language is misleading – the subject *is* drowning, just not underwater. Interrogators are instructed to pour the water when a detainee has just exhaled, so that he's forced to ingest water directly into the lungs. That's drowning, by any medical definition. Interrogators are also allowed to force the water down a detainee's throat using their hands. [READS FROM MEMO] "The interrogator may cup his hands around the detainee's nose and mouth to dam the runoff, in which case it would not be possible for the detainee to breathe during the application of the water." And here, a little later: [READS] "We understand that water may enter – and accumulate in – the detainee's mouth and nasal cavity, preventing him from breathing."

ANCHOR: So there is a very real risk of death?

DOCTOR: Inevitably, the margin of error is a very slim one. [READS FROM MEMO] "If the detainee is not breathing freely after the cloth is removed from his face, he is immediately moved to a vertical position in order to clear the water from his mouth, nose and nasopharynx. The gurney used for administering this technique is specially designed so that this can be accomplished very quickly." And here's one from the CIA's Office of Medical Services: [READS] "An unresponsive subject should be righted immediately. The interrogator should then deliver a sub-xyphoid thrust to expel the water."

ANCHOR: Essentially, the Heimlich manoeuvre.

DOCTOR: Yes. And where *that* doesn't work – and we know it sometimes doesn't, because the memo specifically refers to "spasms of the larynx" that keep a prisoner from breathing "even when the application of water is stopped and the detainee is returned to an upright position" – a medic would perform a tracheotomy.

ANCHOR: The medics are there to save the detainee's life, then?

DOCTOR: In part, but also to monitor their respiratory state and make a judgement on whether it's safe to go further. Effectively, the medic is helping the interrogator to push the prisoner even closer to the edge. This is calibration of harm by medical professionals – which in any country is against the Hippocratic oath.

ANCHOR: Do we know if anyone has actually died from a CIA waterboarding?

DOCTOR: The implication in the memos is that several have. One memo specifically speaks of "death due to psychological resignation". In other words, rather than fighting the water, there have been subjects who have effectively used the waterboarding itself as a means to commit suicide. And at the end of another memo there's what basically amounts to an appeal for more information, to help refine the process. [READS FROM MEMO] "In order to best inform future medical judgements and recommendations, it is important that every application of the waterboard be thoroughly documented: how long each application lasted, how much water was used in the process – realising that much splashes off – how exactly the water was applied, if a seal was achieved, if the naso- or oropharynx was filled, what sort of volume was expelled, how long was the break between applications, and how the subject looked between each treatment."

ANCHOR: One imagines they didn't look all that well. Doctor, thank you. We should point out that in 2009 President Obama declared the use of the waterboard "a mistake", implying that it is no longer in widespread use by American intelligence agencies.

From MTV Italia:

PRESENTER: Your ninety-second news this afternoon. Journalist and comedian Giancarlo Casamonti today volunteered to undergo waterboarding, in an attempt to prove that it wasn't as bad as it was being painted. He was given two weights to hold, and told to drop them when the procedure became unbearable. He lasted twelve seconds.

From Canale 5:

NEWSREADER: In an opinion poll conducted for Canale 5 by MORI today, people were asked how they would vote if there was a referendum over the future of the Dal Molin military base. An overwhelming majority said that they would vote against the kidnappers' proposals, including many who had previously signed petitions protesting the American presence...

By 4 p.m., when the ubiquitous web counters showed just five hours to go, the torrent of second-hand information and chatter had abated. Now there were only the newspapers' posters of Mia that had been appearing on railings and church doors all across Italy, often accompanied by votive candles and bunches of flowers – shrines that had the unfortunate effect of making it look to the rest of the world as if many Italians considered Mia already dead.

At 5 p.m., a voice shouted across the operations room, "The American President's about to make a statement."

In the hush that followed, the American leader was seen in the White House press room, reading out a surprising announcement: a public apology for the "excess of zeal" of the previous administration, which had allowed the CIA to "mistreat, abuse, and even torture those who should not have been detained in the first place". He re-pledged his own administration's commitment to "a fairer, more rigorous approach to the nation's security", declaring that the use of the waterboard "and certain other harsh techniques" was "a grave error". Finally, he called for Mia's release.

Kat joined in the spontaneous applause. All around her she felt a surge of optimism, even expectation, that this unprecedented gesture would be enough for the kidnappers to claim a moral victory and let Mia go.

But, once the effect of the President's soaring oratory had worn off, she was forced to admit that he had promised nothing specific, or even new.

Soon after six, a dense fog crept in from the sea. On the seven o'clock Rai bulletin, the anchor noted that there was no *passeggiata* anywhere in the towns of the Veneto that evening. Traffic was lighter than usual, and restaurants and bars were empty.

It was, he said, as if the country were battening itself down for some terrible storm.

SIXTY-FOUR

AT CAMPO SAN ZACCARIA, they'd made what preparations they could. The zooming software, it was calculated, would allow their technicians to see an extra ribbon of screen around the webcast equivalent, after three minutes of broadcast, to about one twentieth of the total picture.

There were few who thought it would be enough, but they had equipment set up anyway that would allow them to toggle between the two images at a moment's notice.

The webcast was late starting, prompting a flurry of speculation that it wouldn't happen after all. Then the familiar crude titles appeared.

AS WE UNDERSTAND IT, WHEN THE WATERBOARD IS USED, THE SUBJECT'S BODY RESPONDS AS IF THE SUBJECT WERE DROWNING. YOU HAVE INFORMED US THAT THIS PROCEDURE DOES NOT INFLICT ACTUAL PHYSICAL HARM. THUS, ALTHOUGH THE SUBJECT MAY EXPERIENCE THE FEAR OR PANIC ASSOCIATED WITH THE FEELING OF DROWNING, THE WATERBOARD DOES NOT INFLICT PHYSICAL PAIN.

THE WATERBOARD, WHICH INFLICTS NO PAIN OR ACTUAL HARM WHATSOEVER, DOES NOT IN OUR VIEW INFLICT "SEVERE PAIN OR SUFFERING". IT IS A CONTROLLED ACUTE EPISODE,

LACKING THE CONNOTATION OF A PROTRACTED PERIOD OF TIME GENERALLY GIVEN TO "SUFFERING".

As if the extraordinary assertion contained in these words were not enough – that if waterboarding didn't cause "physical harm", it didn't cause pain; that if it didn't last long, it didn't inflict "suffering" – there then came a second series of titles.

BASED ON YOUR RESEARCH INTO THE USE OF THESE METHODS... YOU DO NOT ANTICIPATE THAT ANY PROLONGED MENTAL HARM WOULD RESULT FROM THE USE OF THE WATER-BOARD. INDEED, YOU HAVE ADVISED US THAT THE RELIEF IS ALMOST IMMEDIATE WHEN THE CLOTH IS REMOVED FROM THE NOSE AND MOUTH.

IN THE ABSENCE OF PROLONGED MENTAL HARM, NO SEVERE MENTAL PAIN OR SUFFERING CAN BE SAID TO HAVE BEEN INFLICTED EITHER.

The image cut to Mia in her orange jumpsuit, strapped to the gurney. Her head was at the lower end, and her feet and wrists were securely fastened.

Later, commentators were to remark on the intensity with which she sought out and held the gaze of the man in the Harlequin mask, turning her head to follow him as he approached.

Some were also to remark on the apparent tenderness with which he placed a towel under her head to cushion it, then wrapped another tightly around her face so that she was forced to breathe through the coarse material. The shape of her open nose and mouth was clearly defined under the cloth.

What was not disputed was that Mia was visibly shaking, and that she clenched her fists in an effort to control her tremors. The kidnapper's arms, too, appeared to be shaking as he lifted the watering can – although that might just have been because it was heavy.

The water flowed in a clear, thin stream over the towel. For a long moment nothing happened. Then, with a sudden gasp, Mia released the breath she'd been holding and inhaled the water. She choked violently, her limbs convulsing, her head shaking from side to side in a frantic attempt to deny the liquid – still barely more than a trickle – access to her mouth.

"Jesus," Kat found herself muttering. "This is unbearable."

But she kept watching, as did every other Carabinieri officer in the room. On and on Harlequin poured. There must have been some kind of stopwatch or monitor just out of shot, because he glanced across at it, as if to make sure he wasn't going a second beyond the agreed time.

After exactly twenty seconds, he stopped. The watchers knew, from the pundits, what to expect next. Although the head of the CIA's Counterterrorism Center had in 2006 personally ordered the destruction of ninety-two videotapes of waterboarding sessions, enough witnesses and victims had described the process for it to have become general knowledge. When subjected to waterboarding, the human body generally responded in the same way: first came vomiting, followed by screaming, followed by sobbing, followed by yet more screaming as the towel was reapplied.

But Mia wasn't vomiting. She was lying quite still, unconscious.

There was a moment of shock in the operations room as people realised what had happened. Harlequin realised it too. Reaching down, he placed his hands on Mia's diaphragm and pumped desperately. Nothing happened.

He put his face to hers. But there was no way he could administer the kiss of life through the mask.

He went around to the high end of the bench, where her feet were, and tried to push the bench out of shot. It was heavy, and the wooden legs caught on the concrete floor. He seemed to be in a state of panic as he strained to get it to move.

Her feet remained just in shot as he disappeared towards her head.

"Go to the unzoomed image," Kat said. The technician punched a button, and the image changed – from the one the world was watching, to the raw image from the source.

There, in the tiny strip of picture Harlequin didn't know existed, they saw him rip off his mask to resuscitate Mia. They saw how he breathed for her; how he pumped her chest frantically; saw, too, how when she finally choked and vomited her way back to life, he cradled her head in his hands, weeping with relief, saying her name over and over again.

And they saw him reach to her forehead and make the sign of the cross over it with his thumbs – an unmistakeable gesture of benediction.

"My God," Saito breathed. "He's a *priest*."

With exquisite timing, that was when Carnivia went dark, the image replaced abruptly by a message informing them that the page they were trying to reach was currently unavailable due to heavy traffic, and that they should please try again later.

They replayed the film on a loop. The man's face was in profile, and they never got a clear look at him. It was, Malli told them, far too little to use image-matching software on either.

"Even so, get the best still you can and isolate it. We'll

circulate it round the other agencies," Saito said. He looked around. "Who's got the database of protestors?"

"I have." Kat had already opened the full list of names from the anti-Dal Molin petitions. Within moments, she'd generated a list of everyone who'd given their title as "Don", "Monsignor" or "Father".

Out of one hundred and fifty thousand names, there were seventy that matched.

"Organise into teams," Saito ordered. "Five officers to a team. Start working the list."

"Sir," Kat said. "Is it possible that he *was* a priest, but isn't any more? It just seems unlikely that a working priest could take the time off to do something like this."

"Possible, yes. Even likely. But in that case, how would we find him?"

Despite the lateness of the hour, she tried the Vatican. To her amazement, the phone was answered. She explained what she wanted, and was put through to someone in the Information Service who told her that, while they did indeed have a database of current priests, they didn't keep a specific record of those who had left the Church.

She thought. "Do you have an older database from, say, ten years ago?"

"I'll have a look," the voice on the other end said. He came back after a minute. "It seems we do."

"And a list of priests who have passed away? Obituaries, for example?"

"Certainly."

"Send me all three lists. I'll collate them myself."

As the operations room emptied team by team, she stayed on, cross-referencing the data. By 3 a.m. she had the names of almost a thousand Italian priests who had left the Church in the last ten years.

The database the Vatican had sent contained a bonus she hadn't thought to ask for: each name had a date of birth next to it. Harlequin looked fairly young – probably in his thirties or early forties: to be on the safe side, she only excluded those over fifty.

Then she ran the remaining names against the anti-Dal Molin petition. Just six names matched.

Algisa Belluci
Edilio Barese
Frediano Caliari
Livio Lorenso
Enrico Ferri
Learco Toscano

She dialled Holly's number, knowing that she'd wake her up.

"Kat?" Holly answered on the second ring. "What is it?"

"We've got a list of seventy-six names that are of interest to us, of whom six to my mind are particularly high value. Can you run them against *your* lists, to see if any of them might have a grudge against America?"

"Sure. I'll do it myself." Kat could hear Holly pulling on clothes as she spoke.

"Thanks. I'll email them across."

"Kat?"

"Yes?"

"Do you think this might be it?" Holly said quietly.

"I'm not sure. But it's the best lead yet."

*

Holly went to her work computer and brought up SIPRNet. Then she took the names Kat had emailed and entered them one by one. As she was also connected to the regular internet, she could see immediately that many were coming up with "Don" or "Padre" attached to them.

But the two that gave her hits on SIPRNet had no such honorifics. She called Kat back.

"It looks like we had dealings with two of your names, Frediano Caliari and Livio Lorenso. Caliari was involved in protests against drone strikes in the Yemen, two years ago. And Lorenso is on a list of people who have downloaded films from a piracy website."

Kat thought. "Is it possible to find out any more about them?"

"We can run them through PRISM. That'll give you a shed-load of data. But there are legal ramifications – not at our end, but you'll probably need to get an anti-terrorism warrant. And I'll need to inform Colonel Carver."

"That's fine," Kat said. "I'll get you the paperwork, if you can get me the information."

Holly must have requested the search even before receiving the warrant, because by 6 a.m. Kat had PRISM reports on both Lorenso and Caliari. Despite being headed "Topline", each ran to over fifty pages.

PRISM was simply data that travelled in and out of the US on its way to and from the USA's biggest technology firms – Apple, Google, Microsoft, Skype, Facebook and others. By siphoning off the data direct from the main cross-Atlantic fibre-optic cables and copying it into huge "data tanks" at its $2 billion Utah Data Center, the National Security Agency could quite legally eavesdrop on foreign nationals all around the world without any kind of warrant. The only legal difficulty came if the NSA shared that data with other governments, since it broke many local privacy laws. And although the data was generally analysed at the pattern level – picking up those who were doing searches for both "bomb-making" and "airlines", for example – it could also work the other way round: put in a name, address, and date of birth, or better still an email address, and PRISM's computers could "ingest", as the spooks put it, every detail about that person that could possibly be gleaned from the last few months' internet traffic.

Both Livio Lorenso and Frediano Caliari used Google, Facebook and Skype. Lorenso also used Apple. He had searched for information about erectile dysfunction and bought a treatment for it over the internet. He regularly visited a number of pornographic websites but, until six weeks previously, had also used dating agencies. As he wasn't computer-savvy enough to clear his cookies each time he used Google, Kat could see everything he'd searched for over the last six months – even which terms he'd mistyped. She could tell when he'd booked a flight and a hotel for two people but hadn't completed the transaction, and when he'd searched for advice on how to propose. And since he used Gmail, which scanned emails to and from its users for keywords that would generate "contextual" advertising, she could also see that he'd emailed recently about a car, a holiday, a loan, bankruptcy, sexual fulfilment, marriage, honeymoons and a restaurant with good reviews in the centre of Milan. On Facebook he'd added six friends in the last month; his status had changed from single to "in a relationship" twice, and he had "liked" about a hundred posts, links and videos, including the anti-Dal Molin petition.

More usefully still, he shopped at Esselunga, Italy's largest supermarket, and had a loyalty card, the data from which was stored on a Microsoft server in Texas. This allowed Kat to see, amongst other things, when he'd bought petrol. His fuel purchases had begun three months previously – roughly the time he'd been picking up ads for cheap auto loans and second-hand-car sites – and had been small and regular. His credit rating had recently gone down, owing to an increase in his loan repayments, and he had registered a new number plate to his address.

The clincher, though, was that Lorenso had an iPhone. He'd bought a number of apps that tracked his location, from one that alerted him whenever he was about to pass a speed camera, to a walking app that recorded how many calories he was burning. From the information that had flashed back and forth between his phone and Apple's Location Services, Kat could see that he'd travelled from Milan to Turin twice in the last fortnight, but no further. If she'd wanted to, she could also have accessed the photos stored on his Facebook timeline with the tag "Turin". She could even have checked out the book about relationships he'd recently bought on his e-reader, and seen what phrases in the text he'd underlined.

Clearly, since leaving the priesthood, Lorenso had been making up for lost time with the opposite sex. She very much doubted he was their man.

Caliari was another matter. His internet usage was sparse and functional. He visited religious sites, left-wing blogs, and bulletin boards about international affairs, particularly the anti-globalisation movement.

He cleared his Google cookies every time he used his computer, suggesting a basic understanding of the need for caution. The content of his emails had triggered ads for nothing more exciting than charities and privacy software. And although he had registered a Skype username and password, he seemed never to have used it. His most recent Facebook "like" was a protest against the opening of a McDonald's in Vicenza.

What was more, about three weeks previously he'd bought a new laptop computer, a USB video camera and a pay-as-you-go wireless broadband dongle from an online computer shop. His very last activity had been to search for shops near to him in Verona selling Carnevale masks. After that, his internet use abruptly stopped.

It was him. It had to be.

Had she had more time to reflect, she might have been uneasy at discovering just how much data was held about her countrymen by the US. She'd had a vague idea that when you ticked a privacy setting it meant no one could see your information, not even the government. But like most people, when she was presented with a four-page "Terms and Conditions" she simply clicked "Agree", trusting the global brand whose product she was using to keep her safe. And she'd always assumed that, if something was too invasive for the US government to do to its own citizens, they wouldn't do it to citizens of other countries either.

Clearly, that wasn't actually the case. She began to understand now why Daniele was so reluctant to open up Carnivia's servers.

Going to Saito, she explained what she'd learned about Caliari.

"Good. Take two officers and a search team and go to his home. If he's not there, break down the door. I'll fax you a search warrant."

DAY SIX

SIXTY-FIVE

IT WAS 7.30 a.m. by the time they smashed in the front door of Caliari's apartment in Verona. The place looked barely lived in, Kat thought as she strode from room to room. A mattress on the floor; crockery and pans still in boxes; a hi-fi system that hadn't even been wired up. The only things he'd unpacked properly were his books. Most, she noticed, were academic tomes on theology – particularly liberation theology – and ethics, but there were also some on anti-globalisation and modern culture: Naomi Klein's *No Logo*, Noam Chomsky's *Hegemony or Survival* and Jared Diamond's *Collapse: How Societies Choose to Fail or Survive*. All were in English, she noticed, suggesting that he was fluent in that language. A poster in the kitchen bore a quote by Mahatma Gandhi: "Earth provides enough to satisfy every man's need, but not every man's greed".

On the table were some printouts. She picked them up and leafed through them. They all appeared to be from the web. On the top one, a paragraph had been carefully underlined:

During World War II, US planners developed a strategy of global control, intended to displace the European imperial

*powers and go far beyond, but in new ways. They had
learned the effectiveness of airpower, and intended to
cover as much of the world as possible with military bases
that could be quickly expanded when necessary, and used
to guarantee control over resources, suppress indigenous
movements that threatened US domination, and install
and protect client regimes. Massive intervention in sub-
verting Italian democracy from the late 1940s is just one
of many examples, benign by comparison with others that
reached as far as near-genocidal slaughter.*

Noam Chomsky.

As the search team got to work, she collected the post from
the box outside and looked through it. There was a letter from
the Carabinieri, asking Caliari to get in touch – evidently, he'd
been on enough lists to get his name flagged up, but not so
many as to cause alarm when he hadn't responded. There was
a credit card bill, which showed no new transactions. But in
the recycling bin, the searchers found a receipt from a hardware shop for timber, rope and metal hooks, bought with cash.

And then they brought her something that made her blood
run cold. A receipt from the Co-op for twenty-four bottles of
nutrition drink and a carton of sanitary towels. He'd paid cash
for those, too.

They had their man.

Panicucci came in from talking to the neighbours. "No one's
seen him for weeks. Even before that, he generally kept himself
to himself. But he told the woman downstairs he was going
away on a spiritual retreat. He'd done that before occasionally,
so she wasn't surprised."

Kat went and spoke to the technician leading the search team. "Bring me anything that particularly relates to travelling around Italy. Maps, itineraries, camping sites… anything at all. We need to find an address."

"Will do."

She concentrated on finding his official documents. Everyone, she reasoned, no matter how disorganised, has a file or a folder somewhere that contains the really important stuff: financial papers, passport, birth certificate.

Eventually she found it – a fat cardboard file, unceremoniously stuffed into a carrier bag. In it were a number of out-of-date travel permits and visas relating to a period of employment by the Red Crescent in Yemen, and an even older letter from the diocese of Verona headed "Grant of Dispensation", accepting his resignation "with great reluctance" and alluding to the "difficulties you have been having with spiritual discipline". Then came some old Telecom Italia Mobile bills, all relating to the same account. A vaccination certificate. A guarantee card for a flat-screen television.

Frediano, where have you taken her?

Struck by a thought, she went back to the vaccination certificate. It dated back twenty years and bore the address of a hospital in Trentino-Alto Adige, the mountainous German-speaking area far to the north.

She got on the phone to Saito.

"I think he grew up in the Alto Adige," she told him. "Can you have someone search the residency records for anyone by that name? There may be a family house he's using."

"Hold on." She heard him giving some commands to another officer. Then, coming back on the line, he said, "Good work. Leave the search team to finish up there and get back to Venice."

*

As they drove down the *autostrada*, Panicucci looked across at her. "Do you think we're closing in?"

"It certainly feels like it. But those mountains are incredibly remote. Assuming that's where he's holed up, I'm guessing it'll take a while to pinpoint the exact location."

Panicucci said hesitantly, "What kind of dongle do you suppose he has?"

What do you mean?"

"I bought an internet dongle myself when I went on holiday, so that I didn't have to pay hotel rates for wi-fi. But even though it was pay-as-you-go, I still had to show ID when I bought it. I asked why – apparently it's a regulation, so the dongle could be linked to my TIM account. All these films he's been uploading... he *must* have needed to top up the data allowance, and probably more than once. If he has a mobile phone account, perhaps the dongle will be registered to it too."

"That's a good suggestion. Add it to the TIM request, will you?"

Back in the operations room, she noticed that people were now looking at her in a different way – no longer with a kind of sly, surreptitious disapproval, but with curiosity, as if reassessing her, and even the odd blatant flash of professional jealousy. But Saito himself was frustrated.

"There are over sixty Caliaris in Alto Adige – it's a common surname up there. And TIM are saying it'll take at least a day to get back to us about the dongle."

"A day!"

He nodded. "It's crazy."

It was extraordinary, she thought, that she'd managed to get hold of Caliari's Facebook traffic faster than his phone company could identify whether they had any records relating to his mobile broadband. She hesitated. "There might be a quicker way."

"Such as?"

"When we were first trying to trace Mia's phone, Second Lieutenant Boland got Daniele Barbo to look it up on TIM's system. He did it within half an hour."

Now it was Saito's turn to look appalled. "Dear God."

"We could do the same thing now," she suggested.

He looked torn. "There's no way I can authorise that, Captain."

"I understand, sir. I'll be back as soon as I find anything."

As she was leaving the operations room, she saw a new film flashing up on the screens. Evidently Carnivia had managed to get itself back online.

The footage showed Mia, apparently recovered, tied to a chair. The caption read:

CIA-FUNDED RESEARCH AT MCGILL UNIVERSITY SHOWED THAT SENSORY DEPRIVATION USING GLOVES, GOGGLES AND EARMUFFS COULD INDUCE HALLUCINATIONS WITHIN 24 HOURS AND COMPLETE BREAKDOWN AND DISINTEGRATION OF PERSONALITY WITHIN 48 HOURS.

ACCORDING TO THE USA, SENSORY DEPRIVATION IS NOT TORTURE.

AT 9 P.M. TONIGHT SHE WILL NOT BE TORTURED.

*

"Daniele," Kat said when she reached the prison. "This beautiful fucked-up mess just got a bit uglier and more fucked up."

She told him what she needed from him, and he nodded. "I can do that."

Opening the laptop she'd brought with her, he logged on to the TIM website. "This is how I did it before," he explained as he typed some code into the "Email address" and "Password" boxes. "I doubt they've got round to fixing the vulnerability yet."

Sure enough, within moments he was inside TIM's system. Then he frowned.

"What is it?"

"I can't access the account details." He typed some more code.

"It's blocked?"

"No," he said, puzzled. "There's someone else in here. Someone who opened the database before I did."

"Can't you open it too?"

He shook his head. "Not until they're gone." He waited, then typed the command again.

"That's better. And we're in luck. Your *sottotenente* was right – there's a pay-as-you-go dongle linked to his main account."

"Can we trace it?"

"He hasn't used it in the past twenty-four hours. But if he uses it again, we should be able to get the cell area, just as if it were a mobile phone."

By noon, using conventional methods, the Carabinieri had managed to eliminate only six Caliaris from their list. At this rate, Kat thought, it would take them weeks.

The problem was that the area was so mountainous, and the villages so scattered, that checking out even one address took several hours. The local units had put all their available manpower onto it, but it wasn't nearly enough.

"Wait," Kat said. "How are they choosing which addresses to check?"

"They're doing the quickest ones first – that is, the ones that aren't too remote, so that we can cross as many as possible off our list."

"We need to flip it round. If he's got an old family property he thinks is perfect for holding Mia, it's because it's unusually inaccessible. It may even be listed as derelict. We should start prioritising the places that are the hardest to get to."

They made the change. But by six, darkness was falling in the mountains, making the task of checking any more addresses almost impossible.

And then, finally, the investigators had the tiny sliver of luck that had so far eluded them.

Somewhere high in the Alto Adige, Frediano Caliari topped up his wireless broadband dongle, ahead of the data-heavy upload he was planning to make later that evening. Although he used a pay-as-you-go card, the SIM in the dongle checked in with the nearest cell phone mast to make sure it could find a connection before authorising the new capacity. The tiny packet of data was automatically linked to the account registered to the ID Caliari had showed when he made the original purchase.

Instantly, Daniele forwarded the information to Kat.

The phone mast was situated on top of a two-thousand-metre-high mountain and covered nearly thirty square kilometres around the village of Frisanco.

On the Carabinieri's list of properties registered in the name of Caliari there was just one in the area of Frisanco: a former farmhouse. It was listed as derelict, and was perched halfway up the mountain, well away from any other houses.

There was a moment's stunned silence as they realised what it meant.

"Listen, everyone," Saito said urgently. "This isn't the end, not by a long chalk. Now we have to work out how to get her out of there safely." He lifted the phone. "But first, I should update our partners."

He spoke for several minutes. But Kat saw how, almost from the start of the conversation, his expression was clouding. By the time he put the phone down his face was dark.

"The Americans are already in the air," he said heavily. "Officially, it's a joint operation. In practice, there are a few of our Special Forces with them purely for political cover. The USAF want to get Mia back themselves."

"How did they know?" Kat asked. "If they're already in the air, and we hadn't told them about Caliari?"

"It seems we're not the only ones carrying out surveillance," Saito said bitterly. "Clearly, they've been listening in on our investigation all along."

SIXTY-SIX

SHE DIDN'T KNOW what had happened. She could remember the pain – the panic of suffocation, and the searing agony as her lungs battled for air that wasn't there. She could even remember the sense of vertigo as unconsciousness rushed towards her. But of her resuscitation by Harlequin, she could remember nothing.

Only that when she eventually surfaced, there was a sharp pain in her chest. She later realised that he'd cracked a rib, restarting her heart.

She'd thought, after that, that this had to be the end. They'd nearly killed her, and by some miracle she'd survived. She'd sensed Harlequin's terror even after she came round. So now, surely, they must see sense and release her.

The Skype incoming-call sound had bubbled on the laptop, again and again. Each time, Harlequin had ignored it.

Eventually, from her cell, she'd heard a vehicle climbing up the mountain, the sound gradually getting louder as it tacked back and forth up the steep roads. She heard a door bang, then shouting.

"*L'ho quasi uccisa!*" That was Harlequin's voice.

Another, calmer voice had replied, "*Si, questo è ciò che accade.*"

I nearly killed her.

Yes, that's what happens.

Then Harlequin yelled what sounded like an ultimatum – a long stream of Italian, increasingly angry, culminating in him switching to English. "Fuck you. I'm quitting. Do what you like. But I'm getting out of here."

The reply was in English too. Because the speaker wasn't shouting, she had to strain to hear. But it sounded like, "Fine. Your choice."

Then she'd heard some strange noises, not loud, but what could have been a scuffle. Whatever it was, it was over in seconds. A third voice – a rasping Italian male that she guessed was Bauta – shouted, "*Che cos' hai fatto? Ma sei matto!*"

There was a pop, like a bottle being opened, then silence.

She heard nothing more for half an hour. Then she caught the sound of something heavy being dragged across the rough floor. It was followed by the rattle of the chain at her door.

The man who came in was wearing the Harlequin mask. But it wasn't Harlequin. He was whistling under his breath.

He gestured for her to stand up, then to unzip her overalls.

When he'd walked all round her he put his hand just below her breast. She flinched, then forced herself to relax. He was checking her ribs. She cried out when he came to the cracked one. He kneaded it for a few seconds, like a doctor, but rougher.

She cried out again, but he seemed not even to notice. Apparently satisfied, he pointed to the overalls again. Then he tied her to the chair and filmed her for a few minutes.

"Where are they?" she said. "What have you done to them? Where's Harlequin?"

Without hesitation he drove his fist into her solar plexus. She doubled up, winded.

As he left, he put his finger to his lips. *No talking.*

*

Through her cell window she heard him moving around outside. Then came banging, the sound of a hammer on wood.

Later still, he opened the door and gestured for her to precede him into the larger barn. In the middle of the room was a wooden box lined with blankets.

Silently, he handed her a pair of earmuffs, then a heavy felt hood. She felt her wrists being secured. Thick, soft mittens were pulled over her hands. She was pushed, firmly but without violence, into the box.

As she lay down, she sensed some kind of lid being placed over her. She could dimly hear nails being hammered in – she counted four.

Then there was silence. The deadest, most absolute silence she'd ever known.

She tried to concentrate on the pain in her solar plexus. It was at least something to hold onto, something that existed. But after a while even that seemed to ebb away from her.

Strange patterns danced in the darkness in front of her. She tried opening and closing her eyes, but it didn't make any difference to what she saw. After a while, she couldn't even tell whether her eyes *were* open or closed, and she started to panic.

I will not go mad, she told herself. *I will not.*

She began to hallucinate. She was on a fairground ride, watching the stalls below as she spun round and round. She was in a small boat at sea, feeling seasick. She was already dead, and this was her coffin. She was underwater, slowly sinking to the bottom. Distantly, she heard popping noises, like firecrackers, and couldn't tell if they were real or just another figment of her brain.

SIXTY-SEVEN

THEY'D BEEN PERMITTED to share the live feed from the Americans' drones and helmet cameras. In the crammed operations room, Kat watched along with the rest as the twelve-man Special Forces team flew low and fast in two helicopters up the quiet Alpine valleys.

When they were two kilometres away from the farmhouse, six men abseiled down from the first helicopter, like spiders dropping from their webs, and continued on foot.

After a brief reconnaissance, their leader gave a signal. Flash-bang grenades were hurled through the farmhouse windows, while men simultaneously entered from the roof, upper windows and doors. There was a brief, confused firefight, the bullets appearing like white blotches on the night-vision feeds. One by one, in the terse operational jargon of the Special Forces, it was confirmed that the hostiles were dead.

There had still been no word of Mia. In the operations room, it felt as if everyone was holding their breath.

Then a soldier approached a big wooden box and ripped the top off. Inside was a hooded, gloved figure. The hood was removed, and Mia's face appeared on the screens, dazed from the stun grenades but alive, her eyes silvery as a cat's in the green hue of the cameras.

Back in the operations room, an exultant cheer went up from dozens of throats at once. Kat hugged the nearest person, who happened to be Panicucci. Over his shoulder, she saw Aldo Piola sink his head into his hands with relief. General Saito punched the air, then got swept up in a big group of dancing officers, their arms around each other's shoulders like Cossacks doing the *prisyadka*. All around the room, men openly wiped away tears.

SIXTY-EIGHT

"GIOITE!" SCREAMED THE Italian headlines. "REJOICE!" echoed the media around the world.

Mia, it was announced in a statement from Camp Ederle, was safe and well but would not be giving any interviews, at least not until she'd undergone a lengthy period of medical and psychological assessment.

Sitting between Colonel Carver and General Saito at a hastily convened press conference, Major and Nicole Elston gave a brief but emotional statement of thanks to the Italian nation; to its press, its people, and above all its security services, whose rescue of their daughter had been a textbook example of international cooperation in the war against terror. They now requested a period of privacy in which to be reunited as a family.

Saito, in a short but statesmanlike speech, emphasised that in the modern world terrorism was no longer a national but an international threat, and that to combat it, global alliances were more necessary than ever. He thanked the many agencies, from CNAIPIC to the US Special Forces, whose help in retrieving Mia unharmed had been invaluable.

Colonel Carver's statement was even briefer, and was to the effect that America's enemies should learn from this that there was nowhere to hide.

It was quickly discovered, by journalists with close links to the Vatican, that Caliari had left the Church some time ago because of "problems with spiritual discipline"; it was discovered, too, that he had been in Yemen, working for the International Red Crescent at the time of a controversial missile strike in 2012 that killed a thirty-five-year-old aid worker called Hussein Saleh.

It was equally quickly clarified by the Yemeni government that the missile in question had been fired not by the American RQ-4 Global Hawk drone that troublemakers claimed to have seen circling the target, but by an unspecified plane of the Yemeni Air Force.

In his blog, Raffaele Fallici took the opportunity to point out that,

> *Sources close to the investigation are saying that it was the CIA, not the Carabinieri, which located Mia; not least through electronic intercepts and surveillance. Once again the Italian security services have been found to be one step behind their American counterparts. This new, online world requires a new, online police force – and we are fortunate that we appear to have the necessary expertise amongst our allies, since our own government has been too incompetent to develop it on its own account.*

> *I notice, too,*

he wrote further on in what was quite a lengthy piece,

> *that Mia is said to have suffered no lasting damage from her ordeal. In part, this is undoubtedly due to her own extraordinary courage and resilience. But it also gives the*

lie to all those bleeding hearts who claimed that the processes she was subjected to amounted to torture. For, as we now all know – being, thanks to the media, experts in every aspect of the CIA's position – "torture" means precisely to "cause to suffer lasting harm or trauma". I, for one, am not ashamed to admit it: I was wrong. America should not allow the bleatings of its liberals to deflect it from its mission, on which not only its own domestic safety but the safety of the whole free world now depends. We should not forget: America is not the enemy. Radical Islam is the enemy, and it is one against which we must stand undivided.

Within days, the encampment of reporters and anchormen at Dal Molin had delivered their final pieces to camera, many echoing similar sentiments, and the headlines were filled with a scandal involving the Spanish royal family instead.

"It's perfect," Piola said. "Absolutely perfect. An ex-priest, a little bit crazy, with a grudge against America. And a dropout who owed him everything." The second kidnapper had been identified as Tiziano Capon, a former drug addict whom Caliari had befriended whilst working at a centre for the homeless in Verona. "As far as the general public are concerned, the security services are heroes. The American Secretary of State has even praised the Carabinieri's professionalism, which is code for appreciating that we are somewhat sore at not having been allowed to lead the raid on the farmhouse. The desk clerk at the Stucky tells me they've taken more bookings in the past twelve hours than they did in the whole of the previous month. A poster girl is safe, and everyone is happy."

"You think it's a crock of shit too?" Kat said.

"Let's just say, the questions I had during the investigation still remain." He counted them off on his fingers. "Why such a sophisticated operation? Who was really behind it, and why? What about Dreadlock Guy and his tattooed girlfriend? And, most importantly of all, how did Caliari or Capon know about the formation of this radical Azione Dal Molin group they were apparently part of, if neither Ettore Mazzanti nor any of the other protestors told them about it?"

They were both silent for a moment, thinking.

"Of course, it's not just Saito who's a hero," he added. "The word in the canteen is that if you hadn't fought for the zoom idea, CNAIPIC would have killed it stone dead. There's even a certain amount of respect for the way you handled that thing with your home computer. I heard one officer saying it couldn't be you in the photograph, because that woman doesn't have any balls, and you've got the biggest pair in the division."

She allowed herself a smile at that.

"So all in all, things are almost back to normal," he said. He didn't add that "normal" meant he was still living in a hotel room, estranged from his wife; nor did he mention the pang of envy he'd felt when he'd seen Panicucci embracing her after the rescue. A handsome young man of her own age: why wouldn't she end up with someone like that eventually? "The point is, no one will thank us for stirring up more trouble."

"Let's think this through," she said. "Let's say the world is being told a big fat lie, and Mia's rescue is as bogus as everything else about this case. Where does that take us?"

"It means…" Piola took a breath. "It means this is even bigger than we thought. It means that they didn't just arrange the kidnap of a teenager, they arranged the murder of her kidnappers too. It means the people who arranged the rescue are also responsible for the kidnap. It means the Americans are in this up to their necks."

They stopped and thought.

"So just suppose the two of us were mad enough to take on the most powerful, technologically sophisticated army in the world, Capitano, how would we do it?" he asked.

She said, "We'd find a way to rattle them – to make them think we know more than we do. We'd come out fighting, and hope to provoke them into fighting back. It's only when they start to panic that they'll finally make a mistake."

WEEK TWO

SIXTY-NINE

TWO DAYS AFTER Mia Elston's release, Holly Boland took the grey Stefanel dress out of her closet for the second time in a month.

At the Piazzale Roma pontoon an ancient launch was waiting, all mahogany and brass, its sides bearing an elaborate "B". This, she knew, was the Barbo family boat, although the kid in the driving seat who'd been sent to pick her up looked more like one of Daniele's hacker friends than an old family retainer.

The launch sped down the Grand Canal, weaving through the *vaporetti* and gondolas, before turning into a quiet, dusk-filled *rio*, chugging more slowly past crumbling, bricked-up doorways. She loved these sleepy backwaters of Venice, the sense they gave that the city was almost derelict; although that was, she knew, an illusion – the Venetians were simply masters at knowing which repairs could be safely put off.

He was waiting for her on the wooden landing jetty. He hadn't dressed up, although the hoodie was a clean one and the sneakers looked new.

"Welcome," he said.

"Hi."

"The kitchen's just at the back." Then, anxiously, "You don't mind eating here?"

"Here's perfect," she assured him.

She followed him towards an old wooden door at the rear of the ground floor. Stepping through it, she found herself in a tiny, unexpected garden, each side lined with columns like a monk's cloister. It was so small she could have crossed it in three strides.

Off to the left was a kitchen. A vaulted brick roof made it feel like a cellar, but windows that gave onto the canal filled the air with the quiet murmur of lapping water.

If the room was old, however, the equipment in it was not. Ranged along the counter were several items of what looked like laboratory apparatus, while a whiteboard propped against the wall bore a complex equation.

"You do experiments in here?" she asked, curious.

"Not exactly."

He poured two glasses of *prosecco*, so fine and pale it looked almost like sparkling water. "Dinner will be in nineteen minutes."

"Nineteen?" she repeated, a little amused by his exactitude. "Are you sure?"

"Certain."

Daniele was looking better, she thought. The deep-set hollowness of his eyes, so pronounced when he'd first been released, was easing now, and his blinks and twitches, though still frequent, seemed more like punctuation to his thoughts than something which could overwhelm them at any moment.

He didn't do small talk, but they discussed Carnivia. He was buying more servers, he said, with the Conterno reward money. "But this time I'll hide the mirror sites better. One in Switzerland, in some quiet Zurich cellar. One in San Marino. Perhaps even one in Montenegro."

A timer behind them chimed, and he got to his feet.

"What are we eating?" she asked.

"Duck pasta. Smoked eel. And calves' liver." They were all classic dishes of the Veneto. "And a 1961 Oddero from my father's cellar." He placed a dusty bottle on the table, then checked one of the machines, which whirred faintly as he opened it.

"And the art?" She indicated the whiteboard. "What's that about?"

"That?" He looked at it and smiled. "That's very useful. The correct way to boil an egg."

The formula was intricate and, to her, quite incomprehensible.

$$t = 0.0152c^2 \ln\left[2 \times \frac{(T_{\text{water}} - T_{\text{egg}})}{(T_{\text{water}} - T_{\text{yolk}})} \right]$$

"Our cook had all sorts of superstitions and customs. She always pricked one end of the egg, for example, before she put it in the pan," he explained. "So I did some research to see if there was a more scientific way."

"And was there?"

"Yes. Obviously, the most important factor is the circumference of the egg." He pointed to the "c" in the formula. "Then the ambient temperature, "T". But it turned out that heating the water to a hundred degrees is too much. You need to cook it at a much lower temperature, but for longer."

"So the way to boil the perfect egg," she said, "is *not* to boil it?"

He nodded. "That's when I bought my first temperature bath." He indicated one of the pieces of equipment behind her. "I'm using it for our dinner tonight, in fact."

"Which course?"

"All of them." He got up and went to the counter. "The pasta should be ready. It's had four hours."

She couldn't see what he was doing until he put the food on the table. It wasn't beautiful – there was nothing elegant or chef-like about Daniele's presentation – but she could tell immediately that this was going to be like no dinner she had ever eaten. On her plate were four small tubes the thickness of fountain pens, anointed only with a small puddle of green olive oil.

She cut into one. Dark sauce gushed out, releasing an intense gamey aroma of duck.

"Neat," she said. She put a forkful to her lips. "My God! That's... that's..."

He nodded. "I know."

In some strange way she couldn't quite get her head around, the pasta was inside out – the rich, strong sauce encased by the pasta, instead of the other way round.

He poured them both some wine. "It needs this. The amino acids in the duck match the Maillard reactions in the wine."

"Daniele..." She struggled for words. "I'm just astonished to discover that you can cook."

"Well, I only cook twelve recipes. But those, I've hacked and rehacked until they're perfect."

If the pasta was unusual, it was nothing compared to the calves' liver. *Fegato alla Veneziana* was the signature dish of the city. Holly had eaten it many times, and although every housewife and restaurant cooked it a little differently, the basic formula never varied: onions, simmered over a low heat until they became translucent; liver, cut into strips and dusted with flour, then quickly fried in a mixture of oil and butter; the two tossed together with a splash of white wine vinegar.

Daniele's liver, however, had been cooked for twelve hours in the temperature bath, and was flavoured with star anise and lavender.

"Liver and lavender both contain the same sulphur molecule," he explained. "Put the two together, and they amplify each other."

"And the star anise?"

"Contains estragol, which brings out the natural caramel in the onions."

It was delicious – as meltingly tender as fillet, but with incomparably more flavour. Her favourite course, though, was dessert. When he told her it was a combination of salted chocolate and smoked eel, she almost refused to try it, but in fact it was heavenly: a dark roll of paper-thin chocolate, lightly salted, on top of a mousse whose pungent smokiness and sweetness she would never have identified as eel. It was served with a tiny glass of Torcolato, a Venetian sweet wine that was almost brown in colour, its age belied by explosive, fresh aromas of mango and raisin.

As the meal progressed, Holly noticed how Daniele's eyes made contact with hers more frequently. He asked about her father, and it felt quite natural to confide her guilt about not seeing much of him. Though he didn't recognise her any more, she told Daniele, his strokes having robbed his brain of whatever it was that made him a person, she felt bad for her mother and siblings that she wasn't closer to home.

"When I was a teenager," he said slowly, "I thought I hated my father. But recently, I've come to understand how similar we are. The obsessiveness with which he collected his paintings, for example. If I had a son, and I thought he'd simply sell Carnivia after my death, would I let him? Possibly not."

"Is that the kind of work you do with Father Uriel? Therapy about your father?"

"In part." He hesitated. "And some other exercises too."

"Like what?"

He looked at her. "I'll show you, if you want."

"OK," she said doubtfully.

He cleared the plates from the table as he explained how the exercise was structured. "You can't look away, though. No matter how intense it gets."

She leaned forward, as instructed, and fixed her eyes on his. To begin with she felt mildly amused – *Well, this is a weird way to end the evening.* But even before the first minute was up, she recognised that the amusement was simply a form of self-consciousness. Beyond it, there was only an extraordinary sense that she was somehow opening herself up to him, and he to her, the tiny muscles of their eyes carrying on a non-verbal conversation of their own, in a language she couldn't understand. More than once, whatever was being silently discussed made her want to drop her gaze, or blush, for reasons she couldn't quite fathom; sometimes, too, she found herself thinking, *Wherever did* that *come from?*

Or, *Hope he doesn't realise I just thought about* that.

When they began mirroring each other's movements, their eyes still locked together, she felt as if they were dancing in perfect synchronicity across a ballroom of the mind. Every tiny movement of her hand or neck, every stretch and tug of the cashmere dress against her skin, had the softness and intensity of a caress. The back of her neck flushed, and her earlobes burned.

Behind her a timer chimed. "Truth," he said softly.

"You first." She was suddenly shy.

He thought. "There are so many things I want to ask you.

But the only one that matters, I don't want to ask. In case the answer's no."

Lost in confusion, she didn't respond.

"Is there anything you want to ask *me*?" he added.

"When you do this with your surrogates... is it the same?"

He shook his head. "No. It's intense. But not like this."

"And do you..." She stopped, unsure how to word this. "Where does it end?"

"You want to know whether I have sex with them?"

"I guess I do, yes," she confessed.

"Father Uriel thinks it might be helpful. But I've not gone that far yet. Although there is one surrogate in particular I find very attractive."

"I can never tell when you're joking," she murmured.

"That's because I never do." After a moment's thought he added, "Why? Do you think I *should* go to bed with her?"

"No," she said. "I think you should probably go to bed with me instead."

SEVENTY

SERGIO SANTINI STRODE out of the airlock into the dim glow of the Archivio Segreto, where the friar, Tonatelli, was waiting for him. The two men talked as they went, Santini impatiently pulling on a pair of cotton gloves as they did so.

"Well? Do we have it all?" he demanded.

"It's impossible to say with any certainty," Tonatelli replied. He sounded weary: for the first time, his voice betrayed his years. Santini knew that he'd been sleeping down here of late, his whole life dedicated to the task he'd taken on. It was a curious feature of the Vatican: in a city-state where almost no one had a family, the temptation to work twenty-four hours a day was hard to resist. Men wore themselves out and died in the Curia's offices, their lives literally spent in the attempt to ensure the continuation of the papacy's influence. "But we've followed every obvious reference. I'd say we've got most of it."

He made it sound like a weed, Santini thought, or an infection: something that had to be scraped out so that not even the tiniest trace of it remained, lest it spring up again unfettered. But perhaps that was not so very far from the mark.

"I've put it in here," Tonatelli added, showing Santini into a meeting room. A security guard stood at the door, and the glass walls had been covered up for privacy.

Santini walked in, and stopped dead. The glass walls hadn't

been covered at all, he now saw. They were simply lined with row upon row of boxes: boxes that were stacked floor to ceiling, four deep.

"But... how much is there?" he asked, astonished.

Tonatelli pointed to each of the walls in turn. "From 1945 to 1947, four hundred and sixty-five reports. From 1948 to 1950, six hundred. From 1951 to 1953, two thousand and thirty-five. We stopped there, for the time being."

Santini reached into a box and pulled out a document at random:

It was discussed how in Emilia-Romagna a certain Quirico Buccho, a communist, has been secretly attending confession. It was debated how best to counter Signor Buccho's hypocrisy. In conclusion, the matter is being brought to your attention...

It was dated May 1948. He pulled out another:

A woman in Friuli, Camilla Conti, reports to the priest that her husband refuses to attend Mass, having fallen in with the communists...

And then this:

This man has openly said that he will vote communist in the forthcoming election. As he is the local schoolteacher, there is concern that he may be a person of influence in the community. It has been suggested that he is not a physically courageous man, and might be persuaded to change his mind...

Here was a similar report from Portugal, another from France, yet another from Spain; some of them were even written in Latin, in those days the universal language of the Catholic clergy. All reporting on suspected communist activity.

The local doctor, an atheist, has been heard to espouse radical ideas...

The sermon explaining why it is our parishioners' duty to vote for the Christian Democrats has been well received: however, if I might bring some additional points to Your Grace's attention...

"Well?" Tonatelli said quietly. "What do we do? Destroy it? Put it all back?"

Santini looked around him. "Neither, for the moment," he said at last. "There's someone I need to talk to."

He went to a small, discreet *palazzo* situated just a short walk from the Vatican, and gave his name to the receptionist. After a few minutes he was shown to a quiet corner, where a white-haired man was waiting for him.

"Thank you for agreeing to see me," he said.

"Not at all." The man, who was Santini's predecessor at the Vatican Information Service, had seemed neither surprised nor alarmed when Santini contacted him. "I imagine the job is keeping you busy?"

"Busier than I could ever have imagined," Santini confessed. "And rather more stressful. The burden of secrecy..."

The white-haired man nodded. "It gets easier, believe me."

"There is one matter in particular I wanted to ask your advice about. It concerns Archbishop Montini, as he then was. His Holiness Pope Paul VI."

The other man's expression gave nothing away. "Soon to be Saint Paul, I understand. He has already been declared a Servant of God and Venerable by his successors. Now there are reports of miracles being done in his name."

"What I'm wondering," Santini said quietly, "is whether as well as being a Servant of God, he was also a servant of the CIA."

"Ah." The other man was silent for a moment. "I always wondered who would be sitting at my old desk when that resurfaced."

"*Resurfaced?* So it was known about before?"

"Of course. You couldn't have run an operation like that without it being common knowledge at the time, at least within certain circles."

"And this operation… what was it, exactly?"

"Nothing less than all-out war against the communists," the white-haired man said simply. "A war in which, from the vantage point of history, victory now looks as if it were easy; almost, perhaps, inevitable. But believe me, it didn't appear that way at the time. It was a desperate struggle, and it called forth a great – some might even say, a desperate – strategy in response."

"The Christian Democrats."

"The Christian Democrats," the other man agreed. "Essentially, an alliance between the two greatest powers of the West: the Catholic Church and the USA."

"Some might say there was little that was either Christian or Democratic about it. Not when it meant priests spying on their own parishioners. Or those parishioners effectively being instructed which way to vote. Not when it meant the Mafia rigging elections, and the Curia passing information on dissenters to the security services. Who in turn clearly passed it back to the Mafia in some cases, for enforcement."

"Nevertheless," the other man said firmly, "it was successful. Before you rush to judgement, judge it on those grounds."

"And Montini? How did he come to authorise all this?"

"He was, as you say, connected to the CIA – what they call 'an asset'; probably the most important one they had. But when you say 'servant' – that, I think, is to misunderstand the relationship. The Vatican's interests and the CIA's coincided at that time. Don't forget, Montini had seen how Pope Pius was criticised for not having done enough against the Nazis; indeed, he criticised Pius himself on those grounds. I think he was determined not to make the same mistake in the Cold War. After all, what would have become of the Church, if it had been forced to give up the Vatican? These were terrible questions for any man to face."

"There's a South American saying," Santini said. "'*Cuando la CIA va a la iglesia, no va a orar.*' When the CIA goes to church, it doesn't go to pray."

"Indeed. I'm sure it was a difficult partnership to manage. As for how it started, that was well before my time. I do know that it dated back to the last days of the war. That was when, according to the files I saw, Montini was assigned an OSS codename: Vessel. It was a measure of how important he was to them that an entirely new OSS section, X-2, was set up to run him and analyse the information he produced."

Santini spread his arms. "Tell me. What should I do?"

The other man smiled. "I always think how apt it was that Our Lord made knowledge, not sin, the deadliest fruit in Paradise, and the only one which led to man's expulsion from that blessed place. What should you do? What we all must – accept that you have lost your innocence, and guard the secrets of the past so that others may not lose theirs."

"In other words, do nothing? That sounds like taking the easy way out."

"Believe me, when it comes to the effect on a man's soul," the white-haired man replied, "doing nothing can be the very hardest thing of all."

SEVENTY-ONE

FIRST THING IN the morning, Daniele produced two boiled eggs, cooked in the temperature bath for six hours. As he'd promised, they were perfect.

She wondered when he'd put them on: while she was sleeping, or before?

It was only one of many surprising things about that night; too many to process now. And what was even more surprising was that she found herself content, at this moment, not even to try.

Holly Boland, you have a wild side after all.

Amongst many other things, they talked about Mia.

"Everything makes sense," she told him. "Every question has an answer. And yet, somehow, it still doesn't add up."

"Mia's your egg," he said.

"In what way?"

"Like when I found the formula for the perfect boiled egg, and discovered it wasn't quite perfect. So then I couldn't stop until it was."

She considered this. "I guess."

He finished his egg and, turning it upside down, put his spoon through the bottom of the shell.

"Why do you do that?" she asked.

"If you don't break the shell, the Devil can stay trapped in there. Our cook taught me that."

She looked at him curiously. "Are you *sure* you never make jokes?"

"Certain."

"To get back to Mia... What's still puzzling me is why it was her who was singled out. Although I've looked and looked, I can't find any reason why that should be the case."

He thought. "Maybe there's another way in which this is like my egg. You know how the solution turned out not to be boiling it at all? Maybe you need to turn this on its head."

"But looking at this the other way round doesn't really get us anywhere." She stared at him. An idea had just floated into her mind. "Unless..."

"Yes?"

"Unless it wasn't her they were torturing," she said slowly, the enormity of what she was saying hitting her with each syllable. "Unless it was *him*."

They got the biggest whiteboard he had.

"You're sure you don't mind?" she asked anxiously.

He shook his head. "That's the Riemann Hypothesis. It's been around since 1859. I'm not going to solve it this afternoon."

She wiped the board clean of the formula he'd drawn on it, then drew two stick figures, one male and one female, together with their names, *Mia Elston, Major Elston*, and drew an arrow from daughter to father.

"Vicarious torture has been used for thousands of years, particularly on those who are so physically and mentally tough they'd resist all normal methods. But by the same token, those people have a strong image of themselves as protectors of their loved ones. As the officer commanding an RSTA troop, Elston would have known all too well what Mia was going through – he would have undergone something similar himself, as part of SERE Level C. And Mia's the apple of his eye. He hated being told she was at Club Libero, for example."

"Which, perhaps, was precisely why they chose it."

Nodding, she wrote, *Club Libero*, illustrated with two more stick figures. And then, because she was Holly Boland, the girl with the newly discovered wild side, she drew another stick figure having sex with them. Underneath she wrote, *Drugs? Abduction*. She drew a second arrow from that group to Mia's father.

"Elston hates drugs – Specialist Toomer told us that." She drew another figure. "Elston reports to Colonel Carver. Carver had the reports from Mazzanti, the Azione Dal Molin double agent, delivered direct to him." She wrote *Carver, ADM*, and another arrow.

One by one she went through them all – *Marco Conterno, the Order of Melchizedek, Carnivia* – mapping the connections. "And Joe Nicholls," she added. "A soldier Elston helped get clean from drugs. Who he went to visit recently, just to remind himself what it was all about. Elston denied there was any connection to the kidnapping. But what if there was, and he just didn't want me to know about it?"

She wrote, *Joe Nicholls/Drugs*.

"Then there was something called Exodus. A classified rendition programme in Afghanistan. Elston seems to have only been tangentially involved, however."

She added *Exodus*, drew a final line, and stood back.

It was meaningless. All the connections led to and from Major Elston, but some vital bit was missing.

"When people talk about Riemann," Daniele said, "they

sometimes talk about 'the golden key'. It's the part you have to hypothesise, the missing piece that makes sense of what you do have." He pointed to an area of empty board between *Carver* and *Elston*. "What would make sense of this?"

She shook her head, frustrated. "That's what I still can't figure out."

SEVENTY-TWO

"YOU WANT TO do what?" Saito said incredulously.

"To investigate the killings of Frediano Caliari and Tiziano Capon," Piola said calmly. "As part of a linked investigation which also encompasses the deaths of Ester Iadanza, Cristian Trevisano and Max Ghimenti."

Saito passed a hand across his face. "This is madness. Just when everything was... was..."

"Was all neatly wrapped up, and everyone was happy," Piola agreed. He pointed to the small cross in Saito's lapel, a crucifix whose stubby downbeam turned into a sword. "Congratulations, General. I see that you have been elected to the ranks of the Worthy Brethren. I'm sure you'll be a great asset to them."

Saito shot Piola and Kat a suspicious look. "This investigation. What would it entail?"

"We'll need to interview all the men involved in Mia's rescue. And their commanding officer, Colonel Carver. Oh, and many of the politicians who have supported the American bases over the last sixty years." Piola paused. "If we're right, there's been a large-scale and continuing conspiracy to deprive the Italian people of their right to make a democratic decision about the American military presence here. We want to find out why."

"Dear God." Saito seemed almost to have lost the power of speech. "Dear God," he repeated.

He insisted on accompanying them to the meeting with the prosecutor. By a stroke of good fortune, the magistrate they were assigned was Flavio Li Fonti, a protégé of the legendary Felice Casson, the Venetian magistrate who in 1989, while investigating the deaths of three *carabinieri* in a bombing, unearthed Operation Gladio, NATO's clandestine network of right-wing Italian guerrillas. Li Fonti's own speciality was Mafia prosecutions, as a result of which he still had an armed guard accompanying him wherever he went. While he was certainly no pushover, he was a far cry from some of the craven, politically motivated prosecutors Kat and Piola had worked with in the past.

He heard them out, occasionally making a note on a legal pad in front of him. Piola made his case in careful, measured language, but Li Fonti wasn't fooled.

"So you want to rattle their cages," he said when Piola had finished. "In the hope that some useful evidence may get dislodged."

"We want to spread the investigative net quite wide, certainly," Piola said cautiously.

"It's the wrong approach," Li Fonti said. "The answer's no."

Kat felt disappointed. She'd hoped for more from this dashing, energetic man with sad eyes.

"It's the wrong approach because, if you're correct, you'll both get killed long before you achieve anything," Li Fonti added. "Stop trying to be heroes, and start trying to be effective. Dig into the evidence that already exists, and look for discrepancies. Identify the weak links, the people who have nothing to lose by talking to you, or who are sick of lying, or who might want to swap a confession for immunity. But most of all, find me some *proof*, however small or insignificant. Then we'll use it to kick up a shitstorm. But not the other way round." He looked at his pad. "Begin with the skeleton, Colonel, since your suspect there, Major Garland, does at least have the advantage of being dead. And speak to your politician, this Sandro La Sala. After all, it's possible there's a perfectly innocent explanation for Signor Ghimenti's death." He looked at Kat. "And you, Captain, should focus your efforts on examining Mia Elston's rescue. But don't go straight to Colonel Carver. Trawl through the technical stuff. I assume the farmhouse has been searched?"

"There's a forensic team still on site."

"Good. Find me some discrepancies, Captain. Something I can *use*."

Back at Campo San Zaccaria, Kat put in a request for copies of all the technical reports from the search teams at Frisanco. Then she set to work tracking down La Sala. She checked the register of deaths first, since if he'd been a partisan during the war he must be at least ninety by now, but there was no record of a death, and no obituary online. It seemed he must still be alive.

From the electoral records she found an address and phone number in Lapio, in the hills south of Vicenza. When a woman answered the phone, Kat asked if she could speak to Signor La Sala.

"He doesn't come to the phone," the woman said. "I can give him a message."

"Are you his wife?" Kat enquired.

"No."

"His housekeeper then? I'm with the Carabinieri—"

There was a click, and the line went dead.

They drove out to see him anyway. Kat had forgotten how lovely these hills were, a green swathe that interrupted the flat Veneto plain like the spine of a scaly dragon. They'd travelled only an hour or so from Venice, but they could have been in a different country: a place of rolling vineyards and tiny, pocket-handkerchief-sized fields, where even the farm machinery seemed to date back to a time before the war.

Lapio was a small village overlooking the Lago di Fimon, a bucolic stretch of water where a few fishing boats drifted sleepily. There was nothing rustic about La Sala's residence, however; an aristocratic villa surrounded by vines and olive groves.

"Not bad for a former communist," Piola murmured as they turned up the long drive. But Kat noticed how the olive groves on either side had a neglected air, as if their owner had lost interest in tending them.

The doorbell was answered by a nun in a grey habit. "Can I help you?" she asked.

"We'd like to speak to Signor La Sala," Piola said, showing his ID.

"I doubt he can talk to you. He's not been well for some time."

She led them into a beautiful drawing room that was clearly little used for its original purpose now. Medical equipment and hospital linen were stacked around the walls. A handbell rang in an adjacent room, and a thin voice called, "Is someone there, Maria?"

"It's the Carabinieri," she called. "I've told them you're not well."

"Bring them in."

They followed her into what must have once been the dining room. A bed, the sort that could be electronically raised or lowered at each end, had been set up by the window, overlooking the lake. In it lay a frail-looking old man.

Piola introduced himself and Kat, and explained that they wanted to talk about an incident that had happened during the war.

"The war? I can remember the war," La Sala said weakly. "It's the last few years I have a problem recalling."

"It's about a man known as Max Ghimenti," Piola said, sitting down in a chair by the bed. "You see, we found his body, or the remains of it, in a makeshift grave near what was once the old Dal Molin runway."

"Max Ghimenti." The old man's liver-spotted eyelids fluttered. "Wasn't he captured by the Germans?"

It was a rhetorical question, but Piola answered firmly. "No, he wasn't. And I understand that you were with him when he died."

Another pause. "I don't... recall."

"Mr La Sala," Piola said, more gently. "It's quite clear to me that there's no prospect whatsoever of you standing trial for any crimes that you may have witnessed, or been an accomplice to, or committed. But it would help us to understand the circumstances of Max Ghimenti's death if you could explain exactly what happened. Whatever it was, I don't believe it was something you would forget."

A small sigh escaped La Sala's lips, as if he was too weary to dissemble any longer.

"We know it involved the Americans," Piola continued. "Major Garland of OSS, for example?"

The silence went on so long that Kat wondered if La Sala

was asleep. Then, his eyes still closed, he said, "There was a plot."

Piola leaned forward. "Yes? Whose plan?"

"Our comrades in Yugoslavia. A group of them came to see us. Bringing orders from Tito himself, and approved by the Party. To claim the Veneto for the workers when the Germans withdrew."

"You make it sound very simple," Piola said. "Presumably there would have been resistance?"

The old man's head bobbed on his pillow. "The Badoglini – the monarchists – would have tried to stop it. But we communists outnumbered them. And we were popular. It was just a matter of speed and surprise. Town halls and police stations would have been occupied, strategic roads and bridges held. The red flag would have been flying over Venice before anyone knew what was going on."

"Who stopped it?"

La Sala gave a tiny shake of his head. "It was betrayed. All the leaders were killed, apart from myself. And the Americans made sure that after that, we were never entrusted with any more heavy arms or mortars."

"Why did the Americans spare you?" Piola said. "I understand why they eliminated Ghimenti and the others. But why not you as well?"

Again La Sala shook his head. "You don't understand. It wasn't the Americans who stopped the plot. It was me. I was the one who betrayed it."

"You!"

La Sala sighed. "The Germans were one thing. Even the Blackshirts – I could kill them, because they'd shamed our country. But I couldn't have fought my fellow partisans – the monarchists and the Catholics. When I heard those Yugoslavs discussing their plan, and Max and the others agreeing, I knew I had to do something."

He fell silent for what seemed like an age, then roused himself again.

"There was a church where we used to sleep. I did it there. One bullet in the head for each of them. Max woke up, but I'd taken the precaution of emptying his rifle."

"Then what? What did you do with the bodies?"

"I asked Major Garland to take care of them. We were on our way to meet him anyway. He got them away from there, and I went back to my group with the story about Ghimenti being ambushed."

"Thank you," Piola said quietly. "I'm very grateful to you for clearing this up."

La Sala nodded. "I don't have long left. It's a relief to get this off my chest."

"Well, in the circumstances, we won't need a formal statement," Piola said. "If you'd just sign my captain's verbatim notes, we needn't trouble you any further."

He gestured at Kat, who brought over her notebook. She had to hold it up in front of the old man's face, then guide his hand to the right spot. The signature was shaky, but still just legible.

Piola was quiet as they got back into the car. Kat glanced across at him. "So you were right," she said. "All except the detail of who actually shot Ghimenti. But effectively, he was the first victim of the Cold War, just as you said."

"I may have been right about some things," Piola said. "But La Sala was lying to us, all the same."

"Why do you say that?"

"When Dr Hapadi examined Ghimenti's skeleton, he found a bullet in the right shoulder. It had gone right through

Ghimenti's head, from a point just above the left ear. The gunman would have been standing just behind Ghimenti, who was forced down onto his knees." He sighed. "In other words, it was a left-handed gunman. And La Sala signed that confession with his right hand."

"What makes a ninety-year-old man give a false confession on his deathbed?" she said, puzzled.

"Someone very determined to take the truth with them to the grave."

"But why—" she said, and stopped dead. "Those nuns."

He nodded. "A man who believes that he'll get his just reward in heaven. A man who thinks he's protecting his Church."

Back at headquarters, the forensic reports had come through – page upon page of diagrams and photographs from Caliari's farmhouse. Kat went through it, cross-checking it against the feed they'd watched from the SWAT team's helmet cams. It was heavy going. The forensic units never knew when a conclusion might be challenged in the courts, and therefore aimed to make their reports as scientifically detailed as possible.

"Ah, Capitano Tapo. May I have a word?"

She looked up. It was Colonel Lettiere. Behind him was his sidekick, Endrizzi, holding a stack of files marked with Post-it notes.

"Another victim, I take it?" she said.

"Not exactly." Lettiere smirked. "General Saito has asked me to go through my notes on your case one more time. On reflection, we may not have been quite as diligent as we should have been in protecting young officers like yourself from Colonel Piola's advances."

"Forget it," she said. "I'm withdrawing my complaint."

"Really?" Lettiere affected to look shocked. "That is of course your prerogative. But it will make little difference to my investigation, which has now broadened to include Colonel Piola's affairs with other subordinates." He gestured to Endrizzi, who opened a file and handed it to him. "The affairs you yourself told us about, if you recall, the discovery of which prompted you to consider breaking off your own relationship with him. It seems he is something of a serial offender in that regard. And the Carabinieri takes very seriously indeed the need to provide a safe and harassment-free working environment for female officers." He walked off, barely suppressing his smirk.

Prick. She could see exactly what Saito was doing. The moment Piola's investigation into the kidnap threatened to become an embarrassment, he'd use Lettiere's report to have him suspended, and probably Kat as well, leaving Li Fonti with nothing to base a case on.

She turned back to the papers from the farmhouse search, flicking through until she found the autopsy reports. Neither Caliari nor Capon had any tattoos. In the margin she wrote, *Tattooed Girl? Dreadlock Guy? Where are they?*

Then, buried deep in the document, she found something else that had her reaching for her pen. Caliari's location had been identified when he topped up his wireless broadband dongle. The report noted that he'd added a gigabyte of extra data on that occasion. The total amount of unused data on the dongle when it was analysed was just under 5GB – the maximum possible.

Which meant, she thought, that the curious thing about Caliari's fateful top-up was that it hadn't even been necessary.

She thought back to Daniele's puzzlement when he'd discovered someone besides himself hacking into Caliari's TIM account. When she'd heard that the Americans had been spying on the Carabinieri investigation, she'd assumed it must have been them, following the Italians' evidence trail.

But what if it was more than that? What if the trail itself had been laid by the Americans? Could someone have decided it was time Mia was rescued – and, equally, that it was time for the kidnappers to die?

She went back to the autopsies. Both men found at the farmhouse had died from gunshot wounds to the head, fired from a distance of a few metres. Guns were also found near both bodies, confirming statements by the rescuers that they'd heard gunfire as they entered the property. But, curiously, no member of the rescue team had claimed the kills as their own.

She went back to the helmet-cam feed and went through it frame by frame. It was odd, she thought: first bullets were flying everywhere, and then there was footage of Special Forces soldiers standing over dead bodies. But those bodies were never actually seen alive.

Could both victims have been shot just before the rescue, by another kidnapper? A kidnapper who fired some shots and then melted away, forewarned, just as the rescuers approached? In all the confusion, the rescuers would simply have assumed that the kidnappers were killed in the crossfire.

She went through the report one more time. There was nothing else that either confirmed or contradicted that theory. But at the very least, she had her discrepancies.

SEVENTY-THREE

HOLLY TRANSFERRED HER spidergram to a wall of her sitting room. Then she sat on the sofa opposite, staring at it.

Someone had tortured Major Elston by kidnapping his daughter. The agonies Mia had been subjected to might have been mild by comparison with what real detainees suffered, or even with a SERE exercise, but a man like Elston would have heard the screams from detention cells in Afghanistan and Iraq. He would know how much worse it could get. His imagination could be relied upon to do the rest.

A decorated war hero. A man of firm principles who was revered by his men. What had he been doing, or threatening to do, that generated such an extreme response?

There was, she realised, only one logical explanation.

She went straight to Gilroy.

"I should have realised sooner," she told him. "Elston's a *whistleblower*."

"A whistleblower?" he echoed, trying the thought for size.

"Or was threatening to be. Right at the beginning, when the first film came out, he said something like, 'How do I get in contact with them?' He meant, 'How can I tell the kidnappers that I'll do a deal?'"

"It's a good question, though. How did he?"

"Through me." She shook her head, annoyed at her own stupidity. "I was giving Colonel Carver regular updates on Elston's condition. And then I told Major Elston I'd been to see Joe Nicholls. I suspect that may have been what prompted the major to go direct to Carver, to tell him that he'd do whatever Carver wanted, if it meant getting Mia back. I even saw them together – I overheard Carver doing the deal." She paused. "I think whatever the major discovered, it has something to do with drugs."

"Well, he certainly won't risk speaking out now Mia's safe and sound. The best we can hope for is to find the evidence some other way."

Holly thought. "I need to speak to Mia."

She called Nicole Elston and asked if Mia would like to see some of the thousands of cards and gifts that had been flooding into Civilian Liaison since her rescue. Nicole said she'd just go and check. She sounded like any mother consulting with a busy teenage daughter over her schedule, Holly thought. It was hard to believe that this chatty, bright woman was the same person as the near-catatonic, medicated shell who'd endured the torment of her daughter's kidnap.

Nicole came back on. "Sure, she says to come round."

It was hard to believe, too, that the teenager Holly met at the Elston's house was the same girl she'd last seen on film suffering the kidnappers' abuses. Mia was wearing a woollen skiing beanie when they first sat down, but when she took it off Holly saw that the shaved hair was already growing out, and her voice was firm and strong. Thank heaven for the resilience of the young.

It was Mia who began talking about the kidnap. Holly let the teenager do it her own way, merely prompting with the occasional question.

Mostly she talked about Harlequin. It was clear that, while the teenager had deliberately forged a bond with him, the attachment had gone two ways.

"My friends say he was a monster," she said with a shy laugh, twisting the beanie in her hands. "But I know he wasn't all bad."

She needed permission to grieve for him, Holly realised. Aloud she said, "Caliari made his own choice, which was to deprive you of your liberty and mistreat you. But it's always too simplistic to divide people into monsters and heroes. Some of the very worst acts are done by principled guys. And maybe some of the heroes who rescued you are scumbags."

"I guess." Mia didn't sound convinced.

"Are you getting any counselling?" Holly asked.

She made a face. "My parents want me to see the school counsellor, Mr McConnell. 'Cos we already know each other."

Holly nodded. "I met him. The one who stares at your legs, right?"

Mia laughed. "Right."

"If it would help..." Holly hesitated. "A friend of mine sees a psychiatrist who's also a priest. My friend says he's very good. I could put the two of you in touch."

"Thanks. I'd like that."

"And your father?" Holly prompted gently. "How's he?"

"Dad's OK. He's not one for the big emotional homecoming, but we had a hug and a long talk, so..." She nodded. "He wants me to repledge – that whole purity thing? Not sure about that. But we'll work something out."

"Can I ask something, Mia?"

The teenager shrugged. "Sure."

"Was there a period recently when your father became especially protective towards you?"

Mia nodded. "Yep, for sure. It was right after his last tour. After he came back he kept sitting me down for little talks about security. How I mustn't give my name to anyone online. Be careful when you go out, be careful who your friends are, blah blah. He even wanted me to friend him on Facebook so he could see who *my* friends were." She rolled her eyes. "Like that wouldn't creep them out."

"Is that when you got yourself a Carnivia account?"

"Pretty much."

"Did the kidnappers ever mention Carnivia?"

"Only one of them spoke to me at all. The other two... one only spoke Italian, and the other just whistled."

"The other *two*?" Holly looked at her, perplexed. "From what I read, there were only two kidnappers."

Mia shook her head. "I know that's what they're saying, but I already told them – there was another one who borrowed Harlequin's mask sometimes. Everyone says I must have been mistaken, because they only found two bodies, but..." She shrugged.

"And you never saw this man's face? Nothing that could identify him?"

"Nope. I could only tell when it was him because he did this whistling thing under his breath."

"Like music? A song?"

"Yeah." She thought. "At the time I didn't recognise it. But the weirdest thing is, I heard it on the base radio yesterday. I'm pretty sure it was Springsteen. 'Born to Run'."

Back at her apartment, Holly checked the official reports. They were quite clear: two kidnappers had been shot dead after shots were fired at the rescuers from inside the house.

On the spidergram she'd transferred from Daniele's kitchen,

she added three stick figures underneath Mia. Two she put crosses through. Under the third she wrote: *Whistling Man. Springsteen?*

She wrote a quick email to Kat, telling her what Mia had said. Then she got into her car and headed north, towards the mountains.

SEVENTY-FOUR

THIS TIME SHE gave no warning she was coming. Joe Nicholls answered the door in gym clothes, a light sheen of perspiration on his face. She'd clearly caught him in the middle of a workout.

"Boland," he said, surprised. "What can I do for you?"

"I've got a few more questions."

"I thought Mia was safe and sound."

"She is." She gestured at the door. "Can I come in?"

As he led her past his ski gear into the kitchen, she paused to check out the hall area. Tucked behind the door was a large military backpack. She hefted it experimentally. It weighed at least eighty pounds.

He turned and saw her. "What are you doing?"

She flashed a quick smile. "Pack's pretty heavy."

He grunted. "Sure."

In the kitchen he sat down without offering her coffee.

"Well, you didn't lie to me, Joe," she said. "You just didn't tell me anything that really mattered."

"I don't know what you're talking about," he said neutrally.

"Something happened in Afghanistan. Something that involved you and the major. My guess is, you told him about some irregularity or cover-up you'd come across, he checked it out on his next tour, and then he came back here to tell you

you were right. Whatever it was, it has a bearing on what happened to his daughter."

For a long moment he looked at her, clearly weighing up whether to tell her or throw her out.

"I know about Exodus," she added. "I just don't know how it got Mia kidnapped."

"Major Elston's a hero," he said at last. "Bravest man I ever met."

"I know."

He sighed. "We were doing snatches for the intel guys – at least, that's what we were told. Go into insurgent territory, pick up a target, get the hell out. Routine stuff. We called it the Taliban Taxi. Except they weren't – Taliban, that is. Not always."

He looked at her to make sure she was following him. "Sometimes we took an interpreter along, to defuse any confrontations. Anyway, this one guy we picked up started jabbering away, so we asked the 'terp what he was saying. Turned out he was claiming he'd been snatched because he ran the opium collection point for a local businessman."

"Sounds fair enough," Holly said casually, although her ears had pricked up at the mention of drugs.

"Maybe, but the US Army didn't have a poppy destruction programme at that time. Our orders were to leave the farmers alone, so as not to push them into the arms of the Taliban. Anyway, the target started saying the real reason he'd been lifted was because he didn't work for Karim Sayyaf."

"Who was...?"

"The local big cheese. Warlord, tribal leader, and the guy whose help we'd enlisted to govern the local population."

"So the implication was that your man had really been accused because of some turf war between Afghans? That must happen quite frequently, I imagine?"

"Sure. We gave the targ a few taps with a rifle butt to encourage him to shut up, delivered him to base, and thought no more about it. But then it happened again – a target who claimed he'd been snatched only because he wasn't one of Karim Sayyaf's lot. It happened enough, in fact, that it was starting to look like a pattern."

"So you told the major?"

Nicholls shook his head. "Not at that stage. But I did check the files, to see what had happened to these guys after we'd picked them up. My assumption was, if they were really nothing to do with the Taliban, they'd be given a grilling, sit around in the cells for a while, then get kicked out. But when I looked, I found the first one we'd brought in had been marked 'Transferred to Project Exodus'. So I checked another, and that was the same. All of the opium guys were marked the same way."

"And what is Exodus, exactly?"

"At first I assumed it was some kind of anti-drugs pro-gramme. But in fact, opium production in that area increased five-fold in the time we were there. Mainly because it was all concentrated under one man – Karim Sayyaf. Besides, when I looked through the files, I realised Exodus wasn't just about our prisoners. Most of the detainees written up for it were medium-value targets who'd been interrogated, told us what they knew, and were now just hanging round the system, waiting for a decision on whether to charge them or send them home. Cell-blockers, we called them, 'cos they just took up space."

Holly frowned. This wasn't what she'd been expecting to hear. "And that's what you told the major?"

"Affirmative. He asked me to write it all down, said he'd look into it next time he was out there. I mean, picking up

Taliban is one thing, but if we were just helping some local poppy-grower corner the market, then the US Army was being made a fool of, right?"

"So you wrote your report. Then what happened?"

"I got shot." He looked at her, waiting for the inevitable next question.

"You think, because of what you wrote?"

"No evidence of that. No evidence of anything, in fact. Except that the bullet went in my right leg." He paused. "At the time, it was my left side that was facing the enemy."

"And your military career was finished. All because you asked a few questions about a local warlord who was getting too much help."

"Pretty much." He shook his head. "Man, I struggled when I came out. I don't have family of my own – Red Troop was it. Started taking drugs myself. The rest you already know. The major would have helped me anyway, he's that kind of guy. But I think he felt responsible."

"The pack by the door... that's some kind of escape kit, isn't it? In case the guys who shot you come back."

He nodded. "On skis I'm as fast as any man."

"Where would you go?"

He pointed a finger into the sky. "Up."

She suddenly realised. "That pack's a skyhook."

He looked impressed she'd worked it out. "And a parachute. Prevailing wind here would take me straight over the border into Switzerland. Unless they bring their passports, I should be all right."

She thought it over. "But what I don't get is why anyone would go to such lengths to silence you both. A blue on blue, then a kidnap... I can't believe Karim Sayyaf's the first warlord whose support we bought."

He shrugged. "Maybe I've got it all wrong, then. Maybe that bullet was a coincidence, and what happened in Afghan had nothing to do with Mia."

"No," she said. She was thinking about her spidergram, and the blank spaces that needed to be filled. "The operation to silence Major Elston was huge. So what they were protecting must have been huge too." A thought came to her. "How much weight can a skyhook carry?"

"About two hundred and fifty pounds, depending on conditions. Why?"

"Nothing." There was no point in endangering Joe Nicholls further by sharing the suspicion that had just flitted into her mind.

But he was already ahead of her. "You're thinking some kind of Iran–Contra thing?"

She nodded. "Maybe."

Back in her father's time, Iran–Contra was the revelation that rogue US intelligence officers under Colonel Oliver North were illegally selling weapons in Iran and using the money to buy aeroplanes in Nicaragua; aeroplanes which were used to ferry cocaine, which in turn was sold to raise more money for weapons. Was it possible that something similar could be happening here – that the US Army's support for a pet warlord had extended to getting involved with his drugs business? And if so, how was the money being used?

"But we're a long way from proving anything like that," she added. "Best not to theorise ahead of the evidence. Did you keep a copy of your report?"

He nodded. "It's buried outside, under the woodstack."

She glanced out of the window. Night had long since fallen.

"If you want to sleep on the couch, I'll get it in the morning," he added. "The ground will be frozen solid now."

"OK, thanks," she said. She'd have liked to have had the report in her hands straight away, but she couldn't very well ask him to take apart a woodstack and dig up frozen ground in the middle of the night. The morning would have to do.

She woke around four, too wired to get back to sleep. Bits of that spidergram kept swimming in front of her eyes. Carver. Elston. Project Exodus. Drugs... Mentally she added some new names. Karim Sayyaf. Skyhook...

Tantalisingly, more bits of the solution kept slipping into her mind, only to vanish and dissolve when she tried to analyse them. Elston had been silenced to prevent him from revealing the military's support for Karim Sayyaf, that much was clear. But it was also clear that Elston himself didn't have the whole picture. There was something more, there had to be.

Late though it was, she decided to phone Kat and talk it through.

When she dialled, it started to ring, then failed from lack of signal. They were in the mountains, after all. She wandered through into the room Joe used for his workouts, noting the gym equipment and weights ranged around the walls, holding her phone up to check the bars on the screen.

Joe's own phone was on a low shelf, plugged into a charger. She glanced at it, to see how many bars he was getting.

Several, but he was with a different provider. She was about to move on when she noticed something else.

Nicholls' phone was the sort that displayed unread messages. There was one now. It read simply:

Copy that.

"Copy that" – military shorthand for "message understood".

She picked it up and clicked on the previous message, the one sent by Joe. That, too, consisted of just two words:

She's here.

Oh, Joe Nicholls, you fucking fucker.

Loyalty to the army, she guessed, and fear of more reprisals, had trumped loyalty to Major Elston. But there was no time for thinking about that now. No time for anything. Swiftly she pulled on the rest of her clothes, then crossed to the window.

Below, in the main street, was a black van. Parked, no lights. *Watchers? Or a snatch squad?*

As she watched, a light flashed inside the van, a phone screen coming to life.

They wouldn't send a team all this way just to follow her, she realised. What was the betting Kat's Dreadlock Guy was at the wheel right now?

She ran to the hall. Ski boots, a jacket. Skis. She weighed a third less than Joe, and the ski boots didn't fit her feet too well, but at least they'd fit the skis.

"The prevailing wind's into Switzerland," he'd said. *"So long as they haven't brought their passports."*

As she opened the door, icy air blew in. Joe's voice called sleepily from his bedroom, asking what she was doing. "Having a cigarette," she called back. She doubted he'd believe her, but if it slowed him up by just a few seconds it would help.

The skyhook pack weighed almost as much as she did, and for a moment as she stamped into the skis she thought she'd topple over backwards. If she did, she knew she'd never get up again.

Crouched forwards to balance the pack's load, she strained at the poles to get herself moving.

"What the fuck?" It was Joe, silhouetted against the door. "Boland, what the fuck are you playing at?"

She was moving now, desperately flailing at the ground

with the poles, but it was agonisingly slow. If she could only get some momentum, the weight of the pack would become an asset rather than a drag.

She heard him curse as he ran barefoot after her into the snow. And then, with a final push of the poles, she was moving; enough to push off with her skis, left-right, gathering more speed as she crested the flat ground outside Joe's house and swept down into the woods beyond. There was a path that led away from the village – she had no idea where, but she had no choice: downhill, and quickly, was the only option.

She was a strong skier, thanks to her father's insistence that they had to make the most of their time in Italy by going every year. With her light frame, she'd been racing black runs since she was thirteen. But never with a weight like this on her back, and rarely at night. Luckily the snow bounced back what little light there was: she simply avoided any patches of ground that weren't white, and trusted to her knees to deal with the bits that were.

As she passed below the village, she heard the sound of a van being driven at speed. Going up to the house, she guessed. Then they'd come after her. She hoped Joe didn't have many spare skis.

After a few minutes she came to the edge of the woods. Below her a road zigzagged down into the valley. If she was really going to do this, it had to be here, before she left the shelter of the trees.

Taking off the skis, she dragged the skyhook pack off the path and examined the contents, using her phone as a light. The heaviest item was a large gas cylinder. Then there was a harness, with a coiled steel hawser attaching it to the balloon. The parachute was the ultra-light reserve type, weighing only a couple of pounds or so. She got into the harness, clipped the parachute to the front, and jerked open the ties around the hawser. She had no idea how the inflation mechanism worked, but trusted in the US Army's propensity to keep things idiot-proof.

The words of the cook who'd watched the training exercise with her flashed into her mind. *"They say it's a hell of a buzz. Mind you, they say that when they're safely back on the ground."*

There was still no sound of a pursuit, but she knew Nicholls, at least, would ski silently and fast. If she waited until she heard him, it would be too late.

She fitted the balloon to the canister and yanked the handle. Instantly the rubber bulged, the balloon's creases vanishing as the rushing gas filled it. Within seconds it was straining upright, held down only by the canister's weight. Then with a shriek it tore itself free and was soaring into the air. As the hawser unspooled she adopted the position she'd seen in the training exercise: braced for the jerk, arms folded tightly across her chest.

The tug winded her. And then she was flying, the woods dropping away, the balloon's urge to climb balanced now by her own dead weight. From the trees below, sparkles of light showed where someone was firing at her. No, not at her, she realised as the hissing bullets went high over her head – at the balloon, an even easier target. She was so high already that the fall would kill her.

They must have realised it too, because she heard a shout and the firing stopped.

So they don't want me dead. Or at least, not here. It was hardly reassuring.

She looked at the ground, now hundreds of feet below. How high should she allow herself to get? She knew reserve parachutes were designed to open at relatively low altitudes. But if she left it until the standard skydiving height of two thousand feet, she'd be too cold to open it at all. Already she could hardly breathe.

Too low, though, and the parachute would simply set her down a few yards from where she'd inflated the balloon.

Make a decision. In a crisis, the indecisive die first.

Swiftly followed, of course, by those who decide wrong.

She'd wait until a thousand.

Decision made, she mentally went through what she was going to have to do. Release the balloon, freefall, then deploy the parachute.

Then just steer myself over a border the precise location of which I don't even know.

Holly Boland, you don't make life easy for yourself, do you?

At one thousand feet she released the balloon. That was hard. It might be pulling her upwards to certain death, but every nerve and sinew of her body shrank from unhooking and committing herself to gravity's embrace.

She committed, and fell. This was the point at which her old instructor had told her to shout "Geronimo!". On this occasion she dispensed with the shout, and pulled on the parachute ripcord. The plastic billowed around her, flapping in her face, thin and flimsy as a supermarket carrier bag, and for one heart-stopping moment she thought it was going to tangle or tear. Then it blossomed, just as it was meant to, into an oblong canopy over her head, cupping the air and slowing her fall.

She pulled on the front straps, and found her body angling obediently to the north. In the distance she could see the lights of another village.

Reasoning that it was almost certainly over the border, it seemed as good as any place to aim for.

She drifted down as slowly as she could, tacking to and fro, milking the breeze for every yard of distance. When she landed she was within a few hundred yards of her objective, the col just a black shape behind her.

As she unclipped the parachute, headlights clicked on, bathing her in light.

It seemed Joe Nicholls' colleagues had brought their passports after all.

SEVENTY-FIVE

KAT WAS SHOWN into the Damasco Suite of the Hotel Metropole, where her host was waiting. "I'm sorry I'm late," she said, slipping into the chair he indicated.

Vivaldo Moretti waved her apology away. "I've just spent a most enjoyable twenty minutes anticipating every moment of our evening. So in a sense, the pleasure has been mine already."

"Anticipation will be all it is," she warned.

Vivaldo Moretti smiled. "Then I'm fortunate that what I was imagining was so very wonderful." He indicated the table in front of them. "I've taken the liberty of allowing the chef to choose the dishes. It is, apparently, 'tra-contemporary' cuisine. That is, each dish contains both traditional and modern elements."

Kat inspected her plate doubtfully. It contained a cocktail glass of strawberry puree, next to a square of polenta topped with a mound of bean mush, and finally a fried courgette flower which had been stuffed with some kind of minced fish.

"Thank you for agreeing to meet me," she said, picking up her fork. "I wanted to talk about a man I believe you may have worked with in the past. Sandro La Sala?"

"Indeed. I wouldn't say we knew each other well, but I certainly observed him at close quarters often enough. What do you want to know about him?"

"General impressions, first of all."

Moretti considered. "Politically speaking, a plodder. But an effective one. And, of course, he was fortunate in his friends. That generation of politicians – the ones who fought in the war – tended to sort out their differences quietly over dinner at Gino's, not in the pages of the newspapers."

"You say 'his friends' – I suppose you know he was a member of a so-called charitable organisation called the Order of Melchizedek?"

Moretti nodded. "As are many politicians."

"But not you?"

Moretti said thoughtfully, "You know, there's something very seductive about secrets. And even more beguiling is the notion that there's a kind of brotherhood, an elite of the initiated, where powerful men will share their secrets freely. To be told that you could be amongst them – to get 'the touch', as they call it – that's flattering; intoxicating, even. And of course, you're always aware, or are made aware, of the other benefits such an association could bring. Election expenses, office costs, the services of bright young researchers, not to mention favourable coverage in the media. The power such networks gather to themselves is real enough. And when it really matters, they make sure the inner circle closes ranks."

"And that's what the Order of Melchizedek is, in your opinion? The 'inner circle'?"

He shrugged. "Melchizedek is one version of it. P2 was another. The Vatican is part of it, the intelligence services are riddled with it, certain exclusive clubs and dining societies overlap with it, and even one or two rather specialised brothels. It has no name, exactly – call it 'influence', call it 'corruption', or simply be blunt and call it 'power', because it is all those things and more." He shook his head. "In answer to your previous question, no, I was never part of it."

"How did you avoid it?"

"By being so disreputable that they thought I would disgrace them. And by being so shameless that I had no secrets to be blackmailed over."

"Was La Sala blackmailed, do you think?"

"I don't believe so. It was always whispered of him that he was a great patriot – a war hero of some unspecified kind. Who knows? Perhaps, as a communist who'd crossed to the mainstream, his paymasters simply chose to promote him in order to encourage others who might be tempted to follow the same path. In that world, nothing is ever quite what it seems."

"When you say 'paymasters', you mean the CIA, don't you? Or at least, people within the Italian intelligence services doing their bidding?"

A waiter entered and replaced their empty plates with two more, equally elaborate creations – pigeon with a lychee puree and chocolate shavings for her, braised beef with vegetable mousses for him.

"I will say this," Moretti said when they were alone again. "I've noticed, over the course of a long and scandalous career, that no one prospers long in this country if they take a stand against the Americans. Oh, the odd grand gesture is acceptable, particularly if it makes a splash in the newspapers. But when it comes to matters of trade, or foreign policy, or security, it's generally safer and more profitable to follow the same position as them. Plenty of Italian companies have ridden a long way on their coat tails. Conterno, for example."

"Conterno? How?"

He lifted his hands. "Military contracts. Dozens, even hundreds over the years. It all started with rebuilding the factory in the caves at Longare, the one that made the aeroplane parts for the Nazis. Later came the bottling plants, the irrigation projects, and most recently, the reconstruction projects in Iraq and Afghanistan. La Sala had a seat on the Conterno board, by the way, so he raked it in that way too." He looked at her quizzically. "Are you going to tell me why you want to know all this?"

"I'm trying to work out what it is that links the death of a communist partisan in the last months of the war with the American military bases around Vicenza."

He nodded slowly.

"Do you have any suggestions?"

"Just this," he said. "Obviously, all the American bases in Italy are important to them, in different ways. You've got the submarine base at Sigonella, the naval base at Livorno, the airfield at Aviano, the munitions and equipment stored at Camp Darby, to name just four. But of all of them, during the Cold War, the garrison at Vicenza was strategically the most important."

"Why?"

"Because it was guarding their nuclear weapons," he said simply. "From the 1950s onwards, the Soviets had a massive advantage in conventional weapons, particularly tanks. The thinking was that when Italy was finally ripe for the taking, the Red Army's divisions would stream over the Eastern Alps, down into the flat plains of the Veneto." He gestured to the floor. "This is where NATO would have held them back. And since NATO had far fewer tanks, it would have been necessary to do it with tactical nuclear weapons. In the fifties and sixties, that meant the kind of munitions that had destroyed Hiroshima and Nagasaki – huge, potentially unstable bombs that had to be dropped from planes. And other, even bigger armaments called nuclear mines, that were designed to be placed under the Alpine passes."

"My God," she said. "Venice would have been a wasteland – another Bikini Atoll."

He nodded. "Indeed. But the reason the Americans needed Vicenza in particular is that, uniquely among the towns of northern Italy, it offered somewhere to store those weapons, out of range of any tactical air strikes by the Soviets."

"I don't understand. Where?"

"Underground," he said. "That munitions factory Conterno operated at Longare was one of the Nazi's largest so-called 'tunnel factories'. Even then, it occupied over thirty thousand square metres of caves and quarries, deep under the hills. After the war, Conterno enlarged it still further and remodelled it into an underground facility for nuclear storage. And not just nuclear storage; there were command centres down there, a hidden tank division, barracks for soldiers, water plants – an entire military garrison, quite self-contained, awaiting the day that nuclear war broke out."

"Is it still there?"

"I understood that it was decommissioned in the 1980s, after the end of the Cold War. But for decades before that 'Site Pluto', as it was called, was the jewel in the Americans' nuclear crown. They would have gone to any lengths to protect it."

She thought. "That's interesting. It may even be a link to Ghimenti's death – his body was found in a pile of rubble that Dr Iadanza said was spoil from a local quarry. But if Site Pluto was decommissioned, as you say, why would they still care about protecting it today? There must be dozens of old bunkers like that dotted around Europe."

"I don't know. But I've observed that in Italy, the secrets of the past have a way of becoming the secrets of the present." He pushed his plate aside. "A grappa, perhaps, Captain Kat? I don't know how you feel about this ridiculous food, but personally I'd rather eat no more of it. The Michelin inspectors may like all these mousses and foams and other forms of flavoured air, but one can't help feeling that's because it reminds them of what's inside their favourite car tyres."

She laughed. "Or is it just because they're French?"

"And what do the French know about food?" he agreed. "Or love, for that matter?" He looked at her fondly. "I like you, Captain Kat, and I should very much like to express my admiration by taking you to bed now. It would be, as it were, a pleasant and leisurely way to continue our conversation, and to delay the moment when the evening has to end."

Rather to her surprise, she found herself tempted, at least for a microsecond. The man was old, physically ugly and utterly preposterous, but being bathed in his charm was like sunshine on bare skin. A little reluctantly, she shook her head. "Not tonight, Vivaldo. I have this case to wrap up, and I wouldn't be relaxed enough to enjoy what you have in mind."

"Perhaps on another occasion, then."

"Perhaps," she said, and was rewarded by the delight in his smile.

SEVENTY-SIX

"TAKE THE HOOD off," a familiar voice said. "I want her to see me."

The heavy felt hood was pulled from Holly's head. Blinking in the bright light, it took her a moment to focus on his face, particularly as the ropes to which her wrists were shackled were fastened above and behind her, forcing her to arch her body backwards.

Carver.

He stepped forward so she could see him better. "Boland," he said, rolling the name around his tongue like wine. "Bo-land."

"What am I doing here, sir?" she croaked through dry lips. "Why am I restrained?"

He grinned. "Oh, very good. But it's a little late to be playing the dumb blonde with me now. And much as I like hearing you call me 'sir', it's no longer appropriate. As of this time you should not consider yourself a member of the United States Armed Forces."

"But that's exactly what I am, sir."

He shook his head. "No. A *mystery*, Boland, is what you are. Absent without leave. Vanished without trace. Missing, but not in action. Or at least, that's what you'll be when someone bothers to report you gone. For the time being you're just like every other Exodus." He leaned forward, so that his face was very close to hers. "Mine."

"Sir, what is Exodus?" she said, struggling to keep her voice calm.

"She wants to know about Exodus," he said, turning to the other two men in the cell. Both were thickset, crewcut, in their early thirties. Both were wearing army fatigues. Under the rolled-up sleeves she could see the winged-death's-head tattoos on their biceps. "Do we tell her?"

Neither man answered. The decision was his: they were simply the audience.

"Exodus is need-to-know," he said, turning back to her. "In fact, that's not quite true. There are quite a few people who really ought to know about it who don't know jack shit. Including the President." Pleased with his own answer, he reached out and twanged one of the ropes, testing it for tightness.

Surreptitiously, she tried to examine her surroundings. A small cell, one wall made of steel bars. The walls on either side were breezeblock, the one at the rear bare rock. Beyond it, through the bars, she could just make out more cells, all identical, stretching away as far as the eye could see. In some of them she could see bright orange blobs. There were no windows, and the walls overhead arched into the rock. It was cold, about twelve or fourteen degrees.

She was in a tunnel, somewhere deep underground.

One of the orange blobs moved. In a distant cell a dark face lifted, caught her eye, then quickly looked away again.

There was no surprise in those eyes, no recognition; no emotion of any kind except dull fear.

Prisoners. Hundreds, perhaps thousands of them.

"Exodus is a *solution*," Carver said. "See, our great President leaves office in 2016. He's thinking about his legacy. And right now, he'll go down in history as the man who said he'd close Guantanamo but didn't. So he's got one hundred and sixty-four detainees sitting in Guantanamo he doesn't know what to do with, and the clock's counting down." He stuck out a finger, then a second. "That's problem one, Boland, but it's chickenfeed compared with problem two: Afghanistan. Ever since Guantanamo became a tourist trap for every liberal blogger and do-good journalist in America, we've been sticking our detainees elsewhere. Places like the detention facility at Bagram Air Base – that's three thousand of the suckers, right there. But guess what? Now we're pulling out of Afghanistan, we've got to hand the jails back. And some of those detainees... well, let's just say a few might have stories to tell about their time as our guests that we'd rather not see splashed all over Al Jazeera. So that's another clock ticking. Then there's Iraq, Yemen, Somalia, the occasional troublemaker like yourself, a couple of guys off the construction site who had to be quietly vanished..." He stuck out a third finger, then a fourth, all the way onto his other hand. "Plus all the people we used to ship off to our friends in Libya, Egypt and Syria. You get the picture. Tens of thousands of detainees, and nowhere to put them."

"This is a detention facility," she said.

He considered. "Kind of. But not exactly, not in the usual sense of the term. What this place is, is a grey area. An administrative black hole. An overflow pipe. Or as I like to think of it, a human trash can. No one ordered it, exactly; no one discussed it, but a need arose, and *voilà*." He gestured at the ceiling of rock above them. "This is what under the carpet looks like, Boland. A long, long way under the carpet." He turned to his men again, inviting them to chuckle.

The implications of what she was hearing were only just sinking in. "How many?" she said, appalled. "How many human beings will you keep down here without rights? What will happen to them?"

"Here?" He looked around. "This place could hold a couple of thousand, if we pack 'em in tight. Most of what we've got here already are what we call husks – they've been through the process, not much fight left in them. Not much of anything, really. Get a system set up, it only takes a few dozen men to take care of somewhere this size. But Exodus isn't just this place. There are container ships criss-crossing international waters, a couple of so-called research stations in the Antarctic, a desert oilfield that doesn't produce any oil… Exodus is a *franchise*, and a pretty damn successful one at that." He ran his palm over his head. "As for what will happen to them, the answer's nothing. We've got an exercise facility in the quarry, our own water supply – no sunlight, of course, but a vitamin D shot once a year takes care of that. You're looking at a nice, quiet retirement home for jihadists. The only way they'll leave here is in an urn."

She suddenly realised she was handling this all wrong. The less he told her, the more she'd preserve the slim possibility that he might let her go. Otherwise, she'd face the same fate as all the other human debris that had been tossed down here.

As if reading her mind, he said, "Truth is, most of the time it gets pretty dull for the guys running this place. Particularly after what they were used to doing, before America lost its balls. So I'm not at all displeased to have you as our guest here, Boland. You'll be a nice addition to the facilities." He leaned in very close. "Our very own R&R."

He stood back to enjoy the expression in her eyes. "But first," he added, "we'd like to know everything you know, where it came from, and who you've told. Franklyn here will take care of that."

The burlier of the two men stepped forward, whistling under his breath.

SEVENTY-SEVEN

"KAT? IT'S DANIELE BARBO."

"What can I do for you, Daniele?" Kat knew it must be something out of the ordinary for Daniele to have called her.

"I'm worried about Holly," he said abruptly. "She hasn't been in touch for days."

Kat was surprised to hear that Daniele and Holly were even in contact, let alone that he expected her to call regularly. "She's not returned any of my messages recently, either. But I imagine they're pretty busy over there. Either that, or she's finally having wild sex with a lapdancer."

There was a long silence. "What do you mean?"

"I mean that when she does finally come out of the closet, it's going to be a pretty momentous event," Kat explained patiently. "But I'm sure she'll be in touch soon. What was it you wanted to say to her? If you tell me, I'll pass the message on."

She was answered by a click.

She sent Holly a quick email saying that she should get in touch and added a jokey PS. *Your admirer's getting keen...*

As she pressed "Send" her eye was caught by the previous message, the last one Holly had sent to her.

Kat, I spoke to Mia today. There seem to be some discrepancies between her account and the official version. In
particular, Mia talks about a "whistling man" who wore the
same mask as another kidnapper. This one never spoke,
but whistled Springsteen under his breath. Does that ring
any bells your end?

She'd replied, but heard nothing back. And then there'd
been that failed call at 4 a.m. An odd time to phone, unless it
was something important.

She phoned the base and asked to talk to Holly's ranking
officer in Civilian Liaison. Holly had mentioned First
Lieutenant Mike Breedon on several occasions: Kat knew she
liked and trusted him.

The mellow Virginian voice that came on the line sounded
anxious. "She's not been at her desk for twenty-four hours.
Usually I kind of let her get on with things, but she's always
careful to let me know what her schedule is." He paused.
"Usually in fifteen-minute segments, colour coded, and with a
note reminding me what my own schedule is too."

"Something's wrong," Kat said. "It must be."

"Could the Carabinieri maybe send someone to check her
apartment?"

"I'll go myself," Kat said. "Text me the address, will you?"

It turned out Holly was renting an apartment on the top floor
of a building right in the historic centre of Vicenza. As was
usual in these places, there was a concierge-cum-handyman
who held duplicate keys.

Inside, it was even tidier than Kat had expected. In the
kitchen were four separate chopping boards of different
colours, carefully labelled "Meat", "Fish", "Chicken" and

"Vegetables". Cookery books – Kat had never read a cookery book in her life, let alone bought one, since she'd picked up all the recipes she needed from her mother and grandmother – were ranged on a shelf in alphabetical order. In the bedroom, the bed was made with military neatness, and even the clothes in the dirty laundry basket had been carefully folded.

Kat thought back to the incident that had precipitated her rift with Holly. Although both of them now chose to pretend that it had been over a frying pan, the truth was a little more complex than that. Soon after Holly had come to stay with her, after the end of the Bosnian case, they'd gone out to Kat's favourite Venetian *bacaro*, where, towards the end of the evening, they'd found themselves being chatted up by two good-looking young men, Philippo and Andreas. Since Kat had got on well with Andreas, and since Philippo and Holly seemed to be in a similar situation, Kat had naturally suggested when the bar closed that they all go back to her apartment. After a bottle of wine had been opened and consumed, however, it became clear that there was a small problem, in that there was only one bedroom; which was to say, Kat's.

Kat had taken the opportunity to murmur to Holly, when getting another bottle, that she would presently slip off with Andreas, leaving the sitting room to Holly and Philippo.

Holly had stared at her. "I'm not planning on *sleeping* with him, Kat."

"Oh." Kat considered. "Well, that's awkward. You'd better send him home, then."

However, it hadn't quite worked out that way, and somehow Kat had ended up in the bedroom with both Andreas and Philippo. And somehow they'd made a bit more noise than was strictly necessary – which was nothing at all to do with making a point to the repressed American who was trying to sleep on the couch just the other side of the wall; but might, she later reflected, have been taken that way.

Next day, Kat had gone straight to work. While she was out, it transpired, Holly had decided to give the place a much-needed clean – which, in turn, had absolutely nothing to do with feeling that the whole apartment was now morally tainted by the previous night's excesses. With her usual methodical efficiency, she'd sorted, scrubbed and scoured everything in sight. Unfortunately, that had included Kat's cast-iron frying pan, a family heirloom given to her by her grandmother, Nonna Renata. Kat was extremely proud of the ancient, black-ened patina that enabled the pan to perform its function with nothing more than an occasional wipe and a drizzle of good Garda olive oil, and her fury when she returned that evening to discover that her house guest had not only imposed her anal American neuroses on the clutter of Kat's lovely kitchen, but had ruined her grandmother's pan in the process, had been terrible to behold.

Kat had been on a short fuse in any case since discovering just how difficult her complaint against Piola was going to make her life, and that evening all of her pent-up anger had erupted in one long but satisfying tirade. Things were said that could never be unsaid, some of them even postulating a link between Holly's fondness for cleaning products and her lack of sexual interest in men. Stung, Holly had offered to move out. Kat had told her it would be better if she was gone within the hour. And, somewhat to Kat's surprise, she had been. It was a relief in many ways – the tiny apartment had never been going to accommodate two such different personalities – but a faint suspicion in Kat's mind that she might herself have been in the wrong had, not for the first time in her life, turned into a fierce determination that if so, she didn't give a fuck.

Only later did she discover that she actually cared very much indeed. She had been thanking her lucky stars, ever since Mia's kidnap, that Holly had taken the initiative to reignite their friendship. They might be chalk and cheese, but something about their relationship made their differences irrelevant.

Kat went through to the living room. Beyond a glass door was a tiny little terrace, with fresh herbs growing in pots, and a table with one chair, angled south over the terracotta rooftops towards the Berici hills. She pictured Holly sitting there, drinking her single cup of coffee every morning, perfectly content, and felt a sudden stab of anxiety.

It was when she turned around, though, that she stopped short. The pictures had been taken down from one wall and replaced with the neatest, most organised spidergram Kat had ever seen.

Carver. Elston. Drugs…

She scanned it carefully. There were connections she herself had made, as well as some that were unfamiliar. She raised her eyebrows at the stick drawing of the Club Libero swingers – that, at least, was surely out of character.

Two more stick figures caught her eye, male and female, marked "Daniele" and "Holly". It occurred to her to wonder if she'd said something rather tactless to Daniele earlier. Oh well: there'd be plenty of time to rectify that later. The important thing now was to find Holly.

I've just spoken to Mia, Holly had said in her email.

She punched a number into her phone. "Mike," she said when Holly's boss answered, "Can you find out for me where Mia and her father are now?"

They were at Vicenza High School, came the word back. At a social function, not to be disturbed.

Kat went right ahead and disturbed them.

As she drove into the parking lot she saw a banner tied over the gate. "Ninth Annual Purity Prom!" And, in smaller letters, "Special Homecoming Gala Invitees: Mia and Major R. Elston".

A military band was playing at the base of a raised stage, and a number of pre-teen girls in full prom gowns were trying their hardest to look like Scarlett O'Hara. Some even sported Bo-Peep hats and elbow-length gloves, while their fathers were resplendent in ceremonial dress. Retirees and veterans marched stiffly to and fro, medals pinned to puffed-out chests. Posters tied to the trees and railings exhorted the guests to "Pledge Purity!" and, more incongruously, "Once You Pop You Can't Stop".

She pushed through the crowds, looking for Major Elston. A huge cheer and a round of applause went up, and she saw Mia stepping onto the stage. She edged closer to listen.

"Hey, everyone," Mia began a little awkwardly. "In a minute, some of you guys will make your purity vows. Just like I did a few years back." She paused. "You know, my dad and I have been talking about this, and we've agreed I made the decision to do that before I was really old enough to understand what it meant. Before I realised that the only person you can make a promise like that to is yourself.

"So, if you want to pledge not to do the big S-word thing until your wedding night, then go right ahead – I honour and salute you, and I wish you every success. But equally, if those ideals aren't right for you, don't feel bad." She stopped, blushed in confusion, and added, "I guess that's all I've got to say. Except that I've got the best dad in the world."

The teen princesses applauded her a little doubtfully, glancing up at their own fathers for some indication that these sentiments were acceptable. If their fathers thought they were not, they gave no sign of it.

As the first father–daughter pair was called to the stage, Kat made her way to the side, where Major Elston stood with his arm around Mia's shoulders.

"I'm sorry to disturb you, sir. It's about Second Lieutenant Boland."

He glanced at her. "This is not an appropriate time, Captain. I'm with my family."

"I understand that. But it's an emergency. She's missing."

"You told me once that runaways generally turn up, as I recall."

She swallowed. "I was wrong. Major… Please. You have your daughter back. Help me to rescue my friend."

"Dad…" Mia said pleadingly.

He grimaced. "Very well. Walk with me, Captain."

He took her to one side and listened, his face darkening, while she explained.

"I can see why you're concerned," he said quietly. "Believe me, I think she's in very great danger. But I'm afraid I really can't help. I simply have no knowledge of where they might have taken her."

"There's nowhere on base?"

He shook his head. "You've seen for yourself how busy it is. There's no way someone could be kept round here against their will without people knowing."

Shit, she thought. *Shit. Holly, where are you?*

SEVENTY-EIGHT

SHE FELT MORE tired than she'd ever felt before. It wasn't just not being allowed to sleep. What she hadn't appreciated was that pain – endless, continual pain – was itself exhausting. She had endured what felt like hours of walling; hours of being slapped in the face and belly and tits; of being choked; of being pulled up by the arms and then suddenly dropped; of being hosed down over and over with chilled water and left to shake with cold. After all that, she had no resistance left in her. All she wanted to do was sleep; if necessary, forever.

But she also knew she had to fight for time. She had to believe someone would come looking for her. Her only possible strategy was to stay alive until they did.

And these, she knew, were just the preparatory stages – what the CIA called "establishing a baseline state". After each of Franklyn's sessions, Carver came to look over his man's handiwork. It had been Carver who'd cut off her clothes – "Are you culturally modest, Boland? I sure hope so"; Carver who told her, mockingly, that "No blood, no foul" didn't apply down here; Carver who informed her about the sensory-deprivation tank that could fry a person's brain in hours and the electric-current baths that could do the same to their flesh, both without leaving a mark. And it was Carver who had selected the music to be played at deafening volume in the facility's sleep-deprivation cell. Beyoncé's "End of Time". The words and the crashing rhythm still hammered through her head.

"You know, Boland," he said now, inspecting her as she hung by her arms. "It's a shame about those tits of yours. Frankly, I've seen more impressive fried eggs." He stopped, struck by an idea, and turned to Franklyn. "Could we give her a boob job, Sergeant Franklyn?"

The other man considered. "Can't see why not, sir. Get the implants by mail order, I could sew 'em in easily enough."

"Well, how'd you like that, Boland?" Carver demanded, leaning close. "We're going to make you beautiful. You'll thank us before we're done."

She knew – hoped – that he was just trying to needle her, but if so, it had worked. Gathering all the saliva her dry mouth could provide, she spat in his face.

Grinning, he scraped her spittle off his cheek with a finger and put it in his mouth. "Mmm, tastes good. I hope there's more where that came from. You'll be needing it." Almost gently, he smoothed her hair out of her eyes, tucking it back behind one ear. "We could break you in ten minutes if we had to, Boland. But who wants a broken plaything? Frankly, your defiance is currently the sexiest thing about you." He stepped back so he could see her expression. "You know, there'll come a time when you're so thirsty you'll beg me to spit in *your* face. So hungry, you'll beg me to come in your mouth. So lonely you'll plead for a touch or a contact, no matter how much pain it comes with. But I really hope that time doesn't come for many years. No matter what we do to you."

He turned to Franklyn. "Have we boarded her yet?"

The other man shook his head. "I was just getting round to it."

"Carry on, then. I haven't got all day."

She was strapped to a trolley, the same trolleys they used to transport hog-tied prisoners down the endless tunnels. A towel was wound around her face.

Before the towel claimed her vision, she saw Franklyn hooking a hose up to a spigot in the wall.

They left her for what seemed an age, but was probably only a few minutes – they'd know what the anticipation would be doing to her mind. She couldn't help it: she was already shaking with fear.

The first touch of the water was gentle, a cool sensation on her parched mouth. But that was only Franklyn soaking the towel. She held her breath – it wasn't a conscious decision but an instinct, her body saying, *No*.

But she could only hold it so long, and they knew it. When, finally, she drew a breath, a great gasping inhalation of the air her body was screaming for, it wasn't air she sucked in but water. Water filled her throat and lungs like cement, a bolt of pain that only made her gasp for more air.

And there was none, only more water.

She thought her lungs must explode. She felt the hammering in her ears, the retching spasms in her larynx. It was like the moment when you swam underwater as far as you could and realised you had to get to the surface, fast.

But here there was no surface.

Abruptly, the flow of water ceased. For a moment she thought it was too late, that she was going to lose consciousness. But then, with a massive effort, she forced herself to fight for air. Spluttering and gasping, she vomited up what was in her lungs, the water spluttering out of her in a fountain, and she was alive.

"Again," she heard Carver say.

The second time was longer. The third time was longer still, and she died. She came back with Franklyn's hands pummelling her chest, and a pain like a car crash somewhere in the region of her heart.

"Again," Carver said calmly.

As Franklyn picked up the towel, his boss leaned over her. "You're tougher than you look, aren't you, Boland? Fifty-two seconds is quite impressive. But you know, we don't play by the CIA rules down here. If I want to bring in a taser, or even just a nice heavy truncheon to spice it up a little, I can. So why don't we take a break, and you can tell me everything that you and your friends the Carabinieri have figured out? It's only a matter of time, after all."

But time is all I have to shoot for.

"Sir, I don't report to traitors," she croaked.

"Traitors?" He laughed, a bark of amusement at her presumption. "How am *I* a traitor?"

"You've betrayed every principle of the military code."

"Oh, Boland. Boland. How shall I punish you for taking that tone with me?" He looked her over. "Well, let's come back to that. But in response to your pathetic allegation, I am the furthest from being a traitor of any American you'll ever meet. I am a *patriot*, Boland. A patriot who understands that being obsequious to our adversaries only emboldens them. A patriot who understands that the national interest can only be served by those who act outside its legal constraints. A patriot who knows that America will only survive if it retains its strength. I love my country, you dumb little whore, and that is why I am prepared to lie and torture and murder to protect it."

Harlequin probably said much the same thing to Mia, she thought. Just in very different words.

"Do you know why I let those idiots work over Elston's girl?" he demanded. "It wasn't only to stop that fool of a major from getting on his high horse. It was to show the world what we do to those who oppose us. For years we've been trying to hide the evidence, like it's something to be ashamed of. Destroying the CIA's tapes of waterboard sessions. Pretending the black sites and the rendition flights don't happen any more. Denying that we do what we need to do. But I'm not ashamed of those things, Boland. I'm *proud* of them. Those waterboard tapes are my favourite late-night viewing. Right now every would-be-mujahedin teenage raghead in the Middle East has seen what happened to Mia and maybe – just maybe – is thinking to himself, if I mess with the US, that could be me. So tell me this, Boland: is America more vulnerable today because of what I did? Or safer?"

"Sir, you're an obscenity," she said.

Almost casually, his hand flew out and cracked her across the face, first one way, then the other. "If you weren't strapped to that gurney, Boland, I'd rip your ass open right now and shove a cattle prod up it." He smiled. "Course, I'm not saying that I didn't enjoy what happened to that girl. Miss Mia Elston, the great virgin of Vicenza. I saw her strutting round the base in her cheerleader outfit, looking so cute, like butter wouldn't melt in her mouth. And all that abstinence crap. She knew the effect she had on men. She loved it, you could tell. Loved the power she thought it gave her. But what you whores don't realise is that you don't have any power over us, not really.

Only what we choose to let you have." He looked across at Franklyn. "Enough of this. Get me the juice. We're going to do the double."

They brought in a truck battery and clipped the electrodes to her breasts with crocodile clips.

"This one's not in the manuals, Boland, so let me explain how it works," Carver said, leaning over her. "Franklyn here administers the water – sixty seconds. It's pretty much guaranteed to kill you." He touched one of the crocodile clips, enjoying the way she winced as the sharp teeth tugged at her. "Which is where the juice comes in. It brings you back, but not in a nice way. I've heard sometimes people beg for the water again, just to stop the juice. That's if they can talk at all."

"Sir, I'll tell you what I can," she said, accepting defeat.

"Go ahead."

"I know that it was some kind of Iran–Contra-type operation. You were shipping drugs from Afghanistan. I'm guessing you were using the money to fund Exodus."

He nodded. "Very good, Boland. Even with a tame contractor like Conterno, places like this cost money, and it had to be kept off the books somehow. We tidied up the poppy supply in our part of Afghan, organised a few shipments to the right people here in Italy, and froze out the Taliban in the process. Win-win."

"And Major Elston found out."

"About the drugs, yes. The least important bit. A mere detail in the great scheme. He'd have exposed the whole of Exodus if he'd gone public. So he had to be persuaded to change his mind. Mazzanti's report landed on my desk at just the right time. A radical protest group, planning on kidnapping American kids? Hell, yes! After that, it was just a matter of logistics." He spread his arms. "Which is kind of what we do here anyway. Of course, we had to manage the Carabinieri side of things. I must admit, you had me worried, when you came and told me they were on to Mazzanti. But the reward kept them looking in the wrong direction." He leaned forward. "Now, listen to me very carefully, Boland, and answer this as truthfully as you can. Did you write any of this down? Report it in any way? Mention it to anyone?"

She hesitated, thinking. She'd spoken to Gilroy about some small pieces of it, and Kat too of course. They were both insiders, so it was unlikely Carver would go after them. But there was someone else she'd discussed her suspicions with Daniele. The owner of a site on which people could post whatever secrets they possessed.

"No, sir. No one," she said.

"Boland, Boland." He shook his head in mock sorrow. "You are a terrible liar, do you know that?" He gestured at Franklyn. "Let's get started, shall we?"

SEVENTY-NINE

SHE WENT BACK to Holly's apartment, to the spidergram and the neatly made bed. The answer was here somewhere, she was sure of it.

Holly, tell me where you are.

But nothing had changed. The spidergram was just as she had left it. *Carver. Elston. Exodus...*

Kat stepped out onto the tiny terrace and rested her hands on the parapet, her head bowed in despair. *I'm failing you,* she told her friend silently. *I am a captain in the Carabinieri and being clever about bad people is my job. But I just can't work out where they've taken you.*

She raised her head and gazed over the rooftops at the Berici hills. It was astonishing, she thought, that the Americans had concealed a nuclear-weapons command bunker under their placid surface for so long.

Connections sparked and fizzled in her brain like firecrackers. *Of course.*

"Site Pluto," she said, pointing. "Here."

According to the map she'd spread across Piola's desk, Pluto was just a small US storage compound at the foot of the Berici hills, a few kilometres south of the main base.

"The reason it looks so small," she added, "is because this is only the entrance. The site itself is under these hills, in a series of old caves and quarries. During the war the Germans housed a factory down there, building aircraft parts and munitions, that employed three thousand workers. Even then, it extended over thirty thousand square metres."

"And now?"

"Pluto was officially decommissioned after the Cold War. But as part of the recent building work at Dal Molin, they slipped in a refurbishment." She showed him the plans he himself had got from Sergeant Pownall. Pluto was marked "Explosive Materials Disposal".

He began to understand now why the construction programme at Dal Molin had been working to such a punishing schedule, and why the consortium might have chosen to use illegal labourers who'd ask no questions. "'Explosive Materials Disposal.' I take it that's Carver's idea of a joke. Did you take a look?"

She nodded. "Two armed soldiers turned me back. Which in itself is strange, given that all the other US installations around Vicenza are under Carabinieri guard."

"Do we have any proof she's there?"

"None at all. But it's the only place left, and if she *is* there, we're running out of time."

He made a decision. "Very well. Come with me."

He took her to see General Saito and the prosecutor, Li Fonti. He recounted her story almost word for word, but with one addition: in his account, Kat had spoken to two separate witnesses in Longare who reported seeing a van drive up to the gates of Site Pluto, and a woman in US fatigues being hauled roughly out of the back.

"And you're quite sure of this, Captain?" Saito turned anxiously to Kat.

"Absolutely, sir."

He looked no less worried. "If we get this wrong…"

Piola said firmly, "And if we're right, a small number of rogue Americans have made fools of us in front of the whole world. If we find and expose their corruption, all decent Americans – which I'm sure is the vast majority – will applaud us for it. The reputation of the Carabinieri will be restored."

Li Fonti said, "What do you need?"

"Twenty *carabinieri*, armed with automatic weapons." Piola saw Saito's look of horror. "The Americans have guns," he explained. "If we go in without sufficient force, we're more likely to provoke a firefight than if we're properly equipped."

"Do it," Li Fonti said. "I'll issue the warrant."

"And God help us all if you're wrong," Saito added faintly,

EIGHTY

"WHAT ARE YOU, Boland?"

"I am a trou, sir."

"Correct, Boland. You are indeed a trou. And what do we do with trous?"

"We wear them, sir," she said wearily, the chant from her cadet years still embedded in her brain, even after so long.

"Indeed we do. You will be receiving an STD test shortly, Boland. We operate a nice clean facility here." At that he left her, her shackled arms still fastened to the ceiling.

She hung there, exhausted and defeated. She'd given up Daniele. Despite all her resolve, when it had come down to a straight choice between endless pain or telling the truth, she had told Carver the truth.

"You see?" he'd crowed. "Doesn't it feel good when you stop lying?"

No, she wanted to say. *It feels almost worse than the waterboard.*

She understood, now, the reality behind the bland CIA phrase "death due to psychological resignation". If she'd been boarded again, she'd have gulped the water down and held it. Then again, the detainees the CIA had been referring to probably hadn't had Franklyn standing next to them with his truck battery, ready to jump-start them back to life. She doubted she could even cheat them into letting her die now. Her life had become theirs, to do with as they liked.

What that was to be, Carver had already made all too clear.

"This is a family-friendly facility, Boland. Matter of fact it would be charming to have a few little Bolands running round the place."

Even in his absence, he was there in her head, the things he'd said cascading like cluster bombs.

"I never got to work on Mia myself. Had to make do with watching, like everyone else. Watching, and imagining. I'm just full of ideas for the two of us, Boland. Let me tell you some..."

At first she'd wondered why he bothered with all this. If he was going to rape her, why not just get on with it? But then she'd realised that it wasn't about sex, or not entirely. This was about power. And it wasn't enough simply to have it: the thrill came from reminding her that he had it, as if he must exult in it or it did not exist.

After he left, she was visited by a female guard. The guard wore white micropore gloves and carried a swab in a sterile tray.

"You're pretty," the woman said incongruously as she went about her business. She had the same death's-head tattoo on her upper arm as the other guards.

Holly tried to establish eye contact. "I'm Second Lieutenant Boland of Civilian Liaison. I'm being kept here illegally. You need to raise the alarm."

"Colonel Carver gave orders not to listen to you, ma'am."

"You're a woman. You know what they mean to do with me, don't you? Can you really just stand by and let that happen?"

"I always say the innocent have nothing to fear, ma'am." After that the guard refused to respond to any more questions.

In her exhaustion Holly must have fallen asleep in her shackles, allowing her body weight to hang from her wrists, because she woke to the agony of cramping muscles. As she gritted her teeth, determined not to cry out, she saw that he was there again, watching her.

Coming close, he took her arms and pinched them gently, feeling the muscles knotting under the skin. As if she were some kind of farm animal, and he was judging if she were finally ripe for the knife.

"Guess what, Boland," he said softly. "It's date night."

EIGHTY-ONE

THEY MARCHED IN military formation to the gates of Site Pluto. The officers had their sidearms drawn, and the regular *carabinieri* had their rifles at the ready. But it was the warrant, duly issued by Li Fonti, which Aldo Piola brandished at the hapless soldier in the guardhouse.

"Sir, you'll have to wait while I consult—" the American began.

"No, I won't," Piola said in English. "This is Italian soil, and we are duly authorised officers of the Arma dei Carabinieri. I am showing you this warrant as a courtesy, but if you impede my men or me in any way, you will be arrested and disarmed." Before the man could protest further, they'd passed him, the *carabinieri* fanning out as they approached a massive semi-circular door of reinforced steel built into the hillside.

To one side was a smaller door, open.

Inside, under utility lighting, a tunnel fifty feet high led downhill. Smaller tunnels branched in four directions. Along every one, as far as the eye could see, cages lined the walls.

It's like a zoo, Piola thought as they marched deeper. From cell after cell exhausted, dark-skinned faces stared dully out at them. Most of the detainees were wearing orange jumpsuits. A few clasped battered copies of the Koran. Some were shackled in goggles, so that they resembled bug-eyed orange flies. It was eerily quiet.

From one of the tunnels, faintly, came the sound of Beyoncé singing "End of Time".

"She's down here," Kat said, breaking into a run. Without waiting for a command, the *carabinieri* at her side did the same.

She was the first through the doorway of the little cell. The music had masked their approach, so neither of the people inside heard her at first.

Holly was tied up by her arms to a hook in the ceiling. Her legs had been lashed up too, so that she was hanging in a foetal position. Her fair skin was covered in bruises and her eyes were closed.

Like her, Carver was naked. He was holding a wooden paddle.

He made no effort to cover himself up as he turned to Kat. "What the fuck do you want?" he demanded.

Kat indicated Holly. "Her. I've come for her. And you can get the fuck away from her, you creep."

Holly moaned softly and her eyes opened. Kat stepped forward and took her in her arms. "It's all right," she said. "Holly, it's all right. It's me."

"Kat... Kat..." Holly whispered. "Warn Daniele."

"I'll get some men over to Ca' Barbo. Don't worry, he'll be safe."

"Colonel Carver," Piola said, following her in, "I have here a warrant for your arrest on charges of abduction."

"Abduction of who?" Carver said, amused. He indicated Holly. "She's a US soldier under my command. I have the right to discipline her in any way I choose, including depriving her of her liberty."

"*This* is military discipline?" Piola said, lifting his eyebrows at the man's lack of clothing.

"What *this* is, is none of your business, Colonel."

"Actually, that's not quite correct," Piola said. "For one thing, Second Lieutenant Boland has dual nationality and is entitled to the protection of Italian law. For another, the charge of abduction doesn't only refer to her, or even to Mia Elston. It applies to every single person in this facility."

He had the satisfaction of seeing, first doubt, then fear, fill Carver's eyes. "Handcuff him," he ordered the nearest *carabiniere*. "And get a stretcher for Second Lieutenant Boland."

EIGHTY-TWO

ALDO PIOLA WAITED patiently as Ian Gilroy turned the pages of his report. It was a room in which it was easy to be patient: the frescoes alone could have absorbed his attention for many hours.

"So," Gilroy said at last, putting the document to one side. "What is it you want to ask me, Colonel?"

It had been Gilroy who'd initiated this meeting, calling Piola to say that the US owed him a debt of gratitude, and that if there was anything Piola wanted, he only had to ask. He'd been referring, in part, to the way the drugs-for-detainees scandal had been swiftly hushed up. The whole business, after conversations at the very highest level, had been handed over to the Americans to deal with as they saw fit: the tunnels at Longare quietly evacuated; Colonel Carver transferred to American custody and whisked off to one of the secret tribunals that were yet another unintended consequence of the war on terror. It was better that way, Saito had told Piola: were Carver to be charged in an open court, it would endanger the lives of American soldiers around the world.

Piola heard the echo of some shadowy diplomat in that sentiment. He hadn't pointed out to Saito that not putting Carver in the dock would mean leaving the public in the dark, or that it would send no signal to others like him that they were all subject to the rule of law. Nor had he wondered aloud where the detainees from Site Pluto had been evacuated to. Such were the complexities of leadership, and on this occasion he was only too glad not to have to exercise them himself.

But if that had been Gilroy's primary meaning when he'd talked about gratitude, Piola knew he had been invoking a more personal debt as well. Seeing the way the old man had appeared and embraced Holly's stretcher as the medical team carried her from the caves, there could be no doubt about the closeness between them – almost, he'd thought, like a father and daughter, rather than an ex-spy and his protégée.

And so Piola, after some thought, had replied to Gilroy's offer by saying that he would like to show him a draft of his report into the death of Max Ghimenti, and receive Gilroy's comments on it.

There had been a long silence down the phone before Gilroy had said, "How interesting. I'd imagined you were going to ask for something quite different, Colonel. But yes, I'd be happy to do that for you."

Now Piola looked across the antique rosewood table at the American and said, "I simply want to know how much of it is true. What really happened." He gestured at the report. "Whether I got it right."

Gilroy's expression gave nothing away. "And why do you think I might be able to tell you that?"

"You worked with Bob Garland. If I'm right, he seems to have run the Italy Section as his own private fiefdom. When you took over, you must have inherited many of those secrets."

Gilroy nodded slowly. "It's certainly true that some of Bob's methods were unorthodox." He tapped the report. "Though if you're asking me for a critique, I'd say this document is far too speculative. If one of my analysts had sent me this, back in the day, I'd have sent it straight back with a rude comment in the margin."

Piola waited.

"But," Gilroy said with a sigh, "it is also mostly correct. There *was* a massive effort after the war to steer Italy away from democratic communism. And that did include funding and organising the Christian Democrats. And there were various other organisations and networks through which America did distribute project funds and other forms of influence. Some masqueraded as Masonic lodges, some as the Honoured Society, others were effectively joint ventures with the Church. The Order of Melchizedek was one of the latter."

"I imagine it would shatter Marco Conterno to discover it's a fake."

Gilroy shook his head. "It may have been a fabrication, Colonel. But that's not quite the same thing as a fake. Bob's genius was to see how such networks, once they achieve a certain momentum, become self-perpetuating; their initial success lends them an aura of power, which in turn creates more power, the kind that doesn't have to be bought. Besides, I would hope you wouldn't be so cruel as to enlighten Marco Conterno about the Order's true origins. That young man already has a hard enough burden to bear, knowing what he does about his father and his grandfather."

"That Conterno Costruttori was also a CIA fellow-traveller, you mean?"

Gilroy nodded. "Bob came across Ambrogino during the war. I think the simple truth was, they liked each other. But Bob had been on the lookout for industrialists he could bring into America's sphere of influence, and Ambrogino was shrewd enough to see the advantages of that as well. It started with a request to sabotage the parts the Conterno factory was supplying to the Germans – ironically, the Nazis did Conterno a huge favour when they switched him from making tractors to aircraft and construction. Ambrogino agreed, and the association took off from there."

"And continues to this day, I understand."

The old man's eyes narrowed. "We're here to talk about the past, Colonel. You'd have to ask some youngster what happens now. I'm sure it's all very different."

Piola doubted both parts of that statement – that things were very different now, and that Ian Gilroy knew nothing about them – but he kept the thought to himself.

"But I should also tell you," Gilroy continued, "that your report does contain one rather fundamental misconception. It wasn't Bob Garland who killed Max Ghimenti."

"Who was it?"

"A man you've never heard of. Alvaro Lucci."

"And who was this Signor Lucci?"

"Not 'Signor'," Gilroy corrected. "Monsignor. A parish priest from near Marostica, where the partisans were based."

Piola digested this. "Why?"

"Ghimenti and his fellow partisans used Lucci's church as an occasional hideout and meeting place. One day La Sala came to the priest in a state of agitation and told him about a meeting they'd just had with some Yugoslav partisans. The Yugoslavs had brought an order, signed by the Party leadership, to rise up in the wake of the German retreat and take the Veneto for the communists."

"So Lucci—"

"Alerted the only authority he was in touch with – the Vatican. Where the information passed to one Giovanni Battista Montini, Protonotary Apostolic. Officially, of course, the Holy See was neutral. But this was a threat to its very existence. It was a difficult decision for Montini: he told Bob later that he prayed all night, seeking guidance. Then he sent a note back to Lucci, saying he should stop the plot by any means possible, and that God would forgive him for whatever extreme acts were required. It was a clear instruction to assassinate the plotters."

"A priest committed murder? In cold blood?"

"Yes. The next time the partisans came to the church – on their way to a meeting with OSS this time, trying to trick more weapons out of them to stockpile for their coup – Lucci killed Ghimenti and all the others except La Sala. As a gesture of compassion, I understand, he allowed Ghimenti to pray before he shot him – strange how even a communist can rediscover God in his last moments. Lucci was left-handed, by the way – I imagine that tallies with the archaeological evidence?"

Piola inclined his head, although he suspected that Gilroy already knew perfectly well what the evidence showed.

"So now they had three bodies, the Germans were bound to find them, and the priest was panicking. La Sala convinced him to go to the meeting with Garland in Ghimenti's stead and ask for his help. Conterno took care of the bodies, La Sala went back to the partisans with a hastily concocted story about a German ambush, and Bob Garland had in his hands a note that would change the course of post-war intelligence in Italy."

"I don't understand," Piola said. "Why would it do that?"

"Blackmail," Gilroy said succinctly. "Or, if you prefer a less ugly word, leverage. As soon as he could, Bob made his way to Rome and told Montini he had the letter he'd written to Lucci. He dressed it up nicely, of course – told Montini he was clearly a man of great practicality as well as a man of God; that such a combination of talents was so rare, OSS should be singling out Montini for support; that their aims were, after all, the same: to prevent Europe from falling to the communists. Within a week, Montini had passed OSS valuable information from Vatican officials in Tokyo. And of course, once you have one report from a highly placed agent, you're on your way. They always try to back out after a while, say they've given more than enough. That's when you gently make it clear they're yours for life. But there was no doubting Montini's worth. His recruitment made possible the whole post-war strategy of aligning the Church and the centre-left in Italy."

"And he went on to become Pope Paul VI," Piola said. "During one of the most intense periods of the Cold War, too. I suppose America helped?"

"Let's just say, we did what little we could. But what Bob had told Montini was true: he *was* an unusually clever and pragmatic cleric. I truly believe he was the right man for the job."

"And La Sala was richly rewarded for his betrayal too. What happened to the priest?"

"He chose to serve out his life in the same parish church, in the area where he had probably saved every church and every priest from destruction. He received the Star of Bethlehem, but so far as I know he never wore it, or even revealed that he'd been given it. And when you accuse La Sala of betrayal... it's more complicated than that, Colonel, isn't it? He betrayed his comrades, certainly, but he was loyal to his country. Ghimenti was loyal to his cause, but he was also a traitor who would have torn Italy apart." He indicated Piola's report. "And where you accuse the Americans of plotting, murdering and betraying their allies, in fact the reverse was true. America helped to save Italy from a group of renegade Italians who were bent on destroying it."

Piola was silent for a while, thinking over the implications. "I jumped to a conclusion," he admitted. "I so wanted to believe that America was responsible for Ghimenti's death, it didn't occur to me that the reality might be more nuanced."

Gilroy nodded.

"But then again," Piola added, "everything else you've told me – the plots, the manipulation of elections, agents inside the Vatican… When the things your country *are* guilty of are so extraordinary, it's hardly surprising that every extraordinary allegation is laid first at your door."

"True," Gilroy said. "When I took over from Bob, my first years as Section Chief were largely spent undoing the excesses of the past. But I don't judge him. Italy was the battleground where the Cold War was fought, just as it would have been the theatre of conflict should the war have turned into a real one. I can't tell you how many crises and near-misses there were during those years. And yet it survived. Sometimes it feels like a miracle."

"*Sempre crolla ma non cade*," Piola said, quoting the old Venetian proverb.

"'It's always collapsing but it never falls down.' Indeed."

"And Dr Iadanza and Professor Trevisano? Why were they killed?"

Gilroy shrugged. "Not because of some plot seventy years ago, certainly. My guess is, Dr Iadanza had realised that the rubble beside the old runway had been quarried from the caves at Longare. As the archaeologist attached to the construction project, she was uniquely well placed to make that connection. The last thing Carver would have wanted was someone snooping round Site Pluto."

"When I asked you to read my report," Piola said, curious, "you said you'd thought I was going to ask for something else. What was that?"

"Oh… I thought perhaps you were going to ask me if I

could have a word with your *generale di divisione* about a transfer to Genoa."

Piola's surprise must have been written all over his face. He had told no one about his plans. But then, he thought, Kat knew his wife's family came from there. If she'd mentioned it to Holly, and Holly to Gilroy...

Gilroy smiled, enjoying his astonishment. "Do I take it you've made no decision yet?"

"No," Piola said. "Not yet."

"Well, let me know what you decide." Gilroy stood up, and came around the desk to offer Piola his hand. "I'd be very happy to use what little influence is still left to me. Or, indeed, to help you remain in Venice, if that's what you'd prefer."

EIGHTY-THREE

THEY SAT IN the old music room at Ca' Barbo, the lights from Carnivia's newly upgraded servers pulsing softly behind them. Holly was wearing similar clothes to Daniele today: a hoodie, sneakers, jeans. She didn't feel quite ready yet to put on the uniform of the US Army again, the uniform Carver had been wearing when he'd cut hers off.

Truth to tell, she wasn't sure she ever would.

"I'm taking each day as it comes," she told him. "No schedule, no plans. And I'm seeing Father Uriel. He's helping a lot."

"I'm glad," Daniele said. He added, "I've stopped seeing him myself."

"Why?"

His eyes had a curious, distant quality. "Now I've had a chance to think it through, I'm not sure I actually *want* to develop empathy. I think perhaps, during Mia's kidnap, I did the wrong thing, compromising my principles for sentimental reasons. Once you start doing that, where does it end? Don't you just end up like Caliari or Carver, believing that whatever you're doing, it's for the greater good? How do you ever decide who's important enough to make an exception for, and who isn't? How do you live in a world where everyone wants different things of you?"

The world he was talking about, she knew, wasn't just the one

450

in which they were sitting, but that other, newer creation inside his servers, for which he alone bore ultimate responsibility.

She said gently, "When people pray, they hope someone will answer. It doesn't trouble them that if he does, God's being inconsistent."

"Perhaps." Daniele was silent a moment. "Anyway, I've made another inconsistent decision. I've barred Ethereal from Carnivia."

"Can you do that?"

"It required a major rewrite to the code. But even if the effect is largely symbolic, it will let people know that there are limits to what they're allowed to do. And I've plugged the holes that allowed Mulciber to look as if he was hacking it. It turns out he'd built some administrator privileges into the coding when we collaborated on it. They won't either of them be able to do anything similar again."

"I'm pleased. But you know it won't stop people wanting to control or destroy it, don't you?"

"I know." He glanced at her, then added, "There's something I need to ask you."

"Yes?"

"When you were missing, Kat said something. It made me wonder if... If perhaps your motives for sleeping with me were more complex than they appeared. If perhaps it was Ian Gilroy who had put the idea in your head." His eyes were fixed on the server screens now, a long way from her gaze.

She sighed. "I did say to Ian that I was interested in you, yes. But the idea that he could tell me who to sleep with is pretty insulting, frankly."

He said softly, "I know that you like and trust that man. And I know that you think I'm prejudiced against him because of his relationship with my father. But try looking at everything that happened in a different way. Gilroy inherited his CIA predecessor's influence – his files on the members of the Order of Melchizedek, his access to the US Military, his seat on the Conterno board. Did he know what was going on with Mia from the start? Did he use you, and your links to the Carabinieri, to scupper a rival – Carver – whose ambitions were threatening his own power?"

She shook her head. "That's paranoid." It was true that Gilroy's name had cropped up from time to time. But it would be crazy to try to read too much into it. The truth, as she understood it, was more like a series of Russian dolls, one inside another. Inside Azione Dal Molin was Carver, and drugs, and Elston, and Exodus. Inside the CIA was Bob Garland, and OSS, and the Order of Melchizedek. And inside them both, the very smallest doll, was The Enemy – once called communism, and now called terror, but the same all-consuming foe nevertheless.

And inside The Enemy was... Her mind briefly glimpsed something, the image of another doll, vanishingly tiny and insubstantial, but her brain refused to go there.

"That's paranoid," she repeated. "I trust him absolutely." She hesitated. "But, Daniele, there's another conversation we need to have right now."

"It's all right," he said. "You don't need to explain."

Even so, she tried. "I need to deal with what happened to me. I can't be trying to have a relationship as well."

"Of course." He hadn't asked her exactly what had happened in the caves, and didn't intend to. Just as he didn't intend to ask whether what Kat had told him about Holly's sexuality might also be a factor in her decision. "I understand, really."

"You do?"

"I've felt like that all my life," he said.

EIGHTY-FOUR

KAT WAS WAITING for him outside the villa, in a Carabinieri car. "Well?" she said, as Piola climbed into the passenger seat. "Were all your questions answered?"

"Most of them. Of course, he may have been spinning me a pack of lies. He's certainly capable of it. But whatever his motives, I can't submit that report now."

"I think that's a good thing. Italy has enough problems in the present, without trying to set the past to rights as well."

"Perhaps." Remembering what else the old spy had said, and how perceptively he had framed the decision Piola had to make now, he shook his head and sighed.

"What?" she said, noticing.

"Nothing." As she drove down the long, gravel drive, he turned to look at her profile. "Kat, you know I'm in love with you, don't you?"

"Yes," she said after a moment's pause.

"And?"

"I think you'll get over it." She added, almost apologetically, "Sir."

They reached the road, and she paused, her hand on the indicator. "Where next?"

HISTORICAL NOTE

Although *The Abduction* is fiction, it draws heavily on several real conspiracies with origins in the Cold War.

The plots to annexe northern Italy for the communists at the end of the Second World War are now well known to historians, as are OSS's efforts to prevent them – efforts that resulted in some American intelligence officers receiving papal honours after the war.

It's also well established that many of the first National Security Council directives concerned Italy, and in particular the need, made explicit in directive NSC 4/A, to prevent the Communist Party from gaining electoral power. Amongst many other stratagems, this involved funding a centre-left alternative, the Christian Democrats. How successful this was may be judged from the fact that the party provided every single Italian prime minister for forty years. It survived numerous bribery and corruption scandals before finally falling apart in the 1990s – round about the same time as the Cold War ended.

Many readers will find especially fanciful the suggestion that Giovanni Montini, later Pope Paul VI, could have been a CIA asset. However, this too is based on fact. Under the codename "Vessel" he is alleged to have passed information to OSS from about 1944 onwards. So plentiful, and so useful, was this intelligence that a new section, X-2, was created to process it. According to one account, X-2 produced almost five hundred reports in one six-month period.

The Order of Melchizedek is a composite, based on a number of similar organisations in post-war Italy. Some, like the Sovereign Military Order of Malta or the Order of the Holy Sepulchre, enjoy extraterritoriality and other privileges that have long proved useful to the intelligence services (OSS's post-war "ratlines", for example, were run using Order of Malta passports); others, such as the "Propaganda Due" Masonic lodge, were attempts to bring together the Mafia, the Italian intelligence services and other right-of-centre factions in an alliance against the left. Amongst P2's members was listed the name of Silvio Berlusconi, many years before he became Italy's prime minister.

America built its first permanent bases in Vicenza in 1955, under the terms of a treaty that remains classified to this day. They include "Site Pluto", a cave network deep under the Berici hills, where nuclear mines and short-range nuclear warheads were once stored (it has long been superseded by more modern nuclear bunkers at Ghedi and Aviano). In 2004 the US Army announced that Silvio Berlusconi's government had approved plans for an additional base at a former Italian military airfield called Dal Molin. The plans prompted strong opposition from some local citizens, approximately one hundred and fifty thousand of whom came together to protest under the banner "No Dal Molin". A small number did break into the construction site at one point, although my "Azione Dal Molin" group is fictional.

At an opening ceremony in 2012 – by which time the site's name had been changed to "Del Din" – the US ambassador credited the speed of the building programme to "the strong support that the United States received from the highest levels of the Italian government".

The quotations from CIA documents on enhanced interrogation are mostly taken from the so-called "torture memos" released to the American Civil Liberties Union in 2009 under Freedom of Information legislation. President Obama symbolically rescinded enhanced interrogation when he took office, although a number of the same techniques are believed to remain in use. Obama's 2009 Executive Order also established an interagency task force to review interrogation policies and "the practices of transferring individuals to other nations". Their report was issued later in 2009, but continues to be withheld from the public.

The same Executive Order announced the closure of the prison at Guantanamo Bay. However, the small print revealed that President Obama wasn't intending to release or even charge the detainees, but simply to spread around the American prison system those he described as "too difficult to prosecute, but too dangerous to release". Congress objected to having prisoners in American jails who were being denied trials, and at the time of writing Guantanamo remains open. Meanwhile, many of the other prisons where detainees have been sent in recent years – notably Parwan Detention Facility at Bagram Air Base in Afghanistan, where approximately three thousand prisoners are currently held without charge – are scheduled to be handed over to local governments.

The references to CIA activities such as the "second strike" policy – which attempts to prevent first responders from going to the aid of drone strike victims – and US cyber-surveillance programs such as PRISM are as accurate as I can make them.

Despite suggestions in 2009 that it would be ended,

"rendition" – otherwise known as "abduction" – remains a legal tool of the US government.

For links to further reading, and information about the other books in the Carnivia trilogy, go to www.carnivia.com.

ACKNOWLEDGEMENTS

Once again, huge thanks to Laura Palmer, fiction publisher at Head of Zeus, for helping to shape the story. And to Anna Coscia and Lucy Ridout; the former for correcting my terrible Italian, the latter for correcting my terrible English.

The mathematics of boiling the perfect egg is based on research by Dr Charles D.H. Williams at Exeter University, which can be found at http://newton.ex.ac.uk/teaching/cdhw/egg/

The quotation by Noam Chomsky on page 348 is excerpted from a longer article at www.nodalmolin.it.